A Noble Masquerade

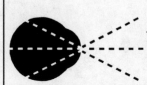

This Large Print Book carries the
Seal of Approval of N.A.V.H.

A Noble Masquerade

Kristi Ann Hunter

THORNDIKE PRESS

A part of Gale, Cengage Learning

GALE
CENGAGE Learning·

Farmington Hills, Mich • San Francisco • New York • Waterville, Maine
Meriden, Conn • Mason, Ohio • Chicago

GALE
CENGAGE Learning

LIBRARY OF CONGRESS CATALOGING-IN-PUBLICATION DATA

Names: Hunter, Kristi Ann, author.
Title: A noble masquerade : Hawthorne house / by Kristi Ann Hunter.
Description: Large print edition. | Waterville, Maine : Thorndike Press, 2016. | © 2015 | Series: Thorndike Press large print Christian historical fiction
Identifiers: LCCN 2016003965| ISBN 9781410488893 (hardcover) | ISBN 1410488896 (hardcover)
Subjects: LCSH: Single women—England—Fiction. | Nobility—England—Fiction. | Large type books. | GSAFD: Love stories. | Regency fiction
Classification: LCC PS3608.U5935 N63 2016 | DDC 813/.6—dc23
LC record available at http://lccn.loc.gov/2016003965

Published in 2016 by arrangement with Bethany House Publishers, a division of Baker Publishing Group

Printed in Mexico
1 2 3 4 5 6 7 20 19 18 17 16

To the Creator,
who has enough depth to make
each of us in His image
and yet still make us uniquely
individual.

Genesis 1:27

And to Jacob,
who is incredible enough
to inspire each
of my heroes in some small way.

PROLOGUE

Hertfordshire, England, 1800

It is never a happy day when an eight-year-old girl's cheesecake lands in the dirt, and she certainly doesn't take kindly to the laughing little boy who put it there.

Fat tears welled up in Lady Miranda Hawthorne's eyes as she stared at the cake now resting forlornly on the ground. Her little hands curled into angry fists at her sides.

"You're a cad, Henry Lampton!" Miranda scooped the cake from the ground and hurled it at the laughing boy, her cheeks wet with tears. There was something satisfying about seeing the creamy dessert smear across his shirt and the smile fall from his face.

Miranda didn't have long to relish her revenge because her mother appeared to lead her away from the party. Mother didn't say a word until the door closed behind them, shutting them into her study.

"Miranda, a lady never expresses her disappointment in public." Mother's admonition was gentle but firm, as it always was.

Even though she knew her mother meant well, Miranda shuddered every time she heard the words, *"Miranda, a lady never . . ."* Occasionally it was *"Miranda, a lady always . . ."* but even then it was something like *"Miranda, a lady always pays attention to her guests, even when she finds them boring."*

Miranda knew better than to speak as her mother lectured. Every time she tried to defend herself, it only made the torture last longer. So she waited until her mother dismissed her.

Instead of returning to the party, however, she ran to her room and threw herself on the bed, punching the pillow at the unfairness of it all.

A white piece of paper on the table by the bed caught her attention. The latest letter from her brother was sure to be more interesting than making a mental list of all the things Mother's lady rules kept her from doing.

When Griffith had left for school two years ago, Mother decided writing to him would be an excellent way for Miranda to practice her penmanship. The first letters had been little more than her name and a sentence about her favorite doll, but over time she and her brother had grown quite close.

Their correspondence had the added benefit of giving Miranda a place to work out her frustrations with her mother.

With anticipation she broke the seal, anxious to hear about her eldest brother's latest exploits.

My dearest sister,

I hope this letter finds you well. Your last letter was long enough to make me very thankful to be a duke. Paying to post that much paper would be costly. Perhaps next time you are bored in church you won't try to kick down the walls of the pew.

Miranda frowned. What else was she supposed to do? The sermon had been supremely boring that day, and Mother had warned her the week before that a lady never sleeps in church. Making Miranda sit still in a chair for an extra hour that afternoon was excessive punishment.

Marsh managed to help us avoid a group of older boys intent on making us do their chores. I continue to be grateful that God provided another young man of high rank here. He's a bit rough around the edges, despite inheriting his ducal title as a child. Almost as bad at being a gentleman as you are at being a lady.

Sticking her tongue out at a piece of paper was the definition of useless, but it made Miranda feel better anyway. No doubt Griffith was doing his best to refine the rough edges of his friend. Their beloved father had taught Griffith well before dying tragically three years ago.

I know it is difficult, but do work harder to control yourself. Mother was beside herself with worry when she found you rolling on the floor laughing over a book you were reading.

The memory brought a curve to Miranda's lips. It had been a very funny book.

One day, Miranda, you'll thank Mother for training you young. It would be helpful if you would try to apply her teachings.

Did he think she didn't try — that she

enjoyed being set in the blue velvet chair beside her mother's desk and lectured about ladylike behavior?

Miranda bounced off her bed and crossed to the writing desk under the window. Snatching a quill and paper, she considered how to phrase today's cake incident in a way that Griffith would understand.

She tried to behave. She really did. But how did one contain emotions when they felt happy or sad or scared? Didn't those feelings have to go somewhere?

It was like those stories Griffith was always telling about his friend. Marshington understood that sometimes one had to go around the rules in order to make things happen. Like the time he left the window open so the fifth-year boys' papers would blow everywhere. Cleaning up the mess had made the older boys miss practice that day, and Marshington and Griffith had finally gotten to play cricket without getting balls thrown at their heads.

Marshington would have done more than throw the dirty cake at Henry. He'd have found a way to make the boy get her a new slice. Maybe even an entire new cake.

He'd have saved her instead of lecturing her. Just like he'd saved Griffith from being tortured right out of school his first month there.

An idea took form in her head.

Did she dare?

She dipped the quill in the ink but didn't press it to the paper. It floated for long moments, until a drop of ink dislodged itself to splatter on the pristine surface. With a deep breath, she placed the nib on the paper and wrote.

Dear Marshington,

It was shocking, even scandalous, which made it exciting. Freeing. A small act of rebellion away from the eyes of her well-meaning mother, away from the censuring of her perfect elder brother.

She'd never send it, of course. A lady never posted letters to an unrelated male. But the very writing of his name made her feel dangerous.

As she scribbled the story of the cake incident, with little care for proper wording and no thought to correct penmanship, something unexpected happened. She felt calm. And she began to see that maybe — *maybe* — her mother had a point.

Throwing cake at Henry hadn't done her any good.

But maybe writing to her brother's best friend would.

CHAPTER 1

Hertfordshire, England
Autumn 1812

Lady Miranda Hawthorne would support her sister tonight, even if it killed her. Judging by the pain already numbing her face, that was a distinct possibility. She massaged her cheeks, hoping to make the forced smile look and feel a little less wooden than the bedroom door in front of her.

With a sharp twist of the brass knob, she wrenched the door open and strode into the corridor. Her stride was firm. Her posture perfect. Nothing would make her abandon the endless lessons in ladylike etiquette from her mother.

Then she walked into a wall.

Oh, very well, it wasn't a *wall* precisely. Walls didn't appear in the middle of passageways, covered in wool.

"I do apologize, my lady."

Nor did they speak.

14

Miranda looked up at the obstruction that was in actuality a solidly built man. She retreated a step, putting as much distance as she could between her and the man without retreating into her bedchamber. Up and up her gaze traveled.

The last dredges of sunlight filtered through a large window at the end of the corridor, sending dim squares of gold marching across the floor and up to the man's broad chest.

He wasn't family. All of her relations had blond hair, including those so far distant they wouldn't even claim the connection if her brother wasn't a duke. The dimly lit passageway prevented her from making out an exact color, but the "barricade" before her had very dark hair pulled back into a short queue at his neck.

With a deep breath, she reminded herself where she stood in life. She was a lady of quality. The daughter, and sister, of a duke. Somewhere inside her must lie the aristocratic arrogance she'd seen so many of her friends embody. If this intruder had nefarious purposes, talking was her only defense. Those long arms could haul her to a stop before she went more than two steps.

He'd yet to make a move, though. He simply stood in the corridor while she

15

inspected him.

"Pardon me." Miranda almost clapped with glee at the clipped, snobby tone that indicated she wasn't begging anyone's pardon. "Who are you?"

She tried to look into his eyes, but his direct gaze made her nervous and shook her focus. Taking deep breaths, filling her nose with the curious scent combination of soap and a hint of evergreen, didn't help either. Instead she concentrated on his chin. Within the shadows of the passageway, he wouldn't be able to tell where she focused her gaze. Hopefully.

He held out a black evening coat. "I am taking His Grace his coat for the evening. I had to press it again."

Miranda's eyes narrowed. "*You* had to press it again? Shouldn't Mr. Herbert be pressing the duke's clothing? I'll ask you again. Who are you?"

"I —"

The slam of a door caused both of them to swivel their heads as her brother Griffith exited the master's chambers. "There you are, Marlow."

Miranda's eyes traveled from one to the other. Both were large men, though Griffith was a bit larger. A blond giant with a tall frame and broad shoulders, Griffith's appearance made as big an impression as his title. This new man, Marlow, possessed less height and brawn — not to mention a lack of status — yet somehow, the servant seemed the more powerful of the two.

Ridiculous, considering Griffith was the Duke of Riverton and in his prime.

Griffith's arm curled around her shoulders as he gestured to the human blockade. "Miranda, this is my new valet."

She blinked in surprise. "Where's Herbert?"

Griffith shook his head as he turned to allow Marlow to help him on with his coat. "Dear Miranda. Mr. Herbert is ancient. He retired. He served me for fifteen years, and he served Father for at least thirty years before that. Did you expect him to work here until he died?"

Miranda raised both eyebrows in a glare of disbelief. "No, but I rather thought *you* did. I suggested you give him a pension three years ago."

She turned to properly greet the new valet. When he leaned forward, nodding his head to acknowledge her, a small smile tugged at the corner of his lips and he didn't drop his gaze in a typical servant manner.

Air backed up into her lungs as she looked into his startling grey eyes. She had always considered grey a rather flat and lifeless color, but *mysterious* and *vibrant* more aptly described this man's eyes. A world of secrets swirled in their depths.

Shaking off the fanciful thoughts that could be nothing but a trick of diminishing sunlight, Miranda gave a polite nod to the servant. "I am pleased to meet you, Marlow. I hope you enjoy working here."

"Thank you, my lady." The servant bowed, then adjusted Griffith's cravat. With a slight nod, he stepped aside.

Griffith offered her his arm, and they proceeded down the corridor.

"When did you hire him?" Miranda whispered as they approached the stairs. She stole a quick glance over her shoulder at the servant's retreating form.

"This morning. I've been quite pleased so far."

"I should hope so. If you were displeased with him after less than twelve hours it would not bode well for the rest of his employment."

They joined their mother in the drawing room.

"Miranda, you look lovely."

As her mother's arms wrapped lightly around her, Miranda focused on the love behind the compliment and swallowed the observation that she looked lovely because she was wearing one of the pastel-colored dresses her mother had allowed this past Season instead of the white and cream she had dressed her in for her first two Seasons. Next Season would be her fourth, and Miranda hoped to eradicate the complexion-killing colors completely.

"I'm sorry William couldn't make the trip with you." Miranda sat on the green-brocade-covered settee, knowing they probably had a while to wait before her younger sister, Georgina, joined them.

A small smile touched her mother's lips as she sat next to Miranda. "I am sorry as well. Next time I will visit longer and he will come with me."

Griffith folded his large frame into a club chair. "Will you return for Christmas?"

Mother shook her head. "We've decided to travel to the coast to celebrate. We never did take a wedding trip, you know."

The love her mother felt for her new husband made her look years younger, though the woman had aged better than anyone else Miranda knew. They could almost pass for sisters when she smiled like that. "It suits you, being Lady Blackstone."

"It does. It was surprisingly easy to go from a duchess to a countess, despite what my friends seemed to think." Mother patted Miranda's hand. "I can't thank you all enough for giving us this year."

Griffith rose to kiss his mother on the cheek. "You deserve it, Mother. His children are married. Yours are all but grown. You should be able to set up housekeeping without us underfoot."

Miranda nodded in agreement, though she had to admit the past year had been freeing for herself as well. Without her mother's constant watchfulness and reminders of proper ladylike behavior, she'd been able to relax a bit, enjoy herself, and even make a few new friends. Having her mother back in the house for the past week had stretched Miranda's emotional control.

Mother cast a worried glance toward the door. "Am I doing a disservice to Georgina, though? She's had such an awful time of it since I moved away. Perhaps I should stay. Or bring her back to Blackstone with me."

Miranda had never seen her mother question anything. Her entire life she'd seen the woman as self-assured, confident, unshakable. It pained her to see doubt and guilt in her mother's eyes. Particularly when the guilt came from doing something all of her children had pressed her into doing for herself.

As for Georgina, her jealous, childish antics in London a few months ago had almost ruined the relationship between two of Miranda's dearest friends. Having a *tendre* for a man did not make it all right to spread damaging rumors about the woman he was courting. Pity was not what Miranda felt when she thought about that time. "Georgina's problems were of her own making, and I think she learned from them."

Griffith rested a hand on Mother's shoulder. "And you're here now, when it matters, for Georgina's first dance as a grown woman, even if it is just a small country assembly."

"It did Miranda good to start small. I wanted Georgina to have the same advantages."

Miranda cleared her throat and looked across the room, deciding a red-and-green vase required her utmost attention. The so-called advantage had done Miranda little good. She was still unmarried and likely to remain so for the foreseeable future.

Learning the man you'd planned to marry cared more for a plot of land than for you could do that to a girl.

A statuesque seventeen-year-old in a blindingly white dress swept into the room. It was unfair that though the sisters' coloring was similar, Georgina could wear the pure color and look angelic. She possessed a special glow about her that made her seem a bit untouchable, a little ethereal.

Miranda recalled the energetic young girl in bouncing blond curls. She'd grown up well. "You look beautiful, Georgina."

"Thank you, sister dear. You are looking well this evening. That blue is ever so much better for your complexion than white. I'm glad you were able to add more color to your wardrobe this year."

She'd also grown up a bit spoiled. Had Georgina just attempted to pay a compliment or to remind her sister that she no longer belonged in the group of fresh-faced young women vying for the best husband?

Either way a compliment from Georgina was a rare and wonderful thing. She would accept it as such. "Thank you. I rather like the variety. Perhaps I will stand out amongst all the white now."

Miranda winced as Georgina smirked and their mother frowned. She had meant to keep that last digging observation to herself. Hadn't she? But it didn't require much imagination to think that the gentlemen might find her more appealing now that she didn't look ill.

Unbidden, a memory of the valet's small

smile flitted through her mind, bringing with it a recollection of his scent. Miranda nearly ran for the door, hoping the cool evening air could clear the last of the man's scent from her mind. Her impending spinsterhood must be bothering her more than she realized if a servant was catching her attention in such a way.

Of course, he was a very nicely put together servant.

After a few minutes of conversation, they climbed into the waiting coach, Miranda sitting backward with her brother to allow their mother and sister the forward-facing seats. Georgina pressed herself against the side to look out the window, and her excited chatter rang through the coach for the entire trip to the assembly hall.

A twinge of jealousy hit Miranda in the back of the throat. That kind of excitement and anticipation had deserted her long ago. Society gatherings were now just something she did. Oh, they were still fun in their own way, but they were also rather ordinary.

Mother's steady voice responded to Georgina's lively prattle, but Miranda paid no attention to what she said. Chances were Mother was reminding Georgina of the proper behavior expected of her. Miranda had heard those reminders often enough to quote them in her sleep.

They descended from the carriage for the short walk into the assembly rooms. Mother squeezed Georgina's arm and leaned in to whisper in her ear. Georgina's smile brightened — how was that even possible? — and she nodded before kissing Mother's cheek.

Miranda glanced around the crowd of people making their way into the assembly hall. They all looked familiar. The same faces she'd seen for the past three years.

They walked between the intricately carved wooden lantern stands and up the pathway to the assembly hall. What felt like a lifetime ago, she herself had walked this now-familiar roughhewn brick path for her first adult outing. The loud clatter of carriage wheels and horses settling in to await the evening's revelers had seemed like music then. Now it was simply loud.

Miranda kept her steps slow, determined to take in everything she might have missed before, desperate for something new and exciting.

By the time she entered the room, Georgina's crowd of admirers had already begun to gather. The innocent excitement of the carriage ride had transformed into a well-practiced grace and just a hint of flirtatiousness. Her sparkling white gown already moved through the crowd of dancers, and if the cluster of young men watching her go was any indication, she would be in constant demand for the rest of the evening.

Miranda refused to be jealous, at least not overly so. She scooped up a cup of lemonade and crossed the room to chat with some of her married friends and a group of mothers watching their daughters from the edge of the dance floor.

He'd used at least twenty names over the last nine years, but none had given him as much trouble as this one. Remembering that he was Marlow, valet to one of the most prestigious and powerful men in the country, was requiring an enormous amount of effort.

Now, more than ever, he had to immerse himself in the role. He had to think, act, even breathe as Marlow, valet to the Duke of Riverton. An untold amount of privileged information crossed that man's desk every day. How much of it could be of use to Napoleon was anyone's guess.

The slightest mistake could mean doom for the entire mission. His final mission.

He pushed the thought away, not wanting to think of the number of men who had gotten injured, captured, or killed on their final trip to the shadows. Vigilance would let him actually see retirement from this business rather than only speaking of it.

He refused to die as Mr. Marlow. The name was horrid, which was why he'd chosen it for this mission. It would keep him from getting comfortable, from forgetting that he was in this home as an employee of the powerful Duke of Riverton, not as his friend.

Once the family had departed for the country dance, it didn't take long for the servants to set the house to rights for the night. While the last maids bustled around the upper floors, Marlow occupied himself with preparing the master chambers for Griffith's — no, His Grace's — return.

He'd searched the duke's room upon arrival this afternoon. Every part of him vehemently rejected that his oldest friend had knowledge of the traitorous activities taking place on the estate, but Marlow couldn't afford to ignore the possibility.

Everyone was a suspect at the beginning.

The unoccupied bedchambers were easy to search and quickly discarded from his suspicions. Using those rooms on a regular basis would have drawn someone's notice. His targets were most likely using a much more public area for their nefarious activities. It was always easiest to hide in plain sight.

He paused outside of Lady Miranda's room, hand poised over the handle. A smile tugged at his lips as he remembered her charging through the door like Henry V running "once more into the breach."

The passionate determination on her face had surprised him. He knew he'd been in the shadows for too long, but he hadn't realized the mere sight of honest emotion would affect him so much.

Moments passed and still his hand hovered over the latch. He should go in, search her room. Being a beautiful, emotional female did not exempt her from suspicion. To some it would increase it. His instincts told him she was cut from the same cloth as her brother, but he couldn't afford to trust the vague intuition. His head had to be convinced.

With a jerk, he pulled his hand back. He started to stab it through his hair but remembered it was slicked back into a queue. A vital part of his disguise, the perfect — and annoying — hair style needed to remain impeccable in case someone saw him. He released his frustration by spinning on his heel and jerking his lapels into place.

Miranda's room would still be there

tomorrow. He could start his search in the more public rooms and deal with his strange hesitation later. It didn't mean she was innocent, simply that he was allowing his instincts to dictate which people were more pressing to investigate. He all but knew it had to be a staff member, so he might as well start with rooms most of them had access to.

As he stepped silently down the stairs, he almost believed himself.

CHAPTER 2

"Did I see you dancing with Mr. Ansley?"

Miranda turned to see an excited smile on the face of her friend, Mrs. Cecilia Abbott, formerly Miss Cecilia Crosby. The two women had shared many a whispered conversation in the corner of this meeting room.

"Yes." Miranda shifted so that her shoulder touched Cecilia's and they could watch the room while they spoke. "He wanted to know if my sister enjoyed hunting. Apparently his family is planning a hunt."

"Poor man. He'll never catch her eye with outdoor pursuits."

His lack of title inhibited his suit far more than his affection for the outdoors did, but Miranda loved Cecilia for not pointing that out. "She told me this morning that less open space was one of the things she looked forward to about London. Outdoor events are limited to riding in Hyde Park and strolling through the Pleasure Gardens."

"Hmm." Cecilia darted a glance around the room before looking at Miranda from the corner of her eye. "You also danced with Lord Osborne."

Heat burned in Miranda's throat. She had hoped no one would put any significance on that turn on the dance floor. "Yes, I did."

Cecilia cleared her throat. "And did he ask about Georgina as well?"

Had it been almost anyone but Cecilia, Miranda probably would have lied. Even to her many other friends, she would have laughed and made up a story about how delightful the interlude had been. But Cecilia had no social aspirations whatsoever. She hadn't even gone to London for a Season, choosing instead to stay in Hertfordshire and find a respectable man who loved her for who she was.

Fortunate girl.

Miranda smoothed her glove over her skirts and stared straight ahead. "He asked if we were planning on going to Town for the winter. Offered to take us skating on the Serpentine if it froze over."

"What a dreadful reason to trap oneself in London for the winter." Cecilia's face scrunched into a frown of disgust.

"Mr. Quinn asked if she enjoyed theater

as much as I did." Miranda smiled, and hoped it looked natural. Too much frowning would draw attention. "He at least remembered I enjoy the theater."

Cecilia winced. "They aren't all dancing with you because of Georgina. Or because of your brother, the duke. You do know that."

"Possibly. Although I've received considerable more invitations to dance than the normal group of family acquaintances and friends' husbands provides."

"That's because you've turned down everyone else."

"Not everyone." Miranda watched her sister twirl around the floor, smiling up into the eyes of Lord Eversly, a man who lived nearly twenty miles from the village of Hawthorne. Had he come for the purpose of meeting Georgina?

Miranda had known these men for at least four years, and they'd barely seen fit to speak to her before — much less ask her to dance.

Georgina's horde of admirers had grown steadily throughout the evening. Happiness warred with resentment as Miranda pressed a hand to the beaded details on her gown.

"Is this what it will be like in London, Cecilia? I'm not positive I can withstand the humiliation. Everyone will compare me to her. I'll be relegated to the spinster corner."

Miranda pinched her finger to distract herself. Tears were threatening, and she could not allow them to fall.

"A lady never reveals her emotions in public."

The subconscious reminder of her mother's frequent admonishments felt as real as if the woman herself were speaking in Miranda's ear. It even sounded like Mother's voice.

"You are hardly a spinster. It will only be your fourth Season. More than one lady of considerable means has waited. It's the desperate ones that make it appear that matrimony must be achieved during the first sojourn to Town."

Miranda said nothing. There was some truth to Cecilia's statement. Miranda was more afraid that her determination to find someone who wanted her and not her family connections would keep her from wedded bliss. If her sister found love before she did, what would that mean?

"Besides," Cecilia continued, "can you truly be a spinster if you're turning down offers of marriage? There were two last year, weren't there?"

"Yes," Miranda mumbled, not wanting to think about those insulting offers. Offers that did nothing but solidify her determination not to settle for anything less than a man's complete devotion. Men's desire to marry for political or material gains didn't surprise her anymore, not as it had that first Season when she'd thought herself in love with the Earl of Ashcombe only to find he was in love with a piece of Griffith's property.

"None of that, now." Cecilia hooked her arm with Miranda's. "You're beginning to look maudlin. Let's see what interesting gossip the lovely ladies that truly do belong in spinsters' corner are discussing. Contrary to popular opinion, they are always in possession of the latest *on-dits*."

The huddle of unmarried ladies stood as far from the dancing as possible. After scooping up glasses of lemonade to give the appearance of taking a rest, Miranda and Cecilia strolled a few steps to their left, keeping their backs to the group to avoid disrupting them.

"Did you hear? Mr. Barrister returned from London yesterday, and he said Lady Marguerite is trying to get her nephew declared dead again!"

Miranda glanced over her shoulder at the

women sipping lemonade and ignoring the rest of the room.

One of the women snapped her fan open. "It will never happen. They can't declare a duke dead without any evidence."

Miranda looked at Cecilia with eyes open wide enough to stretch the surrounding skin. This was interesting news indeed. It wasn't every day that someone tried to snag a dukedom for her son. She turned her head to hear better over the music.

"What if he is dead? How long will they wait?"

"His steward says he receives letters from him on a regular basis with instructions on managing the estates and business holdings."

"Anyone could be doing that. Why, I heard —"

"Would you care to dance?"

Miranda jerked abruptly at the interruption, sloshing a bit of lemonade onto her glove. She looked up to find Mr. Barrister himself standing there, his hand poised to accept hers and lead her onto the floor.

"Yes, yes of course." Miranda handed her glass to a giggling Cecilia and put a bit more effort into her smile. "I would be delighted."

She forced her eyes to meet his bright blue ones as they faced each other amidst the other couples. Many young ladies in the area had written very bad poetry about Mr. Barrister's lively blue eyes. They weren't nearly as appealing as stormy grey ones, though.

Her feet stumbled, nearly sending her careening into the woman beside her. Where had that thought come from? She should not be thinking about another man's eyes while she danced with Mr. Barrister. She shouldn't even be thinking about her brother's valet at all!

The next hour passed in blessed uneventfulness, but Miranda still breathed easier when her mother came around to collect her.

"Leaving a bit early keeps the idea of Georgina's youth in mind." Mother wrapped her shawl around her shoulders as they exited the ballroom. "I need a good night's rest as well. I have a long trip home ahead of me tomorrow."

"When are you returning?"

"I'll return to help you pack for London — late February, I suppose. When we return from our trip to the coast, we're going to visit Lord Blackstone's daughter for a bit." She paused, moisture pooling in her green eyes. "She wants the children to call me Grandmother."

"Why wouldn't they? You'll love them as if they were your own grandchildren. And Lord Blackstone will love our children as much as he does those of his own daughters."

Mother gave a little sniff and turned from emotional to stern in a single breath. "Assuming any of you ever get married and have children."

Miranda suppressed a groan.

"A lady of intelligence and breeding has a responsibility to pass that on to the next generation of the peerage. Some say all the brains come from the father, but I assure you that is not the case."

Miranda's groan turned to a grin. Mother was using her admonishments in ladylike behavior to encourage her daughter to wed now. The woman must be getting desperate to marry off her children.

Griffith and Georgina joined them, preventing Miranda from having to come up with an appropriate response.

"What a glorious evening." Georgina settled into the carriage with a deep sigh and a look of utter satisfaction. "I think being an adult suits me. Did you see all the gentlemen?"

Mother gave Georgina's hand a light squeeze.

"You appeared to have a splendid evening." Miranda was proud of the smile she wore. It felt almost genuine.

Georgina's lips flattened. "Very few of them are ones I would consider eligible, of course. We are in the country, after all. There will be more sophistication in London." She speared Miranda with green eyes too mature for eighteen. "Miranda, you could have warned me how wonderful it would be to have so much attention."

If someone had accused Miranda of growling at her sister's admonishment, she would have heartily denied it. No one said anything, though, allowing Miranda to take solace in the fact that if she had indeed emitted an animalistic sound of annoyance, no one else had heard it.

When they arrived home, Georgina twirled her way through the front entrance hall. The light from the candelabra sought her out, making her the brightest object in the room.

Miranda shook her head. Had she been this giddy after her first social outing? Probably. She'd been a success by normal standards, just not the Incomparable her sister looked to be becoming.

With a kiss on her mother's cheek and a wave to her siblings, Miranda started up the stairs. "Good night, everyone. If I miss you in the morning, Mother, have a good trip."

"You're going to bed?" The pout was evident in Georgina's voice. "Can't we talk more? Didn't you find Lord Eversly's dancing divine? I think he was my best partner of the entire evening."

"I didn't dance with Lord Eversly this evening." In fact, Miranda had never danced with Lord Eversly. Not even in London, where they saw each other at functions two or three times a week during the height of the Season. Lord Eversly never had much to do with marriage-minded young ladies. That he had danced with Georgina tonight placed a seal on her top-tier status.

Miranda faced her sister, focusing all her tension into her white-knuckled grip on the banister. The smooth wood provided little to grip, so she curled her fingers until the nails bit into the underside of the wood. "I am glad you had such a wonderful time. I promise we can relive every detail tomorrow."

She prayed a good night's sleep would help her push past this ridiculous resentment so that she wouldn't ruin her sister's good time. The stairs blurred as she viewed them through unshed tears and flickering candlelight.

■ ■ ■ ■

The family made a great deal of noise as they entered the front hall. But why wouldn't they? It wasn't as if they were sneaking about trying to find places someone could hide in order to obtain secret information.

That was his job.

The family's return meant he had to cease his investigation for the evening. Like it or not, his current cover came with a job. It didn't matter that his employer was aware of the entire scheme; someone had to care for the clothes and help Griffith out of that well-tailored coat.

Marlow slipped out of Lady Blackstone's room. Since she was departing tomorrow, he'd had only tonight to search her things, even though it was nearly impossible for her to have a part in the treachery he was investigating.

He pressed into a curtained window alcove as Lady Miranda reached the top of the stairs. She looked lost in thought, almost to the point of sadness. Her deep, fortifying breaths echoed in the corridor.

They didn't matter. She couldn't matter. Her door closed softly behind her, and he proceeded toward Griffith's room, making special effort to maintain his even stride as he passed Lady Miranda's door.

She was a distraction.

Distractions brought failure, and even death.

This particular distraction had almost caused him to miss the opportunity to search Lady Blackstone's room before she departed. He could not allow Lady Miranda to send this mission down the River Tick. The next chance he had, he was searching her bedchamber, no matter how much the idea unnerved him.

He reached the master bedchamber moments before Griffith did.

"How was your evening, Your Grace?" Marlow helped Griffith out of his jacket and began seeing to the remainder of the evening duties.

"Exhausting." Griffith paused in the process of shrugging into a deep-green dressing gown. "How was your evening?"

"Would you care for anything else this evening, Your Grace?"

Griffith grunted. "We're actually doing this, then?"

Marlow bit his tongue to keep from answering. He must be the servant. Anything else was unacceptable.

40

"No." Griffith tied the belt on the robe. "I'm going to bed to get a solid night's sleep while I still can. Georgina will be the death of me once the Season starts."

Marlow bowed, glad that Griffith hadn't chosen to take advantage of the situation and make his job difficult. If only Marlow's other duties could be handled as efficiently, but there was a dance to be played with whoever was using the estate as a cover. Balancing that dance with Griffith's needs was going to be difficult enough as it was.

Marlow scooped up an armload of footwear as he left the dressing room. He could take care of these tonight and free up some time later in the week to do a bit of investigating.

The opposing smells of high-quality leather and feet drifted from the bundle of boots and evening shoes. This job could not finish soon enough.

After preparing for bed, Miranda couldn't bring herself to crawl between the covers and close her eyes. If she didn't deal with these turbulent emotions, they would follow her to bed. From experience she knew that would leave her tired and out of sorts in the morning, lashing out at everyone for most of the day. No, better to sit up a while more and make peace with herself.

As her mother frequently told her, a lady never makes her family suffer because she is in a bad mood.

Did Georgina get the same lessons? If so, she was much better at ignoring them than Miranda had ever been.

Miranda sat at her dressing table, toying with the necklace Sally had neglected to put away. The gold chain spun around on the table, dragging the teardrop diamonds along the polished surface. They dinged against each other, like the couples crossing the floor at the assembly hall. Even the scraping sounds as the chain hit itself and the table sounded like music.

The emotion roiling inside her could be termed nothing but jealousy, and that didn't sit well with Miranda. She was a woman of twenty, soon to be twenty-one, not a girl of twelve. It wasn't fair and it certainly wasn't Georgina's fault. Miranda had turned down more than one opportunity to get married, so she had no one to blame but herself for her lack of a husband and family of her own.

Where was this jealousy coming from? It wasn't Georgina's herd of beaux that left her yearning. She'd had her chance and found most of them lacking in desirable husband qualities. Was it her sister's innocence? The fresh start?

Frustrated, Miranda tossed the necklace into the waiting jewelry box and closed the lid. She felt restless, as if her skin didn't fit quite right or her heart was about to relocate to somewhere in the vicinity of her stomach.

She folded her arms on the table in front of her and buried her head in her hands. "God," she mumbled, "what is wrong with me? Is this really your plan for me? I don't want to be alone."

The splash of a tear against the dressing table sent Miranda jerking upright. Pushing away from the table, she stood. She refused to cry over this. No more sitting and brooding. The thought of climbing into her bed made her shudder, though.

"Tea," she said, banging her hands flat on the table. "Tea is just the thing."

The only problem was the staff had all gone to bed, and Miranda didn't want to wake anyone.

"All right, Miranda. How hard can it be to make your own tea? You've steeped it hundreds of times. Does it matter if you have never actually heated the water? There's no time like the present to get started. Oh, goodness, I don't know what's more pathetic — that I don't know how to make tea or that I'm talking to myself."

Miranda grabbed the candle from her dressing table before starting down the stairs. The house was eerily quiet and completely black. The moon had hung full and bright in the night sky when they left the assembly rooms, but a dense covering of clouds moved in before they reached home. What little light remained was hidden by the heavy curtains drawn over all the windows.

With the family and servants all tucked into bed, the sprawling country house felt cold and lonely, a sharp contrast to the cheerfully homey atmosphere she was used to.

Two steps from the bottom of the staircase, Miranda's foot caught the lace edge of her dressing gown. A desperate clutch at the banister and a bit of quick footwork brought her to the foot of the stairs. She sent a silent thank-you to her dance instructor for teaching her all the fancy steps, allowing her to come through her stumble with no adverse effects whatsoever.

The same could not be said of her candle.

CHAPTER 3

Miranda found herself standing in the front hall in complete darkness. She supposed it was her due punishment for not taking the time to light her small lantern. Only a fool walked around with an unprotected candle. She stuck her hand in front of her face and wiggled her fingers. Nothing. Not even the slightest shadow was visible.

"Well, that will certainly make things more difficult."

Her choices now consisted of finding a flint box downstairs to relight her candle or to feel her way back up the stairs to her room. Retreat didn't sound appealing, so she slowly slid her feet across the marble floor. Leaving the safety of the staircase, she felt adrift in the sea of darkness.

She dropped her now-cold candle stub in the pocket of her dressing gown. Extending her hands out in front of her, she inched her way to the wall.

Who knew darkness could feel so heavy? It pressed against her, pushing her to take larger, faster steps or maybe sink to her knees and crawl. Anything to have something solid against her hands, anchoring her placement in the room.

With a determined sigh, Miranda set out once more, heading to the breakfast room at the back of the house. There was probably flint in other rooms, but she had no idea where the servants kept it.

The curse of an efficient household.

It was slow going, to be sure. One hand followed the bumps and ridges of the embossed wallpaper. The other waved in circles in front of her, seeking out any obstacle.

She pursed her lips and began to whistle. One of the stable boys had taught her as a child, but she never got the chance to practice, since her mother declared the practice decidedly uncouth. Her tune sounded more like a repeated collection of three notes, but it was better than the gloomy silence.

As she eased around the corner she saw a blessed flicker of light spilling from the library door and dancing through the darkness in the side hall. Giddy relief gave way to curiosity. Who else in the household was up? Surely Georgina had retired to her room where she could blather on about her evening to her maid and her pillows. Georgina had never cared much for the library, anyway.

Even though the door was only slightly ajar, causing the light to point away from her, it allowed Miranda enough vision to move down the corridor with confidence. She pushed the door the rest of the way open, expecting to find Griffith looking for some reference book to help him with one of his projects around the estate.

Instead she found Griffith's boots — a whole pile of them on the floor by the settee. Griffith's new valet was perched on the settee, one of her brother's boots balanced across his lap. A book lay open on the table in front of him.

"Marlow?"

He jerked his attention from his book, sprang to his feet, and executed a smart bow in one fluid motion. "My lady, may I be of service?"

"What are you doing?" She seemed to be asking that a lot lately. It was not a question she normally felt the need to ask her servants.

"Polishing the duke's boots, my lady."

"Of course you are." Miranda thought about rolling her eyes, but refrained.

"A lady always maintains perfect composure in front of the servants."

Eye rolling was not ladylike.

Marlow stood completely still, continuing to stare. It was a bit unnerving.

"I am having trouble sleeping." Why did she feel the need to explain her presence? She'd never needed to before, but oddly she felt as if she had intruded on Marlow's private time.

"Would you like me to get you some warm milk? Or perhaps some tea?"

"I was on my way to the kitchen for tea when my candle blew out." She withdrew the stub from her pocket and held it up.

Marlow opened his mouth to say something and then quickly shut it again. After a moment he opened his mouth again. "I beg your pardon, my lady, but do you . . . know how to make tea?"

"Of course." She lifted her chin in an outward display of confidence. "Every lady has steeped tea."

"My apologies, my lady."

They stood for several heartbeats, he silently watching her while her eyes skittered all about the room. Griffith should really think about rearranging the bookshelves. Their current order was not at all attractive.

Marlow cleared his throat. "I believe the kitchen fires have been banked for the night."

"Yes, I am sure they have." Her fingernails were looking a bit rough. Had she been chewing them again without realizing it?

He cleared his throat once more. Did he always do that before speaking? "Do you know how to stoke the fire?"

Admitting defeat, Miranda threw herself into the chair at her little corner desk, relaxing her tight grip on correct ladylike posture and allowing herself to slump into the soft upholstery with a sigh. "No. I don't."

"Allow me, my lady. I shall fetch you some tea." He executed a perfect bow and turned toward the door.

"Thank you, Marlow," Miranda said to his back.

With nothing to do but wait, Miranda fiddled with the quills and papers on the desk before her. The small desk was one of her favorite places to write. A stack of letters marked for friends from London and for a collection of distant relatives sat on the corner of the table, waiting to be franked and sent to the post in the morning.

She reached for a piece of blue paper from the stash she kept on the corner of the desk, the all-too-familiar feeling of emotional

49

upheaval crawling beneath her skin.

Dipping a quill in ink she began to write.

Dear Marshington,

Georgina has had her little debut here in Hertfordshire. She has made quite a few conquests. I have no doubt the admirers will swarm when she reaches London in a few months.

Is it possible to be happy and disquieted at the same moment? I believe I'm truly happy for her success, but all of those gentlemen now fawning over her did not do the same when I came out a few years ago.

Miranda continued pouring out her feelings in a hasty scribble. A smudge here and a blurred word there didn't much matter. No one would ever read the words but her, and she rarely went back to review them.

She should probably burn them but couldn't bring herself to do it. Instead she kept the piles of letters locked away in a trunk underneath her bed.

The letters kept her sane. She'd long ago passed the age where imaginary friends were acceptable. The fact that her friend wasn't actually imaginary, but simply unaware of her existence, was of little consolation.

There was still the idea in the back of her mind, planted there during those impressionable childhood years, that Griffith's old friend would understand.

I know that I am fairly intelligent, passably pretty, and skilled at running a household, although I discovered tonight that I find fire rather elusive, so why doesn't anyone of any worth seem to want to court *me*?

Just once I would like to meet someone who wasn't intimidated by Griffith. Unfortunately there are no other dukes around. They would not be intimidated by another duke. There is *you,* of course, but we have never actually met, so a courtship between us is a bit unlikely at the moment.

Ah well, I think I hear Marlow returning with my tea.

Yrs,
Miranda

Hastily she folded the paper and shoved it underneath the stack of letters as Marlow entered the library with a loaded tea service.

"Your tea, my lady," he said with a bow.

Miranda looked from the valet to the tea service. The comforting aroma of tea spread through her, making her more relaxed with every breath.

She should offer him a cup. It was the middle of the night, with no one around to see them, and if ever the rules of propriety could be bent it was now.

Then again, *A lady is always a lady."*

Bother that. She shoved her mother out of her mind, fighting a grin at the mental image. It would be a few hours yet before anyone else stirred in the house. Besides, there was something addicting about his grey gaze. Almost refreshing in its honest directness.

She moved from the desk to the settee, trying to subtly wipe her hands against her dressing gown. Had they been sweating while she wrote her letter? "Would you care to join me?"

His gaze snapped to hers.

Miranda's heart gave a strange twist in her chest. They were alone. As alone as she'd ever been with a man, servant or otherwise.

She should recant her offer. The memory of those grey eyes had not accounted for how uneasy they made her feel. They seemed to see more than what was actually before him, as if he could look into her soul and pick apart her inner ponderings and motivations. What a ridiculous thought. Something about this man clearly brought out her fanciful side.

"I would be honored, my lady." Even after answering in the affirmative, he hesitated before taking a seat across the low table from her.

Miranda began to pour the tea. She fixed his cup according to his stated preferences and then sat back with her own cup. She'd already thrown propriety to the wind; rigid posture might as well join it.

"How did you come to be in Griffith's employ, Marlow? I wasn't aware he had set about looking for a new valet, although it was high past time. Herbert must be sixty years old."

"We happened upon each other in the village. I had, ah, been relieved of my employment. Your brother took a liking to me, however, and here I am."

"Truly? That sounds so very unlike Griffith," she murmured. Griffith never did anything without thinking it through and coming up with a good reason or twenty.

"Then I am even more grateful for the position." Marlow quietly sipped at his tea, apparently waiting for her to guide the conversation, if there was to be any.

Did she want there to be any? Yes. Yes, she

did. If for no other reason than to pretend she had control over something. "Did you work as a valet before?"

"Yes, my lady."

Miranda took a large gulp of tea and tried desperately to think of something, *anything,* to ask that did not involve work. She really didn't want to know what it was like dressing a gentleman for a living, and especially not in relation to her brother. Having decided that they were going to have a conversation mere moments before, she wasn't quite ready to abandon the effort.

Her gaze drifted back to him, as if just looking at him would inspire an appropriate topic. All it did was make her realize that she'd been wrong when she thought no man could fill out a coat like her brothers did. Marlow was either padding his shoulders or his muscles were straining the seams of his tailored jacket. She cleared her throat and looked back to her teacup. Tiny blue flowers on white porcelain were considerably safer to look at. "Have you any family near here?"

"No, my lady. I am afraid it is only me. There may be a scattering of cousins over in Derbyshire, but I've lost touch with them over the years."

"Did you grow up in Derbyshire, then?"

"No, Kent."

She looked at him in confusion. It wasn't unheard of for aristocratic families to become scattered, with so many of them traveling to London to marry, but the lower classes? "How in the world did you become so separated? Kent is nowhere near Derbyshire."

"A small move here, a large move there, and you end up going wherever the work takes you." He had a faraway look in his eye, and she suspected there was much more behind his statement than the scattering of extended family members. With a sad little smile and a shrug, he went back to sipping at his tea.

"I see," Miranda said, although she really didn't. A servant would have to change jobs quite a bit to jump from house to house and travel all the way to Derbyshire from Kent and then on to Hertfordshire — and Marlow couldn't be much older than Griffith. "What are you reading?"

Marlow glanced at the book open near the stack of boots. "Shakespeare. *Twelfth Night.*"

"Is that the one where the noblewoman pretends to be a servant to the duke?"

He nodded.

"I've never understood how that would work. I mean, I can't even make myself a

55

cup of tea, much less do things for someone else." She glared at the teapot, as if her ineptitude was entirely its fault. "Aside from the practical aspects, there's the fact that you'd have to go against everything you had been taught since childhood."

Marlow cleared his throat. "I believe, my lady, that the idea is that someone will do whatever is needed when the situation calls for it. I think anyone, nobility included, can find hidden talents within themselves when it is required to accomplish their goals."

After several moments of awkward silence, he placed his cup back on the tea tray. "If you have finished, I will see to the dishes, my lady."

"Of course." She quietly placed her cup down and stood. The smile she directed at the servant wasn't as forced as she expected it to be. The interlude had been far from comfortable, but spending time with him intrigued her more than anything else of late. "Thank you for the tea."

With a last questioning glance at the valet, she lit her candle and went back to her room. Amazing how such a little bit of light made the pathway so much easier to navigate.

Her nerves had settled and bed didn't seem such a daunting place anymore. If part of her suspected it had more to do with the tea and conversation than her heartfelt letter, she refused to admit it.

He set the tea service on the worktable with utmost care. What he really wanted to do was hurl the thing into the fireplace. That would wake the housekeeper though. He didn't doubt his abilities to calm any ruffled feathers waking her would cause, but he preferred no one found out he'd taken tea with the lady of the house.

Servants frowned on uppity airs such as that.

Marlow. He was Marlow. He must remember to be no one but Marlow.

He dumped the tea leaves from the pot and plunged the dish into the wash bucket. Why had he told her about his family? Not all of it, granted. The cousins in Derbyshire were a bit removed and mostly on his mother's side. The aunt and cousin residing in London were much closer relations, but he never mentioned them.

Most of the time he tried to forget they were there.

Life would have been simpler if they weren't. If not for his cousin, he'd have never gone to France, never been caught up in the mystique of espionage, and never found himself shining boots at a duke's country estate.

Which meant he would never have taken midnight tea with Lady Miranda . . . and that would have been a shame.

He smiled as he left everything in the kitchen the way he had found it. No one would suspect a middle-of-the night forage.

Thoughts raced through his mind as he returned to the library. He went over every moment of the exchange, examining angles and motivations. Why would she invite him to drink with her? He'd brought a second cup, intending to finish the pot after she had retired. He never expected she'd invite him to sit with her.

The small writing desk caught his eye as he entered the room. She had left it hastily when he returned with the tea. Was she hiding something?

Dread pooled in his stomach. By necessity, everyone in the house was a suspect until proven otherwise, but he had never truly thought Griffith or his family were behind the leaked secrets.

What if he was wrong?

Thoughts of Miranda's charming and generous nature fell to the wayside. With absolute calm he sorted through the papers on the desk. Letters to family and other social equals were of little interest to him. There was nothing out of the ordinary there, and the post had been the first thing the War Office had searched.

His eyebrows rose at the blue paper at the bottom of the stack. It was folded crookedly, unlike the precise lines of the other letters, and it bore no direction.

He flipped it open and couldn't believe his eyes. She was writing to the Duke of Marshington? Breath whooshed from his lungs as he read the letter. She wasn't just writing to the duke, she was pouring her heart out to him. It indicated an intimate relationship.

He sat on the couch and stared at the dancing flames of fire. This changed everything.

CHAPTER 4

Despite having succumbed to sleep mere hours before dawn, Miranda found herself staring at the ceiling as the sun tried to push its first rays past her curtains. Why couldn't she sleep a little longer? She had nowhere to be, no pressing schedule to keep. That was the beauty of being in the country — her time was her own.

She allowed herself the luxury of an enormous yawn as she stood and reached for the bellpull. Her fingers slipped over the embroidered velvet before snagging on the tassel at the end. The awkward momentum sent her stumbling. The pulls had been installed two years earlier. One would think she'd be managing them better by now.

Hoping the light seeping around her drapes signaled a beautiful morning, she crossed to the window. The warm glow of bright sunlight greeted her as she drew back the green brocade. She searched the sky for any sign of impending rain. Not a single cloud drifted through the blue expanse.

A light sneeze turned her face away from the window to see her maid, Sally, slipping in the door.

"Good morning," Miranda called over her shoulder as she took one last look at the beautiful countryside.

"Good morning, my lady."

Miranda turned from the window to see Sally laying out a cream-colored morning dress. Cream. Only slightly better for her complexion than white. With a sigh, she went forward to get dressed for the day. Maybe later she could get out and take a walk with Georgina. She would have to wait hours for that, however, since her sister rarely stirred herself for any physical activity before noon.

Sally was placing a final hair pin when a soft knock sounded on the door. Curious, Miranda went to open it herself, leaving Sally to put away the nightdress and dressing gown. Who could be coming around this early?

Possibly her mother, with some last bit of wisdom or instruction. Or Georgina, so excited that she'd yet to go to sleep? The housekeeper wouldn't seek her out unless there was an emergency.

Her brother's valet hadn't even made her mental list, yet there he stood, looking crisp and professional and not at all as if he'd spent the night polishing boots in the library.

"Oh, good morning," Miranda said. She poked her head out the door and looked back and forth, expecting to see someone else in the corridor as well. "Marlow? Is something wrong with Griffith?"

"No, my lady. He sent me to request you meet him in his study at your earliest convenience."

"He did?" Miranda's forehead scrunched in confusion. When did Griffith start sending the valet instead of a footman?

"Yes, my lady." Marlow bowed smartly and made as if to leave. He stopped short and turned back to Miranda. "I also wanted to let you know that I posted the letters you left in the library. His Grace had some urgent correspondence this morning, and I took care of yours as well."

"Oh!" Miranda smoothed her hand over the ruffles marching down the front of her morning gown. Were all valets this considerate to other members of the family? Herbert never bothered to deliver messages or care for anyone other than Griffith and occasionally Trent, but then again, the man had been old when Miranda had been born.

"Thank you," she said with a small shake of her head. "In his study, you said?"

Marlow nodded and turned to retreat down the corridor. Miranda slipped out the door and followed him. Two steps down the corridor, Marlow stopped and turned, his grey eyes piercing straight into her own.

"May I help you, my lady?"

Miranda blushed slightly. The reaction spurred her to try to regain the upper hand in the relationship. There was no call for embarrassment. She was, after all, the lady of the house, and after last night's tête-à-tête over tea, she needed to remind both herself and Marlow of that fact. "No, thank you, Marlow. That will be all."

Marlow's eyebrows rose slightly even as he nodded and continued down the corridor.

Miranda's blush deepened. *That will be all?* Even she cringed at the supercilious tone of her voice. What was wrong with her? She shook her head and continued down the corridor as well.

He glanced sideways at her as she caught up with him. Miranda turned her head to look at him, her stride remaining purposeful and steady.

"I am on my way to Griffith's study."

"Of course, my lady." Marlow nodded at her as he continued to walk. He appeared to be strolling, even as he kept even with her brisk pace.

"That is where he is waiting, is it not?" Miranda lifted her chin another notch. He was being gracious and helpful, with the appropriate amount of emotional distance, but she couldn't help thinking that underneath that perfect subservient shell, he was laughing at her.

"Yes, my lady. Table."

"Table?"

"Table."

Miranda narrowed her eyes at the man. What was he talking about?

Marlow's hand shot out and grabbed her arm, forcefully steering her away from the wall and toward the middle of the passageway. Heat bloomed where his ungloved hand met the bare skin of her upper arm. She stopped short and glared at him, her insides dancing with the new understanding of why everyone was supposed to wear gloves to a ball.

With a flick of his hand, he directed her attention to the tall, narrow table holding an elaborate floral arrangement that stretched almost to the ceiling. Had she continued on her previous path, she would surely have run into it.

"Table." He swiftly stepped around her and continued down the corridor, leaving her staring at the offending furniture with considerable bemusement.

Miranda turned her face to the sun, soaking in the warmth and unusual brightness. Griffith's suggestion of a long leisurely ride and picnic was brilliant, though she still didn't understand why she'd been summoned to the study for him to suggest it.

The summons from her brother had been unusual. The request to ride was even more so, but she spent so little leisure time with the man who had acted as her father figure for so many years that she wasn't about to complain about the opportunity.

Georgina did not have the same view of things. "As much as I love you, and you know I do," she'd said when they invited her, "you are not enough of an inducement to get me to eat out-of-doors and without a table. There are insects."

Miranda smiled as Griffith settled into his saddle. "It would be nice if Trent were here to join us."

Griffith murmured agreement and led them away from the stable.

He probably missed their brother as much

as she did. Trent was in London, however, reveling in his freedom, visiting his club and friends, and generally having the enjoyable time young, unencumbered gentlemen tended to have.

It was yet another indication of how old she was getting. Trent was not even a full year older than her and he was out of the house before she was. That was not a good sign.

Miranda gave herself a stern admonishment, though she kept the conversation in her mind. No sense making Griffith worry that she was empty in the attic in addition to being a spinster. Besides, one night of self-pity was more than enough. There was a limit to how much she would let herself languish in misery.

It was a new day. She was out with a brother she saw much too little of. She had a wonderful family and fabulous friends. There was really very little to be sad about.

"This is our last chance to do this for a while, I suppose," Miranda said.

Late October was generally not conducive to leisurely mornings outside, but today was lovely and unseasonably warm.

"True. Before we know it Christmas will be here, and after that we'll be heading to London."

Miranda groaned. "That is all Georgina can talk about. I'm sure we'll be attending gobs more functions than the last two years. She will insist upon it."

Now it was Griffith's turn to groan. Miranda had heard him talk several times about how much he preferred the quieter life of the country. The hours, the relaxation of social stricture, and the privacy were all very alluring. He endured the city to be near his socializing family and to fulfill his political obligations in the House of Lords.

"She's already started listing what we will need in our wardrobes," Miranda continued. "She is planning on being out and about every night. I tried to tell her how exhausting that would be. She stuck her nose in the air and called me old."

"And then of course there are all her opinions about her ball." Griffith gave an over-the-top shudder. "Even I have heard about that."

Miranda ducked slightly as her horse walked under a tree branch. "She is determined to be a success. While last night proved she should be more than adequately popular, I haven't got the slightest idea how she intends to become the Season's Incomparable. She is, after all, quite commonly blond and even more commonly empty-headed."

Griffith opened his mouth, presumably to defend his youngest sibling. After a moment he closed it again. He must have realized that sometimes the truth was just the truth, no matter how harsh it might seem.

Her mother's voice started reproaching her in her mind. *A lady never insults her family, even in private.* Miranda mercilessly squashed the mental chastisement.

"Perhaps she plans on snagging a confirmed bachelor."

Miranda laughed. "Oh, most definitely. She has already told me the normal top-tier bachelors would not do. She wants to be utterly admired when she is the centerpiece of the wedding of the Season. She has a list, you know."

"A list?"

"Um hm." The memory of Georgina reciting her list caused Miranda to laugh so hard that her horse skittered a bit to the side. She took a moment to compose herself and her mare. "She has your friend from school on her list."

Griffith raised a brow at her as they worked their way to the edge of the woods. "Cottingsworth?" he said, referring to the Viscount of Cottingsworth in surprise.

Cottingsworth was a good man, and one

Griffith had suggested to Miranda a time or two. She'd never considered him after Cottingsworth commented about how well suited they were because of his connection to Griffith. Picturing Georgina with Cottingsworth only made Miranda laugh more.

Griffith shook his head. "I am stunned that Georgina is aiming for a title that low. I would have said she would never set her sights, at least not initially, on anyone lower than an earl."

"Oh, no, no." Miranda took deep breaths to calm her giggles. "The duke."

They broke through the edge of the woods into a large rolling field of green grass. Birds trilled in the trees around them, and a sprinkling of wildflowers nodded in the slight breeze. Miranda nudged her mare into a trot, preparing to race across the field like they normally did. After a few paces, she realized Griffith had stopped at the edge of the trees. "Griffith?" she said, turning in the saddle.

"The Duke of Marshington?" Griffith asked incredulously. "But, no one's seen him in nine years! He disappeared during our first year at Oxford, and to my knowledge, he hasn't been seen at all, much less at a social function."

Miranda circled around to pull up beside

him again. "She thinks her reputation of beauty and grace will be so astounding it will pull him out of his rustication, wherever he may be."

Griffith looked blankly across the field before a grin split across his face. "I cannot imagine her being . . . er, popular enough to make him come out of seclusion, but one never knows."

"Are you being serious?" Miranda gasped. If her ever-practical brother considered the Duke of Marshington's reemergence being even the slightest bit possible, he must foresee Georgina being more popular than Miranda could imagine. She shifted in her saddle, trying to alleviate the sudden tightness in her midsection. "You think she could do it? You think he'll actually come to London this year?"

Griffith appeared to give the thought careful consideration. "I think," he said slowly, "that if he comes to London this year it will be pure coincidence."

Miranda narrowed her green eyes at him, the dread gnawing at her belly giving way to the nagging prick of curiosity. A slight nudge was all she required to steer her well-trained horse right up against Griffith's. "Have you heard from him?"

She stared her brother down, all but daring him to keep this information from her. Miranda confessed to having a weakness for good gossip and anything related to the missing duke was good gossip indeed.

Marshington's disappearance from Oxford was legendary among the *ton*. His aunt and cousin had frequently made noises about passing along the dukedom, but his steward, manager, and solicitor claimed to receive communications and instructions from him on a regular basis. The dukedom had in fact been managed well over the last few years, prospering and growing and providing a good living for Marshington's grasping relatives.

Griffith nudged his horse into motion, forcing Miranda's mare to step sideways. "I've gotten letters from him a time or two over the years."

Miranda grinned. This was significant information indeed. "Truly?"

Griffith nodded. "I can't tell you where he is, but I do know that Georgina's obvious machinations would not appeal to him. Race you to the lone oak!"

He kicked his heels against the sides of his horse and charged across the field, leaving Miranda scrambling to send her horse flying after him.

If he thought he was going to get by

without sharing more about that little nug-
get of information, he was sadly mistaken.

CHAPTER 5

Miranda frowned into the mirror over her dressing table. Sally was going to have to completely redo her hair. The long blond tresses had become an utter mess during that mad dash across the field. She began plucking the pins out and letting it fall down in chunks around her face.

A small giggle escaped as she took in her appearance. She really did look a fright. There were leaves stuck to her riding habit, mud on her boots, and even a twig tangled into her mussed coiffure. If she didn't know better, she would think she had fallen off her horse. It had been a close thing when she'd ridden through a hedge in an attempt to cut corners and beat her brother to their favorite picnic tree. Dismounting into a mud puddle upon their return hadn't helped her appearance any either.

She pulled the bell to let Sally know she had returned and began peeling off her possibly ruined jacket. Since she didn't want to soil the upholstery on her chairs, Miranda propped a hip against the window ledge while she awaited her maid.

The view from her window was glorious. The meandering trails, hedges, flower beds, trees, and lawns stretched before her, creating the peaceful sense of home. She savored the expanse of grass where she and her siblings had played, the lake she'd learned to swim in, and the stunning collections of shrubs and statuary her mother had labored over the placement of. If she were successful in finding a husband this year, the view would become an occasional pleasure instead of a daily comfort.

She'd never thought about that before.

Miranda trailed a hand along the simple tone-on-tone green brocade drapes where they met the ruffled lace edging. Such a contrast of the fussy and the practical. Did she and Georgina complement each other as well?

Griffith had certainly been shocked when she'd revealed Georgina's list. Little did he imagine that both his sisters were infatuated with the same man. A man they had never even met. It was a testament to how strong Griffith's high opinion had come through in his letters home from school.

While Miranda was clearly the more levelheaded of the two, possessing no ridiculous notions of enticing the man to marry her, a locked trunk full of letters pouring her innermost thoughts out to him did not make her a pillar of sensibility.

Miranda's smile dropped slowly into a frown. Had she gone back to the library to retrieve her letter from the night before? She was normally so careful with her letters. She even wrote them on precious blue paper so her maid would never confuse them for ordinary correspondence.

With a shrug, Miranda continued to pull pins from her hair. She would go get it when Sally finished fixing her hair. A gasp from behind her indicated that the maid had arrived and taken note of her mistress's appearance.

Miranda grinned. She had pulled out only half of her hair pins thus far, leaving her with a tangled blond tidal wave hanging down one side and the mussed and twisted remains of her coiffure on the other, complete with a twig decoration.

"My lady!" Sally rushed forward to take the mussed jacket from Miranda's hands.

"I'm afraid I had a run-in with some shrubbery."

As Sally fussed over the ruined jacket and

her mistress's overall appearance, Miranda fought the niggling feeling that she needed to remember something about her journal letter. Something important. As Sally's hand flitted over the mess crowning Miranda's head, the niggling memory rushed full force to the front of her mind.

Marlow telling her he had mailed her letters this morning.

Where had she hidden the blue letter last night? Had he found it?

"Oh, no! Oh, no, no, no, no, no!"

Miranda tore out of her room, Sally yelling after her. Miranda wrapped her fingers around the railing at the top of the stairs, swinging herself around the corner and down the first two treads. She snatched her skirt up a little higher than was decent to avoid tripping on the hem as she scampered down the stairs.

The path to the library was blessedly empty. Harsh breathing scraped her throat and lungs as she searched the room. She started with the desk, even riffling through the stack of clean blue paper. When it wasn't there, she refused to believe the inevitable. It was somewhere in the room. It had to be.

She was crawling around on her hands and knees to search underneath the furniture when Sally finally caught up with her.

"My lady!"

Miranda ignored her. She felt around the cushions of the couches and chairs. She looked in every container, no matter how unlikely. Did she really believe it had floated from the desk to the inside of a pottery urn on the fourth shelf?

"My lady, please! We need to redress your hair. And your person. No one is going to touch anything in here. We can come back and look for . . . whatever you need later. It can wait."

"No, no it can't." Frantic fingers dove into the hair at Miranda's temples, further tangling the already disastrous arrangement. "Maybe he hasn't actually sent it yet!"

As Miranda shoved by Sally to return to the corridor, possible outcomes flooded her mind. What if he read it? He could show the letter to Griffith. He could share it amongst the other servants.

She tripped her way back up the stairs, one horrible scenario after another crowding her brain. Could he have posted it? Was it even possible? She had no direction for the Duke of Marshington. She hadn't thought anyone did until Griffith mentioned occasionally exchanging correspondence with the man.

Which meant somewhere amongst Griffith's personal effects was the direction for posting a letter to the Duke of Marshington.

Miranda thought she might swallow her tongue in panic.

Flying past her own door, she ran down the corridor toward Griffith's chambers. He would need to change after their ride as well, so it was the most likely place for the valet to be. She started to charge into the room unannounced but the possibility that Griffith would still be in a state of undress had her stumbling to a stop. Really, they both should be spared the embarrassment that would cause.

She dropped her forehead to the wall, breathing heavily and erratically. Hand folded into a white-knuckled fist, she pounded upon the door.

It swung open to reveal the valet standing there, one muddy boot in hand. "My lady?"

Miranda turned her head and became mesmerized by his quicksilver eyes. She blinked to focus her mind on the task at hand. "Did you actually *send* my letters?"

"Of course, my lady. His Grace said his needed to leave right away so I posted them first thing this morning."

Miranda closed her eyes in despair. "Was there a blue letter amongst the others?"

"Yes, my lady. I took the liberty of completing the direction on it so that it could be posted straightaway."

Miranda opened her eyes to find Marlow discreetly looking her up and down, taking in her total state of dishevelment. She must look like some sort of madwoman. Griffith had returned in a similar state of dishabille, but it never looked as bad on a man as it did on a woman. Cursed ladylike expectations.

Her head dropped limply back on her shoulders. The plaster patterns on the ceiling swam before her unfocused eyes. She wanted to sink down onto the floor in despair, but too many of her mother's how-to-be-a-lady lessons had been drilled into her to allow her such a release. "Dear God," she whispered, "please let the postman lose it!"

"My lady?" he asked.

Miranda simply shook her head in response. Small arms wrapped around her shoulders. Sally must have followed at a more correct, sedate pace. Her maid tried to guide Miranda down the corridor by turning her shoulders. Without a protest, Miranda allowed Sally to lead her away.

The letter was gone. It had been delivered to the posting inn and would be — Miranda's eyes snapped open.

"Wait!" Miranda called.

Marlow pulled the door back open.

Miranda lurched toward him. "Was the post about to leave?"

"I beg your pardon, my lady?"

"The post. Has it already left for London?" Miranda felt as if part of her was standing three feet away, perfectly coiffed, wondering what in the world had come over the crazy woman who now had her hands fisted in the valet's jacket lapels.

"Yes, my lady. He planned to leave for London straightaway, since His Grace . . ."

Heaviness filled her ears, like the pressured quiet when she dove into the lake or swam with her head under the water. Whatever else the bewildered servant said was lost. She heard only a low moan as she gave in to the urge to collapse against the wall.

The letter was going to London. Someone was going to see it. There was no way to keep such a scandalous *on-dit* hidden. Not only was she writing intimate personal letters to a man she had no connection or relation to, she'd confessed to jealousy over her sister. Any hope she had for a modicum of social success this year was lost.

Sally tugged at her shoulders. Miranda looked up to see her maid and Marlow exchanging worried glances. No wonder, that. She'd tossed ladylike decorum aside like last week's newspaper.

Finally, with considerable assistance from Marlow, Sally was able to right her mistress and point her back down the corridor toward her room. The maid looked over her shoulder. "Never mail the blue ones."

Miranda allowed herself to be led back down the corridor to her chambers and sat obediently at the dressing table. A welcome numbness worked its way up from her toes to the top of her head. Practical thoughts once more began to surface.

If anyone had the right direction it would be Griffith, and his valet must have access to it. Perhaps the duke's personal correspondence sat in a pile for days or even months. It was sure to be lost amongst the host of other missives the missing man got and mysteriously answered at his leisure. By the time he read it, she could be safely married.

Maybe he wouldn't read it at all. Even if he did, why would he care?

With a sigh, Miranda wondered for the second time in as many days where the Duke of Marshington was. He was in for quite a surprise when he got her letter. *Dear God, please let him be far, far away, where the letter can never reach him.*

Ryland Montgomery, the Duke of Marshington, was much, much closer than Miranda could have imagined. He'd tried to bury his true identity and truly become Mr. Marlow the valet, but everything about this job made that difficult. Finding the letter and handling the questions it raised made it impossible.

"Was that Miranda?" Griffith asked. He lifted his chin to allow Ryland to finish tying his cravat.

"Indeed it was, Your Grace."

Griffith sighed. "Do you have to talk like that when we're alone? It's rather, well, disturbing."

Ryland snapped a light brown coat in the air and held it out for Griffith to slide his arms into. "I do apologize, sir, but the safest of disguises are the consistent ones."

"Marsh," Griffith began, reverting to his friend's nickname from school.

"Marlow, sir." Ryland inclined his head in a small bow before turning to gather the dirty riding clothes. If his good friend didn't start treating Ryland like a valet, someone was going to be suspicious. While a valet and his master could grow quite close, no one would believe that intimacy occurring in a mere two days.

Griffith sighed. "Marlow. I know I agreed to this whole farce because you told me it was a matter of national security, but we haven't really discussed what it is I'm supposed to do."

Hoping his oldest friend would let it pass, Ryland continued setting the dressing room to rights. The large form of an irritated duke was hard to work around though.

Ryland looked hard at Griffith for several moments. The man in front of him was one of the very few people in this world that Ryland could say that he loved. Griffith would never know how much his friendship had mattered during those unbearable school years.

That friendship had been tested greatly in the last decade, and the man deserved a boon. It wouldn't hurt to shuck the servant demeanor for a few moments behind closed doors.

"Okay, Griff." It felt good to slip into his own skin and personality, if only for a brief time. Dangerously good. "Someone on your lands is gathering and transporting secrets to France. There's a great deal more to it, but the less you know about that, the better. I don't want you acting suspicious around anyone and cluing them in to my presence."

"There are spies on my estate?"

Ryland nodded.

"And you're planning to find them?"

Wary of the direction the conversation was taking, Ryland nodded once more.

Griffith leaned against the doorjamb, blocking the path out of the dressing room. "I still can't believe you've spent the last nine years as a spy for the War Office." He shook his head. "You're probably a great one, though. You always were incredibly observant."

Ryland waved a dismissive hand in the air. "We'll cover my past once I get through this mission. Suffice it to say, the War Office provided an opportunity when I felt I most needed one, but now I'm ready to come home. I wasn't even going to take this mission until we discovered it involved your lands, which brings us back to the matter at hand."

"You plan on finding a spy by pressing my clothes and shaving my chin? I still don't think I'm comfortable with that. Are you sure you know what you're doing?" Griffith ran a hand around his neck, as if ensuring himself it was still in one piece after Ryland's morning ministrations.

"I would hardly have asked you for the

position if I didn't." Ryland raised a single brow. He'd never shaved anyone other than himself, but false confidence had gotten him through stickier situations. "Was there anything else before I return to being Marlow?"

"What did my sister want?"

"She seems to be missing a letter." Ryland turned back to the soiled clothing, afraid his friend would be able to read more than he wanted to admit. Did Griffith know what was in those blue letters?

"A blue one? I don't know what she's constantly scribbling on those papers, but she is certainly protective of them."

Ryland froze, still avoiding looking at Griffith. "You don't know what she's writing?"

"No. I will admit to being curious about them, but she's never seen fit to share them with me." Griffith leaned toward the mirror, inspecting Ryland's handiwork on the cravat.

Ryland took advantage of his altered position and stepped around his friend to take the clothing out of the dressing room. The sooner he removed himself from this conversation, the better.

"Ryland," Griffith said in a low voice. "Why would she think you would know where her letter was?"

Deciding his best defense was to revert back into his servant persona, he turned back around with a bow. "I do beg your —"

"Enough." Griffith hauled Ryland back into the dressing room with one hand and slammed the door with the other.

Ryland forced slow breaths through his nose as he faced off with Griffith. The fresh scent of soap mingled with the more pungent aroma of Griffith's riding clothes.

Griffith jabbed Ryland in the shoulder. "New rule. In this room you are not Marlow. I realize there are prying eyes everywhere else in this house, but in here, it's just you and me, however awkward that may be."

Several moments passed while Ryland and Griffith stared at each other, measuring the other's determination. Griffith's gaze was green stone, hardened by years of responsibility and maturity. The old soul from their school days had grown into itself.

If Ryland wanted to stay, he was going to have to give in to this request.

"Very well."

Griffith nodded, looking a bit stunned that it had been so easy to gain Ryland's acquiescence. What Griffith didn't know, couldn't begin to understand, was that Ryland had almost forgotten how to be himself. It was one of the reasons he wanted out.

Propping his wide frame against the washstand, Griffith pinned Ryland with serious green eyes. "Now, why does Miranda think you have that paper? Are you investigating my family?"

Ryland plopped down into the chair he used to set out Griffith's clothes. He extended his booted feet and crossed them at the ankles. That gave the appearance of comfort, didn't it? Hopefully it would be enough of a change of character to make it seem that he was being totally natural. "I'm investigating everyone, Griff, including you. I've already cleared your family though. It didn't take very long to see that the evidence pointed in a lower direction."

"And the letter?"

"She wrote it in the library last night."

Griffith's eyes narrowed. "You were polishing boots in the library last night."

"Yes."

Griffith rubbed his finger along his thumb, an old habit Ryland instantly recognized. The man was agitated. It wouldn't be long until he couldn't contain the nervous energy to his fingers. Ryland sat back to enjoy the show. It was oddly entertaining to watch the enormous man pace in the small confines of the dressing room. It took only three paces before he had to turn and start the other way.

"You were in there together? Alone? At night? I don't like this, Marsh. I didn't think of my sisters' reputations when I agreed to this."

With a sigh, Ryland rubbed his forehead. He should explain without making Griffith dig for it. It wasn't in his nature, and life had taught him that he was better off keeping his mouth shut, but Griffith was closer than a brother to him, and he deserved better.

"Griff, I'm a servant here. She couldn't sleep. She came downstairs. I made her tea. She was writing the letter when I returned from the kitchen. She drank her tea and went back to bed. If it had been any other servant you wouldn't think a thing of it."

Griffith sighed. "That's true."

Ryland stood and clapped a hand on his friend's shoulder. "Now, if you'll excuse me, I have an alternate personality to resume."

He gathered the dirty clothes and left the room before Griffith could ask him any more questions. The blue letter seemed to burn a hole in his jacket pocket the entire way down the corridor.

Curiosity, a spy's greatest asset and deadliest liability, made his fingers itch. Ignoring the letter wasn't a possibility. He had to learn more. The only question was how?

CHAPTER 6

He found her in the upstairs parlor watching plump raindrops splatter and roll down the window pane.

All afternoon Ryland had told himself not to seek her out, that his curiosity must be ignored and the mystery of the blue letter was best left alone. He couldn't seem to help himself, though. He'd reread that letter at least ten times, and every time it raised more questions. Why him? How long had she been writing her feelings this way? Were the letters always addressed to him?

If so, where were the rest? Because he was finding himself very distracted by the desire to know more about the woman who had poured her emotions onto that paper.

And Ryland never got distracted.

"Are you feeling better?"

Miranda jumped. A brief wince was the only betrayal of how much she must not want to see him. "Very much so, thank you."

"I didn't tell His Grace about your, er, collapse."

She nodded, eyes fixed upon the rain. "Thank you."

He should leave. Simply being here was overstepping the boundaries of his role. She thought him a valet. If he were to say more, push more, even stay in the room a minute more, he would be vastly overstepping his station in her eyes.

"I feel I should apologize, my lady." That was good. Ladies always loved apologies.

She shook her head. "Do not trouble yourself. You were merely being . . . efficient."

Ryland's eyes widened. That was incredibly generous of her, considering he'd had to open the letter to see whom she had addressed it to. Had she forgotten that part?

"I don't know how it was at your previous station." She turned and the anger he'd expected was evident in her face. "Here we do not open personal correspondence, even with the best of intentions."

He bowed. "Understood, my lady."

Her eyes were the same color as Griffith's. Strange how different the shade looked in the face of a pretty woman than in the face of a man. He needed to get out of there. Fast.

"Did you read it?"

Ryland stopped and faced her, lowering his gaze from hers for the first time. He locked his eyes on the velvet bow on her sleeve. Sleeves were safe. "I beg your pardon, my lady?"

"The letter. Did you read it? I know you opened it."

"I . . ." What to do? Lie and leave or tell a small bit of truth and maybe help her sort out the bundle of unasked questions she'd spilled the night before? "Parts, my lady. I humbly beg your forgiveness."

She was silent for a while. Much longer than he was comfortable with. If she went to Griffith demanding his dismissal, he'd be in a tough spot.

"Did you share it?"

"No!" The word scraped out, harsher and louder than he intended. The aristocratic duke he'd hidden for the last decade had crept out in that single moment of outraged denial.

Miranda only nodded.

She looked sad.

This was dangerous. He knew a lot about Miranda. Even before this case necessitated his investigating her, he'd known about her from stories Griffith shared of his family.

Now faced with the woman she had become, he felt drawn to her. Wanted to sit beside her on the blue-and-white-striped sofa and talk about all the troubles she'd laid out in her letter.

But he couldn't. Not as Marlow. An idea began to bloom in the back of his mind. It was insane. Perilous, even, considering the mission he was on.

In any case, he couldn't leave her here, on the verge of tears. He had to give her something to chase away the agony. "If I may, my lady."

She nodded, a resigned look on her face.

"I know I am but a valet." *And a duke, but we won't consider that at the moment.* "I know little about moving around in society." *Certain amount of truth to that. A decade of sneaking and hiding kept a man out of touch.* "But any man who prefers Lady Georgina's company to your own isn't considering anything below the surface."

Her lips twisted in a wry smile and her eyes cast down to the worn wooden floor-boards.

You've cork for brains, Ryland. You just told the woman her sister is prettier.

"What I mean is that they are looking only for easy conversation and surface social niceties." He cleared his throat. Might as well throw everything out there and completely jeopardize his cover as valet. He was truly going to have to avoid this woman after this encounter. "You're more than passably pretty."

She looked up, eyes wide, that same twist of the lips still on her face. "You didn't read the entire thing, hmm?"

Repeatedly. Until I have parts memorized because I wonder what about me made me the target of such confessions. "I merely glanced at it, my lady."

She nodded and turned back to the window. "I thank you for your thoughts, Marlow. Perhaps one day I'll meet a man of my station who feels the same way."

Ryland wondered how a man of servant status would consider that comment. His first instinct was to be affronted at her dismissal of Marlow's opinions simply because of his status, but the truth was, any other view on things would have thrown a servant-class Mr. Marlow into very strange and unexpected territory. Her dismissal was much more along the expected lines.

He left the room, cursing himself for seeking her out in the first place. What had he been thinking? God's grace alone had kept him from shredding his cover back there. He ducked behind a curtain, taking a moment to pray for God's wisdom and protection. More than one miracle had kept him alive and whole during the past ten years. All he needed was one more with his name on it.

It continued to rain for the next week. Fat, plopping drops drifted lazily down from the clouds one day. Shards of water sliced through the air on another. Even when there was no actual precipitation, grey clouds shrouded the sky and a fine mist made a walk in the garden a drenching endeavor.

Miranda sat at the breakfast table, watching raindrops meander down the window. She pushed the coddled eggs around on her plate without thought. Her shoulders slumped, her back slouched, and a small pout marred her face. Even with her mother living hours away, she could still hear the lecture on proper posture ringing in her ears. She ignored it. She was tired of rain.

With a sigh, she pushed her plate aside and sat back against the ornate wooden arches of the dining chair. As long as it continued to precipitate she was stuck indoors, writing letters and applying herself to embroidery and pianoforte plunking. She needed something to break the monotony. Her siblings certainly weren't providing her with much entertainment. The most exciting thing she'd had to do all week was avoid Griffith's new valet — a not surprisingly easy endeavor.

Griffith had plenty to keep him busy — rain did not affect the expectations of a duke. He had spent the last several days holed up in his office, working diligently on whatever it was that kept his many estates running smoothly. Whenever he needed anything, he sent his new valet for it. Marlow had been running all over the estate.

Georgina could think and talk of nothing but the coming Season in London. While Miranda was determined to be happy for her and refused to let jealousy reside in her heart, she saw no reason to test her fortitude more than she absolutely had to.

A rustle accompanied a soft set of footsteps down the corridor. Miranda sighed and adjusted her posture into a more appropriate position.

Georgina entered the room with a delicate yawn. The ruffles of her morning dress fluttered in the air as she spun in a small circle. "Do you like it?"

Miranda raised a single brow. "Is that one of your new dresses?"

"Yes. Isn't it pretty?"

"Indeed. It's also meant for London." Miranda turned her attention to her plate and took a small bite of eggs.

Georgina shrugged. "Mother isn't here. Besides, what could possibly happen to it? I'm hardly going outside in this weather. I'll probably spend the rest of the morning playing the pianoforte and working on my embroidery."

Her excitement over the very activities Miranda was dreading inspired a short laugh. She had to acknowledge the veracity of her sister's statement, though. It was highly unlikely that anything would happen to the dress. She felt rather petty for having brought it up in the first place.

The butler entered as Georgina settled into her seat across from Miranda. A stack of correspondence filled the silver platter in his hand. "The post, my lady."

"Thank you, Lambert." Miranda set her toast to the side and began sorting through the stack. She could have Lambert sort through them, but she liked having an idea of everything that went on in the house. Taking over the housekeeping duties after her mother remarried had given her a sense of accomplishment when she'd desperately needed something to value about herself.

There were two letters addressed to Georgina. Miranda slid them across the table, knowing they would be ignored for the time being. Georgina handled all of her correspondence, what little there was, in complete privacy. A time or two Miranda had wondered if she chucked the things into the fire, unwilling to be bothered with anything that wasn't immediately pressing in her life.

There was nothing for Griffith — hadn't been for more than a week now. Somehow Marlow got to the post before anyone else and pulled anything for Griffith out of the stack.

Was it normal for valets to be so involved in every aspect of their master's affairs? The question was quickly banished to the back of her mind. She may be bored silly, but she still didn't need to concern herself with Griffith's valet.

She frowned again at the rain. Perhaps it would clear this afternoon and she could go visit some of the crofters. Mary Blythe was supposed to have a baby soon.

There was a bill from the dressmaker, an invitation to a country house party, and a handful of personal letters from friends she'd made in London. Answering those would give her something to do with her morning.

The last letter had no identifying marks and the handwriting was decidedly masculine. Her brow puckered in confusion. It was clearly directed to her, not Griffith. A cousin, perhaps?

The seal was plain pressed wax, without a crest or even an initial pressed into it. She eased her fingers under it, nodding and making affirmative noises to whatever Georgina was blathering about. It had something to do with society and London and her planned coming out in a few months. Georgina was quite capable of performing a dozen monologues on the subject, so there was no real need for Miranda to contribute to the conversation.

She picked her mug of chocolate up to take a sip as she flattened the paper on the table. A glance at the contents was all it took for her to start sputtering and choking as she inhaled the hot, sweet liquid. Her hand flailed in front of her mouth as she tried to regain her breath and composure. One errant swing knocked the edge of her plate, sending eggs, toast, and marmalade flying through the air.

A loud shriek accompanied Georgina's scurry out of her chair as she avoided the shower of breakfast food. She frowned at her sister. "You made your point. I'll go change my dress."

She swiped up her letters and left the room, muttering under her breath about overbearing siblings.

Miranda dismissed her sister's pique. She'd been bound to upset the younger girl at some point in the day. Right then, though, she had a much bigger problem requiring her attention.

With both hands, she held the letter up and read it again, disbelief, shock, and terror careening their way through her heart. There was no greeting on the letter, but there was no doubt that it was meant for her and her alone.

Do we know each other?

Regards,
Marshington

A second dollop of wax rested beneath his name, his seal clearly pressed into it.

The letter had reached him. The Duke of Marshington, whose location was the subject of a thousand London rumors, was apparently not very far from Riverton. He had received and responded to her letter in a mere week.

She buried her face in her hands, crumpling the paper. She could still smell the ink on the parchment. How close was he? Not that his location really mattered. He could be sitting at this very breakfast table and that wouldn't alleviate her problem. What was she going to do?

Breathe. In. Out.

Using both hands to brace against the table, she rose on shaking legs.

Deep, slow breaths. Do not panic. Do not faint.

A footman entered and stumbled to a halt as he saw the scattered remains of her breakfast. His face screwed up in confusion before composing itself back into its appropriate servant's blandness. The conversation downstairs would be interesting this morning.

"There was a slight mishap. . . ." Miranda allowed the sentence to trail off. There was really no getting out of this situation with her dignity intact. Food was strewn all about the room and it was clearly from her plate.

"A lady never gives the servants something to gossip about."

"Oh . . . bother!" She scooped up the stack of mail and fled the room.

She locked her gaze to the floor, watching the toe of her slipper peep out from beneath her hem with each step she took. Up the stairs, down the corridor, a quick dash into a guest room to avoid a passing maid, and then, finally, the blessed privacy of her room.

Once inside she leaned back against the door and took a few moments to just breathe.

"It is simply my imagination. All of it. I never sent him a letter accidentally. I never received one." She looked down at the crumpled paper in her hand and groaned. "Why am I lying to myself? My life is ruined!"

If the Duke of Marshington finally chose to come out of hiding and showed that letter to anyone else, Miranda would become a total social pariah. There would be nothing that could save her. This man she had never met held her future in his hands. It was a very sobering thought.

She paced back and forth across the Aubusson carpet she had treated herself to at the end of her second Season, when she had come back to the country without a single marriage prospect in sight. At least not one she was actually willing to consider.

"I can fix this. There must be a way to fix this. Think, Miranda!"

That single line written by a missing aristocrat seemed burned into her vision. Wherever she looked, she saw it. *"Do we know each other?"*

"What kind of a silly question is that? What would it matter if we knew each other? I could not send a letter like that to any man, even if I had known him from childhood."

Her feet stopped their erratic pacing near her small writing table. She didn't write there often, preferring the larger windows of the parlor and library to brighten her writing space. A small stack of paper rested in the shallow drawer, though, and a quill and ink were always kept ready.

She fell into the chair with a thud. With trembling hands, she smoothed the duke's letter on the table in front of her.

"I can do this. Pretend this is a London ballroom and I have to smooth over an awkward moment with an eligible gentleman." The most awkward moment ever created.

Slowly, carefully, she placed a piece of clean, white paper on the desk in front of her. She slid the quill into the ink with utmost precision, careful not to drip excess ink on the paper. Everything about this response had to be perfect.

Moments passed.

Silence descended upon the room. Even the faint click of the rain upon the windowpane ceased.

The ink began to dry on the tip of her quill.

With a groan, Miranda yanked a blue paper across the desk and began scribbling, pouring her heart out in a river of black ink.

Marsh,
You will be aghast over what I have done. I have inadvertently sent you a letter. It is extremely embarrassing to know that my first introduction to you is through an emotionally raging journal entry. What must you think of me?

What else could the man think? There had always existed the high probability that they would meet one day. Writing to him for the past several years was too tempting for fate to resist. Not that Miranda believed in fate, but apparently God had decided she needed to be taught a lesson about using people without their knowledge. Or something. There had to be a lesson in there somewhere, because it could not be happening just to ruin her life.

The thing is that I have been writing to you for years, ever since my brother told me stories about you. You were my fictitious, yet real, companion that I could tell anything to. I have a trunk FULL of these letters. I can't believe I actually sent you one!

What is worse is that you must be in the district somewhere to have gotten my letter and replied so quickly! I don't know how Marlow knew where to send it.

And now I have to reply. I can't not reply. Marsh, what am I going to say to you?

I hope you don't mind that I think of you as Marsh. It is what Griff refers to you as when he speaks of you, which isn't often. He wrote of you when you were in school, of course. What am I doing? I have to write you a real letter!

Having churned out much of the chaos within her head, Miranda took a deep breath, and set the written tumble of craziness off to the side. What could she possibly say to explain what the duke had received? She had to think of something fast, because if he was nearby he was probably in contact of some form with Griffith, and the last thing she needed was her brother knowing she wrote to his friend as if she were some child with a *tendre* for one of her big brother's playmates. Even if that was uncomfortably close to the truth.

With a deep breath, Miranda straightened

up in her chair. She shook the ringlets back from her face and set her teeth with determination. She returned her attention to the white paper and picked up her quill again.

Your Grace,

I am deeply ashamed at the letter you received. I cannot imagine what you must be thinking. Please know that it was never meant to be posted, and I hope that, should our paths ever cross in the future, you will be able to forget this ever happened.

It is a silly childhood habit I have of spilling my thoughts to people I do not know. I find it much more cathartic than the mere keeping of a journal. It was a simple misunderstanding that caused this rambling to wind up in the post.

My deepest apologies.

Yrs,

Lady Miranda

Miranda read and reread what she had written. It was calm and collected and most importantly did not sound as if she *always* wrote to the Duke of Marshington, but that she wrote many different people. That was much better — in her opinion, anyway.

By the time she had finished reading and

checking it several times, the ink had dried and she could fold the note for posting. She wrote the duke's name on the front and then froze. She would have to locate Marlow to discover where to send the letter. Feelings tumbled through her faster than she could recognize them.

How did she feel about seeing him again?

Since their encounter in the parlor last week, the man had been avoiding her as diligently as she had been avoiding him. Considering how often they'd bumped into each other those first two days, it was surprising that she had only seen him at a distance since then.

She tapped the folded letter against the desk. Where would Marlow be in the middle of the morning? Hopefully he was still in Griffith's room. They would be assured of more privacy if he were there.

The crooked lines of her journal letter caught her eye as she stood. She should lock it away and not risk anyone else finding another letter, but she was already losing her nerve to send the real one. A book from her bedside covered most of the letter, hiding the paper from all but the most determined of snoops.

She straightened her dress, took a deep breath, and marched determinedly to the door, real letter in hand. If she had to waylay every servant in the house to find Marlow, she would. A quick jerk of her wrist pulled open the door without requiring that she slow her pace. Nothing would stop her from getting this letter posted this morning.

Then she got punched in the nose.

CHAPTER 7

Ryland lurched as the door he'd been about to knock on disappeared only to be replaced with Miranda's determined face. His fist, already in motion, connected with her nose.

"Oh!" Her gasp corresponded with his surprised outcry.

"My lady!" Thank God he hadn't called out her name. No doubt he had years of covert experience to thank for that.

Miranda collapsed backward on the floor, both hands flying up to cover her nose. Her eyes were shut tightly against the pain that was sure to be shooting through her face.

He winced as he crouched down next to her.

"Are you all right?" That sounded appropriately desperate. Griffith was not going to take kindly to the news that Ryland had knocked his sister to the ground. If he had been a real valet, he would be very afraid of dismissal at that moment.

She pulled her hands away from her face and frowned. "I'm bleeding."

Her voice was flat, probably still stunned. Ryland would be willing to bet the girl had never been struck in her life. There probably hadn't even been a switch in the nursery growing up.

He peeked at her hands to see a few small spots of familiar bright red. He had not hit her as hard as he feared then, for blood was not streaming from her pretty nose. Ryland shook his head. The last thing he needed to focus on was how pretty Miranda's nose was, even with a few spots of almost dried blood around the edges.

She held her hands up for him to get a closer look. "I'm bleeding!" she said again, with considerably more feeling.

"Well, not much, truth be told. I've seen considerably worse."

That was probably not the best thing to say.

She glared at him. A tense few moments passed where Ryland had nothing to do but stare into narrowed green eyes. He could think of far worse ways to spend his time, but her eyes belonged in the same category as her nose: currently off-limits. Once this mission was over, he could consider spending a great deal of time focusing on her features, but right now it was a bad idea.

He fully expected a thrashing, emotional setdown. All evidence he'd seen thus far indicated she was a boiling pot of high emotion, cleverly concealed behind a shield of ladylike behavior.

"I suppose I should put something on it. Trent always puts meat on his nose when he gets busted up." A delicate shudder passed through her frame before she continued her monologue.

Her practicality nearly knocked him off his feet.

"This is going to be revolting. I like my meat thoroughly cooked and covered in sauce. That is an entirely English sentiment, I know, but I have never been anywhere else, so I cannot really bring myself to care."

Did she even remember he was in the room? He never knew a well-bred lady who talked to herself. It was rather endearing. "The cold is said to help, my lady."

She jerked her face back toward his, blushing. So she *had* forgotten he was in the room. A rather humbling thought, that.

One hand whisked through the air, as if pushing the awkwardness aside so she could focus on what was important. "Would you see that this letter gets sent? You can direct it however you did the one last week."

Years of keeping emotions from his face made it easy to hide his pleasure at the idea that she'd answered his letter so quickly. Confusion soon followed, however. Her hands were empty. Nothing was on the floor around her. Unless she was sitting on it, he didn't have a clue where the letter she was talking about was. "What letter, my lady?"

Miranda frowned at her empty hands, then looked around much as he had just done. She gestured toward her writing desk across the room. A white rectangle rested halfway between him and the chair. He raised a brow at the haphazard pile of remaining correspondence littering the floor but chose not to say anything.

"Over there. Addressed to the Duke of Marshington."

As he bent to retrieve the letter, he heard her groping her way to the bed. Was she dizzy? She apparently needed the assistance of the sturdy furniture to stand. He respectfully gave her a few moments.

While he waited he took in the rest of the writing desk. A small corner of blue paper peeked out from underneath a slim volume of poetry. He battled back a grin. Had she written two letters in response to his single line?

A soft, feminine groan had him jerking

back around to face her. Miranda stood, one hand on the bedpost, one pressed to her forehead.

"I barely tapped you," he grumbled under his breath. He'd lost more blood shaving himself in a hurry without a mirror, so it must be the emotional trauma causing her to weave her way across the floor. He'd seen enough injuries to know that even mild ones could knock a person senseless.

"What was that?" she mumbled.

"I was merely wondering if I might be of assistance, my lady." Ryland threw the letter onto the desk and crossed the room to steady her. A soft scent he couldn't quite place tickled his nose. It wasn't floral in nature, but it suited her well.

"Just help me get downstairs."

He held her arm while she took a few slow, shaky steps on her own. At the rate she was moving, it would be time for dinner before she made it anywhere.

"If I may, my lady." Ryland scooped her up in his arms, appreciating the feel of her clasping his shoulders in surprise and, perhaps, a bit of fear. She probably had not been carried since she was a little girl.

"Put me down!" she hissed.

"My lady." Ryland knew his tone was belittling, but he couldn't help it. When he opened his mouth, it sounded as if he were talking to a child. "This is the fastest way to convey you to your desired location."

"Put me in the family parlor, then. You can fetch Sally and have her bring the meat up to me." Another shudder racked her body.

Ryland was much more aware of it this time, since she was in his arms. He began to sweat.

"Of course, my lady."

After gently depositing her on the sofa in the family's private parlor, Ryland bowed himself out the door. He sent a footman to find Sally before returning to Miranda's room to retrieve the letter.

Feeling a little guilty about throwing her morning into chaos, he gathered up the dropped letters beside the desk. He traced a finger over the vine running through the carpet's pattern. It was vaguely reminiscent of a splendid carpet in his own home in London. At least, the carpet had been in the library the last time he had been home. It was possible his money-hungry cousin had sold it, but he doubted it. He paid his steward and estate manager obscene amounts of money to keep his greedy relatives in check.

He placed the stack of letters on the desk,

then picked up the white letter she'd asked him to mail. The corner of blue peeking out from under the book of poetry caught his eye once more. With a grin, he pulled it out and looked over both letters. She thought to give the Duke of Marshington a brush-off, did she? The formal tone of her intended letter didn't suit his purposes at all.

The blue paper found its way into his pocket and the white one replaced it under the slim book. This was sure to muddle Miranda's mind a bit, but the slight knock to the head would have her wondering if she were remembering things clearly.

He was halfway back to the door when it occurred to him that he was in Miranda's room.

Alone.

He'd felt no discomfort going through Georgina's things and only a bit uncomfortable searching Griffith's room, but the idea of invading Miranda's private chambers felt wrong. Wrong enough that he almost continued walking from the room. It wouldn't be the first time an agent's personal feelings had gotten in the way of his job — which was why Ryland jerked open her closet door and searched every pocket, bag, and hem-line.

His search wasn't as thorough as it might

have been but it was enough to satisfy his professional guilt. Dropping to his knees he did a quick look under the bed, surprised to find a large, shallow trunk.

All of the luggage trunks were kept in another area of the house. Why was this one here?

It was incredibly heavy as he pulled it out. And it was locked.

Heart pounding, Ryland grabbed a couple of hair pins from the dressing table and went to work on the lock. The last thing he expected when he popped the lid was paper.

Letters to be precise. Hundreds of them. All addressed to the Duke of Marshington.

As much as he wanted to, he didn't read them. What he was doing with the recently written letters was bad enough. He didn't need to compound the problem.

There was one bit of curiosity he had to satisfy though. Digging in the back of the trunk he found the oldest letters, written on plain white paper. He flipped one open to look at the date.

1800. The woman had been writing to him for twelve years.

How was he ever going to live up to the ideal man she'd created in her mind?

Miranda waited until the last possible mo-

ment to go down for dinner. She success-
fully avoided meeting with Griffith and
Georgina in the drawing room beforehand,
but there was no way to avoid the actual
meal unless she begged off as ill, which
would create a host of other problems.

Georgina's nose wrinkled as Miranda took
her seat. Miranda feared it wasn't a reaction
to the unpleasant aroma wafting up from
the onion soup. She'd avoided looking in a
mirror, not wanting to know if her encounter had left a mark.

"What happened to you?"

Miranda sighed. Her sister's question
brought Griffith's scrutiny. "What did happen to you? There's a bruise across the
bridge of your nose."

She couldn't tell him his new valet had
done it. He'd probably drag Mr. Herbert
back from retirement. "A bit of a clumsy
moment is all. I didn't even bump it that
hard. It must have hit exactly right."

Georgina snickered into her serviette as
Griffith's eyes narrowed. "What hit you
exactly right?"

He sounded calm, but he looked suspicious. She'd never been very good at telling
lies.

"The, um . . ." She spied a painting on
the wall across the room. A woman reclined

on a chaise with a book in her hand. "Book!"

His eyebrows shot up. Georgina's snickers turned into a laughing cough.

"A book?" he asked.

"Yes!" Miranda shifted in her seat, feeling confident in her inspired story. "I was reading in bed and I fell asleep and the book fell right onto my nose."

Griffith ate some soup. "What book was it?"

He wanted to know what book it was? Miranda shoved a spoonful of soup into her mouth, wishing it were something that required a large amount of chewing. A bite of soup only delayed the conversation for a moment. "It was . . ." Another frantic visual search of the room brought nothing to mind. "Shakespeare."

"Shakespeare?"

"Yes."

They all lapsed into silence as the soup was removed and the next course placed on the table. Miranda felt ill simply looking at it. She'd never view meat the same way again.

Georgina grinned. "I've always loved his work. Which one were you reading?"

There should be a law against bratty younger sisters. Georgina couldn't name three Shakespeare plays if her life depended on it. *"Twelfth Night."*

Where had that come from? Oh yes, that was what Marlow had been reading in the library the other night. Fitting choice, then.

Griffith stared at her. *"Twelfth Night?"*

"Er, yes. But I'm not very far into it, so I can't make much discussion about it."

Miranda began to worry about her older brother. He looked deep in thought, as if he were trying to remember something that was just out of his mental reach.

With a shake of his head he gave her a tight smile. "We should talk about something else, then."

Miranda stuffed a bite of meat into her mouth. This was going to be a very long dinner.

Griffith's bed was exceptionally comfortable. Ryland was going to have to look into getting himself a mattress like this one when he got home. Of course, it could have been the years of sleeping in hovels and low-class rooms that made the high-quality mattress seem that much more comfortable.

The large four-poster walnut bed, however, he could do without. It had been in the family for generations, and Griffith frequently described it as horribly ugly, but the last six dukes had slept in it, and he was a sucker for a sentimental tradition.

Ryland shrugged and settled farther back into the pillows. What was he going to do with Miranda's letter? He had to answer it, of course. It was only a matter of time before she realized the wrong one was still on her writing table, and no one would receive a letter such as the one in his hand and not respond somehow — it was simply too absurd! He'd established a week-long response time, so he had a few days to figure it out.

He glanced at the clock. Probably an hour before Griffith required anything of him.

What a ridiculous assignment. His friendship with Griffith made maintaining his disguise extremely difficult. He'd always been able to immerse himself in the role before, forgetting his true past for long stretches of time. That was an impossibility on this assignment. Sometimes it felt as if he and Griffith were back at Eton, before the world took them in such different directions.

It also didn't help that the mission wasn't going very smoothly. He'd searched every room of the house, and his suspect list was considerably narrowed. Within a week the Office should be able to send him anything they knew about the people on his list. There was something bothering him, though. Something missing, but he didn't know what it was.

He didn't like not knowing.

He had determined that at least one upper servant was involved. Someone had thrown a letter into the fire in the drawing room the upper servants shared. One corner hadn't burned. And while Ryland wanted to know what the rest of the letter had said, there was enough there to know someone had been receiving instructions that weren't friendly to the Crown.

Finding that letter had taken more diligence than he would have thought. The scullery maid came through twice a day to sweep out the burnt ashes. Who knew what other clues he'd missed because of her dedication?

Besides the house servants, he had several grounds workers he wanted to look into more. Everyone in the stable was suspect. What better place for moving messages than one with ready access to some of the best horses in the country? He'd seen how often they took the horses out to exercise them. It would be a simple matter to rendezvous with another spy.

The stable staff's quarters were more difficult to gain access to, their proximity to the stable meaning constant activity in and around the rooms. Like it or not, he was going to have to get Griffith involved, have him do something that required all the grooms to leave the stable at the same time.

Until then there was little to do but keep an eye out for more mistakes and wait for the Office's report on whether or not any of the people on his list were more than they seemed.

Patience, the quality most needed in work like this, was running thin for him. He didn't want to wait for opportune moments or for his culprit to make a mistake.

He reached into his pocket to look at the singed scrap of condemning instructions, but his fingers wrapped around the neatly folded square instead. Pulling out the blue paper, he smiled.

Focusing any thought on his friend's younger sister was ill-advised, but he couldn't seem to stop it. The idea that she would choose him as the target of her journal amused him to no end. What had Griffith put in those letters home from Eton? Somehow he doubted they had detailed Ryland's many scrapes and run-ins with the school authorities.

Set to become two of the most powerful

personages in the land, the two of them had tested everything to see how far their titles could get them. Nothing horrendous, of course. Ryland could thank Griffith's faith and steady influence for that one.

The door opened and Ryland jerked to his feet. His eyes flew to the clock. Was dinner completed already?

Griffith stopped a few steps into the room, eyeing the mussed covers. "You're in my bed," he muttered.

"It's more comfortable than mine," Ryland returned.

"I would imagine so, since I am the duke and you are the servant in our little play."

Ryland shrugged. He refolded Miranda's letter and slid it into his pocket.

Griffith's gaze concentrated on Ryland's pocket. "Didn't I see you reading *Twelfth Night* earlier this week?"

CHAPTER 8

Ryland lifted an eyebrow as he moved behind Griffith to help him out of his coat. What had happened at dinner? "I was reading it. It's possible you saw me."

Griffith spun around before Ryland could remove the jacket, his eyebrows lowered ominously. "What's in your pocket?"

"Some personal notes." Well, that was true after a fashion. "I have many suspects to keep track of." Mentally he cringed. He hadn't lied, not really, but he hated how easily he had deliberately misled his friend with his disconnected statements. Yet another sign that it was past time for him to get out of the information-gathering business.

"Miranda's very protective of that blue paper." Griffith began shrugging out of his jacket, whatever suspicion he'd had apparently appeased.

Ryland moved to assist him once more,

124

glad it took him out of visual range for a few moments. "It was convenient."

"Don't let her see you using it. She guards that stuff like gold."

Not surprising. Tinted paper was expensive but not worth as much as the words she wrote on it.

Ryland examined Griffith's white shirt. Streaks of sauce marred the fabric. "Bit clumsy tonight?"

"Must be."

"How convenient that it only spilled in places your coat could cover."

Griffith began examining a small thread on the edge of his trousers. "I've always been rather lucky."

Laughter threatened as Ryland envisioned the scene. Had the duke removed his coat? Shifted it to the side? Ryland flipped the coat inside out, looking for matching streaks. Had he simply shoved the food inside? "You did this on purpose."

Griffith grinned, free of any trace of the earlier tension. "I would hate for you to get bored."

Ryland shook his head and set about his work. His nightly duties didn't take long. As he left the room, he looked at the dirty shirt with a grimace. A decent effort and a lot of time could probably get it clean. Instead of going down to the laundry to soak it, he retreated to his own room, one floor up from Griffith's. He shoved the garment under the mattress. He'd buy Griffith a new one when this was all over.

Two hours later, Ryland was still awake, lying on his back, staring at the ceiling. While it was true that Griffith's bed was considerably better than the one Ryland had been assigned, he had no cause for complaint. In the past decade he had come to appreciate the opportunity to sleep on anything other than the ground. Many a night had been spent tucked into a copse of trees or snuggled into a rocky crevice.

Truth be told, the personal connection was the biggest drawback to this assignment.

He closed his eyes and began mentally composing his response to Miranda's letter.

Life was a very strange thing. As a servant he could knock on her door, be alone in a room, or even go with her on an outing, but he couldn't talk to her as an equal. The unexpected boon of the letters gave him a way to do that.

It was probably mean of him to toy with her. It was definitely not the gentlemanly thing to do.

He grinned as sleep crowded the edges of

his mind.

It may not be nice, but it was definitely fun.

Miranda flattened herself against the wall and slowly reached over to grasp the doorknob. She eased the door open and looked both ways down the corridor. Finding it empty, she left her room feeling utterly ridiculous. She couldn't seem to help it. Ever since Marlow had arrived, the portal to her room had been a much more eventful place than she was accustomed to.

After he conked her on the nose a week before, she took extra precaution exiting her room. Sometimes, like today, she eased the door open. Other times she hauled it open and scurried out of the way in case something lay in wait on the other side. It was enough to make a young lady feel very foolish. Then again, so was getting hit in the nose by a servant waiting to knock on your door.

Thankful that no one had noticed her irregular exit, she walked down the corridor, ready to accomplish her tasks for the day. Cook wanted to go over menus this morning. She also needed to find the gardener and have a word with him. The grounds had been looking quite shoddy of late. At least one of the undergardeners was doing a halfhearted job. Her only hope was that he was lazy and not a drunkard. Lazy was much easier to fix.

"Good morning, my lady."

Miranda shrieked as she heard Marlow's voice behind her. She whirled around. "Marlow." She took a deep breath. "Good morning."

"I'm glad I found you, my lady."

"Oh?"

He held out a small stack of letters. "The post was late this morning. I have pulled His Grace's out."

She stared at the stack of paper in his hand. It had been one week. Had the duke written back? What would he say? Her very future lay in the hands of a man she had never met, a man most of her acquaintances had never met.

"My lady?" Marlow pushed the letters toward her once more.

She should take the letters. They weren't going to bite her. She snatched the folded parchments from his hand. "Thank you."

One eyebrow rose in silent inquiry, but all the valet did was bow and continue down the corridor.

Miranda watched him go. She couldn't remember having many encounters with

Herbert, but Herbert had been a rather unassuming fellow. He did his job and kept quietly to himself.

Marlow was not at all like his predecessor. She couldn't fault the execution of his job; at least she had heard no complaints from Griffith. The man seemed to be everywhere, though. Maybe she just noticed him more. She had to admit that her eyes were drawn to him whenever he was in the room. Something about him didn't fit. Something seemed off.

With a shrug at her groundless notions, she flipped through the post. There it was. In the same bold black writing as before, with a plain seal on the back. Her hands shook as she made her way back to her room. She sank onto the chair of her writing desk with slow, precise motions. With great care, she set the remaining letters on the desk. Sally didn't need another scattering of letters to wonder about.

Two deep breaths fortified her enough to break the seal and open the paper. Still unwilling to read it, she smoothed it on the desk surface, flattening out the creases and blocking the writing with her hands.

No sense putting it off. The words weren't going to change.

Dear Lady Miranda,

I confess that I am flattered by your letter, if a bit confused. As you are aware, I have removed myself from society for the last several years. Normally I do not answer correspondence in a timely manner so as to augment my secrecy. I trust you to keep my whereabouts as our own little secret, given you have such a high regard for me. A trunk full of letters you say? I would be intrigued to read them.

I do apologize for the fact that our unorthodox introduction has flustered you so. I don't believe you meant to send me that last letter, seeing as you ended it with the intention to write me another one. A real one.

You fascinate me, my lady. I find myself anxiously searching the post for a little blue piece of paper. I have not looked forward to something this much in a long time. Please do not let your embarrassment cause you to cease our correspondence. I cannot see you blush through the paper.

And while you can call me Marsh, I fear your brother is the only one who still does. How are you amusing yourself in the recent turn of weather? Rain rarely curtails my own activities, but the drenching we have endured lately has been inhibiting.

Regards,
Marsh

"No," Miranda whispered. "No, no, no, no, no!" She could not have sent him another journal letter! Tightness gripped her chest and made it difficult to breathe. Her hands fluttered in front of her face, as if they could magically change the past or rewrite the words on the paper in front of her.

Calm down. I must calm down. As the man said, he couldn't see her blush through paper, which meant that he couldn't see her have conniptions either.

Deep breaths helped her pounding heart ease enough to allow her to think. She had written both letters here, in her room. Then there had been the horrific experience of having her nose busted by Marlow.

Marlow. Marlow had mailed the letter. He had mailed a *blue* letter. Hadn't Sally told him never to mail the blue letters?

She ran for the door, but a loud crash brought her to a stop. The desk chair lay behind her on the floor. She should prob- ably right it. With a wave of her hand, she ignored the overturned furniture and left the room. With a bit more speed than was prudent, she charged down the stairs.

Where were all the servants? Irrational desperation was beginning to well up in her stomach. Finding Marlow would not unsend the erroneous letter, but it would settle her nerves to figure out what had happened. A footman was entering the great hall as she finished descending. "Marlow!"

"Er, no, my lady. My name is Charles. May I assist —"

"No, no, have you seen Mr. Marlow?"

"Yes, my lady. He was going into His Grace's study."

"Thank you, Charles." She forced herself to walk sedately around the footman. It wouldn't do for the servants to start thinking she had lost her senses.

Again.

It might get back to her mother.

Griffith's study sat next to the library, a short walk from the main hall. How should she start the conversation with Marlow? She turned the knob and pushed open the door without much thought.

Ryland jerked his head up to find Miranda standing at the door, her mouth pinched at the corners and a determined set to her chin. He was fortunate enough to be sitting to the side of the door, out of her immediate line of sight. Her attention was arrested by Griffith, standing by his desk, book in hand, mouth slightly agape in surprise that his sister would barge in without knocking.

Easing to a standing position so that he wouldn't draw attention to himself, Ryland prayed that Griffith would be able to cover his being in the study. While it wasn't the ensured privacy of the dressing room, they had thought the study safe enough to have a hushed conversation about what Ryland needed Griffith to do.

They hadn't counted on Griffith's sister barging in.

Griffith's eyebrows lowered. "Is something wrong, Miranda? Is Georgina all right?"

She shook her head and placed her hand on her forehead. Her eyes closed on a sigh. "No, no, everything is fine. I am so sorry to have barged in like that, Griffith. I was, um, looking for someone."

"I'm afraid it's only myself and Marshlow."

Ryland hoped Miranda didn't notice Griffith stumble over his assumed name.

"Actually, Marlow is the one I need to talk to."

"You need to talk to my valet?" Griffith

speared Ryland with a direct look. "Has he been causing problems?"

Ryland kept his face void of expression. Was she going to mention the letters?

"Oh no. He's been ever so helpful with a special, er, project of mine. I just need to know how a certain phase went."

Griffith's eyes narrowed. Ryland tried to subtly shake his head, though what message he was trying to convey was unclear, even to him. He only knew he did not need Miranda getting suspicious about his relationship with his "employer."

"May I borrow him for a moment?" Miranda continued.

"Of course. We've finished our business anyway." Griffith turned back to his desk, appearing to dismiss the servant without a second thought.

Ryland strode out the door before Griffith could throw any more questionable glances in his direction. There was sure to be an inquisition in the dressing room later that evening.

"How may I be of service, my lady?"

Miranda looked up and down the corridor before grabbing his hand and pulling him into the nearby library. Her hand was small and delicate in his own, the skin cool and soft. Memories of their late-night chat niggled at the side of his attention. He tried not to remember that though it had clearly been awkward, she had tried to relate to him as a servant.

She would never know how much he had learned about her in the space of that shared cup of tea. He was just beginning to acknowledge to himself how much he liked what he was learning.

"You mailed my letter."

He knew, of course, which letter she was referring to. It was probably best if she thought he didn't. "My lady?"

"Last week. After you . . ." She trailed off and gestured toward her nose. "After the incident. You mailed a letter for me."

"Yes, my lady."

"It was blue."

"Yes, my lady."

"Why would you mail the blue one?"

"I assumed since the last one I sent for you was blue that it was the proper letter."

She closed her eyes and sighed. "I thought Sally told you not to mail the blue ones?"

"I do apologize, my lady, but I didn't see any other addressed to the Duke of Marshington." Ryland paused for a moment and then decided to try to draw her out more. "Begging your pardon, but why are you writing letters you don't want to send?"

A blush began creeping up the sides of her neck. His cheeks burned with the effort of holding back his grin. How would she handle the question? He doubted she would confess her journaling tendencies to him.

A shadow crossed the floor as someone passed in front of the glass doors leading from the library to the garden. Miranda's gaze shot toward the door, relief pouring over her features.

"I have to go. That was the gardener." She began moving toward the doors. "I have to speak to him. The west garden is in terrible shape. We may need to hire another under-gardener. I think one must have taken leave." She opened the door and paused. Her mouth opened, but she apparently decided against saying anything else, because she went racing after the gardener.

There was a missing undergardener? Did that mean anything? He could have quit. Maybe he did shoddy work. Of course, a gardener would have run of the grounds. Could retrieve and hide notes and packages. He'd been watching them as best he could, but with even more freedom than the grooms, they were hard to keep track of. And difficult to tell apart when viewed from the house.

Ryland resisted the urge to run his hand

through his hair in frustration. More places to examine outside. It was going to be difficult.

He turned to find the butler standing inside the library door, one eyebrow raised in derision. How had he not noticed the man had entered the room? Berating himself for not listening for footsteps in the corridor, Ryland gave the man a slight bow. "Mr. Lambert."

"Mr. Marlow, what are you doing in here?"

Good question. For that matter, what was the butler doing in the library? "I was discussing something with Lady Miranda."

Lambert gave a pointed look around the now empty room.

"She left out the doors there in search of the gardener."

"Ah, I see. Well, there's much to be done belowstairs. We can't be dallying in the library." The man turned on his heel and led the way from the room.

What had the butler been doing in the library? If one was considering freedom of movement, the butler had the most when it came to the house itself. Someone was searching Griffith's papers and correspondence for information, and it would have to be someone above being questioned by the other servants.

Ryland followed Lambert from the room. At last he had a suspect he could focus on.

CHAPTER 9

Ryland's gut clenched as he flipped through the post and found a letter from Griffith's old school friend, Sir Gilbert Hughes. Since the real Sir Hughes was holed up in Wales drawing disastrous wildlife sketches, the Office had felt safe using his name in their coded communications with Ryland.

He hoped this post would contain the information he needed to seal his investigation. It had been six frustrating weeks since he'd come to Riverton, four since he'd narrowed his suspect list down to four. But last week he'd finally figured out what was bothering him about the whole setup. No one seemed to be in charge. Even the letter in the fireplace had indicated that someone was giving instructions from elsewhere.

While they certainly wanted to shut down the passage of information, it was important they destroyed the head of the snake as well. The idea of anyone getting away with treason made him ill.

As much as he'd resisted pulling Griffith into this mess, Ryland had finally admitted it was the easiest way, and his friend was more than willing. Griffith had been adamant that they do whatever it took to close the information leak. He'd even gone into horse racing to aid Ryland's investigation.

It was a good thing no one dared question the eccentricities of a duke, because when Griffith declared he wanted to race all of his horses against each other to decide which would be a good one to enter in the races next season, no one challenged him. They'd simply emptied the stable of both horses and grooms and took them to a distant field to determine which steed was fastest.

And Ryland had searched every nook and cranny of the stable. A good thing, too, because he learned one of Griffith's grooms was the son of an aristocratic Russian Napoleon supporter and an English baron's daughter. But was the half-Russian blue blood shoveling horse manure to aid his father's cause or avoid his father's wrath?

Griffith had been increasingly clumsy with his correspondence for the past three weeks, leaving letters lying around here and there. Nothing of importance yet — mostly business inquiries Ryland had gotten from a good friend of his who made a living managing investments. Colin McCrae had sent regular details about a mining venture. The mine was doomed for failure but whoever was reading Griffith's letters didn't need to know that.

They'd mixed these letters in with meaningless personal correspondence from distant family members so there would be enough variety to keep from raising anyone's suspicions.

Ryland opened and quickly decoded the letter, years of practice restraining his grin. Finally everything was in place to catch themselves a traitor. It was time to place the bait and hope they caught a fish.

The Office had set up false information drops. Ryland would write four letters to be left in places where each of his four suspects would find one. The letters would ask Griffith to support a new tactic in the war against France. They would then specify a time in which the particulars of this tactic would be given to a messenger.

Four different exchanges had been set up. If someone showed up to the false drops, they'd know who their man was and be able to trace the path and take the entire network down.

It almost made the long weeks of skulking around and pressing Griffith's shirts worth it.

For the next two weeks there would be little to do but wait. Ryland was surprised to find he didn't mind it. His weekly letters to Lady Miranda were quite the diversion.

Hot chocolate scalded Miranda's tongue. She held a serviette to her mouth, trying to keep from sputtering the drink across the table. Her eyes widened as she took in the elaborate mass of curls on her sister's head. "That's a bit fancy for a morning in the country."

Georgina gave a delicate, one-shouldered shrug and crossed the room to admire her reflection. "A lady should always be ready to present herself. I'm trying a few styles to see what I want to do for my first outing. I'll only get one chance to make a name for myself, you know."

Miranda blew across the top of her mug before taking a hesitant sip. "London is still months away."

"True. But it never hurts to prepare. I want nothing left to chance. I do wish I knew who was going to be holding balls at the beginning of the Season. Leaving that strategy to the last moment is so risky."

Lambert placed a small tray at Miranda's elbow. The top letter was addressed with now-familiar bold strokes. It was the eighth letter she'd received from the duke. She grazed a finger across the black ink, a small smile tugging at her lips despite her attempt to hide it. How soon could she leave the room and still be polite?

"Is there a letter from Mother in there?" Georgina reached for the tray.

Miranda snatched the stack of letters up and began flipping through them, not really reading any of them. "I, uh, I don't know. Let me see. Were you expecting a letter from Mother?"

She flipped through the stack once more, slower this time. At the bottom she found the loops of her mother's handwriting.

Georgina plucked it from Miranda's hands. "I wrote her a fortnight ago about a theme for my ball. I want mine selected early, before all the good ones are taken."

"A theme?" Miranda slid the duke's letter into her sleeve before thumbing through the rest of her correspondence. Her ball hadn't had a theme. Unless simple elegance was a theme. "What are you considering?"

"I considered Greek or mythological, but Lady Matilda did that last year."

"Lady Matilda was immensely popular.

143

She married the eldest son of the Earl of Mountieth. There are worse people to emulate."

Georgina frowned. "Emulate? Why should I emulate anyone? I intend to be an original. That only happens with planning."

"Amelia didn't plan it." Miranda hid her smirk with a bite of toast. Georgina wouldn't like being reminded of Miranda's friend who had stumbled into the social scene last year and walked away as the new Marchioness of Raebourne. The whole family knew that Georgina had been hoping to marry the marquis herself. And that Georgina had done everything possible to keep him from marrying Amelia.

Georgina glared but said nothing.

A bit of guilt wormed into Miranda's consciousness. This was her sister, after all. She was supposed to love her, not force her to wallow in past mistakes. "Themes?"

"French."

Miranda choked again. It was becoming dangerous to eat around her little sister. "French? But we are at war with France!"

A wide smile stretched across her face. "I know. So no one else will be doing it."

"Because it is a bad idea."

"No it's not. The *ton* loves all things French. The food, the clothes. I'll make it old France. Before all of this war nonsense."

Miranda set her fork down. "Please, please rethink this."

"It's an original idea, Miranda." She waved the note from Mother in the air. "Mother is sure to love it."

Mother was not sure to love it, Miranda was certain. Georgina was going to be disappointed in the contents of that letter. And Georgina disappointed was more difficult than Georgina excited.

"I think I'll go for a ride," Miranda announced as Georgina sipped her own chocolate, the letter sitting unopened at her elbow. Was she that certain of her mother's agreement? Miranda would have been bursting with curiosity if she had asked for something so ridiculous.

Miranda walked out the door, casting a glance over her shoulder as she went. Maybe Georgina knew her theme was not going to work and wanted to read the news in private.

The wind bit through her riding jacket as she crossed the lawn to the stables an hour later. She circled around to the side paddock, expecting to see the horses saddled and ready.

She was not expecting to see three.

Griffith's large stallion was standing beside her mare, looking bored. Next to him was one of the spirited mounts Griffith kept for company. Did they have visitors? Had Trent come up from Town? She was always glad to have the company of her brothers, but she had been hoping to find a quiet place to read the letter in her pocket.

"Miranda, what are you doing here?"

Miranda whirled to see Griffith and Marlow rounding the corner of the stable. Was Marlow going riding? Herbert had never gone riding with Griffith, but maybe that was only because he was so old. Or maybe he had gone riding and Miranda had never noticed.

"I sent word down an hour ago that I wanted to go for a ride." She gestured to the trio of horses. "I thought you must have heard about it and decided to join me."

He darted a glance at Marlow. "Er, no, but I also sent word down an hour ago. They must have assumed we were going together."

"Oh." Her heart sank a bit. Why was she disappointed? Hadn't she just been lamenting the company of family?

"No matter. Our plans are easily altered. Please, join us." Griffith tugged on his riding gloves.

In no time they were mounted and riding their horses out of the stable yard. Miranda inspected Marlow's seat with quick glances. The man was a very competent horseman. Where had a servant learned to ride so well?

He hung back a bit, allowing Griffith and Miranda to ease their horses ahead of his. It was, of course, the proper thing for a servant to do, but it felt somehow wrong to Miranda. As if he should be riding alongside like their neighbor Anthony, Marquis of Raebourne, used to do before his recent marriage.

"When did you start riding with your valet?" Miranda pitched her voice low and leaned toward Griffith as they crossed through a small patch of trees.

"You and Sally go for walks."

Her mouth fell open, the argument of that being completely different resting on the tip of her tongue. But was it? She did take her maid on walks. Sometimes the choice was between Sally's company and Georgina's. Miranda was sad to say that the maid often won.

She was a terrible older sister.

They rode on in silence over a small rise.

"Your Grace!"

They pulled to a stop. Griffith's steward was climbing the other side of the hill, from the direction of a small cluster of cottages.

"Pardon me a moment." Griffith turned his horse and trotted over to meet the steward.

Leaving Miranda alone with his valet.

CHAPTER 10

Ryland watched Griffith ride away and took the opportunity to pull his mount alongside Miranda's.

"It's a pleasant morning for a ride," Miranda said, with a slight shiver. The wind was worse with them exposed on the top of the hill.

One corner of Ryland's lips tilted. "That it is, my lady."

He nudged his horse forward until he was blocking the worst of the wind. It pulled at his hair, working strands free of the queue and sending them dancing in front of his eyes. It felt good. Free. He wished he could release the whole queue. He really wished he could cut it. That would be the first thing he did when this assignment was over. Get a decent haircut.

They sat in silence a few moments longer.

"I received another letter today."

His head whipped around. She looked

startled that she'd spoken aloud.

Ryland cleared his throat. "I assume you'll have another letter for me to send this afternoon, then. Does that make one a week?"

Miranda nodded. "For the last eight weeks, yes. I thought they would stop after his initial curiosity had been appeased, but he keeps writing. Detailed letters. Personal letters."

"And you respond." He eagerly looked forward to the letters. He was surprised at the restraint it required to wait a week to answer her, but that was the time frame he'd established from the beginning, so it was the one he'd have to maintain.

"Yes," Miranda whispered. "I don't know why. I feel like I know him, though, in a way I've never had the opportunity to get to know a gentleman while in London."

Ryland didn't respond. How could he? Why was she telling him this?

"It's all for naught though. He's in hiding. A few paltry letters with a nearly-on-the-shelf spinster won't make a difference."

If only she knew the effect those letters were having on his future plans. He cleared his throat. "My lady, why are you telling me this?"

A laugh burst from her mouth and a blush

stained her cheeks. "Who else could I tell? You are the only other person who knows of the letters."

"I could give you the direction. Then you wouldn't have to give me the letters." He felt safe making the offer. There were numerous reasons why her posting them herself was a bad idea.

"No. I can't send letters to an unrelated gentleman. Can you imagine the scandal? You can mix them in with Griffith's correspondence. That way only two people in the world know of my horrendous forwardness."

Ryland watched her from beneath lowered lids. The sadness in her voice crept into places he thought well hidden beneath a life-hardened shell. After those first two blundering letters, her writings had always been chipper, confident, and polished. A mere glimmer of the woman he'd studied as he skulked around the house the past two months.

That woman was as unpredictable as she was delightful. Singing in the garden, grumbling at a knotted embroidery thread, plucking the pianoforte keys in a haphazard tune of giddiness.

"I don't know what he writes to you, my lady" — *Dear God, forgive me and let her forgive me for lying!* — "but the regularity of his writing would seem to indicate a marked interest on his part."

"But he's never even seen me. I was still in the schoolroom when he went into hiding." She fidgeted with the reins, threading them through her fingers and then releasing them.

The wind was damaging her styled hair as well as his. A few long tresses fluttered around her face. His hand itched to smooth them back. A tighter grip on the reins kept his hands where they belonged but sent his horse sidling sideways. His knee brushed hers.

"I beg your pardon." His voice was scratchy. He cleared his throat and directed his horse a respectable distance away. "Perhaps it is a good thing that he gets to know you before meeting you. Then you will know his interest is genuine and not based on your beauty."

With any luck that statement wouldn't haunt him when she found out the truth.

Which meant he was doomed. He and luck had parted ways a long time ago.

She smiled and made a swipe at the wayward hairs. "You think I'm beautiful?"

The web of lies he'd constructed slid to the back of his mind. The part of him that knew they were equals, that he was more than suitable, fought its way to the fore, squashing the inner words of caution with a sharp right hook.

His gaze zeroed in on the green eyes he so often avoided connecting with. "I think you are splendid."

"I . . . Thank you." The words were barely audible, carried away on the wind.

Time stretched.

"I like talking to you." Her words smashed together, as if they'd tumbled out in a rush before she could stop them. "When I give you my letters, you always seem to have something interesting to say."

What would she think if she knew he spent hours as he went to sleep at night coming up with what to say when he saw her next? Time he should have spent on the case. It was a dangerous game he was playing, trying to get to know her as duke and as valet. She deserved better.

"Miranda, I —"

"I apologize for the delay. Sudden business with my steward." Griffith trotted up the hill, breaking the trance and reminding Ryland of his chosen role.

What had he been about to say? Did it matter? Calling her by her name was an inexcusable breach of character.

He pulled back on his horse until the animal backed behind Miranda. She'd have to turn fully around in the saddle to see him. "I beg your pardon, Your Grace. I fear I must return to the house. I need to prepare your jacket for this evening."

Griffith's eyebrows shot up as he looked from Ryland to Miranda and back again. Nothing was going to reassure Griffith this time. The man was going to demand answers.

Ryland needed to find some of his own first, though. It was imperative that he solve this case so he could discard the disguise. He nodded at Griffith and turned his horse.

He wasn't going back to the house, though. No word had yet arrived on whether or not his traps had worked. He couldn't wait any longer. It was time to discard a bit of caution in the name of finding a traitor.

She had lost her mind. That was the only explanation. It was time to pack her bags and head to Bedlam.

Miranda stood in the doorway to the library watching Marlow select a book from the crammed bookshelf. He was the most well-read servant she'd ever met.

He was the strangest servant she'd ever met.

154

Which was part of the problem. Even before the encounter on the hill this morning, she'd spent too much time telling herself not to think about mesmerizing grey eyes and kind, profound statements.

"More Shakespeare?" She expected him to whirl or jump or some other reaction that showed surprise. There was nothing. He kept looking at the books. Had he known she was there the whole time, staring at him? How embarrassing.

"Possibly. I haven't decided yet."

"Oh."

Miranda moved to the middle of the room, feeling awkward. She should be at dinner. Her stomach was so tense that she doubted she'd be able to eat a bite until this matter was settled.

At length he turned. His eyes went to the folded blue paper in her hand. "Would you like me to post that for you, my lady?"

"I don't know."

His direct gaze jerked to her face. He stared. What was he looking for? Was he finding it?

She broke the contact first, turning to pace the edges of the room, trailing her fingers along the back of a chair and then the edge of a bookcase. "I don't know if it's wise. I don't really know this man."

"Isn't that the purpose of the letters, my lady?"

"I suppose."

"Will you . . . did you ask him if he intends to come to London next year?"

She toyed with the stiff blue rectangle. "Yes."

"Then, perhaps you will soon know the wisdom of the endeavor."

Miranda slid the letter onto the desk, afraid she'd crumple it if she continued to hold it. She'd poured her heart out in that letter. Treated it like the private letters she used to write.

"You ride very well."

His eyebrows rose. "Thank you."

"Your father was not a servant."

He hesitated before answering. "No, my lady, he wasn't."

"What was he, then?" What was she doing, asking him these questions? It didn't matter that he was the most attractive man she'd ever met and she found herself looking forward to their brief encounters, the insight he provided. Nothing could come of it. Even if he was a gentleman fallen on hard times, she'd have to do the pursuing. He couldn't court her from her brother's dressing room.

The hesitation was longer this time. "He

was a hard man, my lady."

"No, that's not what I —"

"I know what you meant," he said softly. "I'll see to your letter."

"Of course. Yes." Miranda thought she would be sick. Had he seen through her questions? Was he telling her how ridiculous she was being? She hurried to the door, tripping over the edge of the wool rug.

The voices of her siblings drifted from the dining room. She ran up the stairs instead, the headache she'd claimed earlier becoming all too real.

When the footsteps faded, Ryland crossed the room and shut the door. The blue paper screamed at him from the desk. It was thick. Thicker than anything else she'd sent him. He flicked the lock.

He'd just finished checking his second set of hidden information. Three of the four false information letters had been found. Wanting to narrow the field, Ryland had hidden a second set of letters. Only two had been disturbed. It wasn't enough to completely remove suspicion from the stable-hand and the cook, but it was enough to make him focus on the gardener and the butler.

Most assuredly the butler. Lambert was in

this up to his neck.

Satisfied that he'd done all he could do for the evening, Ryland opened the letter.

It was long. Very long.

Half a page in, he had to stop and drop his head into his hands. What was he going to do? The crazy woman had told a duke she was fascinated by a valet.

Three days later Ryland still didn't know how to answer Miranda's letter, but he'd perfected the skill of avoiding her. He hadn't heard yet if they'd been successful at capturing anyone in their information traps, but they would have all occurred by now. Their success or failure was already determined. Once he finished absolving the stablehand of any wrongdoing, they could close down this part of the information exchange.

Ryland assumed his best snobby valet expression and strode into the stable. The abrupt cessation of bright winter sunshine forced him to pause, allowing his vision to adjust. His eyes soon grew accustomed to the dim interior.

Six men busied themselves with grooming horses, polishing tack, and taking stock of the feed bins. Including the groom escorting Miranda on a ride, that accounted for all but one of the stablehands.

158

Ryland stood stiffly in the middle of the central stable aisle. The men's faces reflected derision, dismissal, and every other derogatory reaction in between. His act of a self-important man taking advantage of his close working relationship with the duke was holding. Good. Everyone would leave him alone.

"His Grace wished me to inform you that his plans have changed for tomorrow. He will be riding before breakfast instead of after it."

A loud snort sounded from a nearby stall and a man with shaggy red hair poked his head out long enough to throw Ryland a menacing glance. "Been changing his mind an awful lot lately. You must not be keeping his schedule as well as old Herbert did."

Subdued laughs circled the stable. Ryland allowed his lip to curl as he encompassed them all in a calculated look of disgust. Perfect. He could now account for all the stablehands. "See that his horse is ready."

He stalked off down the aisle. Not the most direct exit from the stables, but he'd made it a point to walk obscure paths wherever he went. It made people less curious when they saw him where he shouldn't be.

In this case, he was heading for one last

look around the Russian's living quarters. The man had received a letter, and Ryland needed to know what was in it. If the letter could exonerate the stablehand, this whole ordeal would be almost over.

He found the missive crumpled in a corner of the small bedroom. After a quick look at the contents, Ryland felt comfortable crossing Jack, as he was calling himself, off the suspect list. The letter was from a friend of Jack's father and the tone was such that the friend expected Jack to be appalled by his father's treasonous activities. The man expected Jack to remain in hiding.

Replacing the wadded-up letter, Ryland made to leave the stable. He knew who his men were and how they were getting information to and from the estate. The innkeeper wouldn't be happy to learn the gardener who was courting his daughter was only doing so in order to pick up and drop off packages at the inn — but the man would not be as angry as Griffith would be when he learned his butler was posting letters in his name, trying to gain access to state secrets.

The shift from the dim stables to the bright courtyard made him stumble blindly a bit as he exited the back side of the stable. He paused and blinked to adjust his eyes.

A sharp pain shot through his skull and his vision went black.

CHAPTER 11

Miranda sat on a rock, thinking of all the ways her situation could be worse. She could be injured. It could be approaching evening. It could be raining. It could be a rainy evening.

Thunder rumbled in the distance.

"I didn't mean it!" Miranda glared at the patches of sky she could see through the bare branches overhead. Sunlight filtered through the sparse canopy, dappling the ground in yellow and orange, but weather could turn quickly in the English country-side.

The prospect of another soaking rain wouldn't be so bad if she weren't stuck on a rock in the woods without a horse. It was embarrassing. Whatever had spooked her normally steadfast mount had done a stellar job of it.

She had not done a stellar job of keeping her seat.

There wasn't even a low-hanging branch to blame for her inelegant flop in the dirt. All she had was her inattention and wandering mind. Her thoughts had been filled with the pointless venture of comparing the Duke of Marshington to the valet of the Duke of Riverton.

The turmoil of emotions had driven her to deliberately lose her groom so she could be alone with her thoughts. Obviously that had been a foolish decision.

"Now what?" She scooped up a stick and poked at the dirt.

She could walk. But the trail meandered, making it wonderful for riding, but incredibly long for walking. Navigating through the woods could get her lost. Parts of it were rather dense and her sense of direction had never been the best. The stick caught on her hem. The cumbersome riding skirt was not intended for walking miles comfortably either.

Another rumble reached her ears, this one closer and longer than the thunder earlier. A smile split Miranda's face.

It was a wagon traveling the old wagon road! She had no idea she was so close. It wasn't much of a road, more like two ruts through a long, rocky clearing, but it cut a fairly direct path back to the house. Miranda began picking her way across the forest floor. It wouldn't do to be found out in the woods without an escort, and she didn't know what kind of person she might encounter, so she couldn't flag the wagon down and ask for a ride, but she could hide in the trees until the wagon passed and then make her way home.

She crouched behind a dense, overgrown holly bush and peered through the leaves to see who was approaching. It looked like one of the undergardeners. Yes it was! A man named Smith. What was the undergardener doing driving a wagon through the woods?

Getting mad at a donkey, if his angry face and hissed words were anything to go by. Clearly the beast of burden was not pulling the wagon as fast as Smith preferred.

Another man who looked vaguely familiar crouched behind him in the bed of the wagon. He was watching the road in both directions and mumbling "Let's go! Let's go!"

"I'm goin' as fast as I can! This old nag won't go any faster." Smith — which might not be his real name given the suspicious circumstances — flicked the reins and bounced in his seat, as if trying to transfer his agitation to the donkey.

The danger emanating from the slow-moving wagon seeped into Miranda's veins, making her heart pound. She held her breath, afraid that even the smallest sound would draw their attention. They looked like dangerous, unhappy men. Were they stealing from the estate? There was some very valuable artwork in the gallery.

"This'll get him moving!" The unknown man snarled out the words as he jerked a long whip from the bed of the wagon. A sharp crack and the donkey squealed and shuffled up into a trot. A second whiz of the whip sent the donkey scurrying toward her, the wagon bouncing along behind.

A foot or two beyond Miranda's hiding place, a small washout crossed the rutted road. Worn away from years of rain, it would have been nothing but an annoyance to a cart moving along at a steady sedate pace. For a frightened donkey trying to outrun its burden it was a bit more of an issue. The donkey did an awkward leap over the four-inch-deep ravine, and the wagon shuddered as its wheels took turns dipping into the washed-out valley.

The wild clatter of the wagon echoed through the lane, disguising the slight rustle of leaves as Miranda pushed her way into the bush, the sharp edges of the leaves biting through her sleeve. She ignored the sting and the sweat riding down her spine.

As the third wheel bounced out of the hole, something large shifted in the bed of the wagon, sliding toward the back edge. She focused all her energy on keeping herself as still as possible as the mystery man scrambled after the load to keep it from falling out the back. A man's head lolled over the end of the cart.

Miranda's stomach churned. Had they killed someone? Kidnapped Griffith? If the men were desperate enough to attack a duke, they were dangerous indeed.

She caught only a glimpse between the bush's branches before the man was hauled back into the wagon bed, but that face had drifted through her mind so often in the past few weeks that she would recognize it anywhere.

Marlow.

She bit her lip to keep from crying out. A sharp, bitter taste — blood — cut through the haze and brought her focus back.

Soil caked between her fisted fingers as she held to the ground, afraid to move from her hiding spot too early.

The wagon was soon out of sight, but she remained motionless until the rumble began to fade.

Fistfuls of dirt flew everywhere as she

scrambled from beneath the bush. Holly leaves pulled at her skirt. The fabric snagged as she shoved her way through to the rutted lane.

What should she do? What could she do? Help. She needed help. Griffith would know what to do. Two steps down the road in the direction of the house, she glanced into the deep ruts, spun around, and looked down in the direction the wagon had traveled. Nothing. Despite the softness of the ground from the previous night's rain, the wagon left no distinct marks. Too many rocks lined the bottom of the ruts.

Even the sound of the wagon was almost gone now.

If she went back to the house they'd never find the wagon. The road split on the other side of the curve. Beyond that, there were countless places they could go and hide.

With a low groan she ripped her jaunty blue riding hat off her head and lodged it in the holly bush. When her groom couldn't find her, he would assume she'd returned home. The chance of them looking for her along the road and finding her hat was slim, but she'd seen God work with slim chances before.

Her hands trembled. A shaky breath rasped her throat.

Was she really going to do this? Chase down a couple of assailants without so much as a riding crop? The picture of Marlow's head lolling over the side swam through her memory.

She wrapped her hands in her riding skirt, dirt smudging the light-blue wool, and set off, muttering a prayer with every step. It looked as if God had a very busy day ahead of Him.

Her feet hurt. She'd given up trying to figure out how far she'd walked in pursuit of the wagon and its beleaguered but blessedly loud donkey.

She was cold. Evening had fallen, bringing a deeper chill to the air.

Being soaked to the skin didn't help either. The rain she'd predicted earlier had arrived with gusto, making her miserable and obscuring her vision. It had tapered off to a mere drizzle now, the scattered clouds letting through the occasional sprinkling of moonlight.

"Positive things, Miranda. Focus on the positive things."

One, her skirt was less cumbersome, as she had ripped several strips of extra fabric off to mark her path. Two, she wasn't walking anymore since the wagon had pulled off the road into a clearing nearly an hour ago.

Three . . . There really wasn't a three.

"I'm wet, I'm cold, and I am incredibly stupid. What was I thinking?"

She had to save Marlow. That was what she'd been thinking. But how to do it? After an hour of considering the situation, she still knew nothing.

Well, she knew that Marlow was alive, or was fairly certain he was. There wasn't much reason to tie up dead people, and the large man was currently slumped against a wagon wheel, arms pinned awkwardly behind him in a way that made her assume he'd been tied to the vehicle.

Miranda was sitting on the ground, shielding herself behind a cluster of prickly shrubs. She had plopped down in the middle of a mud puddle, but by this point a little more rain and dirt wasn't going to hurt. Her vantage point was limited, seeing as how she was looking through a break in the branches that measured approximately three inches square, but she could see the two captors stumbling around the area.

The clearing had once held a stone cottage, but at least half the walls had been carted away and more than half the roof was gone. It wasn't much to look at, but the one corner of remaining roof seemed to be

169

enough of a shelter to satisfy the two men as they settled in for the night.

When one of them tried to build a fire, Miranda gave in to the desire to roll her eyes. Surely captors this clueless could be outwitted, couldn't they?

There was no way to talk around a gun, though. And there was a clear glint of metal in Smith's hand as he gestured around the ruins.

After a brief shoving match, the two men settled in, with Smith sitting up to watch the wagon and the other man stretching out on the ground, presumably to get some sleep. Within moments, Smith's head was falling forward to rest on his chest. Guard duty wasn't enough to keep him awake.

Miranda counted slowly to two hundred, starting over every time she saw one of them move or heard a noise not naturally occurring in the woods. Not that she knew much about forest noises.

When she finally reached two hundred, she decided to keep going until she hit three hundred, just for good measure.

Then she rose from her hiding place, wincing at the cramps in her legs as they took her weight for the first time in hours. She took a step, freezing in place at the snap of a twig underfoot.

"Lord, I don't know what's going on here, but I know Marlow doesn't deserve it. Please, God, help us both get out of here alive."

The prayer didn't ease her fears the way she'd hoped. Simply admitting the worst possible outcome made her throat thicken with her pounding heart. She didn't want to die.

She didn't want to be a coward either.

Marlow must have stumbled into something he shouldn't have, an innocent bystander caught in whatever nefarious activity the other two men had been up to. Then she had stumbled onto their abduction. If Marlow had been courageous enough to try to stop whatever they were doing, she could be daring enough to save him.

A fortifying breath filled her lungs, and she continued on, placing her feet with a bit more care and precision. It was slow going, as she had to keep untangling her ragged skirt hem from the sticks and branches covering the ground, but she made it to the dilapidated stone half-wall before her courage failed her again.

She couldn't see Marlow anymore, but he'd been eerily still the entire time she'd watched him. How bad were his injuries? Would they be able to walk away? Rescuing him was going to be hard enough. Liberating the donkey and wagon would be nearly impossible.

Endless possibilities swirled through her head, clouding her thoughts with fear. Deep breaths and deeper prayers cleared the way for rational thought. If she didn't come up with a plan, she could end up tied right alongside the valet. Until she knew what she was dealing with, she couldn't come up with a plan.

Miranda sank to her knees and started to crawl. Marlow and the wagon were parked beside the lowest part of the wall, the donkey tied to a nearby tree. The poor beast hadn't even been released from his harness.

As the wall got shorter, Miranda's heart beat faster. She was crawling on her belly by the time she reached the end of the wall, where only a single layer of rock remained. A few more feet and she'd be able to slide under the back of the wagon. The shadows beneath should be dark enough to hide everything, including her blue riding habit. If she could untie Marlow from a position underneath the wagon, they would have the element of surprise and be able to slip away.

Hopefully.

The short stretch of ground between the end of the wall and the wagon seemed to grow the longer she looked at it. The wagon might provide decent protection but she would be fully exposed until she got there.

She peeked around the corner at Marlow's slumped body once more.

Sealing the motivating picture in her mind, she closed her eyes and rolled.

CHAPTER 12

Ryland choked on a groan. His head hurt. Every pump of blood sent new shards of pain from the back of his head, down his neck, and across his shoulders.

A flash of blue caught the moonlight to his left, but by the time he eased his head around, whatever had been there was gone. Was he seeing things now? How hard had they hit him?

The slumped-over position was uncomfortable, but he hoped to appear unconscious if they bothered to look. Based on the argument they'd had over who had to be on watch, he didn't think either of them was particularly excited to keep an eye on him.

He tested his bindings again, sending another sharp pain knifing up his arm. It wasn't the first time he'd found himself in a shackled predicament. They'd discarded his vest, so the knife he'd hidden in there was gone. He could still feel the one in his trousers pressing against his calf, but there was no way he could get his leg around to his hands to retrieve the blade.

There was no removing himself from the wheel, but maybe he could remove the wheel from the wagon. Escaping from his captives with a large wheel strapped to his bound arms wouldn't be easy, but perhaps he could smash it against a tree. It didn't feel very strong.

Running his fingers over everything he could reach revealed the wheel was attached to the axle with a simple pin. He thanked God it wasn't one of those newer contraptions that practically made the wheel one piece with the axle.

Removing the pin would be hard enough, if not impossible.

He heard a grunt and froze, darting his eyes around as much as he could without moving his head. Nothing. Not even an animal roamed the dark forest. The rain had slackened and moonlight teased through the branches, but he saw nothing out there.

Abandoning a bit of his ruse, he lifted his head to do a more thorough search of the area.

A rustling came from behind him, beneath the wagon. An animal seeking shelter from the rain?

Then something touched his hands.

Though his fingers were numb to the point of tingling, he hadn't lost all sensation in his hands yet. There was enough feeling left to know that it was not an animal nosing at his bound hands.

It was another pair of hands.

His shoulder screamed at him to stop, but he twisted anyway, throwing his legs to the side in order to angle his body around.

A blue skirt spread along the ground under the wagon. He followed the line of the skirt up to a riding jacket. He couldn't twist enough to see the head, but he knew that riding habit and the body that was in it.

How on God's green earth had Miranda managed to find him?

"Miranda." He kept his voice low, little more than a breath.

The fingers running over his ropes disappeared. More rustling, and then Miranda's dirt-streaked face appeared by the wheel. Ryland was torn between the desire to kiss her or throttle her. Of course, if he had the mobility to do either of those things, he wouldn't be helplessly tied up, awaiting her rescue.

"If we get you out of here, can you walk?"

Ryland nodded, even as he listened for his captors to move. Miranda wasn't experienced at keeping her voice down.

"It's going to take me a bit to untie you. I can't see anything down here."

"Shh." Ryland had to get her to stop talking. Her clearly enunciated *t*'s could be the death of them. "A knife. On my leg."

He'd lined the narrow blade up with the seam in his trousers. Unless someone was doing a very thorough search, they'd pass right over it.

Her head disappeared and more rustling noises drifted through the night. He closed his eyes, praying it wasn't enough to wake Smith or Donkey, as he'd decided to call the guy he'd seen around the town's inn but didn't know by name.

Small hands shot out from under the wagon, hesitating above his feet. Ryland twisted his right leg until the inside seam was facing her, but her hands still didn't move.

"Along the inner seam," Ryland whispered.

Her hands balled into fists for a moment before the fingers stretched for his ankle, pulling the fabric as far away from his leg as she could. Even then, he felt the coolness of her skin as she reached for the knife. He told himself to think of her as he would any other agent, doing what needed to be done to stay alive.

It didn't work. Miranda moved slowly, as if she had to thoroughly think through every move she made. Each time her hand brushed his leg, his breath hitched. Finally she slid the knife out.

The sight of her fingers wrapped around the weapon stole his breath entirely. It was wrong, seeing a knife in her hands. They were hands created to sip tea and embroider cushions. She was being sullied by the entire encounter. He hated it. Knowing that this kind of darkness existed and seeing it with your own eyes were two different things. The price of Ryland's freedom was going to be a piece of Miranda's innocence.

He heard her scramble back to the wagon wheel. "Cut at the knot."

This time he knew why she hesitated. The knot was pressed against his wrist. There was no way to cut the rope without pressing the knife to his skin. "Do it, Miranda."

He kept the knife sharp, so the nick he felt as she slid the knife under the rope didn't surprise him.

Her fingers smoothing over the slight wound did.

It took a long time to cut through the

rope. Ryland kept it as taut as he could, but there was nothing he could do to hurry her along. It was impossible to see what she was doing to know how to instruct her to speed things up.

The tension suddenly released on his arms, and a subdued cheer of victory emerged from the shadows, making Ryland smile.

"Ah, you're awake."

Ryland's eyes snapped forward. Smith was standing on the other side of the low wall, arms crossed over his chest, gun dangling from one hand. Ryland wrapped his hands around the spokes of the wagon wheel so he wouldn't give away the fact that his bindings were gone.

Something pressed against his fingers and he turned his hand to grip his knife. His admiration for Miranda grew even as he called her a fool. She had no way of knowing how skilled he was with a knife, but she had still given him her only means of protection.

Smith snarled. "Well, well, Mr. Marlow. Seems His Grace is going to have to look for another valet. Perhaps Lambert will apply for the job."

Until that moment, Ryland had hoped they thought him a simple valet who had been in the wrong place at the wrong time. But if Smith knew that Ryland knew about Lambert, then he knew that Ryland was at Riverton for a reason.

Which did beg the question of why Ryland was still alive.

"Who sent you?"

Question answered. They knew what he was doing, but they didn't know why. Ryland smirked.

Smith extended the gun.

Ryland threw the knife.

His arm protested the sudden movement, but his aim remained true as ever, sending the knife spearing through Smith's gun hand. The man screamed and jerked in pain, squeezing the trigger and sending the bullet into the wood of the wagon.

Behind him, Miranda whimpered.

Bile rose in Ryland's throat. A few inches lower and that bullet could have hit Miranda.

"What's going on over here?" Donkey came stumbling across the old cottage floor, obviously unhappy about being awoken by the commotion.

Hoping his legs wouldn't give out on him, Ryland pushed off the wagon and jumped to his feet. Two long steps and he was shoving Smith over the short wall, the man still clutching his hand and howling.

Donkey jumped into the fray, and all three men hit the dirt.

Ryland took a punch in the ribs but delivered an elbow to a nose and a kick to someone's knee. Fists were flying everywhere, and he was pretty sure Smith hit Donkey at one point. Rain had turned the ground into a giant mud puddle, making it nearly impossible to gain any footing.

He dug his toe into the mud, preparing to use it as leverage over his attackers.

Then he got a faceful of tree branch.

Over and over the tree branch fell on the group of men. It wasn't thick enough to do any damage but the many small twigs and branches protruding from the limb threatened to stab into his eyes if he wasn't careful.

He threw his right fist toward Donkey's face and plowed into a mess of wet, clingy leaves instead. "What are you doing?" he yelled.

"Helping!" Miranda lifted and lowered the limb again, smacking a startled Smith in the mouth.

"Me or them?" Ryland groaned at the looks on his abductors' faces. The odds had just jumped considerably in their favor.

"What?"

181

Ryland didn't have time to see if her face matched the adorably confused tone in her voice. He had to act fast and get himself and Miranda away from these men. If he were on his own he'd press them for what they knew and who they worked for, but Miranda's survival was more important than that information.

Donkey grabbed the limb and shoved a foot into Ryland's stomach. "Well, well, what have we here?"

Struggling to regain his breath, Ryland knelt on Smith's chest and threw his fist in Donkey's direction. What the punch lacked in finesse it made up for in power. The man's head snapped sideways, and his eyes rolled back before he fell into the mud.

"How can I help?" Miranda's yell pulled his attention. He looked over his shoulder and had to smother a laugh even as he struggled to restrain Smith. Miranda was dancing around on the low stone wall, wanting to help but afraid to get near the man's flailing legs.

Ryland stood and hauled Smith to his feet. With air back in his lungs and firmer control of the situation, his voice was calm. "What are you doing here?"

"Do you really think this is the best time to discuss that?"

She had a point. He punched Smith in the nose, sending him toppling over Donkey on his way to the ground. "Get me that rope."

She nodded and jumped to the ground to retrieve the rope. The gun was nowhere to be found, likely buried in the mud in their scuffle. Ryland looked down at his assailants, now harmless in their unconsciousness.

He'd have some explaining to do.

Then again, so would she.

Miranda was thankful Marlow's calm command gave her something to do that didn't frighten the wits out of her. She scooped up the rope and ran back to Marlow, hiking her skirt up to jump the wall. He was pulling his knife from Smith's hand as she approached. He wiped the blade on Smith's pant leg.

What kind of valet kept a knife in the seam of his trousers?

She tossed the rope at him. He caught it and began looping it around both men's wrists, effectively tying them back-to-back. His coat and vest had been disposed of at some point in his adventure and his white shirt was plastered to his body. She tried not to notice how the muscles bunched and moved as he pulled the rope taut, but she was too fascinated to look away.

Marlow was incredibly strong. Stronger than she'd realized when she'd seen him in his tailored coats. She'd never known a body could look like that, so alive and capable. What would those bunching muscles feel like?

She groaned as she lowered into a sitting position on the wall. The attraction was inappropriate in so many ways that she couldn't even begin to list them all.

"Let's go." Marlow stepped over the wall, hauling her to her feet as he passed.

He stopped by the donkey. Three quick yanks of the knife and the animal was free. A swat to his backside sent him bleating his way back toward the road.

Miranda started to follow the donkey. They could use her fabric markers to retrace their steps and get home. It would take them all night but they'd make it.

Marlow wrapped a hand around her arm and redirected her. Air hissed through her teeth in reaction. His grip loosened instantly, and he shifted his hand to her lower back, pushing her away from the lane and deeper into the woods.

Miranda glanced around, confusion warring with the unexplainable instinct to trust his direction. "Where —"

"We can't go that way. It's not safe."

Her confusion shifted away from wondering where they were going to wondering who she was in the woods with. He had fought very well for a valet. Trent often boxed and was very good at fisticuffs, but even he would have been unable to handily defeat two abductors. And Marlow's skills with the knife . . . ? Aside from the fact that he'd thrown the knife through a man's hand, Marlow had cut through two leather straps and a rope in seconds whereas she'd spent several awkward minutes hacking through his bindings. Who was this man?

"Wait! Wait!" Miranda jerked to a stop, her body screaming in protest about all it had been through in the past twelve hours. Before she got too far from the lane, she had to be sure she trusted him.

"We have to go." His voice was firm and calm.

"But the road is that way!" Her voice managed to rise an octave over the course of a single sentence. She was panicking. She didn't want to panic. She wanted to be calm, collected, controlled. Midnight escapes hadn't been covered in ladyship lessons, though valet training appeared to offer extensive instruction in that area.

"What is going on?" Miranda whispered.

He sighed and began pulling her along, disregarding her cry. "They aren't alone, Miranda. They talked about meeting someone, and I don't have a weapon aside from this measly little knife. So if Lam . . . I mean, if the others show up, we'll be in trouble."

"Trouble . . . I . . . Who are you?"

His silver eyes seemed to emit rather than reflect the moonlight as he stopped to stare down at her. She wasn't sure if hours or mere minutes passed as she stood there, trapped in his gaze, so close that their breath mingled in a frosty cloud between their faces. Why didn't she feel cold anymore?

Rain rolled down his cheek, finding the lines that marked the tension in his face. Her arm hurt, but what kind of pain must he be in?

"Do you trust me?" His voice was quiet but firm.

It wasn't an answer to her question, and yet it was. Something was very wrong here. Things had been strange since the day this man came to work for her brother. Regardless of that, Miranda felt that he was a man she could trust. There was nothing particular to point at, no definite reason that she should place her life in his hands, but she trusted him.

More importantly she trusted herself. Who would have thought she was capable of what she'd done under the wagon? On the road? God had given her sterner stuff than she'd given Him credit for.

"I trust you." She placed her hand in his and they ran.

CHAPTER 13

They ran for hours. Or minutes. Or days.
Miranda lost touch with the concept of time
and focused on putting one foot in front of
the other and not landing on her face in the
mud. They left the woods and crossed fields.
He gave her a break here and there, but then
threw her over hedges and followed her in a
single leap. Whether by design or chance
they never saw any dwellings. They just ran.

By the time Marlow slowed and led them
into a shed, the sun was peeking weakly over
the horizon through thin rain clouds. Miranda leaned against the wall and began to
feel every ache and pain her body had managed to ignore during their midnight flight.

She was too tired to weep but too miserable to fight the tears. They ran unchecked
down her cheeks in a silent flood as her
body collapsed. Strong arms lifted her and
carried her to the back corner of the shed.
She felt scratchy hay against one cheek and

a soft caress against the other. Already, the blessed darkness of sleep was beginning to creep across her mind.

"Sleep, Miranda. I'll keep you safe."

The rough whisper was all the permission her body needed.

She was beautiful. Her hair was an utter disaster, her face smudged with dirt, her riding habit torn and filthy. There was a scrape on her right temple and mud caked halfway up her boots. She resembled a half-drowned street urchin.

And no woman had ever looked lovelier.

He sighed and leaned his head back against the wall of the shed. The chance of the conspirators finding them was small enough that he felt he could allow himself to rest, but he still put himself between Miranda and even the slimmest chance of danger.

There was only one door, and the building wasn't all that large. He had placed her on a scattering of hay near the back corner, a larger pile of hay between her and the door. She was peaceful now, more unconscious than sleeping. When she woke, pain was sure to be her first greeting.

Ryland stretched out his legs, twinges and aches of his own making him wince. He needed sleep as well, though he intended to take his rest in a seated position. It would keep him from falling so deeply asleep that he couldn't notice the door opening or hear suspicious movements outside. He allowed his head to loll to the side so he could look at Miranda once more.

Foolish girl. Every possible reason he could fathom for her to be under that wagon was so unbelievable that he couldn't even complete it. He was grateful, though. Without her, he'd probably still be tied to the wagon wheel — or worse.

He knew his captors had been waiting for Lambert but had no idea what they'd planned to do when the butler got there. Ryland sighed. He'd be lucky if he could find Lambert again. If the man was indeed following his comrades to the ruined cottage, he would find them bound or at least the abandoned wagon. He would soon be fleeing the district, if not the country.

Ryland rolled his shoulders, trying to work out the stiffness from his confinement. Sleep pulled at the edge of his mind, but he held it off a bit longer. He needed to think. Rain was still coming down, which was to their advantage. Whoever's shed they were in would be doing only the most pressing chores this morning.

A few broken pieces of equipment, some hay, and a small stack of farm tools indicated this was a surplus shed. Their unwitting host was unlikely to head this way.

His tongue filled his mouth as he tried to swallow.

Water. They were going to need water very soon. He pushed himself to his feet, stifling the low groan that threatened to emerge. Poor Miranda. She had to be in worse shape than he was. Yes, his head hurt and he'd taken a few punches, but she had walked for miles and crawled beneath that wagon. Nor was her body used to the sort of punishment he regularly put his through.

Two buckets lay amid the broken tools. He shook them out as best he could. The water would be a little dirty, but at least they'd have something to drink.

He eased the door open and slipped outside to place the buckets under the water cascading from the roof.

Light was just beginning to fill the early morning sky. Shining weakly through the clouds, it wasn't bright enough for him to make out more than a few shapes. None of those shapes appeared to be residences, which surprised him. A dense copse of trees extended out to his right. The farmer must have elected to live on the other side for a bit of privacy and shelter from the wind.

There was another, bigger building on the far side of the field, likely the barn. A scattering of cows ranged between the two structures.

The urge to search the distant barn for more food or weapons warred with his desire to stay close to Miranda. After only a moment's hesitation, he jogged across the sodden field to investigate the barn. Knowing that they weren't completely safe, however, had him taking quick glances over his shoulder to ensure the shed remained undisturbed.

Once inside the barn, though, he couldn't see the shed. He sacrificed thoroughness for speed, and after locating a dull knife and someone's forgotten lunch — an apple and cheese wrapped in muslin — he darted back into the rain.

He searched the area as he made his way back to the shed. Everything looked clear.

The door creaked as he reentered the building. The rain was muffled, but he was glad to see it was coming down hard again. It would easily fill their buckets in a couple of hours.

Once the door was snugged back into its frame, he heard the soft snore from the other side of the room. It made him smile.

He settled back down on the floor, making himself as much of a barrier as possible. No one would be able to get to Miranda without crawling over him or over a stack of hay taller than he was. Under the circumstances, it was the best protection he could offer. He leaned his head back against a pile of hay and allowed sleep to claim him.

Ryland woke with a start, taking a moment to determine what had disturbed his sleep.

A low moan echoed from the corner. Miranda was still asleep, but her body must have rested enough to begin to feel the aches and pains. She would wake soon.

Easing himself from the floor, Ryland fought to contain his own moans of discomfort. He checked the water buckets, pleased to find them both full. Rain fell softly now, and the sky had lightened to a murky grey. The storm would pass soon and they could get on with the business of getting home.

Ryland shut the door and lugged the sloshing buckets back to the corner. After drinking his fill and washing his face, he settled in to wait for Miranda to awaken. Hopefully she would sleep for another hour or so.

After all, he had a story to concoct.

Miranda popped the last bite of cheese into her mouth and chewed. Her brain churned, still sluggish from the previous day's experiences. She was trying to get Marlow's explanation straight in her head.

To buy herself more time, she took a long drink of water. The water had been a welcome surprise when she woke. After drinking deeply and washing herself off as best she could, she had poured the remaining water into the other bucket. She turned her bucket over and now used it as a low stool. It was the most ladylike seating position she could find in the shed.

"A lady never sits on the floor."

A lady probably wasn't supposed to crawl on her belly through the dirt either.

"Let me see if I understand correctly." Miranda shifted her legs, trying to find a more comfortable position. Buckets made for horrible chairs. "You stumbled upon Smith and this other fellow stealing something from the house?"

Marlow nodded.

"What were they stealing?"

His eyes darted to hers. It was enough to make her wonder how much of the story was true.

"I couldn't see it," he said.

"But I thought you said you caught them." Miranda's eyes narrowed. She wanted to believe him, because if he was lying she would have to lower her opinion of him. She may not be willing to admit her infatuation with a servant, but she didn't want to blacken his character in order to cure herself of it.

"A few days ago, I saw something that made me curious. I didn't know enough to report it, but they must have thought I did. They conked me on the head and dragged me away."

"You said there was someone else as well. Do you know who?"

"They didn't say his name in the wagon."

He hadn't actually answered her question. She debated pressing him, but if she pushed too much, he might leave her there. She had no idea where "there" was. She decided to accept everything for now, or at least appear to.

"So they put you in the wagon and drove you through the woods."

Marlow tilted his head in her direction. "You would know more about that than I would."

She acknowledged that with a wave of her

195

hand. He could hardly know what happened when he was unconscious. "You were coming to as you got to the clearing?"

"Yes."

"And then what?"

His sigh was more of a deep breath, but it was enough to tell her he really didn't want to go into details. "They tied my hands together, but they didn't have a gag, so I decided to try talking my way out of it. Donkey didn't —"

"Who?"

"The other guy with Smith. Donkey. I decided he needed a name."

He had been rather brutal to that donkey. "I see. Continue."

"Donkey didn't appreciate my humor, and he hit me with the butt of his gun. When I came to again I was tied to the wagon, soaked to the skin." Marlow rolled his head back against the wall and closed his eyes. It wasn't a very subservient position, but Miranda couldn't fault him, given the situation.

She smiled at the disgruntled look on his face. "What did you say to him?"

"I insulted his shoes."

Her eyebrows climbed to her hairline. "I beg your pardon?"

"He had ugly shoes."

There was no making sense of that statement. How could she respond to that?

They sat in silence. One thing, one question lingered in her mind. Could she voice it? So many potential problems could arise from her asking about it.

Finally curiosity could be held back no more, though it came out as more of an observation than a question. "You called me Miranda. Four times."

Marlow had been sitting, head against the wall, arms draped over raised knees, perfectly still for all intents and purposes. But somehow he managed to freeze at her statement. To Miranda it looked as if his breathing halted and his entire body seized up without him changing his position in the slightest. It was more of an impression than anything she could actually see.

In minute increments, his body seemed to relax. He opened his eyes and shot his piercing grey gaze directly at her. Miranda gulped. Why had she given in to her curiosity?

"My apologies, my lady."

She released her pent-up breath. That wasn't so bad. It made way for a good plan. Acknowledge the event and move on with her life, both of them still firmly in their correct social places.

But then he opened his mouth again.

"I can only blame the tense moment in which we found ourselves. I confess that I was not born and raised a servant. It is a position I came to later in life. Occasionally I fall back on old habits. I shall try not to do it again, my lady."

The bucket, which had never been overly comfortable, was now a torture device. Miranda felt like an utter fool. Here they were, in a potentially dangerous and definitely desperate situation, and she was worried about maintaining social status. It was enough to make her sick.

Miranda darted a look at Marlow. She should accept his apology. He was always working, doing things for Griffith long into the evening and early in the morning. He was an exemplary servant and —

Her tongue stuck to the roof of her mouth, frozen before she could utter a syllable. The second part of Marlow's statement was sinking in. He hadn't been born a servant. The implications swirled in her mind, refusing to form a solid thought, leaving her unsure of herself and what she wanted.

"You are, of course, correct, Marlow." She smoothed her skirts to give her hands something to do. What fabric remained of the riding habit had been trampled in the mud. "This is a most remarkable situation. We are relying on each other for our very safety. There is no reason to stand on ceremony. We shall be equals for as long as it takes us to return home."

She felt quite proud of herself as a flash of shock flew across Marlow's face. This was the perfect solution. They could get to know each other better. Surely when the mystery wore off her confounded attachment to this man would fade. Once they returned to the estate, their relationship would return to normal. It was perfect, as long as Marlow agreed.

"My given name is Ryland."

Their eyes met and held for a long moment. Miranda's heart beat loudly in her chest. *Ryland Marlow.* The roar of blood surging through her ears seemed to carry his name, making him even less of a servant in her mind. He didn't seem to move as he stared at her, daring her to make good on her plan.

"Ryland." It came out a strangled whisper as she nodded her head in his direction, as if this were their first introduction.

"Miranda." His voice felt like crushed velvet running over her skin. Maybe the plan wasn't so prudent after all.

CHAPTER 14

A thick drizzle was all that remained of the rain as they left the shed. Ryland poked his head out the door before opening it wide and bowing Miranda through. She swept out, pretending she was entering London's most exclusive ballroom.

Her foot sank in the mud.

"Oh, bother." She tried to tug her heel out of the sucking mire without lifting her skirts. The blue woolen riding skirt was already a lost cause, while her dignity and modesty had yet to suffer a fatal blow. She wanted to keep it that way.

"What's wrong?" Ryland asked. How surprisingly easy it was to think of him as Ryland.

"My boot. It's stuck." Miranda tried once more to tug her heel free. All she managed was to work more of her foot into the ooze.

Ryland knelt by her feet. "Let me help you."

"Have you bacon for brains?" She swatted at his hands reaching for her leg. "You cannot grab my leg."

He sighed. "Then I'll pry out the foot."

"I am certainly not lifting my skirt."

He propped his arm on his raised knee and glared up at her. She crossed her arms and stuck her nose away from him.

Ryland rubbed his hand over his face and through his long hair. He had long since lost the strip of leather tying his hair back and his dark locks were as disheveled as her own. "What do you propose, my lady?" His voice was slurred as if spoken through gritted teeth.

She was being silly, trying to maintain propriety in the middle of a cow pasture. There was nothing proper about this scenario.

"A lady never shows a man her ankles."

Miranda frowned at her mother's voice. A lady was never supposed to spend the night in a shed or walk alone in the woods either. Perhaps it was time for practicality to rule over lady lessons.

"Be quick about it." Miranda squeezed her eyes shut and lifted her skirts the barest of amounts.

Even though she knew it was coming, it still startled her to feel Ryland's strong hand wrap around her ankle. No one but herself and Sally had touched her feet in years. Certainly a man had never had cause to do so.

"On three," Ryland said quietly.

Miranda eased her eyes open and looked down, expecting to see Ryland's bent head. Instead she became snared in his intent gaze. A twirl of excitement flittered from her throat down her spine.

No wonder ladies weren't supposed to let men touch their feet.

"One, two, three."

Miranda forgot to pull her foot until she felt the tugging against her ankle. She yanked, grimacing at the slushy sucking noise that accompanied her foot's freedom.

She stumbled forward, and Ryland landed on his backside.

With a grunt, he jerked to his feet, diverting his gaze to the surrounding area.

"Thank you." She primly set her clothing to rights as well as she could.

"Do you know where we are?"

Miranda looked around, trying to find a significant landmark. They'd had no sense of direction last night, had only run blindly. "I don't recognize a thing, which makes me think we went east. Griffith's lands extend quite far to the north, and the village is to the south."

"So we could be west as well?" Ryland looked at the sun peeking through the clouds, clearly trying to orient himself for heading off in their chosen direction.

"Unlikely. Had we gone west we would be on Raebourne's land. I have spent a great deal of time there the past few years."

Ryland raised a single brow.

Miranda blushed. "With Griffith, of course. The two are quite close. I would never visit the marquis on my own. Besides the man is married now. Happily. To Amelia. You have not yet met Amelia."

She should stop talking, but as the insufferable man kept standing there, one eyebrow hitched up his forehead, condescension oozing from his eyes, her mouth just wouldn't listen to her brain.

"Not that a valet would normally meet a visiting marchioness, but Amelia's different. She meets everyone. Even knows my scullery maid, Lisette. She and Anthony took a belated honeymoon trip. They should be back before Christmas. May even be back now."

Every time she finished a sentence, she thought surely she was done spouting off information he didn't need or care for. But one glance in his direction set her off again, further explaining ridiculous things. She bit her tongue to keep silent.

"What about Crampton's land?"

Miranda shook her head. He knew an awful lot about the local gentry. Did he and Griffith discuss the area often? "The earl's house lies between ours and Anthony's, but his lands do not extend so far."

"Then we head west."

They trudged across the field with the watery sun at their backs. The rain stopped, leaving a thin film of grey clouds floating across a sky that was trying its best to become cheerful. He led her around the farm buildings, taking care to avoid the notice of anyone going about their morning chores.

"Why don't we ask them for help?"

He sent a speaking look across her appearance. "They're from this area. Do you really want them seeing the duke's sister looking like that?"

She sighed. He had a very good point.

Not far from the farm, they came to the top of a small hill. Miranda squealed and clapped her hands as she jumped up and down. "Look!"

Ryland looked where she was pointing, but the only things visible were fields of crops and a crumbling stone tower. Had she lost her mind? "What am I looking at?"

"The tower." She grabbed his hand and started pulling him between the dormant crop rows at a brisk pace. "That's the old watchtower on the corner of Griffith's property. I know where we are."

"Oh. That's good." Ryland needed to get her home so he could track down Lambert, Smith, and Donkey. He shouldn't be enjoying every minute he spent with her away from their normal societal roles.

"It's still a two-hour walk to the house, but at least we'll know where we're going."

Two more hours, then. Two more hours where he was Ryland and she was Miranda.

They reached the crumbling stones at the base of the tower. Miranda veered off, sure of her direction but no longer running. She didn't let go of his hand, and he didn't mention it.

He'd traveled to this side of the estate once, but his search had been concentrated near the house. Miranda would know the landmarks better than he, so he let her take the lead. Though he had to question the meandering path they were taking. . . . "Are you sure you know the way home, my lady?"

Miranda looked up, mud streaked along her cheek. She let go of his hand and grinned. "I thought I was Miranda until we reached Riverton. I am certainly no one's idea of a lady right now. And yes, I know the way home. I also know where all the crofters' homes are and I'd just as soon not run into them in this state."

He looked her up and down, taking in the torn, muddied dress. Her hair was a tangled mess around her grimy face, long tendrils escaping halfway down her back. Her hair was longer than he'd initially thought. "No matter your appearance, you are every inch a lady, Miranda."

"Thank you."

He offered his arm to escort her through a sheep pasture, the woolly creatures paying them no heed. "I think your habit is ruined."

Miranda frowned. "I *know* it is ruined. Sally will faint away when she sees what I've done to it. Thankfully Mother isn't home to see it. This is not the way a lady should look."

"Given the circumstances, I think your mother would allow you some lenience in your appearance."

"Possibly. Although involuntary bodily functions have never been an excuse, so I don't see how a deliberate trek through the woods could be."

Ryland choked on air. *Involuntary bodily*

functions? Really? Surely he was not actually discussing —

"I sneeze constantly. It drives her mad."

He sighed in relief. Sneezing. He could discuss sneezing. It was still a rather inappropriate topic, but he could muddle through it. "You sneeze?"

"Whenever I go outside, it seems. Particularly if it's a sunny day. I can feel in top form and still sneeze. Mother says it will send her to Bedlam one of these days. A lady simply cannot show the world such an unnatural weakness if she wants to be taken seriously."

What could he say to that? There wasn't a whole lot to say about sneezes, and there was virtually nothing he could say about being a lady.

They lapsed into silence, trudging along, occasionally changing directions or climbing a fence. The aches and pains of the night before became more prominent, and he could feel the exhaustion seeping in. Part of him wanted to walk in dazed silence, allowing as much of him to rest as possible. But she had declared them equals for the day, and he didn't want to waste that opportunity.

"Do you often defy your mother's idea of being a lady?" It was a dangerous question.

From the letters he knew that she did, indeed, chafe under some of her mother's stricter rules. He would have to be careful not to betray his knowledge if they followed this line of talking.

She laughed as she kicked a pebble and sent it plopping into a puddle. "I still remember my first lady lesson. I was five, and I wanted to ride like the boys did. She caught me coming back to the stable with a leg on either side of the pony and the groom with me as red as could be. She took me to her office, sat me in that blue chair, and proceeded to tell me how a lady should ride."

The endearing picture made him laugh. Before long the conversation flowed freely from riding to favorite foods and even childhood memories. Ryland had to constantly remind himself to be careful how much he shared. While he was fairly certain he'd be leaving Riverton before the day was through, he couldn't cast aside his disguise until the mission was finished. "How much farther do you think?"

"I don't think it's much farther. We're closer than I thought we would be this morning."

The escaped locks of her hair danced in the breeze. He loved her hair. It was like sunshine. Not the sunshine he saw here in England, but the all-consuming sun found on the open water, traveling between England and France. The vast spread of waves magnified the glory of the sun by reflecting it back on you until the golden glow swallowed you whole. That was her hair.

And when had he become so lyrical? He looked at the soggy landscape. That should displace his poetic tendencies. "It shouldn't take long."

She shrugged and wrapped her arm a bit more securely around his. Her side pressed against his arm, making him wish they were at a party where he could twirl her around the dance floor in his arms.

"What did you do before getting work as a servant?" Miranda asked.

"I beg your pardon?"

"You said you weren't always a servant. What did you do before?"

What should he go with? Lie or partial truth? A lie would be safer, but he was planning on seeing her again when this case was finished. "School." He *had* been at school. Oxford to be precise. For all of two months before the shadows swallowed him up. "I was going to school, but my circumstances changed and I had to go to work."

"How sad. Was there no family to help

you? I know Griffith has sent a few of our distant relations to school long enough to prepare them for a profession. He's even helped some enter the church or the army."

He let her assume his changed circumstances were money related. She'd soon find out money wasn't a problem for him. He'd have some explaining to do then. "I'm afraid I, er, we are the head of the family. There was no one better off financially."

"Oh."

"I had family that needed me." Why was he still talking? He couldn't tell her about his cousin being trapped in France without giving away his identity. "I had to . . . leave the life I knew in order to help them."

"That's very brave."

Silence stretched, and he fumbled around for a new topic to introduce. If they kept talking about family circumstances he was either going to have to outright lie or his evasions were going to become apparent.

She spoke before he had a chance to. "How far would fifty thousand pounds go?"

Ryland lowered his eyebrows as he looked over at Miranda in confusion. "Where are you wanting to send it?"

"Could someone live on that much?"

"Depends how they spent it." He could

not fathom where her question was coming from.

"If someone started life with fifty thousand pounds, would they be able to live comfortably?"

"Of course. Modest, yes, but extremely comfortable. If invested right, fifty thousand pounds would . . ." Ryland trailed off as the significance of the number suddenly struck him. He'd come across the papers while sifting through Griffith's study. Miranda had a fortune of twenty-five thousand pounds from the passing of her father. Her dowry was an additional twenty-five thousand pounds. She could marry a penniless man and they would start life with fifty thousand pounds. He choked on his next sentence and had to swallow before trying again. "Why do you ask?"

Another delicate shrug. She started picking at her skirt. Yet another action that would fall outside of the realm of appropriate ladylike behaviors. "Curious, I suppose, given your school story and all. I've never had to deal much with money. Do you like working as a valet?"

The bottom dropped out of his stomach. Was she actually considering making a match with him? That had to be the catalyst of this conversation. What else could it be?

Shock and pleasure warred inside him. When he showed up in London to court her properly, he wouldn't have to worry about his title being his only appeal to her.

Her face was expectant, waiting. What had she asked him? Oh yes, she wanted to know if he liked shaving her brother's chin and straightening his clothes. "There are worse jobs one can have. All in all it is not a bad lot."

"That's good. I mean, that's a good attitude to have."

"So it is." He was in trouble. She was going to kill him when she learned the truth. The journey her mind must have gone on to even be considering a servant was unthinkably complicated. He didn't for one moment doubt that she'd considered the social ramifications as well as the monetary ones. She was too much of a lady not to be aware of the social ladder.

Who would have thought being a duke could be a detriment to winning his chosen bride?

She sighed. "Maybe I should simply ask Griffith to give me the money. I could set up housekeeping in a little cottage. I've heard spinsters do that sometimes."

Ryland's air left him in a great *whoosh*. So she hadn't been thinking of marrying him. Would he ever understand the female mind?

Ryland looked around, noticing the rock outcropping where the Russian stablehand liked to spend his free time. "I recognize where we are now. Riverton isn't far. What will you do when we get there?"

She laughed, making his heart jump a bit. "Take a bath."

"Miranda," Ryland said softly.

Her face turned toward him, the corners of her mouth drifting down out of their smile. "What?"

"I want you to know something." What was he doing? He should be distancing himself, reminding her what she truly deserved in life. As soon as she was settled in Riverton, he'd be leaving, chasing Lambert and his unknown employer across England.

He couldn't leave her thinking she meant nothing to him though.

She swallowed. Her voice sounded almost choked. "What?"

"You are . . . I have enjoyed this time together."

A weak smile re-formed on her face. "You must be joking. You have enjoyed being beaten, spending the night in a shed, and roaming through farm fields?"

"What I mean is that you are a very special woman. One day, there will be a very fortunate man asking for your hand."

"God willing," she whispered with a shake of her head. "Georgina will be out this Season."

That statement told him more than she would ever know. She may have considered setting up with a valet or even moving out on her own, but she didn't want to do either. Somewhere she'd gotten the idea that her sister's debut was going to hurt her chance at a good match. Ryland wasn't sure when his peers had become so blind, but he wasn't about to complain about it.

They topped a small rise, and the roof of the house became visible over the trees.

"I have never been so happy to see home before." Miranda shielded her eyes for a better look at the looming structure.

They walked in silence as the house grew larger. People spilled down the steps as they crossed the back lawn. A small brunette in a bright blue dress led the pack.

Miranda dropped Ryland's arm and ran forward to wrap her arms around the slight woman. While the women clasped each other, Ryland intercepted a distraught and disheveled Griffith.

The noise from everyone trying to ensure

Miranda's safety and learn what had happened made conversation difficult. Even Georgina was wringing her hands, looking as if she wanted to hug her sister but unsure about the amount of dirt involved in that endeavor.

Miranda worked her way back to his side, dragging a woman in purple with her.

"This is Ry . . . Marlow, Griffith's valet."

Ryland turned to find himself being presented to the small brunette. Why was Miranda introducing him? They were back at Riverton. No more Ryland and Miranda. No more equals.

"Marlow, this is Lady Amelia, Marchioness of Raebourne."

Ryland bowed low, but otherwise did not acknowledge the introduction. He was, after all, a servant. Lady Amelia did not simply nod back as he expected. She scrutinized him, looking him up and down slowly before smiling brightly at him.

"Griffith's new valet?"

"Yes, my lady."

"I see. Marlow, was it? Griffith's been talking about you."

"How long have you been here?" Miranda asked.

"We arrived yesterday, but no one knew where you were. We've been very worried

215

about you." Ryland felt skewered by Lady Amelia's deep brown eyes. "All of the grooms are out scouring the woods. Griffith and Anthony have made several trips out themselves."

Miranda glanced at him, a smile no servant deserved on her lips. "Marlow rescued me."

Griffith looked back and forth between the two of them.

Lady Amelia's eyes widened in shock. "You must be quite the valet."

"I do good work, my lady." What else could he say? He probably should have said nothing.

She watched him for a minute more and then guided Miranda toward the door. "Sally has been keeping water warm so you could have a bath as soon as we found you."

The two women disappeared through the door. Ryland followed soon after them, intent on changing his clothes and doing what he could to determine where his suspects were now. Griffith made his own excuses and followed him. Probably to ensure that Miranda hadn't been more hurt than she appeared.

He left the door open to his little room and began untucking his ruined shirt.

The door slammed.

Ryland jerked his face up in time to see Griffith grab fistfuls of his shirt and shove him into the wall. *What on earth?*

"I assume you're going to marry her." Griffith's voice was hard and menacing, his eyes colder than Ryland had ever seen them.

Ryland shook Griffith's hands off and went to the water pitcher. The contents were cold since they were two days old, but it would suffice to scrub some of the grime from his face. A full bath could wait until London since he would get more road dust on him during his journey.

"Don't be ridiculous, Griffith. I'm your valet."

"We both know what you are and you were alone with her overnight!"

Ryland stared at his enraged friend. "Think, man! Imagine I was one of the other servants. Would you expect her to marry them?"

"Hardly. She'd be better off a spinster than married to a footman."

"Precisely." Ryland ripped off his torn shirt and replaced it with a clean one. He only had the one pair of shoes, so he was going to have to go to London with squishy feet.

"You aren't a footman."

"She doesn't know that."

Griffith stepped up until their faces were inches apart. "Marry her."

"You couldn't force me." It didn't matter that Ryland had already considered courting Miranda. Instinct and self-preservation had him holding his own. Friend or not, Griffith wasn't pushing him around on this.

Griffith threw a punch.

It never landed. Ryland caught Griffith's fist, and the two scuffled across the small room. The water basin crashed to the floor. Griffith had never been a fighter, despite his size, so it didn't take much for Ryland to toss him to the bed.

The two men stared at each other, breathing hard. Griffith finally rubbed a hand over his face.

"You're right. I've never been that scared, though. When you disappeared and then Oscar came back without her from their ride, I didn't know what to think. I never imagined anything happening to my family when you came here to investigate."

Ryland straightened his clothes and headed for the door. "She's safe now and she should stay that way. I'm assuming Lambert has left the estate?"

Griffith sat up on the bed. "Lambert? My butler?"

Ryland nodded.

"He is involved?"

"Yes, my captors mentioned his name."

"That explains his absence. We assumed he had joined the search party for Miranda." Griffith grimaced. "My butler did it. It sounds like a dreadful novel."

"Doesn't it? Now I have to go find him, and his trail is cold and rained on."

Griffith pulled a folded letter from his waistcoat pocket. " 'Sir Gilbert' sent a note yesterday, but you'd already disappeared."

Ryland ripped open the letter, filtering the words through the decoding process. If only this letter had arrived a day sooner. "No one showed up for the drops."

Griffith raised his eyebrows. "Any of them?"

It made Ryland want to throw something. In nine years he'd only twice failed a mission. Without Miranda this third time might have been the end for him. There was more to her than the average young lady. He shook his head. Thoughts of Miranda would have to wait. As delightful a distraction as his letters with her were, it was likely the very distraction that made him sloppy enough to cause Lambert and his cohorts to become suspicious.

He needed to focus and finish this mission before they set up their process at another aristocratic estate. "I'm going to London."

"Godspeed, my friend. I'll pray for you." Griffith rose and shook hands with Ryland.

"I couldn't ask for more." Ryland left the room and called over his shoulder as he trotted down the passageway. "I'm borrowing a horse. I'll leave him in your London stable."

If Griffith responded, he didn't hear it.

Chapter 15

"What do you mean, 'He's gone'?" Miranda sat upright in the bath, sloshing water over the side. She had asked Amelia to make sure someone was taking care of Ryland. He had been through a trying ordeal as well.

Amelia perched on a chair next to the bath and tilted her head at Miranda. "I mean he has left the premises. He has departed. There is no longer anyone with that name residing here at Riverton."

Miranda allowed her maid to help her on with her dressing robe and accepted a length of toweling to blot her hair. "Sardonicism does not become you, Amelia."

A grin stretched across the brunette's face. "Dear Anthony has been teaching me many things."

Miranda frowned. "Dear Anthony should leave you alone. I like you as you are."

"So does he. That's why he married me." Amelia's grin was positively cheeky.

221

Miranda laughed, unable to stop herself in the face of her friend's good humor, but then she returned to the subject at hand. "Surely he has only retired to his room." Miranda could not believe that he was actually gone.

Amelia shook her head. "No, there's quite a to-do in the kitchen about it. Griffith followed Marlow straight up to his room after the two of you returned. Lisette was taking fresh water up for him when she heard them fighting. She fled back downstairs. Moments later, Marlow came bursting through the kitchen. He grabbed some cheese, an apple, and a meat pie before leaving out the back door."

"Maybe he went for a walk?" He should have had plenty of fresh air after their experience, but maybe he was still in shock. She moved to the dressing table to allow Sally to brush out her hair. She could see Amelia in the mirror.

Amelia shook her head. "I saw him riding across the field."

"He took a horse?"

Another nod. "One of the good ones."

Miranda turned from the mirror to better see her friend's face. There had to be some confusion. If Ryland had taken Griffith's horse, he wouldn't be the man she thought him to be. "He took Griffith's stallion?"

Amelia waved a hand in the air. "No, no, he took Trent's horse. The one he was keeping here for when he visited."

"That is not much better. He really took a horse from the stable? What will Griffith think?"

"He doesn't seem very concerned about it." Delicate brown eyebrows pulled together in thought. "He seems much more concerned with having to find another valet. He mentioned something about sending someone after Mr. Herbert."

Miranda groaned. The poor man deserved to retire in peace. He had worked diligently for the master of the house for years. She was sure that she'd heard his creaking bones as he went up and down the stairs the last couple years.

"I wonder where he went." She ran a finger along the embroidery on the edge of her dressing gown. He'd left her. Granted he wasn't anything to her in any official capacity, but they'd had such a nice talk as they walked across the countryside. Was he running from that? From her?

Amelia cleared her throat and rose to take over hair-brushing duties. "Here, Sally, I can do that. Why don't you see to having a tray brought up? I doubt Miranda feels up to going downstairs for dinner."

Miranda sighed. "A tray would be lovely, Sally."

Silence weighed down the room for several moments after the door clicked quietly behind the exiting servant.

"Why do you care?" Amelia finally asked.

"You're the one who is always saying I should remember that the servants are people too."

"And yet you've said nothing about the missing butler or undergardener."

Miranda rose and went to the window. The rain had returned, bringing an early darkness to the countryside. It looked as if tonight's clouds would bring another ferocious storm. She thanked God that she had merely contended with rain on her adventure and prayed that Ryland was already to his destination, wherever that may be.

"Miranda?"

"I want to get married."

Amelia's eyes widened. "To the valet?"

"No. Yes. No. Oh, I have no idea." Miranda threw herself across the bed, burying her face in the silk counterpane.

She rolled to the side as Amelia's slight weight caused the bed to dip. When no words were said, Miranda cracked open her eyelids to try to read what Amelia was thinking.

"I had no idea you knew him so well," Amelia finally said. "No one else seems to know him at all."

"What do you mean?"

"I asked around a bit after hearing he had fled the estate. He distanced himself from everyone, which is not all that uncommon for an upper servant, but it was different. They said he never belonged belowstairs. His arrogance seemed genuine. Your housekeeper's words. Not mine."

Amelia had a way of bonding with people from every station in life. If the housekeeper were going to talk to anyone, it would be her.

"He was born higher. His family became destitute and he had to leave school and find work." Miranda rubbed her hands over her face. This was crazy. The man was gone, and she should not be despairing over that. She should be thankful he left before she could form a serious attachment that would alter her life drastically.

"That would explain a lot of things, then."

Miranda listened to her heartbeat echo in her ears, waiting for Amelia to say more.

"You would be destitute."

"My circumstances would be reduced,

yes, but I would hardly be destitute. I bring a fair amount of money with me. He said a person could live modestly on the income that would bring."

Amelia sputtered. "You . . . you actually talked about . . . I mean, you and he . . ."

"No! No. I hate to admit it, but I'm not very aware of money. I'm starting to think I'll never marry, and I wondered about taking my dowry and my inheritance and setting up house somewhere on my own. Georgina is out this year, and she's going to be so very popular. And . . . I . . ." Tears sprang to Miranda's eyes, and she choked on the sob.

"Oh, Miranda." Amelia's arms wrapped around Miranda's shoulders and she rocked her friend back and forth, making gentle cooing noises as Miranda sobbed.

Miranda began speaking between hiccups and shaky breaths. "I don't want to be — *hiccup* — a spinster, Amelia. I want — *cough* — I want a family, and I don't —" Miranda's heavy crying cut off the remainder of her sentence. She pulled a handkerchief from the table by the bed and blew her nose.

"There are many men in London who would marry you, Miranda. You don't have to settle for a servant, no matter his birth."

"Lord Brigham offered for me last year."

Amelia's eyebrows shot up. Lord Brigham was considered a fine catch indeed. He was handsome and rich and was known to take good care of his business and family responsibilities.

Miranda sniffed. "First, he asked if I thought I had any sway over Griffith's voting decisions. Then he asked me to marry him."

"Well, that wasn't very well done of him." Amelia huffed and crossed her arms.

"No, I am afraid the only men who seem to like talking to me are scandalously below me, or nonexistent, for all intents and purposes." Once Miranda started talking, everything seemed to spill out. She told Amelia about the letters with the duke and her many encounters with the valet. "So you see my romantic prospects are nigh on hopeless."

"I think you need to sleep." Amelia guided Miranda to a more conventional position on the bed. "When Sally returns with the tray, you are going to eat and then go to sleep. While you do that I am going to sit here and read to you so your mind doesn't go off on some despondent bent. In the morning, you'll see that things are not quite so hopeless."

Amelia tucked the blankets around Miranda as the maid returned with a loaded tray. Miranda snuggled into her pillows and began to eat. Amelia went to the desk where Miranda kept the Bible her brother had given her the year before her debut Season. It took a few moments for Amelia to situate herself in the chair beside the bed with the large book open on her lap.

She began to read from chapter twenty-nine in the book of Jeremiah.

" 'For thus saith the Lord, that after seventy years be accomplished at Babylon I will visit you, and perform my good word toward you, in causing you to return to this place. For I know the thoughts that I think toward you, saith the Lord, thoughts of peace, and not of evil, to give you an expected end.' "

Miranda set her barely touched tray aside and eased down under the cover, closing her eyes as she listened to Amelia's sweet voice drift through the room.

" 'Then shall ye call upon me, and ye shall go and pray unto me, and I will hearken unto you. And ye shall seek me, and find me, when ye shall search for me with all your heart.' "

Sleep pulled at her, offering blissful peace and quiet. Her thoughts meandered as she relaxed into the pillows. She'd be a lot happier if she knew that God's plan for her included marriage, because she wanted to seek God. If that involved giving up her dream and expectations . . . did she have enough faith to see it through?

Georgina proved extremely helpful in keeping God at the forefront of Miranda's mind over the next several weeks. As Christmas approached, her excitement could not be contained. She talked of nothing but her debut in London. It was enough to make the stoutest saint beg God for mercy.

Miranda felt the loss of Ryland more than she could have ever imagined, considering he'd never been part of her everyday life. Knowing he wasn't there made the house feel different. She still expected him to pop around a corner just as she did something foolish or unladylike.

He didn't.

The letters stopped as well. She knew it had been a mistake to tell the duke about Ryland, even in passing. She wanted to write him again, find out if he would be in London, but she had never obtained the direction for the duke's letters. It had been her excuse to see Ryland. She'd clung to it jealously and now she suffered for her indulgence.

Her heart pounded when a letter finally arrived — on her birthday of all days — marked with that now familiar bold, slanted script. She tore into the note, anxious for a miracle. It contained only one line.

I have not forgotten you.

What did that mean? It was nice to know, of course. But did that mean she was a pleasant memory? That he intended to seek her out in London? That he wished she'd write him again? Frustration poured through her.

It didn't matter what he meant. She couldn't respond. There was no way to get his direction without explaining to Griffith why she was corresponding with a man she wasn't related or engaged to. Just the prospect of the conversation made her wince.

With no other outlet, she continued to pour her heart out in letters, although she found herself occasionally writing to Ryland as well.

On Christmas Eve, unable to sleep, pen in hand once more, she sat before the brightly burning Yule log and pleaded with the duke to come to London this year. If they could connect as well in person as they did through letters, he might be her only hope of a happy marriage.

She read over the letter, something she rarely did. Despair and self-disgust dripped from the pages. Was that really how she saw herself? Her life? She tossed the journal entry into the fire, watching the pages curl in the festive holiday flame. Maybe she should drag the entire trunk full of misbegotten letters down to give them the same funeral.

Why was it so important that she marry? Between her three siblings and Amelia, there was certain to be enough children around to dote on. She was more than the men she had lost, the men she had never truly had to begin with. She was a daughter, a sister, a friend.

She watched the flame burn until her eyes began to cross and she drifted off to sleep on the sofa.

Weeks passed and the Christmas cheer faded. To Georgina's delight, Miranda focused on the people in front of her. As much as Miranda loathed the constant trips to the modiste for fittings and perusing the shops for matching hats, gloves, and slippers, she enjoyed putting a smile on Georgina's face.

It had the added benefit of providing

Miranda with her smartest spring wardrobe ever.

If Miranda found herself quoting certain Bible passages in an attempt to deal with Georgina's exuberance, well, that was a good thing as well. How else was she to find the patience to listen to one more prediction of what the confirmed bachelors would do once Georgina appeared in the ballroom door?

When Mother returned at the first of March to make final preparations for the family's journey to London, Miranda was able to find a glimmer of excitement within herself for the coming Season.

Maybe God had a gentleman in London for her.

Maybe He had a servant waiting in Kent.

It was possible He had a different future for her entirely, helping the widows and sick on her brother's estate. Whatever it was, she finally felt ready for it. The verses Amelia had read all those weeks ago had become etched in Miranda's brain. She recited them frequently to herself.

The time had finally come to brave London and all of Georgina's potential admirers. She patted the lid of her last trunk, indicating to the footmen they could take it down to the waiting carriage. The prospect of putting her lack of jealousy to the test was both exciting and nerve-wracking. All she could do was pray and hope.

The twitter and chirp of birds and the scent of the first spring flowers greeted her as she walked to the carriage outside the front door.

Mother and Georgina were already within. Griffith and Lord Blackstone — who still doted on Mother after more than a year of marriage — were on horseback, leaning in to converse with the seated ladies. A footman handed Miranda into the carriage and they were off.

The countryside rolled by, a sea of changing fields and budding trees. Life was beginning anew. There was a grand adventure in front of her.

CHAPTER 16

Ryland threw his greatcoat across the bed as he fell into an upholstered club chair by the window. Jeffreys, his valet, scooped the coat up and shook it out while raising his brows in inquiry.

"Nothing," Ryland muttered. Agitation propelled him back out of his seat. He braced himself against the window frame, letting his forehead rest against the cloudy glass. The small four-room apartment served him well as an unobtrusive base of operations. The window looked down on an alley many criminals traversed on a regular basis.

"Whoever he's working for is either very good or very negligent."

Jeffreys frowned at the wrinkled coat. "Negligent, sir?"

"Yes, negligent, and when did you start calling me *sir*?"

"Just practicing, sir."

"In that case, you might want to try using

234

Your Grace instead of *sir.*" Ryland smiled as he watched Jeffreys take a brush to the mistreated coat. The servant's strokes were efficient. The casual observer would not notice that his left hand bore only four fingers.

The fifth was left in a Parisian alleyway, blown off by a bullet meant for Ryland.

"The negligence, Your Grace?"

"Lambert is still here. In town. Doing nothing but drinking and taking the odd job here and there."

"I don't suppose you mean the occasional chimney repair kind of job."

"No. A man paid him to rob an apothecary. Seems he was having trouble getting his hands on enough laudanum."

Jeffreys hung the coat on a peg in the closet. "You let him do it."

Ryland shrugged. "If he disappears, I lose my last connection to whomever his boss is. But the fact that his boss is letting him stay here doesn't feel right. If someone's watching Lambert, they've also seen me. I haven't taken pains to hide from anyone but him."

He shoved his hand through his hair.

A knock at the door gave both men pause. Not many people knew where Ryland was staying. He changed his rooms on a regular basis. Had Lambert or his boss had him followed?

Jeffreys picked up a pistol from the side table and hid it behind his back as he eased the door open. Ryland rose from his seat, ready to fight if the need arose, though he couldn't see through the door from his position.

"Please don't shoot me, Jeffreys. I'm quite fond of this coat."

The familiar voice had Ryland relaxing and Jeffreys laughing as he opened the door wider.

Mr. Colin McCrae strode into the room looking like he belonged in a Grosvenor Street drawing room instead of a set of rented back-alley rooms. A tall hat sat atop his head, reddish-brown hair curling around the edges. Unlike Ryland's discarded greatcoat, Colin's appeared freshly brushed, pressed, and cared for.

Ryland dropped back into his chair, waving an arm toward the only other seat in the room. "What brings you by?"

Colin sat in the wooden chair, crossed his booted feet at the ankles, and placed his hat in his lap. "Other than the joy of welcoming you back to town, you mean?"

"I haven't officially returned."

"And I'm not officially here." The tinge of

Scottish brogue that seeped into Colin's words told Ryland that whatever the man had come to say, it wasn't good.

Ryland sat up a little straighter at that. Colin didn't, strictly speaking, work for the War Office, even though they'd done their best to recruit him when he stumbled into the middle of Ryland's mission five years ago. There were times, however, when certain pieces of information would find their way to Colin and he would see fit to use his incredible business acumen, observation skills, and contacts to assist the Office's cause.

He said *no* often enough to keep the Office from taking advantage of him though. Most of the other agents weren't sure what to think of Colin, but Ryland had always considered him a friend. Saving each other's lives formed a remarkably strong bond.

"You have news?"

Colin nodded. "There've been inquiries about the mine."

"The mine?"

"Yes. The one I sent you information on a few months ago when you asked for a fake investment letter."

Ryland frowned. "The doomed one?"

"It should be. I refused to handle the venture, but I knew a less discerning gentle-

237

man who agreed to see investors. The idea was so abysmal that the venture was soon dead. When you inquired about a fake investment, it seemed easier to pretend Griffith and I were discussing the mine instead of making up something completely new."

"Are you saying it's not dead anymore?"

Colin nodded. "Someone's invested in it, someone who thinks to find something worthwhile in that mud, though Mr. Burke isn't saying who."

Ryland scratched his chin as he contemplated the importance of this development. He'd known there was someone else in the game, someone powerful. This confirmed that he was looking for someone of means, quite possibly an aristocrat. That one of his peers would betray England like that turned his stomach. He'd bought enough secrets from high-powered Frenchmen to know that wealth and title didn't particularly mean loyalty to their country. Treasonous Frenchmen were considerably easier to stomach than treasonous Englishmen though.

"All the more reason to come out of hiding, Your Grace." Jeffreys hauled a small trunk from under the bed and began folding clothes into it. Ryland watched, amusement creeping over his agitation, as his valet quietly stored the room's meager contents in the open baggage.

"And have you also planned where I shall make my debut?" Ryland finally asked.

Jeffreys extracted a small white card from his pocket and flipped it across the bed. Ryland snatched it out of midair, crumpling the corner a bit. It was an invitation.

"She's going to be there?"

Jeffreys nodded. "The servants have been speaking constantly of the various costumes their lords and ladies have procured. That invitation was meant for your aunt. Price said it was a shame she never received it."

Ryland couldn't help grinning. His hulking, unconventional butler had not only gotten him into the party but kept his troublesome aunt out. As he read the details of the event, excitement unfurled in his belly. He couldn't have planned it any better.

God was certainly watching over him.

Colin leaned over and read the card. "There's a she?"

"What is her costume going to be?" Ryland tapped the invitation against his palm, ignoring Colin while he considered the ramifications of attending the ball.

"We aren't sure, though we know it's blue. She and her sister and mother were all seen at the modiste ordering dresses especially for that event. The sister was quite excited. The mother was less so."

"Not surprising. Masquerades are not known for keeping the faint blush of youth in a young lady's cheeks. I wonder at Lady Blackstone letting that be Lady Georgina's first society appearance."

Colin coughed. "Lady Georgina *Haw-thorne*?"

"The hostess, Lady Yensworth, is a particular friend of Lady Blackstone's — otherwise I'm sure they would be skipping the event." Jeffreys pulled a pair of boots from the bottom of the closet. "Are we keeping these?"

The boots were beyond ruined in appearance but still comfortable. Ryland raised a brow. "Why wouldn't we?"

"Your Grace."

"What?"

"Only reminding you that you are a duke. I don't know a whole lot about the aristocracy, but I know they don't wear boots that look like this."

Ryland sighed. He hated to admit that Jeffreys was right. Many of the comforts and idiosyncrasies he'd become accustomed to were going to have to fall by the wayside. A few quirks would label him eccentric. Too many would make him a social pariah.

Colin rose and grabbed Ryland's shoulder, shock covering his normally unreadable features. "You've intentions to court Lady Georgina Hawthorne?"

"What? No." Ryland shifted in his seat.

Colin turned an inquiring look to Jeffreys.

"The older sister, sir."

"Ah." Colin grinned.

Ryland glared at Jeffreys as the valet strode about the room gathering items. He was efficient and loyal, but hardly subservient. Ryland had been slowly filling his staff with people like him. People who'd helped him over the years and needed a safe place to earn a living.

It was also a subtle way of reminding his aunt that the house, title, and power were still his. He grinned, thinking again of Price, the butler he'd installed in the town home. A man the size of the Tower of London, with a face just as craggy. His aunt had been outraged, according to Ryland's steward.

He hadn't considered that his unconventional staff would come back to haunt him. "Why are you telling Mr. McCrae my secrets, Jeffreys? Isn't your loyalty supposed to be to me?"

"Of course, Your Grace. That's why I didn't tell Mr. McCrae that you've been brooding over the young lady since you left your position at her house several months ago." Jeffreys threw the dilapidated boots into the trunk. "Only the least discreet of valets would reveal that you've actually paced the floor as you contemplated what you'd do when she returned to London."

Colin laughed so hard he fell back into his vacated chair holding his right hand to his side underneath the ribs.

Chagrin quickly replaced Ryland's outrage. If Ryland were going to make a successful return to society he was going to need help. Trust Jeffreys to take care of that when Ryland was too stubborn to do it himself.

Six months ago he wouldn't have cared if the *ton* accepted him back into the fold. He ran a thumb over the invitation. It was amazing how quickly things changed.

It was smaller than he remembered, though with seven windows facing the street from the first floor it was still considerably larger than most of the other terraced town homes in Mayfair. The simple three-story facade surrounded the street-level covered and columned entrance, setting it apart from the ornate buildings on either side of it.

It had been a long time since Ryland had

laid eyes on Montgomery House. Through considerable effort Ryland had managed to avoid most of Mayfair for the past nine years. His trusted estate manager kept him abreast of important news.

Jeffreys clapped a hand on Ryland's shoulder. "If we stand here much longer, someone is going to recognize you. You haven't changed that much in appearance."

In appearance, no. But in everything else . . .

"Of course." Ryland cleared his throat and waited for a stately coach-and-four to drive by before crossing the street.

The two men slipped down the stairs to the servant entrance below street level. Entering the workroom was like walking down memory lane. Nurses, soldiers, and even a few reformed criminals welcomed him with smiles and cheery hellos.

Breakfast trays were being readied on one table, and after a brief round of handshakes and hugs, everyone returned to their work. Such a large house required that everyone work diligently to keep it running, even with the enormous number of staff he had hired.

His stomach rumbled as one of the maids, a former battlefield nurse, carried a tray of eggs and kippers toward the stairs.

"Mattie," Ryland called to the French

woman stabbing a spatula at the stove, "would it be possible to have one of those trays brought up to my room? I think I need a little kip before I tackle the social scene tonight."

"Of course, Your Grace." The tall woman softened her thick French accent with a saucy wink as one of the kitchen maids began setting out the makings of another tray.

"Thank you. Send it up when you've finished with the others. No need to delay theirs and make them wonder." Ryland led Jeffreys to the side staircase where the breakfast tray had disappeared moments before. He paused with his foot on the bottom stair. "My room is free, isn't it?"

Cecil, a footman who had been a sly pickpocket and leader of a street gang in his former life, puffed his chest out in evident pride. "Yes, Yer Grace. 'E tried to take it over a time or two but none of us would wait on him while 'e was in there. Wouldn't see to hisself, so didn't take more than a day to boot him back to his old quarters."

"Thank you, Cecil, and to the rest of you. It's good to be home." His glance managed to meet the eyes of everyone in the room before he turned and climbed the steps.

Emotion, surprising and a bit unwelcome,

clogged his throat, making him glad Jeffreys was two steps behind him. That was his legacy, why he'd continued on year after year. He hadn't realized it until that moment, seeing them all together in one room. The good he'd seen in those people and others like them was why he'd taken the risk to fight quietly in the shadows.

The servant stairs hid them for only a while. In order to reach the master's rooms, they would have to pass his aunt's room. The unpleasant task of greeting his relatives could wait. He wanted to bask in the feeling that he'd done some good in the past ten years. With a war on, that was sometimes easy to forget.

Jeffreys had barely shut the door behind them before another servant entered with a pitcher of hot water. Ryland cleaned up and slipped into one of the new silk dressing gowns he'd ordered.

For three months Jeffreys had been slipping clothes and other personal items into the house so that it would be ready for his arrival. There were times when experience at subterfuge came in handy.

The silk felt good. The bed felt even better. The scent wafting from the quickly delivered breakfast tray was almost heavenly. Maybe it wouldn't take as long as he'd feared to adjust back to the life of a duke.

"How do I look?"

Miranda rolled her eyes behind the protection of her blue jeweled and feathered demi mask. It covered her forehead completely and slid just over the bridge of her nose. It was the fifth time Georgina had asked that question since they had climbed into the carriage twenty minutes prior. While Mother rushed to assure her youngest daughter that she looked exquisite in her angel garb, Miranda took the time to adjust a feather that was determined to tickle her nose.

The nice thing about masquerades, particularly masquerades during a girl's fourth Season, was that pastels were not required. The bright blue of Miranda's gown did wonders for her complexion, which she then, of course, had to cover up with a mask. Life wasn't fair sometimes.

"What are you again?" Georgina ran a hand over the gauzy skirts of Miranda's gown.

"The sky."

Mother turned her attention to Miranda. "I thought you said you were a bird."

Lord Blackstone laughed from his corner of the carriage. "Told me she was the ocean."

246

Miranda grinned. "I guess I shall be a woman of mystery, then. Mother, the door is open."

Mother spun her head around to see the footman was indeed waiting for her to exit the conveyance.

Miranda looked up at the house as she followed her mother. The entrance was lit like day, while the rest of the front remained shrouded in darkness. The effect was very dramatic. With a final adjustment to her mask, she trailed her family up the steps and into the home, passing four footmen holding aloft enormous candelabras.

Lady Yensworth greeted them enthusiastically. "I'm so glad you returned to town in time for my little gathering."

Miranda managed to restrain an incredulous laugh. From the looks of things, *everyone* had returned to town for the little gathering. It was sure to be a crush inside. She greeted her hostess with a bow and entered the room, eager to see what kind of decorations lined the interior.

The starkness of the exterior was not mirrored on the interior. Swaths of sheer fabric flowed from the high ceilings, giving the rooms an exotic softness. The second-floor ballroom was exquisite. More candelabras lined the room, these being held by tall stands instead of footmen. Strings of crystal beads hung from them, catching the candlelight and sprinkling spots of sparkle across the room. Lady Yensworth was certainly setting a high standard for the rest of the Season's balls to live up to.

Georgina's pure white gown stood out among the colored dresses most of the women had chosen for the occasion. It wouldn't be long before men were fetching her punch or asking her for a dance. Miranda whipped out her fan and sent her irritating feathers fluttering.

She spied Amelia's pink costume across the room, her arm linked with that of her tall husband, who had donned only a domino mask in addition to his normal evening attire. Anthony might be reformed and completely converted, but certain habits from his jaded, rakish past remained. The couple was in close discussion with two other couples. Rather the women were talking intently while the men gave each other bored half smiles.

Miranda snapped her fan shut and worked her way across the room, the first genuine smile of the evening on her face. Whatever the women were discussing had to be more interesting than watching her sister. There was nothing she could do for Georgina now anyway. It was in God's hands. He would either answer her prayers to protect her younger sister from heartbreak, or He wouldn't.

"Good evening, Amelia. Lady Granton. Mrs. Reeding." She nodded to each of the women who'd chosen masks so minuscule they hardly deserved the name before curtsying to the men.

The men bowed in return.

"If you would excuse us," Anthony said, patting his wife's hand. "There is a card game in the east drawing room."

"Sure to be vastly more entertaining than this commotion. A bunch of fuss over nothing, if you ask me. Probably portly and disfigured." Lord Granton ran a hand over his own ample midsection. "That's why he chose a masquerade."

The men bowed to the ladies once more. Lord Granton and Mr. Reeding departed at once. Anthony leaned in to peck his wife on the cheek first.

"I'll come dance with you later."

Amelia grinned. "A scandalous number of times, no doubt."

"But of course." Anthony nodded to the other ladies and left the party.

It was unusual for any husband to accompany his wife on the dance floor, but

Miranda had a feeling that the newlyweds would not care about social convention.

Miranda waited expectantly for the ladies to fill her in on the topic of Lord Granton's grumblings. Trepidation began to climb up her spine as Amelia glanced at her sideways and then refused to meet her eyes.

"Have you heard? It's the most exciting thing. Sure to be the talk of the entire Season!" Mrs. Reeding fluttered her fan to cool her flushed cheeks.

Icy fingers of fear covered Miranda's shoulders. She didn't know what she was afraid of, only that it felt like this news was going to have a great impact on her future.

Lady Granton leaned in and glanced around. "I heard him over by the punch bowl. He introduced himself to Lord Trent."

"Trent is here?" Miranda looked around for her other brother.

Amelia snagged Miranda's arm, pulling her attention back to the circle. "It could be someone pretending to be him. It's been known to happen."

Lady Granton shook her head, making her mask slide from side to side across her nose. "I saw the ring. That signet ring is certainly authentic. No one would dare to copy it. Not even his cousin."

Miranda was losing interest in the whole

intrigue. Obviously her sense of doom was wrapped up in the drama of the story. "Who?"

Mrs. Reeding leaned in. "The Duke of Marshington is here."

CHAPTER 17

Miranda had never imagined a person could actually feel themselves turn pale. Her skin felt thin and icy even while her pulse pounded through her ears. The rhythmic roar drowned out the next few words of her companions, and she was grateful for the protection the mask offered. Her face was surely the picture of shock and fear.

Distantly, she heard Amelia making an excuse about needing fresh air. In moments the welcome breeze on the terrace drew Miranda from her stupor.

"Did he not tell you that he would be in London this Season?" Amelia gripped Miranda's elbows. Compassion was evident in her deep brown eyes despite the shadows created by the purple silk mask.

Miranda shook her head. "I haven't heard from him since my birthday. The last letter from him was rather cryptic, and there's been nothing since."

"Do you want to leave? Shall I fetch Trent or Griffith?"

"No. No, I shall feel quite the thing in a moment. It was merely surprise that caused such a severe reaction." Several moments and a few deep breaths later, Miranda felt that she could enter the ballroom once more. As appealing as the terrace was, she couldn't stay out much longer and protect her reputation.

Amelia left her to find some punch, and Miranda skirted the edge of the dance floor, seeking clues to identify the men. Each time she couldn't name the man with certainty, she wondered if she was looking at the duke.

A flash of white caught her eye, and her attention was drawn to her sister. Georgina's feet flew through the steps of the lively cotillion. In addition to matchless beauty and incredible charm, the blessed girl had been born with natural grace. Her dancing instructors had declared her their easiest pupil ever.

Miranda followed her sister's shadowed gaze and charming smile over to the young girl's partner. He was unlike any other man in the room. Most of the male occupants were dressed as kings or Roman conquerors if they had bothered to dress with any imagination at all. Many wandered the room in their normal attire, only a mask to mark the occasion as Anthony had done.

Georgina's dance partner, however, had gone an entirely different direction in his choice of clothing. He looked more like a century-old French courtier than anything else. The jacket stretched across his broad shoulders was made from a burnt-orange brocade with white ruffles spilling from the sleeves. Brown breeches topped white stockings and heeled shoes. That he was even managing the dance in the ridiculous footwear was intriguing.

The man was large. Perhaps as tall as her brother Griffith — though she couldn't tell for sure considering distance and the elevated shoes. He wasn't as broad in the shoulder though. His brown hair was cropped very short and his mask covered his face from mid-forehead to the top of his jaw. It was even molded over his nose.

She inched forward, trying to see more of him, and got her shoulder grazed by another couple dancing by. Embarrassment flooded her cheeks, and she was once again grateful for the protection the mask provided. Could the man with her sister be the mysterious duke? Through his letters she knew he was unlikely to conform to society simply because he'd decided to reenter it, but would he be willing to stand out that much?

There was something familiar about the man, though Miranda couldn't think of anyone who wore his hair so closely cropped. Was it the way he moved? The tilt of his head as he led Georgina off the dance floor? Whatever it was, Miranda felt drawn to him. Stepping out with that many layers of lace marching down his chest required a considerable amount of confidence. Confidence that Miranda found herself admiring and envying at the same time.

Perhaps she wasn't trusting the Lord as much as she'd thought. Her first outing back in town and she was adding another name to the list of men she couldn't stop thinking about. First Ryland Marlow the valet, and then the Duke of Marshington, and now the mysterious Lord Brocade. Her desire for a family was drawing her to any man that seemed to be out of the normal mold.

She rose to her toes and craned her neck to follow the couple's progress, but she soon lost them in the crowd. Georgina resurfaced on the dance floor a few minutes later, but with a different partner. A quick glance revealed that Lord Brocade was not among the couples now squaring off for a quadrille.

"Lemonade. Suddenly I'm feeling quite

parched." Miranda's voice was a bit louder than she intended, but none of the surrounding bucks jumped to retrieve her a glass. A woman with a tall powdered wig and wide skirt informed her that the refreshment table was at the other end of the ballroom.

With a sigh, Miranda began working her way through the crowd. She knew the lemonade was on the other side of the room. It was why she decided to get some. She could peruse the crowd while she traveled. The fact that she hadn't wanted anyone to get the lemonade for her did not take the sting out of the fact that three unattached gentlemen had been nearby and none of them had offered.

No orange brocade along this side of the dance floor. She sipped at her lemonade as she worked her way toward the other side.

"You have quite a reputation."

Miranda spun around at the deep voice. Lord Brocade had found her. "I beg your pardon!"

"Amongst the gentlemen fawning over your sister instead of you. You have quite a reputation. I thought you might like to know." A small smile tilted one side of his mouth up.

There was something familiar about the

256

smile. Did she know him? His eyes were hidden by the mask, shadowed too much for her to make out their color. Who was he?

"That is terribly ungentlemanly of you to point out my, er, lack of popularity."

He shrugged. "You said it, not I."

Miranda's mouth dropped open. This man had crashed the party! There was no other explanation for it. No one of her acquaintance would be this rude, even with the protection of semi-anonymity. She opened her mouth to give him the cut direct, but he spoke again before she could formulate an actual sentence.

"Then again, you also said you were only passably pretty, and unless that mask is hiding a disfigurement, I believe you might have a misconception there as well."

She might not be able to see his eyes, but she could certainly feel them. They bored into her. He didn't look to the side or down at his feet. His gaze remained unnervingly constant on her face.

"Who are you?" she finally whispered.

"My apologies. I thought my statements made that obvious." He reached forward and grasped her hand from where it hung limply at her side. A large gold ring caught the glint of candlelight as he raised her hand to his lips. "I am the Duke of Marshington, Marsh to some of my friends."

Miranda's first thought was that if her blood kept rushing around her body like this, she was going to have to see a surgeon. Surely it couldn't be healthy. Her second thought was relief that it was only two men filling her attention instead of the three she imagined a few moments earlier. Finally full realization that she was standing in front of the Duke of Marshington set in, and she considered the merits of fainting for the first time in her life.

"Would you do me the honor of dancing the next with me?"

"Oh! I . . . of course."

The slight smile graced his face once more. "I shall look forward to it."

He kissed her hand once more before melting back into the crowd, leaving her wondering if the encounter had actually occurred.

Ryland slid behind one of the sheer drapings in a darkened corner, keeping his gaze trained on Miranda. When he'd revealed his identity as the Duke of Marshington, her beautiful green eyes had widened under her mask until they were all that was visible through the cutaways. Every move he had made thus far was carefully calculated. That would all end once he stepped onto the dance floor with her. He would have to improvise based on her reactions.

He counted to ten before she moved, jerking her head back and forth, seeking him in the crowd. These few minutes before the next dance were important. They would give her time to adjust and come to terms with being face-to-face with the man she had been writing to for years.

As the quadrille ended, Miranda remained still. People flowed on either side of her. One or two people even stopped to talk to her. If she answered, Ryland couldn't see it. It was clear that she was trying to wrap her mind around the idea that he was actually in the same room as she was.

He pulled at the ruffles near his wrist. One of the problems with having a valet who was more friend than servant was that sometimes they took the opportunity to play elaborate practical jokes. Jeffreys had presented the brocade monstrosity with a grin stretched across his pointy face.

He could try Griffith's tactic of spilling food all over himself to create more work, but Jeffreys would probably do the same thing Ryland had done — throw the shirt away and tell his employer that he was rich

259

enough to buy a new one.

Stained or not, the rag bin was certainly where this ensemble was going. He had never been so hot, itchy, and uncomfortable in his life, and he had been in many uncomfortable situations.

The first strains of a familiar tune reached his ears. He had arranged for a waltz to be played next. It would allow him the maximum amount of time with her as a somewhat captive audience. The time would be necessary to move her past the awkwardness of the letters before revealing the deeper deception of his also being Marlow. Ryland left his hiding place and made his way to Miranda's side.

"My lady?"

She looked at him, hesitating for several heartbeats before placing her hand in his. "It's a waltz."

"So it is." He watched her, knew the exact moment when she decided to throw caution to the wind and get to know him better.

She felt perfect in his arms. He led her around the floor twice before he remembered that he had things he wanted to say to her. There had been moments of physical closeness during their journey through the English countryside, but this was different. Here, in this moment, she was completely focused on him. Her hand in his was not because she needed steady footing but because she wanted to be with him. The knowledge meant more to him than he thought it would.

Dragging his focus from the way her skirt swept around his legs was difficult, but he needed to move the conversation along to accomplish his plan.

Miranda had other intentions. "Why didn't you find me earlier?"

The question was innocent and reasonable. Given what he knew from her letters — and from weeks spent under the same roof — he realized what she was really asking was why he had danced with Georgina first.

"I wanted to get to know you first."

Her pink lips turned down into a frown. He wished he could slide her mask up her face. She looked adorable when she was confused.

"But you weren't talking to me."

"No, but I was learning quite a bit about you. As I mentioned, you have quite a reputation. Not to worry, it's not a bad one."

"Oh."

They swirled around the corner of the dance floor, and Ryland pulled her the slightest bit closer. Her hair smelled like lemons. The deep conversation he'd envisioned would have to wait. His mere existence was giving her enough to deal with in one evening.

"Would you like to know what that reputation is?" Ryland asked.

"I . . . I suppose it would be best to know what others think of me."

He tilted his head to whisper in her ear. "You are exquisite."

Shivers passed through her shoulders and arms and into his own appendages. He continued whispering, using other couples to shield them from the most curious of onlookers. "It's true. They say you are exquisite, and I must agree with them."

"Your Grace, it is really quite unfair of you to deceive me this way."

"Oh, but I'm not. They also say you are determined to remain unwed. I know this to be untrue, but it is certainly in my best interests to let them think it is."

Ryland attuned all his senses into reading her reaction to that sentence. He had all but declared himself to be courting her. How would she react?

She missed a step.

He tightened his arms to keep her from tripping. For a brief moment she was trapped to his side. As pleasurable as the experience was, the couples waltzing around them could only hide so much. In the next step he maneuvered her a more proper distance away.

During his years in France he had slipped in and out of many balls and parties, coaxing secrets from and relaying messages to various attendees. It had kept his dancing skills sharp, particularly when it came to waltzing. While the *ton* was still unsure about it, the French had embraced it.

"May I call upon you tomorrow?"

Her gaze was glued to his. What did she see? Could she recognize him? He had forgotten to continue disguising his voice. It wasn't like him to forget anything about a disguise.

"I would like that." Her smile was shy, but it was beautiful.

They didn't speak for the rest of the dance. After bowing to her and escorting her back to the edge of the floor, Ryland slipped out of the party via the back garden.

Tomorrow he would call on her and everything would be revealed.

Tonight she had been awestruck by him. Tomorrow she was bound to be spitting mad. He climbed into the carriage he had waiting in the alley and made himself comfortable. He had more plotting to do.

CHAPTER 18

"The Duke of Marshington will be coming by today."

Miranda's needle slipped, jabbing her in the finger. She restrained the flinch and the urge to suck on her injured finger. Hearing her sister say the words that had been circling through her own mind all morning was more shocking than the missed stitch. How did Georgina know that he intended to call?

"Darling, it was a masquerade." Mother inspected Georgina's hair and dress, giving a slight nod of approval. Not a blemish could be allowed on their first "at home" day since returning to London. "There are always one or two gentlemen claiming to be the esoteric duke at these things."

Miranda could have informed them that he was indeed the real Duke of Marshington, but then she would have to admit to corresponding with him, and that was certainly not going to happen.

"He had the ring, Mother." Georgina adjusted her skirts as she made herself comfortable on the white-and-gold settee.

This was the most formal of all the drawing rooms in Hawthorne House. Decorated during Miranda's second Season, it was done entirely in gold and white. Fortunately, by then she had convinced her mother to let her build her wardrobe with cream and the occasional light pink or green. The idea of wearing white while sitting on a white couch in front of white-on-white silk wall coverings had been enough to make her shudder. Georgina didn't seem the least bit bothered.

"The ring? I suppose that does make a difference." Mother chose a gold brocade armchair. She settled into it with her own needlework. "Did you bring anything to occupy yourself between callers this morning?"

Georgina arched her eyebrows at her mother. "I don't think there will be any need. Several people mentioned calling on me today. We shall find ourselves quite busy. Especially when word goes around that the Duke of Marshington has come out of his self-imposed exile for me."

Miranda snorted.

Her mother glared at her.

She considered shrugging. It was what she truly wanted to do. In the end, lady lessons won out and she murmured a quiet, "Pardon me."

"You think otherwise, dear sister?"

It was time to remind Georgina that while her older sister wasn't as popular, she was not quite on the shelf yet. "Has it not occurred to you, *dear sister,* that maybe he wants to call on me today? You are not the only eligible lady in this house."

"Oh, I am sorry to hurt your feelings. That was never my intention. But don't you think if you were the enticement he would have come back sometime in the last three years?"

A sudden urge to jam her embroidery needle through her sister's perfect nose gripped her. The mental image was satisfying enough, so she stayed in her seat.

"Georgina, that is uncalled for. A lady never mentions another's unwed status, particularly if they have been socializing for a while. And Miranda, a lady never emits noises more suited to a pig." Mother peeked up from her needlework to spear both of her daughters with her sharp green gaze. Her message was clear. The visits today would set the tone for the entire Season, and she was not going to allow anything untoward to happen.

"Yes, Mother," Miranda said.

Georgina murmured her own agreement.

Ten minutes later Gibson, the butler, announced the first caller.

He was a young gentleman Miranda remembered meeting the year before. She thought he might be a second son, which she knew would hold no appeal to her younger sister. Georgina's rejection could take many forms and Miranda felt sorry for the poor man.

"The flowers are beautiful Mr. Sherbourne. Were you aware that my sister, Lady Miranda, adores carnations?" Georgina's face was the picture of angelic innocence. Her eyes were wide enough to disguise their slight exotic tilt, and her smile was soft and natural.

Miranda wasn't fooled for a moment — bitterness rose up her throat to coat her tongue as her sister's game became clear. Anyone she didn't want was going to be aimed in Miranda's direction. She had to remind herself repeatedly that Mr. Sherbourne wasn't at fault in this little play.

After a moment of awkward silence, Mr. Sherbourne extended the bouquet to Miranda. "A lady should always have a bouquet of her favorite flowers. Please accept these, Lady Miranda."

"Of course. I am honored that you thought of me." Miranda almost choked on the words. The truth was she had never been particularly fond of carnations. She much preferred tulips or lilies.

They talked for a few minutes, Georgina constantly drawing the conversation back to Miranda. The skill would truly have been impressive if she had been helping Miranda land a man she actually wanted. By the time Mr. Sherbourne left he probably believed he'd arrived to see Miranda instead of Georgina.

And so the morning progressed. Wealthy, attractive men with lofty titles or at least the prospect of a lofty title were met with coy smiles and soft laughter while Miranda was all but ignored. Everyone else was shuffled off as Georgina played the adoring younger sister.

A few women stopped by to see Miranda, though more came to visit with her mother. Georgina's friends were all having their own at homes or resting up for the night's festivities. Few of them had been allowed to attend last night's masquerade.

The visitors were a steady stream through the drawing room. No one stayed overly long and everyone mentioned how lovely Georgina looked in her white embroidered muslin. Miranda wasn't having a grand time, but it was not quite as bad as she'd feared.

Then Gibson announced the Earl of Ashcombe.

One glance at Georgina's face revealed her delight. The earl was considered a decent catch. He was quite handsome, and his family had ample funds. The burn of bile rose in Miranda's throat. She could not sit and visit with that man and maintain the ladylike civility her mother insisted upon.

She rose to slip from the room through the side door that led into the dining room, but she wasn't fast enough. The earl entered, his bright green coat catching the corner of her vision, and she couldn't stop herself from stealing a better glance. By design, she had avoided him for the past two years — an impressive achievement considering the closeness of London's high society.

He was still breathtakingly handsome. He was a bit taller than Miranda, which would put him a good head over Georgina. His carriage was perfect, his smile held just the right level of enthusiasm. His eyes met Miranda's across the room and he winked.

The man winked.

She darted through the door, hoping her mother would remember what he had done to Miranda during her first Season. Then she would understand why Miranda had fled and she would do everything in her power to move him along before he could shatter the innocent illusions of another Hawthorne sister.

Ryland sat in the middle of Grosvenor Square, watching the callers coming and going from Hawthorne House. Colin sat next to him, rolling a plucked blade of grass through his fingers.

"Think any of them are here to visit her?" Colin twisted the blade of grass into a circle and tried to toss it around a nearby branch.

"Only the smart ones."

"So none, then."

Ryland laughed at his friend's assessment of the parade of Quality. While he agreed with the sentiment for many people, there were a few men that had better heads on their shoulders. Of course, even a level head could be turned by a woman of Georgina's beauty. Had Ryland not witnessed her shallowness while working at Riverton, he would have been a bit awed as well.

Colin stood. "This isn't a campaign, chap. We either go in or we don't."

Ryland hated to admit that his friend was right. He couldn't treat this courtship like a mission. He was officially retired. As hard as it had been, he'd turned over all of his findings on Lambert and the still-open investigation. It was time for him to move on and let someone else protect the country.

The butler opened the door before they even had a chance to knock. Colin immediately extended his calling card. Ryland had actually forgotten about the practice of presenting cards with one's name on it. Leaving a paper announcing your presence wasn't high on a spy's priority list.

He stuck his hand in his coat pocket and removed a stack of parchment rectangles. Jeffreys had not forgotten. Ryland figured that made up, at least partially, for the atrocious outfit the night before. He held his card out to the butler.

Where Colin's had gotten him nothing more than a quizzical stare, Ryland's card got them immediately issued into the front hall. It occurred to Ryland how easily someone could fake being him. He ran his thumb over the heavy signet ring on his right hand. It had been in the family for generations and was actually the only personal effect he had carried with him on his travels. Dangerous, yes, but he couldn't risk his cousin finding it. It was the only proof he'd had when communicating with his managers.

"If you will wait here, I will announce your presence."

"Hold, man," Ryland said softly. "Who all is in the drawing room?"

"Lady Blackstone and Lady Georgina, sir."

Ryland clapped a hand on Colin's shoulder. "Enjoy their company, my good man. I've business with Griffith to take care of first."

Colin's eyes narrowed.

Ryland headed down the corridor before his friend could protest the arrangement. He knew where the study was, having spent time in the house as a boy. He had come with Griffith to town on a school holiday. Griffith's uncle had traveled with them. None of the ladies in the family had been present.

Trusting that Griffith would be hiding from the horde of callers, he knocked softly at the door. Instead of hearing a call to enter, he saw the door swing open to reveal Trent, Griffith's younger brother.

"Marsh! Good to see you without the mask on. I couldn't believe it when you told me who you were last night." Trent had been a few years behind Griffith and Ryland in school, but they had gotten to know each other some before Ryland's sudden retreat from the country.

"It is good to see you as well, Trent. Is Griffith within?"

"Of course. My sister Miranda is as well. Said she couldn't stomach the simpering anymore and needed a respite." Trent pushed the door the rest of the way open to allow Ryland to enter.

His hopes for arranging a private interlude with Miranda crumpled. The scene when he entered that study was not going to be pretty. It was going to take Miranda a moment or two, but she would be able to put all of his identities together.

And then she was going to get angry. Well, he assumed she was going to be angry. Women tended to go a bit queer in the attic about things like this.

Staying in the corridor would solve nothing, though. The last thing he needed was for her to encounter him there. At least the study provided a modicum of privacy.

Time slowed to a crawl. Everyone seemed to move through water.

The first thing he noticed was Miranda's shy but excited expression. That she had been looking forward to seeing him again gave him courage. He heard Griffith moving around, making introductions, saying some nonsense about the party the night before. Miranda's face filled his vision. As her eyes met his, he saw the brows lower in confusion. He could almost hear her thinking.

She would be trying to explain away what her eyes were telling her.

Every conceivable alternative would be flittering through her mind.

Finally she would settle on the fact that the only option, no matter how ridiculous, had to be true. And that option did not put Ryland in a very favorable light.

As understanding worked its way into her expression, he considered her possible reactions. He thought she might yell. It wasn't the ladylike thing to do, but at her core Miranda was a bit too vibrant for a traditional lady. In moments of heightened emotion he was sure those emotional tendencies would escape. Leaving the room was another option for her. It was the exquisitely rude option for a lady to cut a man in that fashion though. Of course, the ultimate in ladylike behavior would have her properly greeting him and then making excuses about seeing to refreshments.

He didn't think that third option a very

likely one.

The journey across the study carpet took forever. Did time seem slower to anyone else? "Lady Miranda," he said, executing a slight bow.

Miranda's fist connected with his nose.

CHAPTER 19

Miranda shook her hand out. Had she really just hit a man? The sting in her knuckles and the pain in her wrist indicated she had. So did the shocked and angry look on her eldest brother's face.

"That was an option I didn't consider," Ryland murmured. He brought a hand to his nose, a wry smile twisting his lips as his gaze remained fixed on her face.

She grunted in irritation. If she was going to hit someone, couldn't she at least have knocked him over?

Poorly suppressed laughter sputtered through Trent's lips, while Griffith rushed forward, berating his sister. "What were you thinking, Miranda? Marsh is a guest in our home."

"I thought he was your valet. Pardon me, your former valet." The shock dissipated, leaving anger in its wake. This man had played with her and her emotions. She thought through all the conversations. The trip through the countryside.

The letters. The letters were by far the worst. She crossed her arms over her middle, trying to banish the feeling of exposure. She was covered from neck to ankle, but she felt as if she were standing there in only her shift.

Her eyes connected with his. With no guise between them, the full power of his focus nearly knocked her over. She heard Griffith's voice; the angry, confused tone washed through her head but none of the actual words registered. All of her mind's energy was caught up in trying to discern Ryland's thoughts, if that was indeed his actual name. Griffith had always referred to him by his title or the shortened version of it. She made a mental note to find a copy of Debrett's Peerage when this was over and look up his given name.

Ryland's head tilted to the side, but his eyes never left hers. She wondered if he was trying to read her mind as she was trying to read his. He knew so many of her inner secrets. Had he read the other letters? The ones she kept in a trunk in her room? The mere possibility made her want to hit him again. Her emotions were too raw to contain the urge.

She surged forward, her already sore hand raised in a fist.

Griffith's brawny arm snagged her in mid-stride. He hauled her up against his chest, his forearm digging into her stomach. Miranda's arms and legs flung wildly through the air as she tried to reach her nemesis.

"How could you do that to me?" she screeched. It was possible they could hear her in the drawing room, but she didn't care. "I trusted you!"

Those dynamic silver eyes shifted from her face to her swinging arm.

"You'll break your thumb if you hit me that way."

She gave up the ineffectual struggle and simply hung in Griffith's grip. "What?"

He gestured toward her still-clenched fingers. "Your thumb. It's tucked into your fist. You can break it that way. Too much pressure on the knuckle if you hit with any force. I can teach you the proper way."

Miranda blinked. "You want to teach me how to hit you?"

"If you like."

Trent laughed so hard he fell back into a chair.

Miranda could feel Griffith lean to the side, presumably to glare at his younger brother. That never worked. It only ever made Trent laugh harder.

Griffith placed Miranda's feet on the ground and slowly released her. Her heart was pounding, her breathing was too fast — as if she had run all the way home from Hyde Park. The next few moments could change her life.

Ryland had crushed her heart when he walked away from Riverton. Her confidence was in shambles because he had come back as someone else. He had destroyed what remained of her fragile trust in men. He held the power to ruin her socially and publicly embarrass her beyond repair. She had to know the extent of her danger and his intentions.

"How many did you . . ." she whispered. She couldn't finish the sentence. Her brothers were still in the room, and they were listening to every word. There was going to be enough to explain without mentioning the letters. She would have to find another way to determine whether or not he'd found the trunk full of years of private thoughts and ramblings.

"Only the ones you know about," he answered. Chills ran down her spine at the knowledge that he was so attuned to her that he'd known what she was asking. And knew there'd been more letters.

Griffith stepped between them, his head swiveling back and forth to look at both of them. "Would one of you please tell me what is going on here?"

Miranda turned to her brother with a sigh. Curiosity was evident, but there was no shock in his eyes. Wasn't he surprised to see Ryland? It was obviously the same man. The hair was different, but —

She snapped her head back to Ryland. The long black queue had been replaced with short brown hair. "Your hair . . ."

"Silver nitrate," he answered, ignoring Griffith completely.

She'd heard of people using it to color their hair black. When used for excessively long periods it tended to discolor the eyes so he must have used it for the express purpose of fooling the occupants of Riverton. Only Griffith had not been fooled.

Her eyes narrowed as she looked at her oldest brother. The head of the family. The man sworn to protect and care for her. He'd known who Ryland was. The two of them had been eighteen the last time they saw each other, at least to her knowledge. Old enough to be able to recognize each other, even so many years later. And Griffith had kept in touch with Ryland. So he knew. He had brought the impostor into their house for some reason she could not imagine, to trick them all and then show up in London to prove them to be utter fools.

She turned her wrath on her sibling, lunging for his throat. His height meant that she hit his chest instead of his neck, but surprise sent him stumbling back several paces until he bumped against a large footstool. Using one foot to launch off the upholstered stool, Miranda went for his head.

Trent laughed so hard he fell to the floor.

"You did this!" She yelled as she hammered at Griffith's broad shoulders. "You made fools of us! Every one of us! He's no more a valet than I am!"

Ryland snatched her off of Griffith, who had been struggling to shield himself from her blows and shake her off without hurting her. Once more she found herself pinned to a man's chest, but this one did not belong to her brother, and she couldn't have been more aware of that fact.

Lean muscles moved and bunched against her back as Ryland hauled her across the room to the window. His body heat was immense. It felt as if she were standing against a roaring fire. When he set her down and turned her around, her first thought was to throw herself back into the warmth. The emotional upheaval was exhausting her.

He took her shoulders in his hands and leaned down. His handsome face was earnest as he searched her eyes.

"Miranda, I —"

"No. No, I can't do this. I don't know why any of this happened — and right now, I don't care." A look at her brothers revealed worry and confusion. She must look like a madwoman. Even Trent had stopped laughing and looked concerned.

Humiliation swelled as she came to her senses. She had not had such an emotional outburst since she was a child. Years had passed since she'd allowed herself to let go and give her emotions such free reign. Mother had taught her well. Under no circumstances did she allow herself to lose control anymore.

Shame blurred her vision. She would never recover from this. Eventually she would have to face Griffith and Trent — they were family — but Ryland was a different story.

A lady could always avoid any unpleasant person if she tried hard enough, even at an intimate dinner party.

Miranda was a lady. It was time for her to remember that.

She squared her shoulders and stuck her

nose in the air. With conscious, controlled movements, she strolled to the door.

"Excuse me, gentlemen," she murmured as she opened the door. She slipped into the passageway and closed the portal quietly behind her. Maintaining a steadfast grip on her forced calm, she went up the stairs and entered her room, utterly thankful she passed no one on the way.

Then she threw herself onto the bed and cried.

Ryland watched Miranda's stiff back depart the study. He wanted — no, he needed — to explain things to her, but now was not the time. The surprise, shock, and concern mingling now on her brothers' faces revealed that they'd had no idea of the riotous emotions that boiled beneath Miranda's serene surface. The glimpse he had gotten in her letters had prepared him somewhat.

When the door clicked, Griffith turned his attention to Ryland. "Is there something you would like to tell me?"

Ryland debated how much to tell Griffith. In the end the letters weren't his secret; they were Miranda's. He was good at not divulging secrets. His friendship with Griffith was important. His integrity was more so. "I've decided to return to London."

Griffith's eyebrows rose. "So I see. Should I regret allowing you into my home last year?"

"That avenue of information to the French is broken. I consider that a worthwhile outcome." Ryland crossed to the decanter and poured himself a glass of brandy to give himself something to do. Knowing Griffith, it was likely the same brandy that had been here three years ago, when he had made a brief visit to his friend.

"And my sister?"

"With any luck and God's blessing the war will never touch her directly." Ryland swirled the brandy and contemplated the shifting ripples. How long could he stall his old friend? No matter how strong their ties were, family was more important to Griffith. That was as it should be. The fact that Ryland would choose Griffith's well-being over that of his aunt and cousin was more an indication of his lack of connection to his relations than the strength of his ties to his old school chum.

Griffith leaned back against the desk, looking deceptively relaxed. Ryland had seen him use similar tactics in school to lull people into a false sense of security before maneuvering them right where he wanted them. Ryland kept his guard up.

The slightly larger man cleared his throat and examined his hand. "I'm not well trained, but I do know not to tuck in my thumb." His gaze rose to meet Ryland's. "And I think sheer size will give me a little more power."

"I won't stop you."

Griffith tensed, though he remained against the desk. "Are you saying I need to?"

Trent stepped between the two, hands raised, poised to keep them separated should one of them decide to lunge for the other. There was no danger from Ryland. Should Griffith decide to call Ryland on the carpet for misleading his sister, he had no defense without divulging more than Miranda would like. It was alarming, but what Miranda would like was increasingly important to him.

"Now, look," Trent said, his head swinging back and forth between the two older men. "I don't know what's going on here, but I do know one thing. Marsh is an honorable man. Griffith, you have held him up for me as an example of a man triumphing over his circumstances and —"

Ryland bit back a chuckle.

Trent threw him a dirty look before continuing, "— and I am sure that he has done nothing to dishonor our sister." He turned to face Ryland fully. "But if he has, let me take a go at him. I've trained."

Griffith had spoken often about how worried he was about how his younger brother would turn out without a father to guide him through his formative years, but somewhere along that span of time, Trent had become a man under all the joviality and charm. Ryland was glad to know it.

Trent crossed his arms over his chest. "So tell me. Did you hurt my sister? Because I can plant you a facer right now that will leave your ears ringing for a month."

Griffith's hand appeared on Trent's shoulder. "I will handle this, Trent."

"She's my sister too. You may be a giant, but I've seen you fight. We could bring Miranda back down here. At least she can jump on his back."

Ryland grinned, his respect and liking of Trent rising even with the threat of having to engage in fisticuffs with him. It was a rare man who could effectively threaten a bloke and tease a brother in the same breath.

Ryland let his gaze fall to Trent's hand, already starting to curl. Apparently he was taking too long to answer the younger man's question.

Recalling Trent's choice of words wiped

the smile from Ryland's face. Trent hadn't asked if Ryland had been honorable. The question had been whether or not he'd hurt Miranda. Had he? Some of the emotion boiling through her right now was bound to be hurt, but that would go away when he explained everything. Wouldn't it?

The truth was she'd taken his unmasking a bit harder than he'd anticipated, which could be an indication that she wouldn't view the entire business the same way he did.

So what did that mean the answer to Trent's question was?

CHAPTER 20

Ryland prided himself on being an honest man, particularly when not on a mission. It could be said that he had frequently implied things that weren't true, but rarely had he actually lied. It was a fine line, and one that meant little to anyone but himself given his chosen profession, but the line was there nonetheless. He'd gone nine years in subterfuge without crossing it and he wasn't about to start now.

"I think her display speaks for itself. Women don't like to be deceived. I believe she thinks I have misled her and taken advantage of my former position as a servant at Riverton. I believe we can safely say that I have hurt her, though I don't think it is irrecoverably so." Ryland finished his speech and braced himself for the first blows.

Silent moments passed. He began to wonder if Trent was going to choose calm discussion over the effectiveness of a well-placed fist.

"Darken his daylights," Griffith rumbled.

Trent swung his left arm and Ryland braced himself for the blow. The power of the right uppercut to his chin caught him completely by surprise. The pup had been honest as well. He was trained. Ryland was going to have to be a more active participant in this fight than he originally planned. His first line of defense was always his tongue.

"She's probably more miffed than hurt."

Trent feinted right. Ryland narrowly missed the next punch by leaning sideways. He needed to talk quickly before Griffith decided to hold him in place while Trent pummeled. Griffith might not know how to swing a fist properly, but those were genuine muscles filling out his jacket, and Ryland didn't want to fight both of them.

"She thought I was a servant, and now she's found out I'm a peer. It's enough to make anyone feel a bit cork-brained for not seeing it."

Trent paused and considered Ryland's statements, hand raised at the ready. Cautiously, Ryland stopped his backward dance along the carpet.

Griffith stepped forward. "What about the trip?"

Trent's eyebrows rose. "What trip?"

Ryland rubbed a hand across the back of his neck. "I was abducted and Miranda got caught up in the whole mess. It took us a while to get home."

The brothers exchanged dark looks.

"He was with her all night?" Trent asked.

Griffith's nod was grim. "And then he refused to marry her."

As soon as the words left Griffith's mouth, Ryland lifted his hands to defend against what was sure to be a significant blow. Trent's dart slipped around Ryland's raised fists, clipping him on the cheek hard enough to toss his head back, throwing his balance off. Fire sliced through his face. Gentleman Jack was certainly turning out some prime fighters these days. He braced himself for the next blow but then remembered he was in front of the high carved fireplace mantel. Blessed darkness covered him before he hit the floor.

Miranda stared at the ceiling, eyes dry, head throbbing. She didn't know how long she'd been hiding in her room, but her mother was bound to come in search of her soon. Fortunately she could blame her distress on the earl. Mother never needed to know about the rest of it.

That was assuming Trent could keep his

big mouth shut. When it came to getting his sisters in trouble, the man had looser lips than twelve society matrons. If his laughter was any indication, he was going to delight in telling Mother Miranda had actually hit a duke. Two dukes if she counted her brother.

She bit back a groan as the door swung open with a quiet *swoosh*. When no polite tirade on ladylike qualities split the air, Miranda lifted her head to see who had come in. It was her maid, Sally, with a tray of tea and biscuits.

"Bless you, Sally." Miranda pushed herself up against the pillows while Sally arranged the tray. "Did my mother send you? She's probably counting the minutes until she can come and berate me."

"Lady Blackstone has been a bit pre-occupied." Sally leaned over to begin repairing Miranda's coiffure.

"Would you like me to sit in front of the mirror, Sally?"

"I'm sure I can manage, my lady. Your hair needs minimal attention. If the tea restores you well enough, you'll want to return downstairs as soon as possible."

The thought of trying to relax with a cup of tea while Sally leaned awkwardly over the bed was decidedly unappealing. She moved to the chair, bringing the steaming cup with her. Sally followed with the tray.

Once they were situated again, Miranda bit into a warm biscuit. She sought Sally's eyes in the mirror. "My mother is pre-occupied?"

"Yes, my lady. She did ask after you, but I don't think she's had much time or energy to plan your next lady lesson."

Miranda grinned. Sally was the only person who had heard Miranda's term for her mother's constant improvement sessions. Well, Sally and the now all-too-well-known Duke of Marshington. "What has her so engaged?"

"Trying to get the body out of the house without anyone noticing. It took quite a while to come up with a plan that wouldn't attract the attention of everyone in Grosvenor Square."

"The body . . . the . . . Wait, what?"

Miranda jumped up, scattering biscuits across the carpet. She lurched to the door and ran to her brother's study.

Griffith and Trent were still there.

"How could you?" she wailed. "It was a misunderstanding! There had to be a reason — you wouldn't have let him into Riverton without a reason!" She stood in the middle of the room, wringing her hands, trying to hold back tears and losing the fight. Yes, she had been mad at him. Yes, she had wanted to cause him bodily harm. But she hadn't wanted him killed!

Her brothers both rushed forward, hands awkwardly extended to pat her shoulders. Trent was the first to actually speak. "He all but asked us to, Miranda. He had every opportunity to defend himself."

"We couldn't let his hurting you go by unpunished," Griffith added.

Their calmness stunned her. She would never have thought them capable of such violence. "He'll never have the chance to make it right! I'll never get to see if maybe, just maybe, he was everything I originally thought him to be."

Griffith tilted his head, brow knit in thought. "I suppose that is a possibility. Although I know much more about him than you do, Miranda, and I'm not sure I'd have let him court you even if this whole misunderstanding hadn't happened."

"I never knew you were so high-handed!"

"Yes, you did, Miranda. I won't let this emotion cloud your memory. I've been plenty high-handed over the years. I've shown several suitors the door before you received so much as a flower from them."

"But I still *see* them. I'll never see Ryland

again!" Miranda lost her battle with the tears and began crying earnestly. She hadn't yet made up her mind to forgive Ryland, but she hated having the choice removed. Something told her that eventually they would have made peace with each other. Should that have happened, there was the slightest possibility he could have been everything she'd ever wanted.

"You'll see him again, Miranda." Trent extended his handkerchief and then discreetly turned his back. "I doubt we could keep him completely away from you unless we locked you up in the country."

Trent's words cut through Miranda's emotion fogged brain. She took a closer look around the room. There was no weapon, no blood, not even an overturned chair. "So . . . he's not dead?"

"You thought . . . you thought . . . Why did you . . . ? I mean . . ." Trent tried to speak between shouts of laughter.

Griffith shook his head in bemusement.

"Sally said Mother had to get the body out of the house," Miranda grumbled and crossed her arms over her chest.

Griffith got control of himself first. "Trent punched Marsh and knocked him into the mantel. Set the man out cold. Mother was concerned with getting the unconscious body out of the house without anyone seeing it. His friend was here visiting Georgina, so he said he would see that Marsh got home."

"Oh." Miranda felt all kinds of foolish. When would she learn to think things through before letting her emotions jump to conclusions? Of course her brothers hadn't killed anyone. If she had taken a few moments to think before she reacted, she would have avoided making a total cake of herself.

She glanced quickly at her brothers before easing her way toward the door. "Well, I'll be . . . going, then. Since we understand each other."

Griffith raised an eyebrow at her. "I believe you might have some explaining to do. That was quite a scene."

"Well, I thought you'd killed a man!" Miranda's hand closed over the door latch. Escape was nearly hers.

"I meant earlier."

Trent rocked back and forth on his feet, grinning.

"Earlier?" She was lifting the latch. Once in the corridor, he wouldn't chase her with accusations.

"Yes. I didn't tell Mother about it, but I think we need to talk. Had it been anyone but Marsh, your reputation would be shattered."

Had it been anyone but Marsh she never would have had the emotional outbreak in the first place. The latch clicked open.

"Do not open that door, Miranda."

Air rushed from her lungs. She was tired, her head hurt, and she really didn't know what she wanted to have happen next. Until she sorted out her own thoughts, she couldn't answer Griffith's questions.

A soft knock at the door preceded her mother's entrance. "Oh, there you are, Miranda. I need to speak with you. Privately."

She caught Miranda's gaze and tilted her head toward the open portal. Then she turned on her heel and walked off.

Mother's tone was menacing. There could only be one meaning behind that stern tone. Miranda glanced at Griffith before fleeing after her mother. She had never looked forward to a lady lesson so much in her life.

Ryland's first thought was that he was going to be sick. His second was that there was no way he was going to cast up his accounts because he would have to move his head in order to do so. And his head hurt. Twin points of pain radiated torturous pulses across his face and the back of his head. A groan escaped before he could catch it, grating against his ears.

"I was hoping you'd stay out until I got you home."

Ryland struggled to place the voice. The pain acted as a filter until it sounded like someone was speaking through a long tunnel. As the rest of his brain engaged, he deducted that his bed was too small and it was swaying, which meant he was probably in a carriage. Colin had been at the house, so it was likely that he was the other carriage occupant. Ryland forced one eye open to confirm his suspicion.

Colin sat across the carriage, swaying along with the conveyance, a grin giving tell to the fact that he wasn't totally sympathetic to his friend's plight.

Gingerly Ryland raised a hand to feel the damage to the back of his head. He vaguely recalled falling back toward the fireplace after Trent's last punch. His head must have connected with the ornately carved mantel.

He hoped he'd broken it.

Questing fingers found an enormous bump but not the sticky wetness of blood or the sting of broken skin. That was good. Within a couple of days the headache should cease and he could begin squiring his way around town, trying to pin Miranda into a private conversation that would allow him to explain.

The carriage stopped.

"Thank you, Lord," Ryland whispered. He had managed to avoid injuring himself very often, but one couldn't be in his line of work for any length of time and not experience a couple of devastating blows to the head. He hoped this would be his last.

Colin flung the door open and hopped to the ground. "Wait here. Don't move."

As if he would even try. Ryland wasn't fool enough to make things worse unless his life were hanging in the balance. In this case it was just his dignity, and he couldn't muster up the energy to care about that. A peek at the carriage opening showed a disgruntled footman, standing at attention. No doubt he was miffed that Colin had the audacity to open a carriage door and jump down without the aid of the step.

In a few moments Colin returned with Jeffreys. They tried to be gentle, and Ryland helped as best he could, but his vision was still fuzzy around the edges and his body was still slightly disconnected from his brain. Once clear of the carriage they went down to the servants' entrance, which was standing open.

Ryland closed his eyes in anticipation of the noise. Once the door closed behind them, the only sound was the crackle of the kitchen fire. He heard the small clink of china followed by a hastily whispered "Shush!" Easing his eyes open he saw half a dozen servants, jobs set to the side, concern marring their faces as they watched him pass.

"Thank you," he managed to whisper as Colin and Jeffreys approached the stairs. The climb was arduous, but his bed was absolute bliss. Sinking into the feathered mattress, taking all of the strain from his neck, felt better than he could possibly have imagined. Yes, two days of this would have him back to normal for sure.

CHAPTER 21

Guilt settled in Miranda's stomach as she watched her sister and mother dither over the right ribbons to purchase. It didn't matter that they'd already bought out the shops in Hertfordshire, Georgina was determined to start afresh at the stores in London. Their mother was as excited as Miranda had ever seen her, obviously thrilled to have one daughter who found enjoyment in the trappings of the Season.

Miranda had never been as enthralled as Georgina. Even today she'd walked into the shop knowing she wanted a bright green ribbon to trim the hat she was making to go with her new walking dress. She'd walked in, found the ribbon, purchased it, and then waited for the others to finish.

She was still waiting.

Finally Georgina settled on the width and style of ribbon she wanted. There was no question of the color. She hadn't purchased anything that wasn't white in well over a year.

Georgina turned to Mother with wide eyes. "Don't you need a ribbon as well? If you and Lord Blackstone go riding, you'll need a bonnet that goes with your new afternoon dresses."

Miranda bit back a groan as the two floated away from the white ribbons to examine the blue ones.

She strolled deeper into the trim shop, perusing pins and buttons and decorative trims. A collection of beaded lace caught her eye for its unusual blend of elegance and simplicity.

"May I help you with anything, my lady?"

Miranda's head snapped up at the familiar voice. There was Ryland, standing behind the counter with a tape measure draped around his neck and a pair of scissors poking from his pocket. His back was slouched and he was standing in a way that made him shorter than she was.

His swollen right eye was mottled with purple, red, and blue splotches. She didn't know whether to commiserate over the pain or search out Trent to commend his skills as a pugilist. "What are you doing here?"

"Talking to you. Also cutting lace, if you wish to purchase it." He pulled the very trim

Miranda had been admiring from the case and sat it on the counter.

Miranda looked around the shop, but no one was paying them the slightest bit of attention. "Is this what you've been doing for the past ten years, then? Hiding amongst the aristocracy so you can make fools of us?"

"Hiding, yes. Making fools of you, no." He unwound a length of lace and spread it along the counter.

"What would you consider it, then?" She couldn't help but run a finger along the beautiful piece of trim.

"Spying. And most of the time I was in France. Occasionally Spain. I even traveled to India once."

Miranda looked into his face, knowing her surprise must have been written all over her face. Her voice lowered to a whisper. "Why are you telling me this?"

Ryland lifted a brow. "Because you deserve to know."

She swallowed. "When you were at Riverton you were watching us? You thought we would betray —"

"No." He cut her off with a swift snip of the scissors, even though Miranda had not yet said she'd take the trim.

"Donkey. And Smith," Miranda said.

Ryland nodded. "And your butler."

Miranda fiddled with the edge of the cut lace. "If you wanted to talk to me, why didn't you come by the house?"

Ryland lifted an eyebrow at her. "You aren't at home."

It was hard to refute that truth.

"Even if you were, I doubt you'd have agreed to see me."

She couldn't deny that claim either. "How did you get back there? How did you even know we'd be here?"

"This is what I do. I'm a spy, Miranda — or at least I was." He folded the trim and wrapped it in paper. Anyone looking at them would see a clerk — albeit an unconventional one — helping a customer.

She wasn't sure what to react to, his confession that he'd spent a decade submerged in lies and danger or the revelation that he'd walked away from it. Confusion joined the swirl of hurt, insecurity, and embarrassment.

"You can ask me any question you want." Ryland folded the ends of the paper together, forming a package as pretty as that of the most experienced store clerk.

"And you're going to answer them over lace and ribbons? This isn't normal, Ryland."

"My life hasn't been normal for nine

303

years, assuming it ever was." He placed a different roll of trim on the counter.

Miranda looked at the package, at his easy handling of the trims, his understated appearance. The ease with which he appeared to be something he wasn't sparked the emotions swirling inside her into a blaze of hurt anger. "If it was all a lie —"

"I don't lie, Miranda."

Her eyes narrowed. She supposed if one were going by a very strict definition of honesty, he'd truly been her brother's valet for those few weeks. But everything else. Had there been any truth in it? "Then you posted my letters? Where did you send them?"

He winced.

It was all the answer she needed. She turned to leave, intending to drag her mother and sister out of the store whether they were done or not.

Ryland dropped a handful of coins on the counter and scooped up the package of lace. The proprietor was finishing with Miranda's mother and sister as Ryland slipped toward the back of the shop and out the door. The overwhelming stench of the back alley turned his stomach even as the noise echoing from the main street pounded through his brain.

Following Miranda into the shop had not been his original intention when he'd left the house this morning. His bruised eye would keep him from polite society for a few days, at least until the worst of the swelling had gone down, but impatience had spurred him from his bed. Despite the fact that he had officially retired, the entire business with Lambert left him feeling uneasy. He didn't feel like he could truly pursue Miranda until the situation had been resolved — which was why he was slinking through a London alley instead of nursing his head in the quiet of his bedroom.

And when he'd seen Miranda step from the carriage, he had been unable to resist — but he wasn't certain their encounter had done any good. So now it seemed clear his best chance with her would be to solve the case he had left behind.

After walking away from spying, he'd asked Archibald, one of his agents turned footman, to follow Lambert. Most of his reports had been incredibly boring. Yesterday, however, Lambert had received a message from a well-dressed footman. It had been a simple matter for Archibald to pick a fight with Lambert in the tavern and pull the message from Lambert's pocket. He'd stepped away and memorized it before slipping it back in place.

Archibald was still following Lambert. Jeffreys was checking on a few other locations in case the note was written in code. And that was why Ryland was sneaking toward the rendezvous point mentioned in the note to see if anything — or anyone — interesting was there.

Given the fact that whoever had sent the note had used one of his own footmen to deliver it, Ryland was banking on his adversary's arrogance to keep him from using code in his communication.

Although the choice of a popular tea shop as a meeting point was surprising.

Ryland looked over the alley behind the tea shop. He'd rather be inside the shop, acting as a waiter or even sitting in a quiet corner sipping tea. Unfortunately, the possibility existed that Lambert would recognize him. They couldn't take that chance.

The shop was on the end of the street, so Ryland eased around the corner, trying to peek into the windows at the patrons. The tables were filled with London's elite. Even dressed in his finest, Archibald would stick out like a sore thumb. The choice of location wasn't looking quite as ridiculous as it had earlier.

Ryland watched Archibald stride past the shop, a stack of packages in his arms. Anyone looking would think him a footman taking his master's purchased goods back to the house.

Ryland dared to ease closer to the front of the shop, watching the interior for any sign of Lambert.

There he was. Walking toward the back of the shop, just past the window.

Ryland wanted to punch something. He was going to have to enter the shop. There was no way around it. He'd have to wait a suitable amount of time, but he had to see who was in that corner.

Archibald appeared at his elbow, having gone around the next section of buildings to come up the same alley Ryland had. "Where is he?"

"In the corner. Where we can't see."

"What do you want me to do?"

With a grimace, Ryland watched as Lambert came back into view and quickly walked to the door. Whatever the meeting had been about, it had been short. "Follow him. Try to see if he left this meeting with anything interesting."

He pulled the package of lace from his coat pocket and stuck it under his arm before strolling around the corner and into the shop. Lambert was gone, but Ryland needed to see who was sitting in the unseen section of the shop.

The whispers began as soon as he entered. He sat and placed his package on the edge of the table before ordering tea from the prompt waiter. A newspaper had been left on one of the seats at his table. Ryland opened it and pretended to read while taking in the four tables past the edge of the window.

A man and a woman sat at one table, appearing oblivious to everyone else. Unlikely to be them, but Ryland memorized their faces anyway.

Another table was occupied by a woman and a young girl. Ryland prayed that it wasn't them. He had no illusions that women couldn't be conniving, but he hated the thought that anyone would involve a child in their underhanded dealings.

The last two tables held men, sitting alone, drinking tea and reading the paper just as he was. Both looked vaguely familiar, though he couldn't come up with their names. Both were dressed in fine clothing with stiff white cravats and expert tailoring. The only thing Ryland could do was commit their faces to memory and hope their fine clothes meant he might encounter them socially. After all, an introduction was the easiest way to learn a name.

The next day, amongst the flowers and poems for Georgina, a small paper-wrapped package arrived addressed to Miranda. She recognized the interlocking edges from the package Ryland folded at the trim shop.

She slid it into the folds of her skirt and smuggled it upstairs before anyone else had a chance to remark on it. She expected a note of some sort but found nothing except the lace.

All afternoon she expected him to come by, but the day passed without Gibson announcing the man.

Miranda couldn't stop herself searching for him at the ball that night, even though she swore to herself it was only so that she could avoid him. She was still angry, after all, even if a part of her remembered how much she'd missed his letters and the conversations she'd had with him as the valet. The fact that the two men she'd been thinking about were actually one man should have delighted her.

It didn't. Not completely.

He didn't show up the next day either. Every question she couldn't think of while in the trim shop swam through her mind as she suffered through the agonizing anticipation of another afternoon of callers and the harrowing tension of another ball.

That night, as she stood near the wall, watching Georgina and Lord Howard work their way across the dance floor, she consoled herself with the fact that the next day's plans were easier if for no other reason than that they would be the ones going visiting, and she knew the Duke of Marshington's house was not on their agenda.

CHAPTER 22

"Is he here?" Georgina whispered as soon as they crossed the threshold into the drawing room.

Miranda was thankful they were attending a card party that evening instead of a ball. It was difficult to avoid people when one had only one room to work in. The card party was spread through two drawing rooms, a dining room, the main hall, and the library. While the library was informally reserved for the men, she could use it if absolutely necessary.

"I am sure I don't know." Miranda smiled at a couple of people she knew. The other benefit to card parties was that a person could wander the room and look as if she had a purpose. And if she did sit down to a game she could be firmly engaged for upwards of an hour with no need to contrive another activity for herself or drink another cup of warm lemonade.

"No one's seen him in days. I'm beginning to think it wasn't really him." Georgina pouted prettily and then flipped her mouth into a beaming grin as they passed a table holding Lord Eversly and Mr. Sherbourne. Both men sat a little straighter. Poor Mr. Sherbourne.

"Why do you say that?" Miranda hated her curiosity, but she had wondered about his absence as well. Was he still lurking in the shops, hoping she would show up? While she had the benefit of knowing the duke truly was in town, she wasn't about to divulge that to her sister.

"His aunt." Georgina nodded at a gentleman and lady seated at one of the card tables. "She says he isn't at the house. He would hardly return to town and take up lodgings elsewhere when he has that beautiful, enormous home over on Pall Mall."

Having met the aunt and heard multiple unflattering stories of the woman, Miranda could think of several reasons why Ryland would avoid the house on Pall Mall. "There are plenty of gentlemen that let homes for the Season, you know."

"Upstarts. They aren't worth my notice or yours, sister. No pedigree and no title. Who knows how they got all that money? It could be from anywhere, but they think it makes them Quality somehow." Georgina paused in the doorway to the second drawing room, looking over the occupants.

She nudged Miranda in the side and nodded toward the window across the room. "There's one now. Odious man. He came to visit a few days ago after you'd gone to lie down with your headache. I don't know what Gibson was thinking to let him in."

Miranda looked across the room. Three men stood in conversation by the window. Two of them she recognized and knew they would never set foot in Hawthorne House, so she decided Georgina was referring to the third. He was shorter than the other two with a head of reddish-brown hair. He looked like a pleasant gentleman and he irritated Georgina, so Miranda was inclined to like him.

"Introduce me."

"What?"

Miranda looked down at her sister. "Introduce me."

Georgina's eyes widened. "To the odious man?"

"You do remember his name don't you?" Miranda couldn't keep a slight smirk off of her face.

"Of course I do. But if I introduce you,

then he'll think I've been talking about him
—"

"You have."

"— and he'll think that I'm interested.
He'll come to call again." Georgina
frowned.

"Introduce me," Miranda repeated. "Unless you're afraid he'll like me more than
you."

It was quite unfair of Miranda to tug on
her sister's vanity that way, but she really
wanted to meet this man who made her
sister so mad. Georgina drew her brows
together and sucked in her cheeks. She
should have looked ridiculous, but somehow
her cheekbones stood out more and her eyes
seemed more exotic. "I don't think I have
anything to worry about. This way, sister
dear."

Miranda found herself hauled through the
drawing room until they stood next to the
trio of men deep in discussion about some
business venture. That explained how Odious Man had gotten invited to the card
party. The aristocratic life cost money and
men who could help make it were always
welcomed on the fringes of society.

"I apologize for the intrusion, but my
sister insisted we come over here." There
wasn't a hint of derision in Georgina's tone.

Miranda was impressed. Her sister's duplicity was deep indeed. "Mr. McCrae, she particularly wanted to meet you. Lady Miranda, this is Mr. Colin McCrae. I believe you know the other two gentlemen."

Poison. She was going to poison her little sister's chocolate in the morning. While Miranda knew the other two gentlemen by sight, she couldn't remember their names. They were fringe men, usually invited to simply even up the numbers. They were considered third or possibly even fourth tier bachelors that her mother would never direct her to in a social situation.

Georgina smiled sweetly at her sister.

"How do you do, Lady Miranda? I was just telling Mr. Craven and Sir Robert about a shipping company I'm involved in. Very dry conversation, I'm afraid."

Miranda's gaze flew to Mr. McCrae's face. He winked at her. She drew a quick breath in surprise. *He knows! Bless this man.* If he hadn't already been snared in Georgina's web she might consider setting her cap for him herself. It would help her get past the horrible situation with Ryland.

No. Forget that. She didn't need to set her cap for a gentleman. Men were even more manipulative than Georgina. Doting aunt was her future goal.

"I'm afraid I know nothing of shipping." Miranda turned to the other men, their names bringing to mind bits and pieces of information from previous dinner parties. "Mr. Craven, how is your sister? She married last year?"

The man with the thinning hair beamed. "Yes, she did. Doing splendidly. I hear from her occasionally." After a beat of awkward silence, he spoke again. "Sir Robert, do you fancy a game of faro? I believe they are starting one in the library."

Mr. McCrae watched his companions leave with a raised eyebrow. He turned back to the women with a small smile. "I suppose that leaves me to entertain two lovely ladies. Might I retrieve you a bit of refreshment? Or procure you a seat at a table?"

"No, thank you," Georgina said. "I see someone I must speak with. Pardon me." Was it Miranda's imagination or did her sister look a bit flushed?

"Do you need to speak with them as well?"

Miranda smiled at the joyful light in the man's light blue eyes. He knew exactly what had just transpired and it didn't bother him in the slightest. "I believe I am good where I am, thank you."

"I am pleased to finally meet you."

She tried to mask her sudden burst of

surprise. A widening of her eyes was the only outward sign that escaped. At least she hoped it was. "Finally, Mr. McCrae?"

He settled back into the corner, forcing her to completely turn her back to the rest of the room if she wanted to continue the conversation. She did.

He smiled into her eyes and leaned forward, as if to impart a secret. "I've heard about you."

A genuine smile spread across Miranda's lips. There was something very charming about her companion. "All good things, I hope."

"But of course."

"Hmmm." Miranda knew some of the things that were said about her — that she was too cold, too demanding, too choosy. If this man had truly been talking about her, then he would have heard some of the spiteful comments. As it didn't appear he was going to believe them or bring them up, she elected to leave them alone as well. "Have you sat down to a game of whist yet this evening?"

"Sadly, no. I'm afraid I've been too deep in discussions since I arrived. Should we find a table and sit down to a game?" Mr. McCrae tilted his head in a slight bow and made to offer her his arm. He froze as something over her shoulder caught his eye. His arm shifted, raising his hand to cover his mouth as he cleared his throat.

Miranda darted a glance behind her and found Ryland dressed in the first stare of fashion. He would have looked like quite the swell except for the discoloration that remained around his right eye. "Ry— er, Duke! I was not aware that you were attending this evening." She turned to allow Ryland into the small conversational group. Regardless of how confused she felt about him she couldn't be rude to a duke in the middle of a party.

His eyebrow arched over the array of blue, purple, and sickly green that adorned his face. "I'm quickly finding that I can go almost anywhere in London right now. Every hostess wants to claim I attended her gathering."

Miranda frowned. "So you weren't invited?"

"My dear Lady Miranda, do remember I've been away for a while. Hostesses haven't sent me an invite in years." His smile was patronizing, and Miranda found herself tempted to see if she could make his eyes a matching set.

A lady never resorts to violence.

Her mother had thoroughly expounded

318

on that point after the incident at the house the other day. There are many more subtle, cutting ways to exact revenge on a gentleman.

Only Miranda wasn't any good at them. Her ladylike demeanor often felt like little more than a mask. Anything requiring actual skill was beyond her.

Miranda turned to her new acquaintance. "Mr. McCrae, may I present His Grace, the Duke of Marshington? Your Grace, this is Mr. McCrae."

"A pleasure, sir," Ryland said quietly.

Mr. McCrae's smile had not dimmed with the appearance of what many men would consider a formidable presence. "The honor is mine, Your Grace."

The two bowed to each other and then said nothing for several moments.

Miranda felt an arm snake around her elbow. She turned, startled to find Georgina clinging to her side. "Georgina?"

"You looked in need of rescue, dear sister. You couldn't possibly partner both of these fine gentlemen in a game of cards."

Miranda noticed that while her sister might have referred to both gentlemen, she had eyes only for the duke. Giving in to the inevitable, Miranda introduced them. "Your Grace, my sister, Lady Georgina. Sister, may I present —"

"The Duke of Marshington." With an elegant sweep of her arm, Georgina presented her gloved hand. "I know who you are, Your Grace. I always keep up with news of importance."

Ryland did little more than bow over Georgina's hand before turning his attention back to Miranda and Mr. McCrae.

"Lady Miranda and I were about to locate an open spot at a table. We fancied a game of whist this evening." Mr. McCrae offered his arm and Miranda rested her hand on his elbow, fascination blooming. Here was a man, face-to-face with one of the highest-ranking persons in London, and he had not tried to turn the discussion to his advantage in social or business matters.

Georgina's eyes lit. "There is an empty table across the room, but you'll need another pair."

The fact that the young girl, barely a week into her first Season, had perfected the coy art of flirting was impressive and frightening at the same time. Miranda sighed as Ryland fell under the spell of Georgina's delicate features and fluttering lashes.

"May we join you for a game?" he asked, extending his arm to Georgina.

Miranda sighed again. There was no

graceful way out of the request.

They situated themselves at the table.
Miranda sat across from Mr. McCrae with
Georgina on her left and Ryland on her
right. The cards were dealt and the first two
tricks played in silence.

Ryland tapped his cards against the table,
and Miranda felt his eyes on her as she slid
the ten of clubs across the table. His gaze
moved to the card. "Fishing for something,
are you?"

"I beg your pardon!" Miranda sat up
straighter in her chair, outraged. The fact
that she was actually hoping someone would
play the ace so that her king would be the
high card in the suit was irrelevant.

"You aren't supposed to discuss the cards,
Your Grace." Georgina smiled at him,
clearly more interested in drawing his attention than in reprimanding him. She slid the
eight under Miranda's ten.

"My apologies." Ryland watched the cards
as Mr. McCrae slid the knave onto the pile.
"I was simply guessing that your sister was
using a bit of an underhanded play to look
for something that might improve the standing of her hand."

Miranda cut her eyes to look at him
askance. Was that how he justified his ac-

tions? The good of the country made everything worthwhile? Service to England was admirable, of course, but he'd spent a decade deceiving people. How could he compare that to her playing a game of cards? "I am not playing underhandedly, Your Grace."

Ryland considered his cards for a while and then flicked the ace onto the table, sending it sliding into Miranda's lap. "Oh, I'm not complaining. There's nothing wrong with what you've done. I'm sure that's not the best club you have in your hand, though. You presented something lower than your best in order to find something else. Well played."

Miranda felt two spots of heat form on her cheeks as Georgina gathered up the trick. The man was insufferable! How dare he compare her card-playing gambit to his heinous subterfuge? She ran her tongue around her teeth, determined that he not come ahead in this little battle of wits.

"One might think you have peeked at my cards, if you feel so sure of my tactics. Now that would be underhanded playing."

Ryland's eyes met hers, and she was captured all over again by their silvery depths. The skin around his eyes crinkled a bit as they stared at each other. The man was enjoying this! Miranda broke the connection first. "It is your lead, Your Grace."

He extracted a card from his hand but didn't lay it down on the table. "Sometimes knowing something about another person's hand," Ryland said so quietly Miranda was sure only she and Mr. McCrae would be able to hear, "lets you help them play it to its best advantage."

Miranda's eyes were glued to the card as he flipped it into the middle of the table. The queen of clubs. Her eyes flew to his face, but he was staring at his hand, expressionless. She stole a glance at Mr. McCrae, but he only smiled expectantly at her, no doubt assuming she had the king and would be able to take the trick.

Georgina tsked and smiled sweetly at her partner. "That was not well played, Your Grace, but you've been away from civilized gatherings for a while, so I won't complain."

Miranda looked at her hand. There was more at stake here than a simple card game. She had two options. If she played her king, what did that say? Would she be admitting that his knowing her smallest secrets only made him a better match for her? On the other hand, she could play the five and send the message that he may not know her as well as he thought. But then she would also be saying she was willing to spite herself in order to thwart him.

All of this assumed he was interested in pursuing the fledgling connection they had when he was a servant at Riverton.

Miranda's head pounded as she ran her finger back and forth across the two cards. She took a deep breath and raised her eyes to meet his grey gaze. Then she flicked her card into the air.

CHAPTER 23

The delicate *whoosh* of the card drifting through the air echoed in her ears despite the noise of the rest of the party. She maintained Ryland's gaze with a slight feeling of desperation. If he kept looking at her until all of the cards had been played, he wouldn't see her king and then he couldn't draw any conclusions about it.

Georgina placed her card on the table with a *thunk.* "How unkind, Miranda, for you to take advantage of His Grace's blunder."

Miranda raised her eyebrows, keeping her gaze steady on the duke. "I believe His Grace will understand taking advantage of one's situation."

The corner of Ryland's mouth tipped in a slight smile. "One should take every opportunity presented. The unexpected ones are sometimes the most meaningful."

Mr. McCrae coughed. From the side of

her vision, Miranda saw him lay a card on the table and then collect the hand. He tapped the cards on the table a few times before setting them to the side.

Moments passed. Miranda had no idea how long it was, but she was sure that Mr. McCrae and Georgina were beginning to wonder what was happening between herself and Ryland. It was unseemly for a woman and a man to spend such a lengthy amount of time staring at each other, but she couldn't break away.

"Sister dear, it is your play." Georgina's voice was tight with clear irritation. She had made her intentions of snaring the duke plain and was no doubt miffed at his attention to Miranda.

Ryland's smile grew, and Miranda's heart sped up. Smiles had been rare in their encounters before now. His was breathtaking. She had never seen teeth so straight and even. The man was truly blessed.

He nodded toward her cards, his gaze still connected to hers. "You have the next move, Lady Miranda."

"What if I don't want it?" Miranda whispered, forgetting about the card game momentarily.

Georgina huffed. "What do you mean you don't want it? You played the king, Miranda.

Who did you think was going to have the next lead?"

Ryland sat back in his chair and inspected his cards, severing the invisible connection. "What are you going to play, Lady Miranda?"

She felt lost without the silver glow of his direct attention and then looked blindly down at her own cards. Her eyes refused to focus on the numbers, no matter how many times she blinked, so she snagged a card and threw it on the table without knowing what it was.

Once the stiff paper had left her fingers, Miranda slid her eyes shut and swallowed a groan. The silence at the table lasted so long that she peeked between her lashes to determine what she played. Her eyes flew open.

She had played the queen of hearts.

"You behaved like a green girl tonight at that card table." Georgina waited only until the carriage door shut before berating her older sister. "What was all that nonsense? The duke must think you a total jingle-brain."

Griffith froze in the middle of adjusting his coat to allow him to sit more comfortably in the carriage. His eyes darted to

Miranda, but she turned to stare out the window at the other revelers climbing into their own conveyances instead of meeting his gaze.

He cleared his throat. "What nonsense?"

"It started when Marshington —"

"You're calling him Marshington now?" Miranda cut in, hoping to distract her sister from telling the story.

"He is a friend of the family, Miranda, I think certain liberties can be taken in private. This is hardly the dark ages anymore, is it?"

Miranda blinked at her sister's haughty smirk. What could she possibly say to that? When it came to taking liberties under the guise of family friendship, using the name *Marshington* in private didn't compare to all of the letters she herself had addressed to him over the years.

"As I was saying, Marshington made a simple strategic error, understandable given his years away from polite society, and Miranda turned it into some philosophical nonsense. He, being a gentleman, played along, of course." Georgina folded her hands over the reticule in her lap.

"How, exactly, did he blunder?" Griffith's question was directed at Georgina, but his gaze remained fixed on Miranda. It was giving her an irresistible desire to squirm.

The sounds of the party drifted away to be replaced by the rattle of horse hooves and carriage wheels over cobbled streets. Georgina related the tale as she saw it, leaving out parts that she hadn't heard or didn't believe. Had Miranda not been there to know differently, she would consider herself jingle-brained based on Georgina's version of the card game.

"And then she laid the queen of hearts, Griffith. It was such a strange play to make. How could it be construed as anything but a flirtation? I was ashamed for her — really, I was."

Tension eased from Griffith for the first time since entering the carriage. "She played the queen of hearts, you say? And what did you play?"

Miranda rolled her eyes. If Griffith was making this much of that silly card, who knew what Ryland was thinking about it.

"Well, I played the four, because I couldn't beat her queen. Mr. Macroy —"

"McCrae," Miranda said.

Georgina waved a hand in dismissal. "He played the nine, but then the duke played the king, which was necessary to take the trick but made everyone at the table very uncomfortable."

"I was just fine, thank you." It was a complete lie, but Miranda felt she had to do something to temper Georgina's view of the evening.

Georgina reached across the seat and took Miranda's hand. "For someone who has been out in society for so long, I am surprised you haven't learned to hide your feelings better, dear sister. You were quite distinctly flushed. Anyone could see it."

Another flush threatened to heat Miranda's cheeks, but she forced slow, steady breaths through her nose and thought about the rolling fields around Riverton. The calming trick had been working for years when she fought the desire to chuck her lady lessons out the window. She could only hope it was effective against blushing as well.

Then she remembered walking through those rolling fields with Ryland. The blush returned full force. Fortunately, Georgina had moved on by then.

"He couldn't leave the table fast enough once the hand was played out. It was sheer luck that Lord Ashcombe was nearby and took the vacated seat."

Griffith raised his eyebrows and concern drifted over his features as he looked at Miranda. "Ashcombe played cards with you tonight?"

"Yes, and then Miranda got a headache after the next hand," Georgina continued, seemingly unaware of the underlying strain her comment had brought to the carriage. Miranda had never been more thankful for her sister's self-absorption. "So Lady Sarah Wrothington played the rest of the game."

"Has your head recovered, Miranda?"

"Yes, I found a bit of fresh air did it wonders." Miranda nodded to her eldest brother, hoping he understood her acceptance of his concern.

Griffith had always maintained that he felt a bit guilty for his part in the dealings that broke her heart and, possibly more importantly, her trust in the male portion of English society. Blaming him would have been pointless though. All he'd done was expose Ashcombe's true motivations and allow her to see that most men viewed marriage as little more than a business transaction.

Blessed quiet filled the carriage for the remainder of the short ride. Miranda was relieved to be back in the sanctuary of her home. The quiet tick of the clock in the red drawing room was the only sound once the front door clicked shut behind them.

"Will there be anything more, Your

Grace?" asked Gibson, the butler.

"No, I think it's been a long night for all of us. We'll retire. Until tomorrow, then." Griffith turned and led the little group up the stairs.

Miranda made to follow him, but Georgina's hand on her arm made her pause and turn back to her sister.

"When the duke comes to call on me, I expect you to make yourself scarce. I can't have him thinking we're both lacking in the upper garrets."

Miranda shook her head. If the duke came to call on Georgina he wasn't half the man she thought she knew. She would gladly agree to stay away from him should he be swayed into courting the youngest Hawthorne. With a murmur of assent, Miranda headed up the stairs, intent on finding her bed and dreaming of anything besides Ryland.

The following morning Mother arrived as Georgina and Miranda were finishing breakfast. They were to be at home again that afternoon.

Miranda was still a bit irritated with her sister's criticism from the night before, so she was feeling less than charitable about spending another afternoon smoothing the ruffled feathers of discarded suitors. "Mother, why don't you move Georgina in with you? Then you wouldn't have to come over here so early in the morning."

"As much as I love William, he is only an earl, and his house, while nice, is not as impressive as Hawthorne House. Your father was a very powerful duke, Miranda, and I will not lose that advantage when it comes to finding Georgina the best possible match." Mother fixed herself a cup of tea and sipped it slowly while her daughters finished eating. "Besides, as much as William loves me, he's already been through this with his two girls. He deserves a quiet home."

Miranda made her last two bites of toast stretch into five to put off the inevitable. But when no more crumbs could be eaten without censure, she gave in and went upstairs to dress, bracing for the exhausting discussions that were to come.

Mother insisted on overseeing every part of Georgina's preparation, determined that she be as close to perfection as possible. Since she hadn't sat in on Miranda's daily preparations in over two years, Miranda could only assume today's attentions were an effort to keep her from feeling neglected.

Normally, Sally had Miranda ready for the

day within an hour. With Mother and Georgina deliberating over dress choices and coiffure suggestions, Miranda knew it would be at least two hours before the three of them would once again be seated in the white room awaiting callers.

She slid her Bible from the table by the bed, intent on rereading the passages she'd clung to while still in the country. Whatever they selected for her to wear would suit her. She had no intention of catching a gentleman's fancy anyway.

Ryland perused the front page of the newspaper while slowly chewing a succulent bite of ham. He had been enjoying the chef's efforts from the comfort of his room since arriving five days prior, but this was the first meal he'd ventured to the dining room for.

Continuing to avoid his family after showing his face at the tea shop was bad enough. Doing so after attending the card party would be unpardonable. Not that he regretted attending the party. It had proven a very worthwhile endeavor given the interesting verbal parlay over the first hand of cards. He'd also encountered the young couple from the tea shop. Newly affianced, they'd been too absorbed in each other to pay attention to anything else, even when the young lady's skirt got stepped upon, ripping the hem.

Given the choice, he'd attend the card party again, but that didn't make him look forward to the coming confrontation.

"So. You are here."

Ryland looked up into a face so familiar and yet so altered that it sent shock vibrating down his spine. He'd kept up with news of his cousin, Mr. Gregory Montgomery, through the years, but he hadn't actually seen the man since hauling him out of a burning building in France. The years were evident on his face.

They looked similar, had always been mistaken for brothers growing up. Gregory's grey eyes were a little wider set. His ears were a touch bigger. Having continued to lead a posh lifestyle while Ryland risked his life for England had created a more rounded face and thicker middle.

And then there was the limp.

Ryland studiously avoided looking at his cousin's left leg. That the man was alive at all was a miracle. That he walked was unbelievable. The fact that he blamed Ryland for all of it was ludicrous. Ryland was the only reason Gregory was breakfasting in England instead of the afterlife.

Ryland turned his attention back to the

paper. "Yes, I am here."

The clink of china and the rattle of the paper were the only sounds for several moments.

"Are you staying?"

"Yes. I've decided it's time to come home." A story about the discovery of the body of King Charles I drew his attention. While the one-hundred-and-sixty-year-old mystery of where the old king's body was didn't keep him awake at night, Ryland always enjoyed when questions got answered. It was rather amusing that they'd found him tucked in with Henry VIII. A tomb was the perfect place to hide a body.

"Mother is livid," Gregory said.

"I don't see why. My being here shouldn't change her life overmuch. I have no intention of restricting her comings and goings, and my room and office have never been used by either of you." Ryland took a moment to glance up and judge the veracity of his statement. He saw no signs in his cousin that would indicate a breakage of the rules, so he went back to his paper. "The house is large enough we can all avoid each other."

Gregory grunted. "That doesn't seem very familial of you."

"I didn't stop the purchase when you overspent your monthly allowance to buy that hunting horse last year." Ryland met Gregory's eyes with a hard glare. "I'd say that was quite familial of me, wouldn't you?"

Gregory fidgeted in his seat, looking more like an eight-year-old boy than a man twenty years older than that. "Er, yes, I suppose it was."

"It's a fine horse, by the way. You chose well." In truth he had been manipulated. Ryland hadn't stopped the purchase because he wanted Gregory to buy the horse. Ryland had been working at the time and was unable to buy the steed himself, but with plans to return to his former life soon, he'd desired the grand hunter to be part of his own stable. Setting up a man to convince Gregory to buy it had been easier than Ryland anticipated.

And if it made Gregory think he'd gotten away with something or that the duke had extended the hand of generosity . . . Well, Ryland considered that a positive as well.

"Thank you. I've always had a good eye for horseflesh." Gregory visibly relaxed as he shoveled bacon into his mouth.

Ryland barely avoided snorting. Gregory had a terrible eye for horseflesh. He lost more money in a single visit to Ascot than Ryland paid the butler for an entire year.

And Ryland paid his staff very well.

"Mother is still livid, though."

Ryland debated repeating his answer, but decided that would be childish. So he ignored the repeated statement instead.

"She told everyone that you weren't back. That the rumors were wrong, as always. She is furious that you made her look like a fool."

Ryland finished the news and money sections, but if he set aside the paper he'd have to talk to Gregory, so he moved on to the society section, where half of the articles made mention of his return.

Gregory finally got the idea that Ryland wasn't going to engage in welcome-home chatter. He ate quietly, and Ryland could almost pretend he had his home to himself.

And then another voice ripped through the morning air.

"Good morning, Ryland. Pardon me if I don't welcome you home."

CHAPTER 24

Ryland kept the paper raised, blocking him from his aunt's view. "I don't mind at all. I trust you will pardon me as well if I don't tell you how good it is to see you."

Out of the corner of his eye he saw a footman scurry to pull out Aunt Marguerite's chair. There was a clatter of china and then the muffled sounds of his family eating. The crinkling of the paper as he turned the page echoed through the room.

"You should have informed us of your return. We would have had a proper celebration."

Ryland grinned behind his paper shield. He had wondered how long his aunt would be able to keep silent. "I arrived exactly as I wished to, aunt."

"Everyone is going to want to know where you've been."

Ryland read an article about a horse race through Hyde Park.

"What should I tell them?"

It was quite irresponsible to race through Hyde Park. Much too crowded. Regent's Park would have been a better choice.

"Ryland?"

Of course it wouldn't be as convenient since the racers were probably coming from one of the gentlemen's clubs along St. James's Street. Hyde Park was considerably closer.

"Ryland! I am speaking to you!"

Ryland folded his paper and stood, scooping up the additional correspondence sitting on the corner of the table. He looked at his aunt for the first time, noticing how much the years and bitterness had aged her. The once effortlessly elegant and stately woman now looked haggard and desperate. Unexpected pity rose within him.

This was the woman who had spent her entire life trying to belittle him. As the only mother figure he'd ever known, she should have been special, even loved. But he'd spent his entire childhood hiding from her diatribes on how much better his cousin was.

Pity was the last thing he'd expected to feel in connection to her.

He looked from his aunt to his cousin. Ryland's mother had died in childbirth and his uncle had passed a few months later. He and Gregory had been raised like brothers. Gregory was only seven months older. They should have been close.

If the disgust on the faces of his aunt and cousin were anything to go by, Ryland was the only one who even slightly mourned the lost opportunity.

"Tell them what I've told you." He rounded the table and headed for the door.

"But you've told me nothing!"

He paused to smile at her over his shoulder. "Precisely."

Eighteen. Eighteen men had come to the house to offer their attentions to Georgina that afternoon. And eighteen men had all gone away befuddled, no doubt wondering why they'd given their flowers to the spinster sister instead.

"Lady Raebourne is here," Gibson announced.

Miranda sat a little straighter in anticipation. A visit from Amelia was always welcome, today more than ever. She hadn't had a chance to speak in much depth about the situation with Ryland, only a rushed whispered conversation the day after the confrontation in Griffith's study.

The necessary pleasantries seemed to take

much longer than normal. At the first lull in the conversation, Miranda sprang from her seat. "Amelia, have you seen the new roses in the conservatory?"

Amelia's eyes widened briefly before she too got to her feet. "They sound lovely."

"Oh yes," Miranda gushed. "You simply must see them."

She grabbed Amelia's hand and pulled her from the drawing room before Mother had a chance to speak a protest.

Amelia tripped along behind Miranda until they entered the conservatory, then she wrenched her arm from Miranda's grasp. "That was very subtle."

Miranda's eyes narrowed at more evidence of Amelia's newfound sarcasm, but she couldn't maintain her ire. It had been a rather ungraceful exit from the room. She shook her head with a groan.

"Are there even roses in here?" Amelia asked as she wandered the room.

"I believe so, over in the corner." Miranda led the way so they would be in the appropriate location should Mother come looking for them. "He was at the card party last night."

"He's interesting." Amelia grazed a finger along a small, pink bloom.

It was not the response Miranda had

expected. "What do you mean?"

"I mean," Amelia said with a sigh as she lowered herself onto a curved stone bench, "that I'm going to be of little assistance beyond that of a sympathetic ear."

Miranda's thoughts deserted Ryland and the myriad of problems he inspired. Amelia had been raised by her guardian's servants. Local maids had been her playmates, and she'd grown up visiting with half the aristocratic servants in Mayfair. Those same servants had been instrumental in pairing Amelia with her husband, the Marquis of Raebourne. If anyone could find out what was going on in someone's home it should have been her.

How dreadful if her old friends had stopped talking to her now that she was an aristocrat herself. Miranda sat next to Amelia on the bench and covered Amelia's small hands with her own. "None of the servants will speak to you anymore? Oh, I'm so sorry."

Amelia clasped Miranda's hands and laughed lightly. "Oh no, nothing like that, although Mrs. Harris thought it strange when I asked for the local gossip," Amelia said, referring to the housekeeper that had practically raised her. "I mean that none of them know anything about the Duke of

Marshington or his household."

"Well, he's only now returned to London. It will take time, surely."

Amelia shook her head. "He moved into his family home on Pall Mall. That's all anyone knows. His servants don't mingle much with the others in London, and when they do they don't share anything about the household."

"Nothing?" Miranda was mystified. Gossip was currency in London for every class from servant to peer. How was it no one knew anything about what went on behind the walls of Ryland's home?

"Nothing." Amelia gave a slow shake of her head. "It's as if the man simply dropped from the sky."

Miranda couldn't hide her disappointment. She'd been hoping Amelia would be able to give her some insight, some secret information about Ryland to help level the playing field. After all, he knew so much about her private life after living as a servant at Riverton.

It was Amelia's turn to reach out to Miranda and grip hands. "Why don't you tell me how the card party went? You said he was there."

"It all started to go wrong when I sat down to play a game of whist with him. . . ."

■ ■ ■ ■

Account books spread across the desk surface, requiring so much of Ryland's attention he almost didn't hear the knock on the door. "Enter," he barked.

Price, the butler, opened the door, his wide torso filling the doorframe. Ryland glanced up at the man and grinned. He wished he could have seen his aunt's face when Price had come to work here. With arms the size of ham hocks, a nonexistent neck, and scars along the side of his face, he was no one's idea of an aristocratic butler. Ryland had seen him throw a grown man fifteen feet through the air. The man might have kept going, but the wall stopped him.

"What is it, Price?"

"Mr. McCrae is here to see you, sir."

Colin clapped the giant on the shoulder and sidled around him into the room. "You'll have to start using *Your Grace* instead of *sir* if you want to be a proper butler, Price."

Price grinned as he backed out of the room. It made his face look eerily boyish. "I think that's the least of my problems, Mr. McCrae."

Colin made a show of looking over the butler. "You may have a point there."

Price pulled the door closed as Colin threw himself into one of the Chippendale wing chairs that flanked the cold fireplace. He stuck out his booted feet and crossed his ankles. "Didn't expect to see you at the card party last night."

Ryland shrugged as he came around the desk to settle into the other chair. "I couldn't bear to hide out in my room any longer."

"Is your aunt delighted you're home?" That Colin had managed to say that with a straight face was a compliment to his composure. It must be a considerable asset during business dealings.

"Hardly. I think she coddled the eggs with her glare this morning."

"And your cousin?"

Ryland shrugged, and wished he'd had a fire set, even though it was too warm to need one. It would have given him something to look at. He wasn't sure how Gregory felt. Their past experience should have brought them closer, but Ryland knew the other man had attempted on two separate occasions to have him declared dead. While he was certain Aunt Marguerite instigated the attempts, Gregory had agreed to carry them through.

His family was not something he felt comfortable discussing. He had to protect them, he was supposed to love them, but in reality life would be considerably easier without them. A change of topic was in order. "Have you found anything more about that mine investment inquiry?"

"I thought you were off the case. You said you turned everything you had over to another agent." Colin frowned.

Ryland dropped his head onto the back of the chair. "I don't like leaving things unfinished."

Silence stretched.

"You're supposed to be moving on with your life," Colin finally said.

Ryland rolled his head to the side so he could look at Colin. "What do you know?"

"You first. Are you truly getting out of the spying game or is this all some elaborate ruse?" Colin's blue eyes were hard and flat. Ryland didn't often see the side of Colin that made him such a shrewd and successful businessman, but at times like this he was reminded why he'd given Colin so much money to invest over the past five years.

Ryland turned his gaze back to the ceiling. "Out. As soon as this mission is actually completed."

"You wouldn't be the first man to use that lie on himself."

"I've given enough of my life to king and country. But I can't leave this undone. Despite what they say, the Office is counting on me to finish this. No one else knows as much as I do. So I need to know what you know."

Colin sighed. "Not a name. I was able to learn that all of the men in the mining venture are small fish. A title or two, some lower sons, even a few gentry. Your man may think he's got some considerable prestige to protect, but it's not enough to save him from the gallows."

Ryland sighed. He thought of the two men in the tea shop. Sketching had never been his greatest skill, but he grabbed a piece of paper and a pencil and did his best to draw the men's faces.

Colin waited in silence.

"Do you know these men?" Ryland shoved the drawings in Colin's direction.

"You're not serious. Look at those. Do they look anything like the men you're trying to identify?" Colin laughed and tossed the paper into Ryland's lap.

Ryland cringed as he admitted that even he wouldn't recognize the drawings as the men from the shop.

When Ryland asked no more questions, Colin moved on to another topic. "How fares your latest project?"

"I assume you refer to my courtship of Lady Miranda."

"Aye. Unless you've decided the younger sister is more appealing after all."

Ryland's lips curved into a half smile. "Not at all. Are you intrigued by the younger —"

"Are you daft, man? It takes only a moment to tell her head is filled with fashion and frippery. I'd rather court your parlor maid." Colin shuddered.

"Jess is actually quite fetching. She likes to read Shakespeare."

Colin laughed. "Maybe I'll take her for a drive."

Ryland leaned forward and braced his elbows on his knees. "I was wondering if you would take Miranda."

"I beg your pardon?"

"You didn't reveal last night that we know each other."

"Old habits, you know. I never knew what you were up to on the rare occasion that I saw you. Seemed safer to pretend I didn't know you." Colin leaned forward as well, mirroring Ryland's posture. "Please don't tell me you want me to spy on this woman."

"Yes."

"I refuse to interrogate a lady as to whether or not she's forgiven you. Besides, as you said, she doesn't know we know each other."

Ryland examined his fingernails. "You could ask her about the card game."

Colin burst from the chair and paced across the room. "You want me to go to this woman's house, ask her to go for a ride, and then proceed to embarrass her thoroughly so that you can have more information with which to create your plan of attack?"

Colin's knowing him well made things much easier. "Yes."

"No. This is a courtship, not an army invasion."

"One should always know the factors involved when creating a plan of action. Information is power, and I'm going to need all of the leverage I can get to bring her around. She's being stubbornly female about the whole thing."

Colin scoffed. "How dare she?" He glared at Ryland. "Find yourself another lackey. I won't do it."

Time stretched on, the clicking of the

mantel clock the only sound as the two men stared at each other.

CHAPTER 25

"My lady, Mr. McCrae has arrived."

Miranda looked at the butler in surprise. If she were to make a list of all the people returning to partake of Georgina's special brand of refined rejection, Mr. McCrae would certainly not be on it. He had seemed much too intelligent during their conversation at the card party. A glance at Georgina revealed that she was stunned as well.

"Odious man," Georgina hissed under her breath. "I don't wish to see him, Mother."

Gibson cleared his throat. "He asked to see Lady Miranda, milady."

"Oh." Two sets of startled green eyes turned to Miranda. Mother's were glittering and crinkling at the corners with a small smile. Georgina looked dumbfounded.

Miranda couldn't quite resist the urge to preen. Odious or not, Mr. McCrae was rich and attractive and he'd chosen to visit her instead of Georgina. "Thank you, Gibson.

Please show him in."

Gibson bowed and returned to the front hall. Mr. McCrae strode in moments later.

He bowed to Mother first. "Good afternoon, my lady."

"Same to you, Mr. McCrae. I didn't know we would see you again so soon." Her smile was a bit larger than socially acceptable. It warmed Miranda's heart that her mother still believed a match could be found for her eldest daughter, even if it was a mere mister and a Scottish one at that.

Mr. McCrae bypassed Georgina entirely, startling a muffled giggle from Miranda. "Lady Miranda, I know this is quite presumptuous of me, but would you care to go for a drive?"

Mother's smiled dimmed a bit. "I don't know —"

"Yes." Miranda popped up from the settee. "Yes, I would love to."

Mr. McCrae might not cause a stirring in her middle like Ryland did, but he had been a perfectly pleasant companion at the card party. It was worth considering him as a future husband. The fact that she would be unavailable for Georgina to use as a decoy for the afternoon only added to her anticipation.

And as much as she hated to admit it, loving wife and mother sounded much better than doting aunt.

"Oh, well, I suppose it would be acceptable." Mother's light green eyes met Miranda's. "An hour. No more."

Mr. McCrae bowed again. "Of course."

Miranda placed her hand on his arm. Neither spoke as he escorted her from the room and out the door. The curricle looked brand-new. The seat was unworn, and no signs of mending marred the harness connections. Even the wheels looked free of scuffs.

Settling onto the seat, she realized the curricle was exceptionally well sprung. A vehicle like this would not have come cheaply. She watched Mr. McCrae with an assessing eye as he circled the curricle and climbed up beside her.

"This is very nice." She ran a hand along the polished wood.

Mr. McCrae's grin was instantaneous and accompanied by a self-satisfied chuckle. "A friend loaned it to me. I'm considering keeping it. He owes me. I'm doing him a grand favor."

"Oh." Miranda didn't know what to say. The answer was not at all what she had been expecting. On the one hand, the fact that he had gone through the trouble of convincing his friend to loan him such a fine curricle was flattering. That he was considering not returning it showed a lack of character she could not condone, although she knew gentlemen took their debts very seriously.

He clicked at the horse, a tall, sleek creature with a beautiful reddish-brown coat. The curricle glided smoothly into the traffic flowing toward Rotten Row. "I enjoyed meeting you last night. I haven't played such an interesting hand of whist in years."

Miranda flushed. She turned her face to gaze at the passing houses, hoping the edge of her bonnet shielded her face from his eyes. "I confess that I have not either."

Mr. McCrae waved to a few people before speaking again. "Lady Miranda, may I be ruthlessly honest with you?"

"Of . . . of course." Could there really be any other response to a question like that? One could hardly say that she would prefer to be lied to and deceived.

"We both know there was more afoot than a game of cards last night, and we also know that I could never compete with a duke as far as social status goes."

"Mr. McCrae, I can assure you that I find you a most interesting gentleman." Such a bald statement left her flustered and flaming. She tried to fan her cheeks with subtle hand movements in an attempt to dispel the heat in her face and neck.

He cast her a sideways glance before turning back to the road. "It's glad I am to hear that. I was more wondering if you would say that the duke was an interesting gentleman as well. As I said, I don't have much to compete with him."

Miranda snorted, which caused her blush to return full force. "Have you had any dealings with him? Wait, that is a silly question. He's only been back in London for a few days."

"I've worked with him a time or two before."

"You . . . you have? Then you . . . I mean, you do that too?"

He looked down at the reins for a moment. A muffled cough preceded the lifting of his head. His lips were pressed into a tight line. "Do I do what?"

"Er, what he does."

"Manage estates? Hardly. I dabble in a shipping company and manage investments."

"Oh." Miranda found herself confused. If Ryland had been acting as a spy for the past nine years, how had he worked with Mr. McCrae? "Did you invest money for the duke, then?"

He cleared his throat. "I don't like to discuss such matters. You understand."

"Oh yes, of course."

They turned onto Rotten Row, joining the parade of fashionable couples in their open-air conveyances.

"The thing is, Lady Miranda, I'm considering looking into some investments out of town. I know this is terribly forward of me, but I need to know if I should postpone my trip."

"Mr. McCrae, I —"

"Do call me Colin. It's the least I can offer considering how personal I'm being at the moment."

Miranda swallowed. "Colin, I don't know what to say to this. I have known you for a mere day."

She felt trapped as he turned his head to catch her in his blue gaze. It was not the piercing intensity of Ryland's nor the powerful demand for respect she often saw in Griffith's. It was captivating. Like watching the dancing flames of a fire or the repeated licks of the ocean against the sand in Brighton.

He sighed. "There's something between you and the duke, isn't there? You're a beautiful lady, but I have a sense I shouldn't waste my time courting you. Am I right?"

She opened her mouth, intending to deny the charge that her heart was already taken, but nothing came out. Her encounters with Ryland floated through her memory. For the first time she allowed herself to see how genuine he had managed to be, even while playing the servant. Allowing herself the freedom to imagine a future with the duke, she began to smile and cry at the same time. Getting past the hurt and mistrust was not going to be easy, but maybe it would be worth it.

"I'm sorry, Colin, but I think maybe you are. I'm not entirely sure what will happen with the duke, but I owe it to myself to find out." A sad smile curved her lips. Colin seemed like a good man. He didn't deserve to have the woman he was courting thinking of another man.

"I understand. Shall we simply enjoy this sunshine, then, as I take the route back home?"

"That would be wonderful, yes."

They drove on in companionable silence, occasionally breaking it with a remark on a particularly interesting hat or ramifications of seeing certain couples riding out together. They discussed the ball she was to attend later that evening. Miranda participated in the conversation by rote, her mind focused on acclimating to this new way of thinking about Ryland. Was she in love with him? If the answer was yes, what was she going to do?

Colin pulled up in front of her home and jumped down. As he walked her to the door, he looked over his shoulder at the vehicle. "It is a fine curricle, isn't it?"

"It is. I hope your friend will allow you to borrow it again when you find another young lady to take for a drive."

That large, self-assured grin spread across his face once more. "I think I'll keep it. It's the least Ryland can do after putting me in a position to anger such a lovely woman as yourself."

The door opened behind Miranda but it felt as if the pavement had just crumbled beneath her feet.

Colin continued speaking as he bowed to her and backed down the four steps to the street. "Do tell him for me at the ball tonight, won't you? That I'm keeping his horse and curricle? He'll understand."

He tipped his hat.

Miranda stomped into the house. Apparently Colin McCrae was not such a nice man after all.

■ ■ ■ ■

"You're going to break that fan."

Miranda ceased the staccato slap of her folded fan against her arm and turned to find the younger of her brothers leaning against the wall. It didn't surprise her. He'd been her shadow since the card party, waiting to see what would happen next between her and Ryland.

Miranda was beginning to wonder herself. It had been a week since Colin had taken her for a ride. During that time Ryland had kept their interactions brief and public, never giving her the chance to confront him about what he'd done. The conflicted emotions it was causing were maddening.

She glared at her brother. "Do you have a point?"

Trent shrugged and pushed away from the wall, strolling the two steps necessary to reach her side. "That it would be a sad waste of a fan, I suppose. After all, it's done nothing to harm you. Your energy would be much better spent if you directed it at the actual problem, wouldn't it?"

"The problem, as you put it, has not seen fit to make an appearance yet this evening." Her volatile mood had driven her to the corner to sulk and glare at the doorway, daring Ryland to appear. Agitation sent her hand into motion once more, the lace border of her fan doing little to pad the clicking of the ivory ribs as she tapped her arm.

"Maybe he doesn't know you're here." Trent eased a hand toward the fan. Miranda rapped him on the knuckles before resuming her rhythmic motion.

"He knows. Somehow he always knows. He knows when I go shopping so I'm positive he knows when I attend a social event." Her foot joined the fan in announcing her displeasure. The infernal man had driven her to abandon her carefully held ladylike veneer. It terrified her that he had caused such a lack of decorum and he wasn't even in the room. That more than anything revealed how much he must matter to her. It wasn't smart to let him matter to her. She still had questions.

Trent cleared his throat. "Do you want him to show up?"

Did her grin look as evil as it felt? "Oh yes indeed. You see, if he doesn't show up he can't ask me to dance, and if he doesn't ask me to dance, I can't give him the cut direct he so very much deserves."

Her brother's sputter brought a momentary flash of happiness to her mood. "You . . . you intend to cut him here? In the ballroom? If you refuse to dance with him you'll be sitting out everything for the rest of the evening. To dance with someone else would be unforgivably rude."

"Then maybe I'll be unforgivably rude. Unlikely though. I spend more and more time on the fringes as it is. If I find it too tedious, I can always go home." Miranda shrugged and returned her attention to the door. Had she missed him come in while Trent distracted her?

"He's a duke, Miranda!"

"So I hear."

Ryland appeared in the doorway to the ballroom.

Miranda's heart skipped a beat as she took in his broad shoulders and exquisite male grace. He moved through the ballroom easily, despite its packed confines. His height allowed her to keep track of him. His head didn't swing back and forth as most people's would, but she sensed he was methodically searching the ballroom. Maybe it was prideful, but she assumed he was looking for her.

She tried to remember how she felt after Colin had taken her riding. She thought through every question Ryland's actions had raised since she'd returned to London. She did everything she could to remind herself that she was angry at the handsome man.

Memories from the week warred with her disgust for the front of her mind. His tweaked lips when he asked for a recommendation of a good stationery store. Preferably one specializing in colored parchments.

Him "dropping" his greatcoat in front of a woman huddling with two small children outside the opera house. He'd waited until Miranda had climbed into Griffith's carriage, but she'd still seen the caring deed.

Him offering to hold her packages while she and Georgina stepped into Gunter's for ices one afternoon.

She frowned and brought to mind the memory of him talking to her about her letters in the guise of Griffith's valet. If that didn't keep her ire up, nothing would.

Trent stepped forward, abandoning his careless position. "You can't cut a duke."

With another devilish grin tossed over her shoulder, she stepped forward into the halo of candlelight from a tall brass candelabra. "Watch me."

CHAPTER 26

Ryland flicked his eyes back and forth, inspecting the ballroom. His heart beat faster as he looked for Miranda.

He wanted to talk to her, to get past their unconventional meeting and move forward with getting to know one another, but first he had to break through the shell of propriety that he kept bumping up against. Were the little encounters he'd planned enough to remind her that she had, at one point, actually liked him? Were they enough to get her to let down her guard?

Right now he would take any emotion as a sign he was succeeding. Anything other than the pleasant, perfect lady her mother had convinced her to become.

A movement in the corner caught Ryland's eye and his gaze homed in on a breathtaking woman in pale green velvet. She was stepping into the glowing circle cast by a nearby candelabra, a look of mischief on her face as she said something to someone in the shadows behind her. Miranda had always been beautiful to him, but at that moment she was utterly captivating. Her hair had something sparkly woven into the curls that caught the candlelight and gave her an exquisite glow.

Even as her beauty knocked his breath down to his toes, that mischievous look made his heart cheer. It also had him shoring up his guard. She was planning something, and whatever it was, it wouldn't bode well for him. He would have to counteract it before she had a chance to maneuver him into her plan.

Making his way around the ballroom with the efficiency of a man used to getting where he wanted to be without drawing undue notice to himself, he planned his own strategy.

"Good evening, Lady Miranda."

"Your Grace." She curtsied low, the very picture of social grace. Her eyes betrayed the exuberant, passionate woman he'd been drawn to.

"It is quite a crush this evening." He turned to stand next to her and gaze out over the couples spinning and twirling their way through a quadrille.

"Yes, quite. But not so bad as some I've

been to. There is room to move and breathe here, after all."

"You find it hard to breathe at these events, then?" He thought he felt her eyes boring into the side of his head, but he refused to glance her way to verify the feeling. His eyes remained fastened on the dancers.

"At times. I have been to events where the only way I knew my shoes were on my feet was to grip them with my toes."

He made some sort of grunt as a response. Not terribly polite of him, but he wanted to see what she had planned.

"Unless, of course, I was dancing. They maintained plenty of room in which to actually dance."

Another grunt vibrated his lips. He forced himself not to smile as an inkling of her thoughts formed in his mind.

Her fan beat a staccato rhythm against her leg. "The dance floor tonight is especially spacious."

His hand eased up to cover the surge of a smile that broke through before his disinterested facade sealed it off once more. He wondered if she planned on kicking him and stepping on his toes while on the dance floor or if she intended to refuse his request in an attempt to humiliate him. Either way, it was easy enough to foil her plan.

"You're right. The dancing looks particularly inviting tonight." He turned to his left and was pleased to find a woman he had been introduced to at another party the week before. She wasn't exceptionally pretty or popular, but neither was she ignored and reviled. She was perfect for his needs.

Two steps brought him to her side. "Miss Poppyton, might I have the honor of dancing the next with you?"

"Of course, Your Grace." She curtsied and smiled, confusion, surprise, and pleasure flitting across her pale features.

He heard a low laugh in the shadows and angled himself to be able to peek sideways in the direction of his current adversary. Her mouth was set in a thin line. Behind her Trent was bent over at the waist, laughing. He was muffling and controlling it as best he could, but it was clear he found considerable humor in the situation. Good. It would only irk Miranda more.

Ryland offered his arm to Miss Poppyton. A spin around the floor with him would do wonders for her reputation. In the end he was likely doing her a favor instead of using her for his own means. The thought eased what little of his conscience felt uncomfortable walking away from Miranda.

The dance was as enjoyable as it could be. Miss Poppyton held her own on the topics of weather, the ball they were attending, and the exquisite cut of his coat. He didn't understand why so many people felt the need to compliment a man on his ability to find a competent tailor, but he'd had the discussion multiple times since returning to London.

Once the dance was over, he escorted Miss Poppyton back to her mother, where three young gentlemen were waiting to vie for her attention. The blush that graced the young girl's cheeks paired prettily with her shy smile.

He bowed to her mother and then turned to make his way across the ballroom, once again on the lookout for Miranda. She was on the dance floor with Lord Raebourne. The man was a close friend of Griffith's, and he was married. Happily so, if the gossip could be believed. No threat emanated from that corner, then.

Ryland didn't want to lead another young miss out on the floor in an attempt to get closer to his true quarry. Instead he positioned himself near the end of the line of dancers, where he could easily watch her progress her way across the dance floor. The steps caused her to spend a significant amount of time facing him.

She glared.

He grinned.

She turned her nose up at him.

Ryland's grin widened. It was time for them to talk.

Miranda handed her bonnet to Trent's butler. Ryland's behavior at the ball last night still twisted her stomach in knots. Her entire morning had been taken up with reliving those few moments he'd been in the ballroom. How dare he foil her plan to humiliate him and stop this nonsensical feud? The missive from Trent asking her to stop by his house this afternoon was a welcome distraction.

The butler waved her toward the staircase. "Lord Trent asked me to tell you that he was in his study."

With a nod, Miranda made her way up the stairs. She couldn't begin to fathom what Trent could need that required her to come to him instead of him stopping by Hawthorne House. It was probably still the newness of having his own place. He'd moved into the narrow terrace house at the end of last Season.

She knocked at the study door and forced herself to wait for his answer before pushing the panel open. They were so close in age, barely a year apart, she had trouble remembering that they were adults now. Trent was a man of twenty-two with his own home and his own duties. The fact that she was still at the mercy of her family's care while her brother had moved out on his own was a bit depressing.

"Why am I here?" She took in the study with its faded wall coverings and worn furniture. Maybe he wanted her to redecorate.

Trent looked up with a smile tinged with nervousness. Trent never got nervous. This brother went through life with nary a care. If he was worried, then something must be very wrong indeed.

Miranda's already anxious stomach threatened to become ill. "Trent?"

"Isn't it obvious? I need a woman's help." He spread his arms wide and glanced around the room.

She'd noticed as much. But why would that make him look so tentative? "You want me to decorate your house?"

He shrugged. "Maybe a bit here and there."

She groaned. It was one thing to keep house for Griffith. He was, in many ways, her guardian. If she started working on

Trent's home, she could put on her spinster's cap for certain.

"Well, then don't decorate my house. That's not why I brought you here."

Her heart skipped a beat. This could not be good. "Then why am I here?"

Trent gave her a sheepish smile and nodded to the door behind her.

Miranda whirled around to find Ryland leaning in the doorway to Trent's study. Forget skipping a beat, her heart just gave up and stopped altogether. With a shoulder propped against the doorframe and one foot crossed over the other, he looked relaxed.

Confident.

Gorgeous.

His coat only enhanced the strain of his muscles as his arms crossed over his chest. The eyes that haunted her dreams drew her in to his chiseled face and tapered jaw. His features held none of the challenge so evident in their last few meetings. "You're here to talk to me."

Was fratricide legal in England? If not, it should be. Exceptions should be made for cases like this. A girl should have some form of retribution when brothers behaved in such a high-handed manner. Glaring holes in Trent was easier than dealing with Ryland, so she focused on making her blond buffoon of a brother squirm like the worms he used to hide in her bed.

He offered her another sheepish grin and shrugged. "It was time for the two of you to talk this out. You've clearly been miserable since —"

"Trent!" Miranda darted a look over her shoulder and caught the last vestiges of a smirk before Ryland composed his face into a blank canvas once more. She returned to spearing her sibling with her eyes. "Some things are best left unsaid."

"Right, well, you two go about your business. Don't mind me." He eased himself into the chair behind his desk and pulled a book across the polished surface. A moment later he turned the page, looking for all the world like a man engrossed in the poems of Coleridge.

"Your book is upside down," Miranda muttered. It wasn't true, but she was hoping to catch him having to double-check.

Trent ignored her and turned another page.

Ryland strode farther into the room and stood next to her. "He appears to be quite occupied."

"He's faking. His attention isn't on that book at all."

Ryland turned to face Miranda. He was

silent for so long that she felt compelled to turn her gaze in his direction. His eyes looked like silver fire surrounded by billowing smoke. She felt sucked into their depths, thinking she'd forgive him anything if he would just look at her with that much passion for the rest of their lives. It was enough to make a girl feel positively cherished.

"Shall we test that?" His whisper drew her eyes to his lips.

"Test what?"

"His enthrallment."

Miranda jerked back at the reminder that Trent was in the room. It wasn't until she regained her bearings that she realized she had taken a step toward Ryland and leaned in, drawn to the promise of his gaze. "How would we do that?"

He appeared to consider it for a moment. His hand reached out and clasped hers loosely. "I could kiss you."

Miranda's gasp was almost loud enough to cover Trent's pointed cough.

Ryland laughed. "I concede. You're correct. He's listening."

"Of course he's listening. For all of his underhanded nonsense, he is my brother." Irritation that it had all been a ruse to get a rise out of Trent had her crossing her arms over her chest and retreating back another step.

"Trent, could I have a few moments alone with your sister?"

Trent looked up, his normally cheerful face wearing maturity better than she expected it to. "Are you going to propose?"

"Probably not."

"Then no. I believe we shall all stay as we are. You may continue." He dropped his attention back to his book.

Ryland sighed. "May I at least direct her to the far corner where we may converse with a modicum of privacy?"

Trent waved a hand through the air without looking up. "Be my guest. The acoustics in this room are fabulous."

Ryland sighed as he grasped her elbow and propelled her across the room. He angled himself into the corner by the door, leaving Miranda to stand in front of the open portal. She felt very exposed, yet thankful that he hadn't boxed her in.

Neither spoke.

Miranda crossed her arms and looked anywhere except Ryland's face. The wall bore a slight crack between the trim and the wallpaper. One of Shakespeare's plays had been put back on the shelf upside down. Her brother's favorite wing chair was looking a little worn along the arms.

Finally there was nowhere else to look and she brought her consideration back to Ryland. She raised her eyebrows, hoping he would pick up the initiative in the conversation.

He didn't. The complete picture of calm, he stood and watched her.

The only sound in the room came from Miranda's right foot as it tapped sharp staccato beats against the floor. If Trent was still turning pages, he was doing an admirable job of keeping them from rattling.

Finally Miranda said, "I am waiting."

"For what?"

Miranda's foot stopped midbeat. "For what? For . . . for an apology, of course!"

"You won't be getting one."

Miranda's arms dropped to her side and her mouth fell open. Remembering that she was supposed to be a refined lady she snapped her mouth shut. "I see."

"Do you?"

Miranda wasn't sure what to say to that. She had never heard of a gentleman refusing to apologize to a lady. Not a true gentleman anyway. There were always rogues and cads who went about insulting women and refusing to make any amends for it, but even when she'd thought him a valet she'd considered Ryland to be more gentlemanly than that.

"I have nothing to apologize for," Ryland continued.

Trent snorted. "Not the best opening line, old man," he muttered, proving that he had no intention of ignoring the conversation.

"Nothing to . . . I beg to differ, *Your Grace.*" Miranda gritted her teeth, determined to ignore her interfering relation.

"An apology implies regret over something done. If I apologize to you that means I would do it differently if I could. There is nothing about my interactions with you that I would change. With the exception of your involvement in the escape from my abductors, of course. Putting your life in danger is not something I would plan, even if it did lead to a very pleasant interlude as we crossed the countryside." Ryland leaned into the corner and crossed his feet at the ankles.

"But you behaved in a despicably ungentlemanlike manner!"

"What would you have me change, Miranda? You know I could not tell you who I was. It would have wrecked the entire mission."

"I would not have revealed your secret."

"You would have without meaning to. Your

demeanor around me would have changed. But we both know that's not really the issue here." He abandoned his relaxed posture and leaned forward until he was mere inches from Miranda's face.

"Let's talk about the letters," he said. His voice was low, an unspoken dare, a verbal gauntlet thrown between them.

"They had nothing to do with your mission. *Nothing!*" Miranda hugged her arms across her body. He was right, and that stung almost as much as the feeling of exposure over the letters themselves. She wasn't all that upset by his deception and spying, but she felt used and scared when she thought of the letters.

"I knew this was my last mission. I knew I would be in London this year. I knew that I would be crossing paths with you because of my relationship with Griffith. If I had not exchanged letters with you over the winter, what do you think would have happened when we met at the masquerade?"

Miranda stood still, staring at the floor, her lips puckered just shy of a pout.

"I'm waiting, Miranda." Ryland's voice was deep and serious. "What would have happened?"

"Well, I suppose we would have danced much like we did."

"You would have been too embarrassed to do much more than comment on the weather. You would have been thinking about all the secrets you had put on paper in the guise of writing to me. I didn't want that awkwardness between us when we officially met, so I took care of it. You may not like it, but I am not sorry for it."

"You think you spared me embarrassment? How do you think I felt when I realized I had been exchanging letters with *the valet*?" Miranda yelled in his face.

Ryland settled back into the corner with a cocky little grin. She had the feeling he'd been trying to get an outburst out of her. "Angry."

Miranda sputtered. She gritted her teeth. "You are despicable."

"Am I now? What part makes me despicable? That I was so intrigued by you that I didn't want to wait six months to speak with you? That I took the opportunity the letters provided to get to know you in a way we would never be allowed to do in a ballroom? Or is it the fact that I fooled you? Maybe you don't like the fact that I served our country as a gatherer of information."

"Now you're being ridiculous." Her body began to tremble. Even her toes felt shaky. Her voice dropped to a whisper. "Why did you? Become a spy, I mean."

"It was almost an accident, really. School was a trial for me. The sitting still, studying words someone had written for the sole purpose of teaching a particular thing. When we got word that my cousin had been trapped in France when the war restarted, I took the excuse to leave Oxford."

"You went to rescue him?"

Ryland nodded. "I found him trying to buy his way home with information — claiming he was the Duke of Marshington. It didn't have the effect he intended. They beat him and kept him prisoner in a little cottage in the south of France."

Miranda's heart clenched at the look of anguish in Ryland's eyes. She knew he wasn't close to his aunt and cousin, but he obviously felt something for them, even if it was nothing more than responsibility. "But you saved him. I've seen him around Town."

He nodded. "I found him. It took me two weeks of hiding in the palace, listening and digging through partially burned correspondence. I wasn't very good at sneaking yet, so they discovered I was coming and tried to burn the cottage down. Gregory's leg was broken, but I hauled him out of there."

He blinked and the tormented shadows left his eyes. "An agent for the War Office tracked me down and offered to take care of getting us home to England. I told him some of the other things I'd learned while looking for Gregory and the next thing I knew they were training me and sending me on missions. To an eighteen-year-old it was infinitely more exciting than school."

Miranda smiled, picturing his excitement and youth. "I can imagine."

Ryland reached out a hand and skimmed his knuckle along the edge of her smile, as if he'd missed it and welcomed its return. "At twenty-seven it doesn't seem as smart now. That's why I got out."

"I'm glad," Miranda whispered. She didn't know much about what he'd done but knew it had been dangerous. Broken legs and burning cottages were enough to make her afraid for him. Her relief and newfound understanding warred with her irritation and left her feeling confused.

Was Ryland right? Would she have allowed him to court her if the letters had remained secret? His prediction was plausible, that she would have been so embarrassed that she would have avoided his every advance.

Ryland's finger grazed her cheek until it came to rest under her chin and he could force her gaze back to his. "What will it be, Miranda?"

CHAPTER 27

Ryland almost stopped breathing as he watched the emotions play in her eyes. He couldn't identify them but was simply thankful she wasn't hiding them. "Are we going to move on and see if we could have a good life together?"

He tried to think through any additional objections she might have. Anything he could eradicate now would only help his case. "My friendship with Griffith has survived nine years of secrets and long absences. I don't think I need you to maintain that connection. It's you and me at stake here. Nothing else."

Miranda bit her lip, looking as unsure as he'd ever seen her. Despite what most of London thought, he knew he wasn't the best potential husband. And Miranda knew enough about him to know life with him wouldn't be the safe and uncomplicated one she'd grown up with. She'd been raised by a duchess to be a perfect duchess.

He didn't need a perfect duchess. He needed one who could navigate between the world he'd lived in and the world everyone else lived in. Someone who would understand him even when his choices hurt her.

The breath flew from his lungs.

He'd hurt her. Why hadn't he fully realized that before? He was always admiring the fire lying just below that ladylike surface. How could he not have realized that those vibrant emotions could be bruised? It wasn't a temporary thing caused by shock and misunderstanding. It was real.

"I'm sorry I hurt you," he blurted.

She looked like she wanted to grin. "You said you weren't going to apologize."

A bit of the tension eased from his chest, and he breathed a bit easier. He didn't stop his lips from turning up at the corners. "I'm not sorry for what I did. I would do it all again. But I didn't mean for you to find out in front of your brothers. I wanted us to have this conversation the first time I saw you in London. Not weeks later."

"And still in front of my brother." Miranda's smile flashed before her face fell into contemplative lines. "I'll think about it."

Ryland's gaze fell to his toes. At least it

wasn't a no. Her fingers curled and un-curled. Was she trying to get her emotions back under control? Trying to stuff them behind the mask of ladylike perfection? If she allowed him to court her, he had every intention of challenging that composure. No doubt that was one of the things she wanted to think about. "How long?"

"Three days."

He could do three days. "I'll give you three days."

"And you'll stay away from me for those three days. No bribing servants to seat you next to me at dinners or suddenly showing up at balls I'm attending. And you're not to send Colin round to my house either. I'll not go riding with your investigator again."

Ryland wanted to laugh at the indication that his plan had indeed worked. The little things had gotten to her. In retrospect, sending Colin had been more desperate than wise, but it didn't appear to have damaged his campaign too much. "Very well. Three days. I'll come by Thursday to take you for a ride in the park."

Moments passed, heartbeat by heartbeat, as they stared at each other. He should go. She'd asked for three days, and he had every intention of giving them to her, but that meant they had to leave Trent's study.

Three days without the opportunity to do anything. Three days in which she would only have her memories of him to consider.

He'd better make them powerful.

Without warning he dipped his head and brushed his lips against hers. She stiffened in surprise. Ryland lingered until he felt her soften and sigh into the kiss. Then he made himself lift his head, clenching his hands around his trousers to keep from wrapping his arms around her.

"Until Thursday," he whispered.

And then he turned and left.

"Do you think this curl should stay here? Would it look better pulled up around this braid?" Miranda fussed with the bouncing ringlets framing her face. In the mirror she saw Sally pull a face as she adjusted the curl according to her mistress's wishes.

Miranda sighed. Her three days were up and she was a nervous wreck. "No, you were right. It looked better down."

"My lady, you're going to be wearing a bonnet while you ride. He's not going to see any of this." Sally adjusted the curl once more and stepped back, silently declaring she was done with the coiffure.

Miranda stood and then leaned down to examine her hair one last time. "He'll see it when he comes into the drawing room to get me."

"It looks perfect, my lady."

Miranda gave her maid a smile. The poor woman had been very patient with her. First she'd gone through six different outfits. Sally had run downstairs twice to press dresses Miranda thought she wanted to wear. In the end she'd found her way back into Sally's original suggestion. Now it had taken three times longer than normal to dress her hair. Even if it was her job to do so, Miranda decided the woman had displayed remarkable constraint.

"Thank you, Sally. Have Mother and Georgina left yet?"

"I don't know, my lady. I'll go down and see."

Miranda paced while she waited for Sally to return. When Mother and Georgina had mentioned going visiting and shopping this afternoon, she'd begged off, claiming a headache. It suited her well to be alone when Ryland came to call. She didn't know what he would say when he arrived. She wasn't even entirely sure of what she was going to say.

The past three days had been difficult. Despite his promise to stay away while she considered things, she kept looking for him.

Irrational disappointment always followed the realization that he was going to respect her wishes.

Once she thought she saw him across the ballroom, but she wasn't close enough to be sure. If it had been him, he'd spent the entire night in the card room and never once stepped out on the dance floor. She knew because she'd watched for him.

One thing became clear very quickly. Life without Ryland would be pale and lifeless. Was holding on to her equilibrium worth throwing away her best chance to marry for love? Because if she didn't pursue things with Ryland she knew she would never have another chance to find true love again. She would have to settle for one of those respectable men that wanted to increase their holdings or improve their connections.

Someone like Ashcombe.

The thought made her shudder.

Sally returned and verified that, yes, the other two women had already departed. Miranda swept from the room, anticipation building and making her heart thump in her chest. She skipped down the stairs and couldn't resist doing a little twirl as she entered the drawing room to wait for Ryland. Her life would no longer be dull, that was certain. While it was probable that her heightened emotional state would prompt many more lady lessons, it would be a good trade for the potential happiness with a man like Ryland.

She plopped on the settee, allowing herself to bounce a bit. The closer the time came, the giddier she felt. Things were going to work for her this time. God was going to reward her diligence in accepting His plan and being at peace with the idea of being a doting aunt.

After a few minutes, she grew restless and rang for a maid to bring her embroidery. She sat, the focus required to perfect an intricate flower momentarily distracting her. After finishing the cluster of pink and yellow roses, she glanced at the clock to find nearly two hours had passed. The fashionable time for riding in the park was fast drawing to a close.

She shrugged. Being fashionable was not all that important right now. Eventually she would want to parade down Rotten Row at the height of the afternoon so everyone would see that she and Ryland were courting. It would help stake her claim among the other marriage-minded females. Maybe he wished for fewer interruptions today, and so wanted to ride a bit later.

Hoping that the next bit of the pattern

would be as mentally consuming, she applied herself once more to her needlework. A while later, she heard a carriage rattle to a stop. Voices could be heard beyond the window, the words and tones indistinguishable.

Miranda leaped across the room to peer around the drapery. Her mother and sister stood on the steps, directing the servants who were unloading their packages. Heart racing, she spun around to face the mantel clock, unable to believe what was happening to her. The clock didn't lie though. It was getting on into the time for the various evening festivities that would be taking place around town. No one would be going riding in the park this late in the day.

She ran from the room, desperate to get upstairs before Georgina could see her. Of all the ways she had imagined this day going, him not showing had never seemed a possibility.

Had he done some thinking of his own? Decided he didn't want her after all?

Given his impassioned plea in Trent's study and all the little things he'd done since coming back to London, she knew he wouldn't choose to stop his attempt to court her.

Her heart wasn't listening very well

though. She escaped into her room, her emotions and her thoughts battling for control. The door slammed against the wall, leaving a small dent in the plaster. In a spontaneous fit of sensibility, she caught the door before it could slam closed and announce her upset to the rest of the household. After shutting it gently, she resumed her fierce pacing, grabbing a pillow off the bed on one of her rounds.

Punching and squeezing the innocent lump of fabric and stuffing eased a bit of her frustration. Throwing it at the wall and pretending it was Ryland's head was even better. Was this a sign of what life would be like with him? Wondering what he'd gotten himself into? If he'd been unable to leave his life of danger and ended up facedown in the gutter somewhere?

She grabbed all the pillows in the room and hurled them at the wall. Chest heaving, she gathered them up and went at it once more.

Energy spent, she crumpled into a little ball in the middle of the floor. Ryland Montgomery, Duke of Marshington, former valet and spy extraordinaire, would not be an easy man to live with.

But if this was a sign of what life was going to be like with him, perhaps she should put more effort into trying to live without him.

Ryland leaned his head back against the chair and allowed his arms to dangle over the sides. His feet extended toward the low-burning fire, crossed at the ankle. An apple hung from the hook on the mantel, spinning slowly on its string, firelight glinting off the shiny skin as the fruit roasted its way to a comforting snack reminiscent of his days at school. He watched the apple twist until his eyes crossed, and then he let the lids drift shut.

He was the very picture of a relaxed gentleman with nothing on his mind but the next pleasurable pursuit, except perhaps thoughts of his last pleasant endeavor. The truth was something else altogether, but then again it usually was. Survival often depended on appearing one way while doing something entirely different. In this case, his body was relaxed, but his mind was tense.

Flexing his mental muscle to twist and pull and stretch the problem so he could inspect it from every angle was exhausting, but it was the only thing left to do. He had names now. On the surface none of them appeared to be a traitor, but one of them was meeting with Lambert and it couldn't have been with noble purposes.

The couple from the tea shop had married last week before retiring to Yorkshire. The woman with the young girl had turned out to be a governess. One of the men was a baron and the other the second son of a viscount. Both in keeping with Colin's description of the investor — high enough to want more and low enough to feel they had nothing to lose.

And one of them knew he was getting close, though Ryland didn't know how.

The clock on the mantel chimed seven times. The fading tones of the final ding brought a wince to his face. What was Miranda doing right now? Mentally roasting him over the fire like an apple, no doubt. Three times this afternoon, he had drafted a note to send to her, to make some excuse, but he couldn't risk sending it.

He was sure his house was being watched and any messenger would be followed. Even if he could get the message out without detection, the man could be watching Miranda to see if a note arrived. While the man might know about Miranda, he couldn't know the depth to which Ryland cared for her. Ryland couldn't risk doing anything to change that.

He'd already set up a rotation of servants to watch over Miranda's house. They slipped out at odd hours, taking a circuitous route to Hawthorne House. Griffith would probably kill him if he learned what Ryland was doing. He'd considered telling his friend about the potential danger, but didn't think Griffith would know how to properly protect Miranda in this situation.

So he'd send his own people and beg for forgiveness later.

The calluses on his hands scraped his face as he tried to physically wipe away thoughts of Miranda. Beyond setting up a discreet guard, there was nothing he could do. His time would be better spent determining who his enemy was so he could roust the scoundrel and get back to his life.

He hated sitting here, waiting for information. Everything in him wanted to go out and dig around himself. To find things himself. To catch the man red-handed instead of directing the effort from his desk.

The snick of the door latch jerked him into the present. He forced his body to remain loose, while his senses reached out to determine the visitor to his study. One eye opened a crack to take in the hulking shadow slipping in the door.

"Any news, Price?" Ryland eased his eye

closed once more and allowed part of his mind to sift through what he knew about Lambert while he focused the bulk of his attention on Price's report. He was quickly learning that one advantage to staffing his house with former spies and war survivors was the ready source of capable aid when he needed something strange done. Or information gathered.

It might be killing him to not be out there, but he had every confidence that the people he had out there were the best. He'd sent word round to the War Office about their findings. While they claimed to be looking into it, he was fairly certain they were letting him take care of it on his own.

Though they'd probably still take the credit.

He heard Price move across the room to the fireplace. After a few moments of silence the smell of roasted apple drew nearer and the fruit was pressed into his dangling hand. Ryland lifted it to his mouth and let his teeth puncture the wrinkled skin. Warm juice flooded his mouth as he tore off a chunk of the now almost gooey fruit. "Make yourself one, Price. There's a bowl of apples on the shelf behind the desk."

"Don't mind if I do, sir. My mum used to roast apples for us at Christmas. I haven't had one in years."

Ryland tracked the man's movements out of habit. He thought he had left the life where knowing where everyone was in a room at any given moment could mean the difference between life and death. The note he'd received that morning said differently.

After several moments, the other wing chair creaked and sighed as the springs adjusted to support a large weight. Ryland eased his eyes open and continued to munch on his apple.

In deference to the unseasonable fire, Price had removed his jacket. It draped over the back of the chair. With slow movements, Price arranged his bulky body into a casual pose similar to Ryland's. "There's nothing, sir. It's as if the letter just appeared on the front stoop. We can't find a messenger, not even a street urchin admitting to taking a few coins in return for bringing the letter. Jess has been scouring the streets, looking for anyone who knows anything. She slipped back in a few minutes ago."

Ryland frowned. Jess was one of the parlor maids. "Jess is just a girl, Price. I don't want her out there."

Price shook his head. "She's not that young girl you found in a trunk anymore, Your Grace. Watching your parents get hauled off as English sympathizers grows you up real quick-like. Don't forget she's done her own share of work for the Crown since then.

"She had the fortitude for you to smuggle her across the channel seven years ago, and she's not lost any of that since, even if she is still a mite of a thing. It lets her pass as a youngster out on the street."

"I still don't like it." Truth be told, Ryland hadn't liked that any women served with him in the intelligence field. At his core he was still a gentleman, and it went against the grain to allow a female to deliberately endanger herself. It was a care he'd learned to ignore early on in his career but he'd never been able to eradicate it.

Price poked at his spinning apple. "Which one do you think sent the note?"

Ryland fished the paper from his pocket to read it again, though he had the entire short missive memorized.

You will pay for ruining this for me. You've robbed me of everything I worked for. Now I shall rob you. Maybe I'll start with the girl.

"I have my suspicions but no proof." Ryland passed the paper to Price and got up to pace. "He's not professi— Wait. Are my aunt and cousin still at home?"

Price shook his head. "Left an hour ago for the theater."

Ryland nodded and resumed pacing. "Our man, whoever he is, is not a professional. Which is surprising given the strong network of spies he put in wealthy houses across the whole of England. He's too emotional, too close to whatever this is he thinks I've taken. He's out for revenge."

The Office had picked up Lambert two days ago in a smuggler's boat bound for France. Since then the man had talked about everything except who hired him. They were going to have their hands busy for the next few weeks looking into all the servants the man claimed were part of the spy ring.

"That makes him all the more dangerous."

Price and Ryland exchanged glances. As a former smuggler, Price knew about hidden enemies and the cold, calculating nature of the breed. He also knew how dangerous it was when those men left logic behind.

Archibald stuck his head around the study door. "I think we got it, Your Grace. You were right about Baron Listwist."

Ryland waved Archibald into the room as he took another bite of apple. It was the only thing he'd had the stomach to eat all day.

"His fields haven't been planted in two years. The estate's empty except for an old couple taking care of the house and the donkey they use to take them into town." Archibald handed over a list. "Yet all of these creditors said he's paid off his bills in the last six months. Bills he'd run up to the point of being on the verge of debtors' prison."

"Is the estate on the water?"

Archibald nodded. "A nice cove. Deep and calm. It'd be a simple thing to sail in and out of."

Ryland dismissed Archibald and told him to get some sleep. The man looked exhausted. He must have ridden nonstop, alternating between horse and mail coach.

"Does he have a connection to France?" Price asked.

Ryland nodded. "An aunt. She's a member of Napoleon's court. That's enough to make him suspect. The influx of money seals the deal. If he's not our traitor, he's at least doing something criminal, because he's claiming the money came from his estate."

Jeffreys entered into the study, slamming the door behind him so that he could continue across the floor without breaking stride. "There's been another note."

Ryland spun and held his hand out for the paper. "Where?"

"The front hall table. It's the same shaky handwriting."

Price stood up with a growl. "Someone came through my door?"

A grin fought to find a home on Ryland's lips. "I believe it's my door, Price."

"The house may be yours, Your Grace, but that door is mine."

Laughter begged to join the repressed grin. "Let's see what this one says, shall we?"

You never know where I'll strike. Imagine your door without that preposterous butler.

"I think the man's an idiot," Jeffreys said with a shake of his head.

Ryland cast a sideways glance at the "preposterous butler." The servant's ears were turning red. "He has a death wish at the very least."

"First my door and now my person. I'm going to kill him, Ryland!"

Alarmed that Price had reverted to calling him by his given name, Ryland pushed the big man back into the chair. "Calm down.

Remember the attack is against me, not you."

Ryland slowly paced some more, keeping Price in the corner of his eye.

Finally, Ryland leaned both arms on the back of his vacated chair and stared into the flickering flames. Price's forgotten apple spun merrily around, casting shadows on the ceiling. "Jeffreys, send word to the Office that we have our man. They've been letting us run things unofficially until now, and I am willing to assist in his capture, but they'll have to be the ones to make the actual arrest."

CHAPTER 28

Miranda tapped the quill against her lips and stared at the blank blue paper in front of her. Her very skin felt as if it would rip apart at any moment.

Confusion, sadness, a touch of anger, and even a bit of fear swirled around her head. She couldn't make sense of it. Didn't know what she should do with it. And the avenue she'd used for as long as she could remember had apparently been stolen from her.

She couldn't write.

Every time her quill touched the paper, it sat there, leaving a glob of ink behind. How could she write to Ryland about Ryland? The freedom and anonymity were lost. Gone. Never again would she be able to scrawl her feelings out knowing there would be no condemnation for whatever she said. Even if Ryland never saw the letter, he was no longer a faceless friend.

He was real.

And she missed him.

Which sent her emotions careening all over the place once more, because she'd spent the past several months telling God she wouldn't miss a man, that she would be completely happy without one. Yet when Ryland didn't show up that afternoon as promised, she was left pacing the floor.

A light knock on the door brought Miranda to a halt. Her mother's voice drifted through the wooden panel. "Are you ready, darling?"

"What? Oh! Yes, Mother, I'm coming." Miranda snatched her reticule off the bed and headed for the door.

"You look stunning, Miranda. There's color in your cheeks and your eyes are bright. We simply must put you in green more often."

Miranda glanced down at the soft green silk gown, covered with an overskirt of dark green lace. She'd worn the dress on two prior occasions and gotten no such compliments from her mother. Emotional upheaval apparently agreed with her. Her stomach roiled. Well, it agreed with her complexion anyway.

"Thank you, Mother. Is everyone else ready?" Miranda stepped out of the room and shut the door.

Mother led the way down the corridor. "Yes, Trent and Georgina are downstairs. Griffith, of course, is at Parliament this evening. He'll be joining us for dinner after the play."

The ride to the theater was uneventful. Georgina had been allowed to attend plays and such for the past two years, so the novelty had worn off, meaning she wouldn't chatter her way through the entire thing in excitement.

The crush of carriages around the theater took twice as long to maneuver through as the trip from the house had taken. When it was finally their turn to alight, Miranda found the press of the glittering crowd was not much better. She stepped to the side as best she could to wait for the rest of her party to exit the carriage.

A jostling of people to her left suddenly knocked her off balance. She slid sideways into a male body. Straightening as quickly as she could, a blush heating her cheeks, she turned to apologize. Her breath solidified in her throat as she glanced at the man's profile.

"You!" she finally managed to choke out.

He turned to look at her and she found a sudden desire to hide. It wasn't Ryland. She found herself looking into the rounder, questioning face of his cousin, Mr. Gregory Montgomery. He was not someone she knew well and this was the first time their paths had crossed this Season.

"Oh! Pardon me. I thought you were someone else for a moment." Miranda bobbed a small curtsy and moved to join her mother, who had gotten sent in the other direction during the jostling.

"Lady Miranda, isn't it? Lady Miranda Hawthorne?"

She turned with a start, having expected him to merely bow in response and move on into the theater. Turning only her head back toward him, she answered, "Yes. Again, I apologize for the misconception. Enjoy your evening at the theater!"

Once inside the theater, the crowd thinned as people made their way to their seats and settled in for the show.

The heavy amounts of laughter and chortles indicated that it was a good show indeed, but Miranda could barely concentrate on it. She was still agitated and found herself fidgeting constantly. Her fan was moving fast enough to blow out the candle fixed to the back wall of their box.

During intermission, she joined Georgina at the refreshment table just to have something to do.

"We meet again."

She looked up to find Mr. Montgomery looking down on her once more. "So we do. Hardly surprising since it is the same venue as our last meeting."

He smiled. The tilt of the lips was similar to Ryland's but some spark, a sign of inner fire, was missing. Or maybe it was just that she didn't know him well. It was hardly fair to consider the man lacking in inner fortitude when she barely knew him by sight. In fact, before tonight, had a Bow Street runner asked her to describe Mr. Montgomery, she would have failed miserably.

Now, after only a few moments in his company, she could pinpoint that his nose was straight, where Ryland's had a slight bump between the eyes. The chin was rounder than Ryland's squared-off jaw. Mr. Montgomery's shoulders were nearly as wide as his cousin's but did not carry the same easy strength and brawn, making them look awkward over his thicker middle.

Miranda shook her head as she realized that Mr. Montgomery had been saying something to her. She had missed it entirely. "I beg your pardon, would you mind repeating that?"

"I asked if you were enjoying the show."

What could she say? In truth she wasn't

even sure what the play was tonight. "It's quite the comedy, isn't it?"

"I was wondering if you'd be partial to discussing the play further. Do you intend to be at home tomorrow? Might I call upon you?" His brows rose in inquiry, the lifeless smile still in place on his lips.

"Of course. I shall look forward to the discussion." What was she thinking? She had no interest in discussing anything with Ryland's cousin. Was there any way out of her polite acceptance? "My mother and sister are attending tonight as well and will, of course, be sitting with me tomorrow. It shall be a lively conversation for us all."

His smile shrank a bit but maintained its place. "Excellent. Until tomorrow, then."

Miranda forced herself to smile back. It was what a lady would do, after all. She trudged back to her seat, already dreading the next afternoon. As she settled her skirts around her chair, she admonished herself to focus on the second half of the play. She needed something to say when the man came calling.

The curtain rose and her mind wandered away from the action on stage. While she was certain that Mr. Montgomery held no interest for her, the encounter renewed her thinking that Ryland would not be the easiest man to have in her life.

It was time to consider other options.

Miranda was delighted to see the excessive amount of rain falling from the sky the next day.

Georgina turned from the window with a sound of disgust. "No one will be visiting in this weather. It is positively sheeting out there. If this keeps up, Sunday's sermon will be on Noah."

Miranda couldn't restrain the surprise that lifted her eyebrows. Since when did Georgina notice what the sermon was about? Miranda bit her tongue to keep the scathing remark behind her lips as she poked her embroidery needle through the cream-colored fabric. A shadow fell over her work as Georgina's blond curls danced into the edge of Miranda's vision.

"What are you working on?" The breathy whisper tickled Miranda's ear.

"A pillow." Miranda rubbed her wrist against the itch in her ear, careful not to poke herself with the needle grasped between her fingers.

"A pillow? Whatever for?" Boredom etched on her features, Georgina draped herself across her favorite settee. Even without an audience, the girl played the part.

"To bash you in the head with," Miranda mumbled.

"A lady never mumbles, dear." Mother didn't even look up from her book as she corrected her daughter.

Miranda wanted to howl at the unfairness. A lady never displayed her ankles either but Georgina's skirt had ridden all the way up to her knee. Unfortunately, howling would also be in opposition to appropriate genteel behavior which would make two marks against Miranda and would still not cause Mother to look up from her book. "I said that I wanted it to decorate my bed with."

"It's rather pretty." Georgina angled her head to inspect the floral vine creeping along the edge of the fabric. "Will you make one for me? I could put it in my drawing room when I get married."

"I think I'll wait until the grand event is forthcoming."

"I'm sure an offer will be extended any day now."

Miranda's fingers stilled. "From whom?"

"He was supposed to come today, but one would hardly want to be soaked to the skin when approaching Griffith for permission to marry his sister."

"Who is approaching Griffith?" Miranda felt the pinch of the needle as her hand tightened in instinctive trepidation.

"I wouldn't want a proposal from a wet man, either. Even if he did come today, I wouldn't see him."

"Who?" Miranda was nearly shouting now.

"Georgina, dear," Mother said as she turned the page in her book, "a lady never ignores someone's question unless she means to insult the speaker."

The easy manner in which her mother could say such a bizarre statement momentarily distracted Miranda from her sister's news. The rules of being a lady never ceased to amaze her.

"I was trying to build suspense, Mother." Georgina began to pace around the room. "Add some life to this dreary afternoon."

"You could work on something yourself. You mentioned wanting to paint a new fire screen for the upstairs parlor." Mother turned another page.

"I can't paint, Mother. I would have to change. If by some miracle someone does come calling, I would be unfit to see them."

"I suppose, although I don't think —"

"I beg your pardon," Miranda said with a slight wave to attract Georgina's attention. Her mother still didn't look up. "You still haven't answered my question."

"Oh! Well, he's only an earl, but he's a well-respected one, so I should consider it. The Marquis of Linstock is ghastly looking. I don't think I could manage watching that face grow older every day. And the Duke of Marshington is annoyingly uninteresting. With all of that intrigue around him, you'd think he'd be fascinating, but he isn't."

Miranda thought the only thing that could make Ryland uninteresting to Georgina was the fact that he so obviously wasn't interested in pampering her and her pride. It suited Miranda fine to have her younger sister find fault with the duke.

Not that Miranda planned on having anything to do with him. In the early hours of the morning she'd settled on being angry with him. It wasn't a very justifiable anger, but it kept the emotional swirl to a minimum and didn't leave her with an ever-present threat of tears.

Georgina continued as she circled the room once more. "So I decided to put serious consideration to the available earls. There's quite a crop of them this year."

Miranda went down the list. She'd seen four earls making the rounds in the ballrooms. It wasn't a high number, but it was enough to send more than one marriage-hungry mama to the modiste to make more eye-catching gowns for their daughters.

One earl was too old. He was making the social rounds as part of his granddaughter's first Season. While many women would be willing to marry an old man for money and title, Georgina was not in a position to need to do so. Lord Clampton was seen at Gunter's nearly every day with Lady Elizabeth Strosser, so he couldn't be encouraging Georgina.

That left only Lord Grayling and . . . No. The needle slipped from Miranda's nerveless fingers as the last possibility formed in her mind even as Georgina said the name aloud.

"Lord Ashcombe has been most attentive. I think he'll come up to scratch very soon."

Miranda's eyes flew across the room. Her mother was peeking over her book, concern in her eyes as they connected with Miranda's frantic gaze.

"You can't," Miranda whispered.

"Why not? Just because you couldn't get him to fully commit doesn't mean that I can't."

"But Griffith —"

"Pardon me, my lady," the butler interrupted, maintaining his perfect posture despite the water spotting the front of his attire. "Mr. Gregory Montgomery is here."

Mother straightened her spine and slid her book under the pillow behind her. "Is this a farce, Gibson? No one would be out in this weather."

"He is drying himself off in the kitchen at the moment, my lady. I apologize, but it was the only fire lit today."

"Of course, of course." Mother gestured to her daughters. "Sit, sit. Mr. Montgomery will be up soon."

Georgina smirked at Miranda. "It would seem that someone is overly eager to discuss the theater."

A sigh escaped Miranda's lips as she folded her embroidery and stored it in her sewing box. She should be feeling flattered that the man had braved the forces of nature to see her, but all she could drum up was a slight amount of gratitude that she no longer had to listen to Georgina's complaints about the weather or her admiration for Lord Ashcombe.

Gibson entered the room with a steaming tea service, Mr. Montgomery on his heels. The rough weather had ruined what was once a quite appealing ensemble. The cravat alone managed to escape dishevelment. The boots were likely beyond repair, and his hair was matted to his head and beginning to curl at the edges.

If Miranda looked closely, she could still see the family resemblance between Ryland and his cousin, but the bedraggled condition of Mr. Montgomery had a very different effect. She had seen Ryland looking rumpled and grubby, but he had still managed to exude confidence and power. Mr. Montgomery gave the impression of a sick puppy.

Disgusted that she was once again casting Ryland in a favorable light, Miranda directed Mr. Montgomery to a seat — none of the upholstered ones, of course — and began to pour his tea. "Whatever possessed you to venture forth in this deluge, Mr. Montgomery?"

"I make it my business to never back down from a promise. And I did assure you last evening that I would come calling today." He wrapped his hands around the cup of tea and breathed in the steam.

Mother cleared her throat with a delicate cough. "Under the circumstances, we would have understood your delay."

A considerably more tactful statement than the one Miranda was thinking. Honor was all well and good, but good sense was valuable as well.

He shook his head, water droplets slinging

to the carpet. "I wouldn't hear of it."

Moments passed. Did her sister's and mother's thoughts mirror her own? Were they trying to calculate how long they had to entertain Mr. Montgomery before they could make their excuses and send him back into the rain?

Even Mother, Lady Caroline, the epitome of everything a lady should be, looked a bit flustered. There were rules for unwanted company. Piles of them. Did they not apply because of the weather? Miranda choked on air. Were they to be compelled to invite him to dinner?

Georgina glared at Miranda, tilting her head in Mr. Montgomery's direction. Miranda suspected that if they had been sitting on the same couch, kicks would have been involved. "Did you, um, enjoy the rest of the play last evening, Mr. Montgomery?"

"Of course. Such masterful writing is sure to be enjoyable."

"Er, yes. I agree."

More silence.

Perturbed green eyes stared at Miranda over the edge of a teacup. She wasn't Mother at the moment, she was Lady Caroline and she had an amazingly awkward situation in her drawing room. One she blamed Miranda for.

Miranda shrugged, trying to rid herself of the guilt of encouraging this man to visit.

Thunder shook the windows.

Finally Mother took pity on Miranda and broke the silence. "And how are you and your mother adjusting to the return of your cousin? I must have heard a dozen tales about where he's been. Would you care to enlighten us with the truth?"

Miranda sat forward. Did her mother know? Of course she did. There was the small matter of hauling Ryland's unconscious body out of the house. She would have demanded some small explanation from her sons. Was the topic of Ryland supposed to be Miranda's punishment? She would take it. As much as she hated to admit it, this was a subject she could readily engage in.

Mr. Montgomery didn't look quite so eager. "We are, of course, overjoyed at his return to civilized society. He had been . . . Well, I'm afraid the subject isn't fit for tender ears, my lady. With all due respect, I must decline to answer your question."

Miranda frowned. If the man's aim was to elude the potential scandal Ryland's profession would cause, he was doing a very poor job of it. The innuendo implied something much worse than clandestine service to England.

Mother nodded. "I suppose we shouldn't speak of it, then. Perhaps there is another topic more to your liking?"

Georgina plunked her cup in the saucer. "The weather is dismal. You've spent some time in France, haven't you? Is the weather better there?"

So much for not listening to Georgina complain about the rain.

"Yes, France is wonderful. Such a shame that current inconveniences prevent you from seeing it yourself."

"A man trying to infiltrate England is hardly a mere inconvenience, Mr. Montgomery." Miranda's fingers clenched around her teacup. Like many women of her station, she was unaware of the details in the scuffle with Napoleon, but she was not delusional enough to think the war that had dragged on for years and taken life and limb of many men was a mere inconvenience.

"My apologies, Lady Miranda." His eyes narrowed in her direction. "I did not wish to bring the unpleasantness of the battle into your drawing room. Please excuse me for offending you."

Mother waved her arm in the air. "Oh no, she is merely out of sorts because of the rain. Such a downpour brings out her maudlin side."

Miranda huffed. She had obviously not paid enough attention to Mother's lessons in discreet and socially acceptable verbal punches. Maybe she should pull her embroidery back out. This was going to be a very long visit.

CHAPTER 29

Ryland strode toward the drawing room, ignoring the cluster of servants at the other end of the front hall. His valet had been goading him about avoiding his aunt, so he'd decided to appease him and take tea with her. Only pride kept him from retreating.

Gregory was away, having departed early this morning for his club. The rain had started soon after he left and the downpour had likely kept him there all day. But it was early evening now, and Gregory had yet to return to dress for the evening's festivities.

The rain had made the arrest of Baron Listwist an absolute mess. The man had nearly gotten away with a well-planned escape route. Ryland had tackled him, and they'd both slid down the muddy embankment to land in the Thames.

It had felt good to finally be doing something instead of waiting around.

Unfortunately the rain also kept him from making amends with Miranda. Now that the threat was over, he wanted to look his best when he asked her to allow him to court her.

Fortunately, the precipitation would also keep the horde of curious callers away from Ryland's door. There would never be a better time to extend the proverbial olive branch to his aunt.

Ryland strode into the room, forcing himself to appear relaxed. The smile on his face was fake, but he dared anyone but his closest companions to figure that out.

His aunt was sitting near the window, reading. Even when she thought herself alone, she didn't appear relaxed. Her posture would please the strictest of governesses, and she was dressed in the first stare of fashion from head to toe.

"May I join you for tea, Aunt Marguerite?"

She looked up, unable to keep the surprise entirely off her face. "Of course. I suppose I should ring for additional refreshments, then."

"I already informed Price I would be joining you."

"Since you mentioned him, could we discuss some of your staffing choices?" She toyed with the corner of her book, riffling the pages before setting the volume on the table next to her. "You must admit that your upbringing was not one that would necessarily prepare you for domestic management."

Ryland pinched his leg as he settled onto the wide couch across from his lone female relation. "Father never thought it an important part of my education, I admit. Perhaps he thought you would teach me. That would have been something for a mother to do, after all."

Marguerite patted her hair. "It was a failing on my part, I suppose, but I was busy raising my Gregory. All the more reason for me to guide you now."

He couldn't keep all of the skepticism off of his face. Hopefully she would misinterpret it as insecurity. A handful of nurses had raised Gregory. Marguerite had been too busy trying to act like his father's wife. She'd kept house for them, acted as his hostess at parties, even saw to some of his correspondence.

She turned in her chair to fully face him. "For instance, this stipulation you have that keeps me from maintaining the staff of my home —"

Ryland cleared his throat.

"Our home," she corrected with a frown.

"As your aunt, I should be seeing to the staff instead of your steward. What does he know about maintaining a staff? His choices are abysmal."

"Before you continue, aunt, I should tell you that I have hand selected every member of this house's staff. They were hired at my discretion."

"My poor nephew, how inattentive I've been."

Price entered the room, his shoulders filling the doorway, arms bulging as he held the laden tea tray in front of him. He positioned the tray on the table and set about filling plates for the room's occupants. Despite the size of his hands, he managed to handle the delicate china with grace and elegance. Not a clink was heard as he shifted cups and plates.

"I believe we'll serve ourselves, Price, since it is only my nephew and myself." Marguerite's smile was thin and sickly looking. It didn't really deserve to be called a smile.

"Of course, madam." Price bowed and left the room.

Ryland marveled at the man's patience. He'd been faced with this derision for the past eight years? How had he managed to avoid strangling the woman?

"Preposterous man for a butler," Marguerite mumbled as she poured tea.

Ryland mentally jerked at the words that so closely mirrored the ones from the note. His aunt couldn't be threatening him, could she? Was he wrong about the notes being from the baron?

He cleared his throat, suddenly interested in this interlude with his only female relation. "Price is a good man."

Marguerite passed Ryland a cup of tea. He took a sip and frowned. Sugar. Lots of it. He had always taken his tea with milk and no sugar. He thought he recalled Gregory always spooning the sweetener into his tea though.

"He is not a proper butler. The man doesn't have a neck, Ryland."

Ryland shrugged. "No one will be able to choke him to gain entrance. The staff isn't going to change, aunt. I have my reasons for hiring them. If you don't care for them, you're welcome to spend time at Marshington Abbey."

He'd left the country estate entirely in the care of his trusted steward. Memories of a torturous childhood were all that waited for him in its hallowed halls. It would take a miracle for him to enter its doors and not hear the awkwardness of Aunt Marguerite trying to pretend the four of them were one happy family. No, Ryland wasn't ready to set foot in Marshington Abbey, so he was more than willing to let his aunt live there.

"And miss the Season? You remember that everyone who is anyone is in London right now, don't you?" His aunt's voice brought him back to the London drawing room.

"Yes, aunt, I timed my return to coincide with it. It is time for me to see about extending the line, after all."

"Gregory has set his eyes on a prime candidate. Should you decide not to marry, he will be glad to continue the line."

Ryland grunted and watched the rain cascade down the window. He took a large bite of one of the sandwiches Price had left. If his mouth was full he couldn't make disparaging comments about his cousin's ability to handle the responsibilities of the title.

This tea had been a horrible idea. The next time Jeffreys admonished him for ignoring the remains of his family, he'd deliberately rend his trousers. If the valet was kept busy he couldn't stick his nose into Ryland's personal life.

The visit plagued her long after Mr. Montgomery departed. Was it the man or the situation that had made it so terribly awkward? It was obvious that Mr. Montgomery was interested in courting her, but the very idea made her feel ill. Was there no possibility of her moving on from Ryland?

She was doomed to settle for lonely spinsterhood.

Which was what she'd already told God she was prepared to accept.

Apparently she'd lied.

With a nervous glance at the storm raging outside, she took a few steps away from the window. There was no reason to tempt God to strike her with lightning. His aim was sure to be better than Mother's.

Maybe her siblings would produce lots of nieces and nephews for her to cherish. She could make Georgina's wedding present pillow say something about her children having England's best aunt.

A horrible thought flitted through her mind of her having to suffer the company of the Earl of Ashcombe in order to visit Georgina's children. He sat at the head of the table, counting his money while Georgina huddled at the foot, a pale ghost of her former vibrancy, worn down by his constant statements about how worthless she'd be if she hadn't brought money and land into the marriage.

Very well, that statement had actually been made to Miranda when she'd confronted him about asking Griffith for the land, but she imagined he viewed Georgina in a similar fashion.

No. Miranda might be forced at some point to contemplate a marriage of convenience, but Georgina's heart was not yet given, not truly. She'd suffered childhood infatuations but never looked into the eyes of someone and seen her own soul. Miranda was positive about that. Georgina was still too animated about her marriage prospects to have loved and lost.

A rush of sisterly affection sent her on a search through the house.

Miranda found Georgina painting in the solarium.

"Don't marry Ashcombe." The words were strangled, escaping as little more than a whisper. It was imperative that she make Georgina see the impossibility of that choice.

The paintbrush didn't pause. "Whyever not? He's extremely eligible. I would of course prefer a marquis or a duke or even one of those foreign princes, but they seem to be out of town. If I must settle for an earl, let him be a rich and popular one."

"But he's awful."

Georgina stopped painting and cast a scathing look at Miranda. "Because he didn't want you? There are a hundred reasons why he might not have offered for —"

"He did."

"No, he didn't."

Miranda sat on a stool beside Georgina. "Yes, he did. He went to Griffith to work out the details."

Georgina turned back to her painting but didn't apply the brush to the canvas. "What happened? Obviously you didn't marry him."

"He wanted . . ." Miranda braced herself for the fresh pain of remembered rejection. It didn't come. Had she finally after all these years moved on? Let go of that torment? Relieved laughter threatened, but she held it back. She had indeed moved past the hurt. It wasn't only because of Ryland, but also because of the realization that she was important.

She was loved.

God had created her the way she was for a reason. And if there wasn't a man who could appreciate that, then what other reason did she have to marry? That was why she couldn't encourage Mr. Montgomery or Colin or anyone else who might never

425

appreciate her underlying passion.

The same underlying passion Ryland had praised in one of his letters last fall.

She looked at Georgina. Could she teach her younger sister the same truth? "He wanted land. It was his condition. If the estate from Papa's mother wasn't included in the dowry, he would rescind his attentions."

Georgina set about mixing a dollop of white into a small pot of red paint.

"He didn't care about me. All that mattered was what he could gain from Griffith through the match."

Silence.

Miranda's shoulders slumped. There was nothing more she could do.

"He must have cared a bit. He was willing to marry you." The words were so quiet Miranda almost missed them.

"He was willing to marry Griffith's connections." Miranda licked her lips. "He's still willing to marry for them."

Moments passed. Neither moved for a long time. Then Georgina picked up her paintbrush and stabbed it angrily at the canvas. "Get out."

Her heart heavy, Miranda returned to her room, prepared to spend a quiet night with a novel. When had she and Georgina grown so far apart? Sadness at the distance weighed on her shoulders, but it wasn't enough to temper the joy at finally feeling free even in the face of spinsterhood.

Back in her room she rang for tea. The room wasn't chilled, but the constant rain made it dreary. Mrs. Brantley kept tea trays at the ready when the weather was like this, so no more than five minutes passed before a maid carried the tea service into the room.

"I'll serve myself. Thank you." Miranda smiled at the young girl.

After a slight curtsy, the maid backed out of the room.

Miranda blew her ringlets out of her face as she poured tea into the waiting cup. What was she going to do now? As much as she wanted to consider Ryland a lost cause, she couldn't. If he came back, asking her forgiveness, would she give it?

A roll of thunder made her jump as she replaced the teapot, sending a splash of tea across the tray.

His words about apologies had stayed with her since that afternoon in Trent's study. Apologies implied the desire for things to turn out differently. If he did indeed apologize for missing their ride, she would forgive him. He would never lower himself to apologize unless he meant it.

As she sipped her tea, she noticed a square of paper on the tray, partially covered by the teapot, a bit of it in a puddle of spilt tea. How odd.

With a frown she plucked the paper from the tray, shook off the tea, and opened it. Shaky handwriting scrawled across the scrap of parchment.

Your family I shall spare, but you will feel the pain. And no one will save you.

Miranda bobbled her teacup, sending drops of tea splashing to the floor before she managed to plop the cup back onto the tray.

She studied the paper, reading the short missive over and over again. What did this mean? Why would someone threaten her? Or was the note intended for Griffith? The note said they would be spared, but was her family in danger?

Her teeth sank into her lip as she looked to the window, still streaked by falling rain. The fragrant steam from the tea that had been so calming mere moments before now seemed ominous, the bearer of bad tidings.

One thing was certain. She needed help. Someone who knew how to deal with something such as this.

As she pulled her cloak around herself and snuck down the stairs, part of her acknowledged that she was using this as an excuse, but she didn't care. If she took the note to Griffith he would assure her he could take care of it, but Miranda had her doubts. Griffith was a man of business and politics. He was completely upfront about everything. What did he know about protecting them from an ominous threat? She would rather err on the side of caution and protect her family.

And there was one man she knew would know how to do that.

CHAPTER 30

Price returned to the drawing room. Was it Ryland's imagination, or was the man puffing himself up to appear even larger than he already was? Aunt Marguerite's lips thinned into a belabored frown. Ryland decided to give the man a bonus.

"Your Grace, I'm afraid your presence is needed in the library."

Ryland sighed, took a gulp of tea, and grabbed another sandwich as he stood. One more thing to thank God for when he prayed tonight.

He left the drawing room, and Price fell into step beside him.

"Jess found something when she was lurking in the streets this evening."

Ryland nearly choked on the ham in his mouth. "She went out in this?"

Price shrugged. "She wanted to keep an eye on Grosvenor Square a bit longer. She said something didn't feel right."

Ryland began to get nervous. He'd had that same feeling ever since he'd washed the Thames from his hair. "What did she find?"

A large blunt-fingered hand gestured to the study door.

Ice skittered down Ryland's back. "She brought it back?"

Price nodded.

Ryland opened the door just enough to slip inside, careful to keep anyone from seeing anything they didn't need to see. Jess stood near the French doors, water dripping off the moth-eaten wool cap she wore as part of her disguise. Next to her was the last person he expected to see in his study.

"Hello, Ryland."

He blinked. "Miranda?" Panic surged through Ryland's blood as he watched Miranda wring her hands. She stood in the corner wearing an expression he couldn't decipher. Was she scared? Angry? Sad? It didn't matter. If Jess had brought Miranda here, something must have gone horribly wrong.

He looked at Price and then Jess, but both of them were too experienced to allow anything to show in their expressions. The information was going to have to be pulled out of them. "What is she doing here?"

Price nodded in the direction of Jess, a dirty bundle of rags with stringy blond hair, as she plopped down in one of the chairs flanking the fireplace. "Jess brought her in through the back. She swears no one saw them."

Jess shrugged and reached for a nearby dish of peppermints. She popped one in her mouth and then indicated Miranda with a wave of her hand. "She was planning to sneak over here anyway. I assumed you'd prefer she actually make it undetected."

Ryland's gaze homed in on Miranda. He was going to throttle her. Never mind that she had no idea what danger could have surrounded them had the baron not been arrested — she was here alone, which meant she'd been planning on coming unescorted. That was reason enough to be mad at her. "You were coming *here*? Alone? What were you thinking?"

He could see the instant her befuddlement was overcome by anger. Her hands went to her hips, her brow lowered, and her mouth pulled tight at the corners. Her eyes bored into him as she took a deep breath and spit out a tirade.

"What was I thinking? Maybe I was thinking that you owed me some answers. It's possible I wanted to tell you what a cad you are for leaving me to wonder if you'd ended up in a ditch somewhere. Now I think I'll call you on the carpet for having me *watched*! I'm assuming this person works for you." She stalked across the room and stood behind Jess's chair. "She practically abducted me out of Grosvenor Square! I had one of those filthy mittens stuffed in my mouth. There is dirt between my teeth."

She sidestepped the chair so she could continue advancing on her target, which appeared to be him. Her finger was now stretched out, stabbing the air to make her point. Five more steps and it would be boring into his chest.

"I was hauled through places I never knew existed, fearing for my life because she certainly saw no need to enlighten me as to where we were going."

Her scent, the enticing combination of roses and rain, reached him before she did, making it difficult to concentrate on her words. Never before had he faced difficulty concentrating during dangerous situations.

She glared back at Jess before poking her finger at him again. "Believe me, if I'd had anywhere else to turn I would steer clear of you, but the only thing underhanded about the individuals of my acquaintance is how low they'll stoop to snag the last of the white silk at the dressmakers! You, on the other hand, spent nine years doing heaven only knows what!"

She was beautiful. His brainpower and focus were needed for much more pressing matters, but he couldn't seem to get past the thought that she was gorgeous. And brave. And strong. And he really needed to think about something else.

A bit of branch clung to the side of her head, its four spindly twigs forming a lopsided crown. Dirt smudged her flushed cheeks. What path had Jess used to get her here? Her chest heaved with the effort of propelling air in and out of her lungs with considerably more force than necessary for normal breathing.

He flushed as he pulled his gaze back to her face.

She swallowed hard, pulling herself back into a more decorous posture. "Now, would you please send your man for some tea? There really is an awful lot of grime in my mouth."

He tilted his head toward Price and heard the man open the door and slip out. Ryland's eyes narrowed as he watched her swallow again and shift her eyes away from a direct connection with his own. The realization that she was scared hit him in the gut with the force of one of Price's punches. What had she said about needing his under-handed experience?

Taking her elbow, he led her to the vacant fireside chair. He squatted in front of it and took her icy hands in his own. "What happened?"

"I-I was walking across the square. I slipped out the servant door so that Gibson wouldn't see me. This, um, young lady —"

Jess snorted out a laugh.

"— appeared out of nowhere and asked me for a coin. I didn't give her one, but she persisted in walking next to me. I don't know how she knew where I was going —"

"I didn't. Not really. You said you were on urgent business to meet a friend. You was shaking and frightened." Jess shrugged and chomped down on the mint. "If you wasn't coming here, you shoulda been."

Ryland cleared his throat and swallowed a smile. "Jess, why don't you go get cleaned up and out of character. I'm going to have a hard enough time as it is convincing Miranda that you are actually a gently born lady."

Jess grinned, revealing wide straight teeth blackened to make them appear crooked and broken at a glance. "As you wish, guv'nor."

Jess slipped out the door with a jaunty salute. Ryland hooked a foot on the leg of her vacated chair and pulled it closer to Miranda's. He shifted to sit in it without losing his hold of her hands.

Miranda's eyes seemed fixated on their joined hands. "She stuffed a mitten in my mouth and hauled me into the bush. We went down I don't know how many alleys — although I'm sure we circled behind Brooks' at some point. Then we ended up here."

She shrugged. One hand slipped free of his clasp and began tracing the fine white line of an old scar that ran along the back of his hand and across his thumb. While Ryland didn't mind the caress in the least, he felt certain it was an indication that her concentration was elsewhere. Most likely on whatever had driven her to him in the first place.

"Why were you coming here?"

"I found a note."

The icy fear that had ridden his back earlier stabbed through his skin and seized his heart. The door clicked open and he jerked, shifting to the edge of the chair, ready to pounce on the intruder if need be. It was only Price with the requested tea and a plate of sandwiches. Telling himself to at least appear relaxed, Ryland rolled his shoulders and eased back in the chair.

Miranda slipped her hands from his and busied herself with the tea. She slid a cup in his direction, fixed the same way he'd requested it of her that first night in her brother's library. It was possible that lady-like decorum had drilled in her the need to remember how people took their tea, but he chose to believe that even then she'd noticed the attraction between them. At least enough to take note of how he took his tea.

He cleared his throat and his mind. "A note? Did you bring it with you?"

It had to be a coincidence. There could be a million reasons why someone would threaten Miranda. She was connected to the powerful Duke of Riverton after all. Hope plummeted as he saw the shaky black scrawl on the paper she pulled from her sleeve.

"I think someone is after Griffith."

Ryland paused in the process of reaching for the note. It wouldn't be out of the question for Baron Listwist to have threatened more than one aristocrat if he'd been panicking. He hadn't seemed like a panicked man that morning, though. "And you received it today?"

She nodded. "This evening."

He slipped the note from her fingers.

With the slightest jerk of his head he called Price over. The man leaned down, eyes on the note, ears ready for instruction. "Send someone to Grosvenor Square. Have them keep an eye on Griffith. And the rest of them as well."

Price nodded and left the room once more, shutting the door behind him. Ryland stared at the door latch. It didn't matter that the matter was sensitive and possibly dangerous, he shouldn't be alone in the study with Miranda. That she wasn't calling him out on it meant that she was too flustered to notice or had already decided in favor of his suit, despite his not showing up for the agreed-upon ride.

Either alternative left him shaken, so he focused on the note instead.

"Where did you find it?"

"On my tea tray. We decided to stay in tonight, with the poor weather and all. I rang for tea. When the weather is bad, Mrs. Brantley always keeps a tea tray ready so all she has to do is pour hot water into the pot and have it delivered. I suppose someone thought the tray was meant for Griffith and tucked the note on it."

Ryland frowned. It was plausible, but very sloppy. There was no way of knowing the tray would get to the intended target. Why risk such a note falling into unintended hands?

Her cup rattled in its saucer, and she carefully eased it onto the table. "I don't think it's the first note."

That caught his attention. "Why not?"

"Because he doesn't say why he's mad. Don't they normally say why they're mad? How else can someone rectify the situation?" Miranda's eyes were wide. She wrapped the fingers of both hands around her steaming teacup and pulled it to her lap. It was nearly full. Had she drunk any of it?

He fought with himself. How much to tell her? Should he let her believe there were other notes or enlighten her of the fact that once a lunatic got the idea in his head that he'd been wronged and vengeance was required, nothing was going to rectify the situation. In his experience, if the problem had deteriorated into anonymous, vague threats, someone was going to get shot before the whole thing ended. He preferred making sure it wasn't him or someone he cared for.

Their eyes met. He couldn't lie to her. All of his adult life had been spent in shadows, but he'd held on to his integrity with a death grip. The idea that he was about to bring more fear into her life made him cringe, but there was no help for it.

"I don't know that —"

He was cut off by the sudden opening of the door.

Miranda jumped as the door clicked shut almost as soon as it swung open. She peeked around the back of her wing chair to see who had entered. A slight maid hastened across the room. Her dress was light brown and it was covered nearly to her ankles by a crisp white apron. "Your aunt is coming."

The sentence was still sinking in to Miranda's brain when Ryland jumped up from his chair. He kicked open the door to a cabinet resting below his bookshelves. He slid the tea service in and swung the door closed.

The maid hauled Miranda out of the chair and across the room to the solid walnut desk. The massive piece of furniture rested directly on the floor on three sides. Miranda found herself shoved down into the knee space of the desk, the maid squeezing in behind her, blocking her from the opening.

"Who are you?" Miranda hissed. *Really.* Ryland had the strangest staff she'd ever seen, and she had been privy to some interesting households.

A single blond brow inched up the forehead of a face that could have graced a porcelain doll. The door clicked open just as the maid was opening her mouth to answer. She snapped her teeth shut. Her arm shot out and stuffed a corner of her apron in Miranda's mouth.

Surprise made a more effective gag than the apron. This beautiful waif was the rugged street urchin Jess? Surely Ryland didn't employ two women that would so quickly resort to stuffing fabric into Miranda's mouth to ensure silence.

Movement on the other side of the desk reminded her why the need for silence existed.

"Do you intend to stay in this evening? There is a break in the weather, and it looks as if I shall be able to go out after all. Perhaps you would like to join me." It was a woman's voice, presumably the aunt.

"I believe I shall decline, aunt. All the rain has put me in the mood for a good book," Ryland answered.

"So I see. Hmmm, by a lady. Sounds . . . delightful." Her tone indicated that it sounded anything but.

Miranda clapped her hand over her apron-filled mouth to stifle a giggle. In his haste Ryland had grabbed a novel as his shield.

She wondered if it was the same book she'd read earlier this year. It had been authored simply "by a lady."

Jess's eyes jerked in her direction. Apparently satisfied that Miranda wasn't going to give away their location, she turned back to watching the edge of the desk.

"It is," Ryland answered.

Silence dragged on for several moments. Miranda's leg began to cramp. She thought about moving it, but a glare from Jess convinced her that she was better off in pain. Finally the aunt made a comment about having the carriage brought around and the door opened and closed once more.

Jess's arm shot out to hold Miranda still. The scraping sound of a page being turned echoed through the quiet study. Miranda glanced at Jess, who appeared to be waiting for some sort of signal from Ryland. Was his aunt actually still in the room?

The door swung back open with a *whoosh*.

"One more thing," said the aunt.

"Hmmm?" answered Ryland, sounding for all the world like a man absorbed in his reading.

"When Gregory returns, tell him I've gone to Lady Chevelle's dinner after all. He may join me there if he wishes."

"Why don't you tell Price? He's much

more likely to see him than I am."

Did the woman hiss? Miranda wriggled her toes in her slipper, trying to stave off the prickly feeling spreading from her ankle.

After a moment, light footsteps crossed the floor. The swish of fabric indicated the woman had yanked on the bellpull. "There. When that infernal butler comes, you can relay the message. If you insist on employing him, you can deal with him."

Footsteps crossed the room once more, and the door slammed shut.

With nothing better to do, Miranda started counting. She had just reached ten when Jess slid out from under the desk, dragging the apron from Miranda's mouth. With considerable effort, Miranda unfolded herself and followed.

Ryland's hand appeared, offering her assistance in rising.

"What was that about? She never comes to this room." Jess busied herself extracting the tea service from the cabinet.

"I believe I made her suspicious with my friendly overture this afternoon."

A grin split the maid's face as she set the tray back on the table. "An overture? Toward your family? Are you feeling all right?"

Ryland shrugged. "It was Jeffreys' idea."

Miranda watched the exchange with equal

parts awe and foreboding. Free of her urchin disguise, Jess was indeed a beautiful woman. With a silk dress and the proper coiffure she would compete with Georgina in any ballroom in London. That she and Ryland were so familiar with each other was disturbing, to say the least.

Jess poured more tea into the cups. "Jeffreys doesn't understand that some families don't get along. Not families like ours, anyway."

Miranda couldn't handle any more. Jealousy unlike anything she'd experienced toward Georgina welled within her. This woman had more in common with Ryland than Miranda ever would. "You two seem awfully familiar."

An impish grin crossed Jess's face. "It's not surprising. We were married, after all."

CHAPTER 31

Ryland groaned as he watched Miranda's eyes grow wider and wider. The sudden narrowing of her gaze to dagger-like slits indicated the full import of Jess's sentence had finally sunk in. He sent Jess a scathing glare of his own. She shrugged and plopped down on a chair.

He reached out and grasped Miranda's shoulders, intending to use force if necessary to make her hear him out. "We were never married. We only *pretended* to be married in order to stay alive. It was only once and only for a month."

Miranda's eyes jerked wide once more. "A month? You lived with her as husband and wife for a month?"

"No! I mean, yes, we gave the appearance of it, but no, we didn't. I mean . . . That is to say . . ." Ryland struggled to find the right words to convey his relationship with Jess. "We didn't, ahem, complicate things."

Miranda blinked at him.

"The entire setup was a complete sham."

A frown joined the blink.

"It was seven years ago. She was only fifteen."

The frown deepened to a scowl.

Ryland sighed. Fortunately, the anger seemed to have left her eyes, but confusion had followed in its wake. What else could he say? Miranda had been sheltered her entire life. He couldn't just come out and say —

"He's trying to tell you we never consummated the fake marriage. There were no shenanigans or relations while we worked together." Jess rolled her eyes and leaned her head back to stare at the ceiling.

A blush stained Miranda's cheeks a most becoming shade of rose. Obviously she now knew what he meant, even if she didn't truly know what it *meant.* While he could never have brought himself to make such a bald statement to a lady, he was grateful that Jess had been able to clear up the confusion. Sometimes her brash behavior was actually helpful.

"Really, Ryland, are you sure you want to marry her? She seems rather soft."

Most of the time though, it wasn't helpful

at all. "Shouldn't you be cleaning something?"

"Probably." Jess grinned. "That is what you pay me for, after all."

He made himself count to ten. He reminded himself that Jess did it on purpose. She thrived on riling people up and watching the aftermath of their explosions. "Get out, Jess."

She hopped to her feet and executed a jaunty curtsy. "Of course, Your Grace."

He felt Miranda relax under his hands as Jess skipped out the door. His fingers flexed, massaging the supple muscles of her upper arms. The scent of roses drifted to him again as she swung her head around to face him. Did she have rose oil put in her soap? Drop rose petals into her bathwater? He reined his mind in and forced himself to focus on the problem at hand.

Threatening missives needed his attention, not thoughts of Miranda's bathing habits.

All thoughts of the notes vanished when he looked down into Miranda's face. She was biting her lip, the slightly crooked front teeth raking across the tender surface.

His pulse jumped.

Moisture gathered in the corner of her eye. "You want to marry me?"

He was going to fire Jess. Or send her to

his country estate. Maybe turn her back over to Napoleon.

"Ryland?"

"Miranda, I —" He looked into her gaze and felt something slide into place with a single blink of those big green eyes. "Yes."

The smile that spread across her face was a more welcome sight than the English shore had been when he'd returned home from France.

He intended to say more about why he couldn't propose yet and how she deserved a proper courtship, to temper her expectations until he could deal with the eminent threat of a Bedlam candidate threatening English dukes.

But when she smiled, the rest of that didn't matter. He lowered his head and took that smile as his own.

There was no brother in the room this time, no formality, no ensuing argument, no rush. He took his time to savor the soft feel of her lips, the small gasp, and the blessed moment when she leaned in to kiss him back. He made himself keep his hands gripped around her upper arms. His mind clung to the fact that they weren't even betrothed yet, not really. Care had to be taken. He shouldn't even be kissing her, but he could find nothing in him willing to pull away.

She shifted, and he told his fingers to loosen so she could pull away. But then her fluttering touch landed on his arms. The grazes of her hands shyly making their way to his back. He wrapped his arms around her shoulders and hauled her closer.

Warmth. Warmth invaded every part of Miranda's body and soul. Emanating from the blissful pressure of Ryland's lips and his snug embrace. Not knowing what else to do, she mimicked his movements, wrapping her arms around him as best she could, and pressing her lips firmly against his.

She heard a low rumble in the back of her mind, but its significance was lost under the sound of blood rushing through her ears. Whatever it was, she felt like cursing it, because Ryland's lips drew away. She forgave the intrusion when he didn't let her go, merely pressed her head to his chest and rested his chin in her hair. One arm remained locked around her shoulders while the other soothed her by rubbing her back.

"What is it, Price?" Ryland's voice sounded different with her ear pressed to his chest. The echoing rumble reached her before his actual words did. The sensation

449

was far from unpleasant.

"Another note, sir."

The rubbing stopped. Ryland eased himself away and turned toward Price. A chill crept over her, making her legs shaky and unsteady. She sank into a nearby chair.

Price had turned his back to the room, finding the books on the shelf by the door vastly interesting. Ryland crossed the floor in three strides, his body seeming to hold itself tighter with every step. She realized she was watching him shift from gentleman to spy. It was a tad disconcerting.

"Where was it?" He slipped a folded white paper from the butler's hand.

"The silver tray by the door."

Price's words pierced Miranda's kiss-induced fog. She jumped to her feet. "You're getting notes too? Like the one I got?"

The frozen finger of dread chased away the last of her euphoria and caused small bumps to spring up along her skin. Clutching her arms across her stomach, she told herself to be strong. She was learning how strong a man Ryland was, and if she wanted a future with him she was going to need significant fortitude herself.

Ryland glanced at her with a stoic expression. Gone was the passionate gaze of moments before. Now he looked almost hard.

Cold. "Yes."

She waited, but no further explanation was forthcoming. He turned back to the note, murmuring something to Price in tones too low for her to hear. The butler nodded and swung his bulky body back toward the door. Ryland folded the parchment and tapped it against his lips. Silence thickened the air. He didn't speak. He didn't turn.

Cold was no longer a problem. Strength ceased to be an issue. Miranda was positively rigid with anger. How could he block her out like this? What part of him thought "Yes" was an adequate answer to the inquiry concerning a potential threat to his well-being?

He took three steps toward the door and put his hand to the latch.

"Not another step." The words sounded foreign, a lower, deeper tone than her usual voice.

Ryland froze with his hand extended. Moments passed where the only movement in the room seemed to be the clenching and releasing of her fists in time with her heavy breaths.

"I need to take care of this, Miranda."

"You need to tell me what's going on."

His knuckles paled as his fingers tightened

on the latch. "I'll protect you, Miranda. And Griffith. You have nothing to worry about."

Something broke inside Miranda's chest. A wall that she had spent her entire life building. Until that moment she hadn't realized how much of her natural exuberance and emotion had been repressed by her commitment to expected and correct behavior. But with Ryland she didn't need that wall. She knew she could be herself and he would delight in her freedom.

"Nothing to worry about?" She strode across the carpet. It took both hands and a significant amount of her weight, but she spun him around to face her. "What about you? What am I supposed to do while you go in search of the man looking to fill you with lead?"

Their eyes met, and for a moment she thought he would relent and tell her, show her that he wanted to partner together in life. He broke the look first and turned to glance around the room. "The tea is probably still hot. Why don't you —"

"Tea? You want me to sit and have some tea."

"Well, it would pass the time."

She wanted to hit him. Better yet, she could grab the vase off the bookshelf behind him and beat in his brain box with it. All of

452

her life, men had been taking care of everything for her. She didn't even know how much her last trip to the modiste had run. The bill had been sent directly to Griffith, and she'd never seen it.

Now Ryland expected her to simply sit and drink some tea while he went in search of a vengeful madman. The proper, dutiful position was no longer acceptable.

"I will not drink *tea*. If you won't tell me what is going on I'll go find out myself." Miranda spun around and stalked to the door, but her hand never made it to the latch.

Ryland whipped her up in his arms. In any other circumstance she would have blushed furiously at the romantic intimacy of the action. Romance was the furthest thing from her mind as she beat his shoulders and kicked her legs, determined not to be left out.

He threw her in a chair and blocked her in with his arms. Leaning down until his nose nearly touched hers, he whispered, "You will not leave this room. If you so much as poke your head out the door, I will tie you to this chair. If you require something to make your stay in my study more comfortable, ring the bell and Jess will see to whatever you need."

As if Miranda wanted anything more to do with the troublemaking maid.

"Do you understand?"

"Oh, I understand. I don't agree, but I understand."

He sighed. "I'm posting a guard. Don't. Leave."

He pressed a quick, hard kiss to her lips and then backed toward the door. He felt for the latch behind him and slipped out. A second later the click of the key told her he'd locked her in.

She began to pace the room, trying to work off some of the restless energy coursing through her legs, making them tingle. There wasn't much she could do, locked inside Ryland's study. She could think, she supposed, but she didn't have much information to ponder.

A flash of white on the floor caught her eye on her second trip around the perimeter of the room. She knelt to retrieve the folded paper. It was Ryland's note. Now she would know what the killer was threatening him with.

The paper tore a bit, and she cut her finger in her haste to open the missive. Sucking on the injured appendage, she held the paper open with her free hand. Disappointment filled her. This wasn't Ryland's note — it was hers. Or rather Griffith's.

She plopped down in the chair Ryland had deposited her in earlier. The note fluttered from her fingertips to the tea tray, landing at an awkward angle against the half-filled cup. It looked like a little lean-to shed. Amused by the thought, she took the linen napkin from beneath the other cup and began folding it to make a house to accompany the shed.

The jostling of the tray had caused the tea to slosh out of the cup, leaving a light brown stain on the napkin. She twisted her creation to use the tea mark as a door. The effect was rather cute.

She sat back to look at her makeshift diorama. Maybe she could find some scraps of paper and fold some animal and people shapes to populate her cottage. A thought niggled at the back of her mind, telling her something was wrong with the picture in front of her.

Leaning back in the chair, she turned her head one way and then another, trying to look at the disheveled tea tray in different ways. The appearance was that of a normal tea tray. It looked very similar to the one delivered to her that evening, starting this entire debacle, right down to the puddle of spilt tea.

When she'd found the note the corner of it had been splattered with tea —

She sat up and snatched at the note, knocking her napkin cottage over as well. There was no tea on the note — only her blood. This *was* the note Ryland had gotten.

Confusion filled Miranda.

Why would two men be given the same threatening letter?

Ryland waited at the door, listening to Miranda's movements within the study. The echo of stomping feet and disgruntled mumblings approached the door, and he braced himself for another argument. When the sounds shifted in the direction of the corner bookcases, he allowed his muscles to slowly relax. Air rushed through his lips in a silent sigh. The chink of the teapot and the slight squeak of chair leather indicated Miranda had accepted her confinement and settled in with a book and a cup of tea.

He waited for another moment or two before making his way down to the kitchen to meet with Price and Jeffreys. If their note-sender wasn't Baron Listwist, they needed to figure out who it was — and quickly, before the man moved on to threatening the entire aristocracy.

Memories of the recently shared kiss flitted at the edge of his mind, tempting him to forget the operation and return to the study.

Wanting this entire business behind him the next time he held her in his arms spurred him down the creaky side stairs into the servants' domain. Besides, Miranda would probably throw the teacup at his head if he so much as peeked inside the door.

He was nearly to the kitchen before he realized that he was smiling. The curve of his lips felt large and a bit ridiculous. Considering he rarely allowed more than a smirk to indicate his humor, a full-fledged lovesick grin was bound to draw attention he didn't need or want. It was hard not to smile when he thought of Miranda's barely concealed passion, though. For years she had hidden it beneath a sheen of ladylike predictability. It was nice to know he inspired more emotion than her carefully crafted shell could contain.

Still, the smile had to go.

He smacked himself on the cheeks, the hard, calloused palms grating against his face as he screwed up his nose and fought to gain control of his facial muscles. Feeling composed and in control once more, he strode into the kitchen.

It was empty save his three cronies. They sat around a rough wooden table, Price filling up one bench while Jeffreys and Jess shared the other one. Ryland reached a hand into his pocket to pull out the notes as he approached the table.

Only one paper resided in his pocket. He wrapped his fingers around it, trying to remember where the other note might be. He must have dropped it in the study. With a silent prayer that Miranda wouldn't find it, he flattened the one note onto the table.

Three sets of hardened, experienced eyes stared back at Ryland. He was the leader of this mission. "The same note showed up at Griffith's house. If I can figure out why, I think we'll have our man."

CHAPTER 32

Miranda twirled the paper in her hand, shadows from a nearby candle causing the words to go in and out of focus. Whoever was making menacing overtures wasn't very creative. Sending the same message to two different peers seemed a very foolish thing to do.

Of course, leaving it on a tea tray in hopes that it would be delivered to your target was quite foolish as well. Whoever penned the scrawling black words must have a few attics to let. She hated to think that any of their staff would be driven to attack the family, but who else could have left the note?

Wind whistled by the closed French doors, sending a spattering of rain against the glass panes. It was a miracle that she had managed to arrive at Ryland's home without mishap. She should have been soaked to the skin and shivering from the swirling night wind.

Huddling deeper into the chair, she stared at the candle flame until it became a yellow and orange blur and her eyes began to feel dry and crusty. There was something she was missing. Something the wind and the rain kept trying to bring to the forefront of her mind.

"Lord, this would be much simpler if you would just tell me. Maybe write it down or make it appear in the tea." Well, maybe not the tea. She'd heard tales of people thinking the future could be discerned by tea leaves. It seemed illogical and a bit unnerving to her.

A quill and ink set on the desk caught her eye. *Writing.* How many times in her life had she organized her thoughts and figured things out by writing? At least half of her letters to Ryland had served that purpose.

Paper and quill at the ready, she sat at the desk and started to write. Out of habit, she started the paper with *Dear Marshington,* but nothing else came to her. Even in a situation as difficult as this one she couldn't push past the inability to write letters the way she used to.

"Okay, then, I'll talk to him. He's probably still in the house. I'll find him, and we can talk this out. He'll realize that I can help him."

Her fingers grasped the door latch and pulled. The door rattled but didn't open. He had indeed locked her in. For a moment she debated banging on the door, but after they'd gone through such pains to hide her presence from his aunt earlier, it didn't seem the wisest course of action.

She eyed the glass doors on the other side of the room but dismissed them immediately. There was no guarantee that she could get back into the house if she exited that way. She could find herself stranded between the row of homes and the wall bordering Carlton House's vast gardens. The option was not appealing.

"I shall simply work it out myself, then."

She bounced slightly as she dropped back into her chair, staring at the familiar note and willing her brain to work.

It didn't.

Frustrated, she popped back out of the chair and began to pace. She eyed the quill one more time but knew that was no longer an option. Until she invented a new mythical friend, it seemed her journaling days were over. Her hands found her hips and she huffed, making her sagging ringlets dance around her head. She needed someone to talk to.

A quick scan of the room revealed a

surprising lack of portraits. What peer's study wasn't overrun with portraits of the title's previous holders? A small globe sat on the shelf, its metal base glinting in the firelight. She draped her napkin over the top like a hat.

It would have to do.

She paced back and forth in front of her new friend and began talking. After repeating everything she knew, nothing was any clearer than it had been fifteen minutes prior.

"I don't understand. It always works at home. What am I missing?"

Ryland stabbed his hand through his hair. "What am I missing?"

Jess looked around at the men's faces. "Perhaps you could ask —"

"I'm not asking Miranda. I will not involve her in this." Ryland bit off the words, cutting short the suggestion Jess had made five times in as many minutes.

"She is the one who found the other note." Jeffreys examined the toes of his shoes, avoiding Ryland's murderous glare.

"No. I will not put her in any more danger than she is just by being here."

Jess sighed and dropped her forehead to the table. "You would only be talking to her,

Ryland."

"No."

"All right, then. I'm going to bed. Unlike you lazy blokes, I have to get up and stoke the fires in the morning." Jess pushed away from the table and headed for the stairs. "I suggest you all turn in as well. There's obviously a clue we have yet to find and I doubt it's here in this kitchen."

"Jess." Ryland leaned against the table, his shoulders slumped beneath the rare feeling of desperation. "One more time. Let's go over everything one more time. Then I'll need you to help me get Miranda home. She can't stay the night in my study, and I can't take her myself."

Tense silence filled the room. Jess finally returned to the table. "Okay. When did the first note show up?"

"It's ridiculous, really," Miranda said to the globe. "Why the tea tray? It could have gone to anyone. Mrs. Brantley always keeps several at the ready when the weather is bad because we are forever ringing for tea to warm our insides. It's not always worth the hassle of lighting a fire."

She paced back and forth, hands clasped behind her at the small of her back. Five steps to the edge of the carpet, turn, five steps to the other edge, repeat.

"Ryland obviously doesn't have the same philosophy. Of course, his house seems to be a bit draftier than ours. He should really look into fixing that.

"It was under the teapot, so whoever left it was in the kitchen. That makes nearly every servant an option. We didn't have the paper this morning. Gibson said it was because even the delivery boys were having trouble slogging through the weather. It really makes me wonder what drove Mr. Montgomery to drive out in it. It took him nearly half an hour to dry off in . . . the . . . kitchen . . ."

Miranda stared at the note. What if it hadn't been meant for Griffith? What if it hadn't been for anyone at Hawthorne House? That would explain Ryland receiving an identical note. If the culprit thought he'd lost the first one, he could write a second one. And who had more to gain from Ryland's untimely death than the next in line for the title?

Ryland didn't know that his cousin had been to visit Miranda. He would never think to tie Mr. Montgomery to a threat on Griffith. He could be in mortal danger right now! If Miranda was right, and Mr. Montgomery had decided he would rather be referred to as "His Grace," then the killer had free rein of his target's house.

She ran to the door, prepared to bang on it until she broke through if that's what it would take to get Ryland to listen to her. Her hand stalled inches from the door. Was Mr. Montgomery home? No one had said he was home, but if you were planning on murdering someone wouldn't you claim to be elsewhere?

Banging wasn't an option. She couldn't risk gaining Mr. Montgomery's attention before attaining Ryland's. She knelt and pressed her eye to the keyhole, hoping to see the guard Ryland had promised. There didn't appear to be anyone outside the door. Had he counted on the mere threat of a guard to keep her inside?

She tried the latch. It was truly locked.

She flattened to the ground and peered underneath, looking for a shadow or shoes. Though how she could know whether or not they belonged to Mr. Montgomery was beyond her.

Nothing.

What else could she do? She stood and looked around the room, praying for inspiration. The embroidery of the bellpull caught the firelight, mocking her. Why hadn't she started there? Despite Miranda's lack of affection for the woman, Jess would be able to get the information to Ryland.

Miranda's stomach churned at the thought of the disdain on Jess's face when Miranda had to admit she needed the other girl's help. It wasn't Miranda's fault she was raised as a normal person. Everyone couldn't be spies.

She stomped her way across the room and yanked on the pull with a force fed by the surge of agitation. The top of the pull slapped her in the head before falling useless to the floor. It wasn't the first time she'd dismantled a bellpull with an overly enthusiastic tug, but it was certainly the most inconvenient.

No bellpull, no guard, no way of making sure Ryland was the one who heard her if she yelled. All her life Miranda had been told to be a lady, to do as instructed, to stay out of trouble, but Miranda could never live with herself if she stood in this study while Ryland's cousin tried to kill him.

What would her mother do if she were locked in the study with an urgent message? Miranda frowned at the tea. Her mother would have gently rung the bell and then finished her tea while she waited.

What would Jess do if she were locked in the study with an urgent message? Probably pick the lock.

Miranda kicked aside the useless bellpull. She couldn't be a lady like her mother or a partner like Jess, but she could find a way to help Ryland. Rain pelted the doors leading to the back garden. There was more than one way into the rest of the house. With a deep breath, Miranda flung the doors open and darted into the rain.

"That's it, Ryland. We'll have to wait until we know something else. I'll go see Miranda home for you." Jess rose from the table once more and made her way to the stairs.

"Don't ask her anything, Jess." Ryland rolled his neck back and forth.

"Is she such a hothouse flower, then? If she's so delicate, what do you see in her?"

Price placed a heavy hand on Ryland's shoulder. "She's been gently bred, Jess. Remember how you were. I remember hauling your carcass out of a pond when you didn't consider that a dock could have been rigged as a trap."

Jess huffed and looked the other way. "All right, I won't ask her anything. But if she can't handle this, Ryland, can she handle being married to you?"

She darted silently up the stairs. Ryland hated that she'd asked the question he'd been ignoring. Even if he never did another minute of spy work, Ryland would never be the same as his peers. What kind of life was that for Miranda?

"Shall we retire, Your Grace?" Jeffreys stood as a servant awaiting instruction. Considering that five minutes earlier he had been hotly arguing for an inquisition of the entire household, his servient posture struck Ryland as funny. He understood Jeffreys' underlying message though. It was time for Ryland to remember that he wasn't a spy any longer. He had chosen to resume his duties as a peer of the realm.

"Yes, Jeffreys, I think that would be best." Jess came falling back into the room. "She's gone."

Ryland's heart froze, his breath evaporated.

"Was there a struggle?" Price came forward and slapped Ryland between the shoulder blades.

"There's a globe with a napkin on it, but it doesn't look like it put up much of a fight."

Ryland tried to wrap his mind around that statement, but it was stuck back at *"She's gone."*

He could figure out the globe part later. Right now they had to find Miranda.

"Spread out. Price and Jess, start from the study and work your way back. Don't forget to check the garden. Jeffreys, have my horse saddled and brought round front. I'll search the roads."

Ryland raced up the stairs, intent on gaining the front door as quickly as possible. He paused in the front hall and took a detour around by the study. Sure enough, there sat a globe with a napkin on it. In spite of the danger, a grin split his face. He was fairly certain Miranda could handle a life that wasn't quite normal.

Chapter 33

Running from the warm study into the rain had not been her brightest moment. Worry for Ryland made her do things without considering the ramifications. Even if she found a way back into the house, was Ryland even still there? Had he left to search for clues? To confront the enemy?

Rain had long ago seeped through the final layer of her clothes, making her ambivalent to the stream of water coursing down the back of her neck. Much more annoying were the lank strands of hair the wind kept flinging across her eyes. What had once been light, fashionable curls framing her face were now heavy, sopping hanks of hair, whipped hither and yon by the dancing wind, occasionally catching on her lashes, and once entangling in a holly bush.

She tried every door and window on the ground floor, but all of them were locked and none of the rooms held Ryland. Her best chance was the front door. Returning to the study would gain her nothing. She needed to find Ryland.

Unfortunately getting to the front door was easier said than done. Montgomery House shared walls with its neighbors, making a trip from the back to the front of the house a long walk. A long walk through a series of gardens where anyone could lie in wait for her or sneak up behind without her noticing.

"Think like a spy, Miranda. Show Ryland that you can play at his party. I may not be as proficient as Jess, but I will not let her be the only courageous woman in his life."

She listened to the sounds of the garden. It seemed to pulse, with occasional periods of extended rustling as a long, angry finger of wind stabbed through the hedges. If she varied her pace, she should be able to make the same sort of unpredictable noise pattern. Maybe she could avoid drawing attention to herself.

Making her way from garden to garden proved easier than she expected. In the dark, she couldn't make out the delineation in the wall to mark the change from house to house. Some of them had walls and fences, others hedges or pathways. Sooner than she expected, she saw the decorative gate around Marlborough house, indicating she'd reached the western end of Pall Mall.

Stepping onto the footpath alongside the cobbled road, she attempted to shake out her skirts. The soggy muslin clung to her legs and the lightweight cloak did little to hide the indecent fit of her wet gown. She quelled at the thought of Ryland seeing her like this.

"A lady never goes out looking less than her best."

Years of lectures and training told her to go home as quickly as she could. But if Ryland didn't know who his enemy was, he could put himself in danger inadvertently.

Traffic was incredibly nonexistent. Had the weather been better, the roads would have been crowded with carriages returning from the night's festivities. The most dangerous part of her walk was going to be the expanse across St. James's Street, where many of the gentlemen's clubs were. If anywhere was going to be filled with people, it would be there.

Sure enough, a curricle pulled onto Pall Mall from St. James's as she walked past the intersection. She wanted to run but restrained herself. Running would only make the curricle driver more curious about her.

"Well, hello!"

Miranda glanced around the side of her hood, intending to continue walking without acknowledging the greeting. Her eyes made out the shadowy face, nose, and cheekbones highlighted by a small carriage lantern, shielded from the rain by the half top of the curricle.

Her feet froze. Water numbed her toes and she realized she was standing in a puddle, but still, she couldn't move. Of all the things she had considered, running into Mr. Montgomery wasn't one of them.

She had to move. Walk on. If she kept her hood up and her face averted, she could avoid the light from the gas streetlamps. Her only hope was to make it to the safety of Montgomery House before he recognized her. As that was probably Mr. Montgomery's destination as well, she prayed that Ryland or his butler were very close to the front door.

The curricle kept pace with her, and it became increasingly difficult to evade the light from the lampposts. Ryland *would* have to live on the most well-lit street in London.

Miranda turned her head as she passed another lamppost, using the movement to see if she could guess Mr. Montgomery's next actions. Lightning suddenly illuminated the street, causing her to blink at the sudden brightness. Miranda turned her gaze to the heavens and then to Gregory's face, locking eyes with his startled gaze. "Truly, God? You couldn't have waited another five seconds?"

In that instant, he had recognized her. What would he be thinking? What reason other than the truth could he come up with for her being so near to Ryland's house, alone, at this time of night?

"Lady Miranda?"

Her feet screamed at her to let them run toward Ryland's house. Another part of her brain told her to stay calm. If she drew attention to the fact that she was now terrified of this man, he would know he'd been discovered. Who knew what he would do then?

She would brazen it out. "I'm sorry, sir. I cannot stay. Unfortunate circumstances force me to seek shelter at my brother's home. You understand."

Blood pounded in her ears as she fought every instinct she had. Calmly turning her back on him, she crossed the street as if she were headed home instead of toward Ryland's. Her breathing grew harsh and loud, combining with her pounding heart to obscure all sound. Was Mr. Montgomery driving away? Walking after her?

St. James's Square came into view.

"Breathe. Walk. Breathe. Walk." Miranda repeated the mantra. If she could maintain these two things, she would make it to Trent's house. She crossed into the park area of the square without incident. The trees at the far side of St. James's Square beckoned her. Beyond them, she could lose Mr. Montgomery by taking a number of different streets and alleys to cross over to Mount Street.

She looked over the square as she emerged from the small park. Empty. Damp air filled her lungs as she took her first full breath in five very long minutes. All she had to do was jog down York Street and she could wend her way over to Mount Street with no one the wiser.

Just beyond the square, however, York Street was blocked.

Mr. Montgomery tipped his hat. "I cannot allow you to walk in such horrific weather, my lady. Allow me to escort you home."

Water dripped off the brim of Ryland's hat as he rode through the rain. He covered the length of Pall Mall and was making his way along the back alleys and side streets. Alarm

475

was now spreading through the Hawthorne household, but that couldn't be helped. He'd had to know if Miranda had somehow made it home, and it was either break into his friend's house or bang on the door until the butler was roused.

Banging on the door was considerably more efficient.

She hadn't made it home. Nor had she gone to Trent's house. It would be a while before Trent would know of his sister's disappearance since he was waiting the storm out at his club as far as his valet knew. That meant she was likely somewhere in between.

It was possible she had ducked into the house of a friend, but who would she trust that much with her reputation? For it was sure to be ruined after roaming London alone. Not that he cared. He would marry her anyway. If blemished reputation mattered to him, he would never have done anything as scandalous as become a spy.

An hour later, he slipped in his front door, shucking his dripping overcoat and gloves. Not wanting to spread more water through the house than necessary, he sat on the floor to pry off his wet boots. After several minutes he gave up and stretched out on the cold marble floor.

He needed to think, and he desperately needed some sleep, but being defeated by a pair of soggy boots left him despondent. It wasn't the first time he'd ridden through the rain. Had his boots been so much looser before? Probably. He'd generally worn peasant clothing when on a mission and those men didn't have the luxury of a valet to pry tight leather from their legs.

Ryland's eyes drifted shut. *Where is Miranda?*

"What in the name of . . . Are you dead?" Aunt Marguerite's voice seeped into the edges of his brain. Was she talking to him?

Something hard and blunt poked him in the ribs. He managed a grunt.

"Are you really going to oblige me by expiring in the middle of the front hall? Is there blood? Are you shot? I don't want to ruin the floors in here."

More poking. It hurt. Ryland snatched the offending object and flung it across the hall. The sound of glass breaking was followed by a scream from his aunt. The demise of a vase distressed her more than the potential death of her nephew. How touching.

Ryland frowned. In fact, she seemed to relish the possibility of his untimely end. Maybe he should continue the charade, though after that splendid display of reflexes, he'd be hard-pressed to convince her of his impending doom.

What would she expect of a person when they were about to die? Ryland had seen more than his share of death over the years, but he doubted Aunt Marguerite knew anything about it. If he put on a good show, she would probably believe it. He groaned as low and loud as he could, before thrashing about on the floor, slipping through the growing puddle of water. Slowly he calmed the thrashing to the occasional twist, keeping his breathing as shallow as possible, in case she was watching for the rise and fall of his chest.

"Ryland?"

He twitched. His knuckle cracked against the marble floor. He bit his tongue to contain the groan.

"Ryland?"

She had retrieved the cane and started poking him again.

"Are you breathing?"

The pokes traveled to his chest. Ryland held his breath.

"It worked. I can't believe it worked. Oh, my bright, bright boy. I don't know how you did it, but you won't regret it."

Booted heels clicked on the marble as she circled Ryland's body.

"A witness. I need a witness."

Fabric grazed his cheek as she settled near his head. What was she doing?

"I despise getting wet," she mumbled. And then she wailed.

Ryland almost gave up the game when the ear-splitting scream rent the air. If he didn't know any better, he'd swear that the woman crying about his demise was authentically upset. His aunt was quite the thespian.

Steps rushed from all corners of the house. Hushed murmurings of "Your Grace?" came from every direction. Ryland waited for something, some sign that he had enough to solve the mystery of his aunt's desire for his death. There had never been any love lost between them, but he'd never truly wished her ill. The same apparently couldn't be said for her.

"Ryland? Your Grace?"

A sigh of relief almost escaped Ryland's lips. Price had returned.

His aunt managed to speak and sob at the same time. "I heard the door and thought Gregory must have returned, but then I saw . . . him . . . here . . . Oh, what could have happened?"

Regret that he could not witness the splendid theatrical production himself nearly made Ryland smile. Why hadn't he thought to roll over in his thrashings and hide his face? Next time he pretended to die, he would do so on his stomach. It would be much easier.

"My lady, I . . ." Price sounded more perplexed than concerned.

Aunt Marguerite hiccupped. "I suppose you'll have to see to the body, Price. It can be your last official duty."

"My lady?"

"Well, my son Gregory is the duke now, so I'll be managing the house. You are dismissed. Without a reference."

The tableau was almost over. Was there anything to gain by pretending any longer? He couldn't perpetuate the scam for several days. She would be expecting a visit from the Prince's committee and a funeral.

Perhaps more could be gained by scaring his aunt out of her wits. Ryland sat upright. "Don't heed that, Price. I think I'd like to keep you on as butler."

Aunt Marguerite's scream was sure to leave everyone's ears ringing for days. It was a good thing that she was sitting on the floor. Ryland didn't extend his arms to catch her as she fainted.

CHAPTER 34

Ryland rose to his feet with Price's assistance. His eyes narrowed as he took in his aunt's form, sprawled across the hall floor, skirt trailing through the puddle he had left behind.

"Should we move her, Your Grace?"

He should say no. He wanted to say no.

"Yes. Put her on the sofa in the drawing room. Bind her and set up a watch. Until Miranda is safely home, my aunt is to be kept confined as a person of suspicion."

Price nodded but paused for a long moment before scooping up the prone body and crossing the hall. Ryland watched them go, trying to process the fact that his last-remaining family wanted him dead. His aunt had crowed over his passing and seemed to think Gregory had orchestrated it. One hand speared through his hair, the clammy feeling reminding him that he was still soaked to the bone.

"Jeffreys!"

The valet strode from the direction of the kitchens, several folds of toweling in his arms. "Would you care for a towel, Your Grace?"

Ryland felt a smile tug at the corner of his lips. How could he find humor when Miranda was missing? He took a towel and rubbed at his hair, face, and arms.

"May I take your coat, Your Grace? Perhaps if we remove some of the wet items, the towels will be more effective." Jeffreys set the remaining towels on the floor and moved to divest Ryland of his sodden outer garments.

The half smile was firmly in place as Ryland watched his ruined coat get neatly folded and set upon the floor. "You shall make a right fine valet, I think."

"I'd like to think so, Your Grace. I've laid dry clothing out already. I shall be up to assist you as soon as I can find somewhere for these, er, garments."

Ryland jogged up the stairs and down the corridor, doing his best to avoid the rugs. Despite shedding boots, jacket, cravat, and waistcoat, he was still dripping. A slow smile stretched his lips as he took in the scene in his dressing room. The nondescript garb of a country farmworker draped across a straight-back chair, laid out as elegantly as his finest evening wear.

His spy clothes. He hadn't realized Jeffreys had kept them. Sliding his legs in the worn brown trousers felt comforting, and not only because they were dry. This was a case, a job. If he could remember that and treat it like one, Miranda would be safe within hours, if she wasn't ensconced at Hawthorne House already. Until he heard otherwise, he would assume the worst.

Three sharp knocks rolled through the room. Ryland jerked his white shirt down before bidding the knocker to enter.

Jess opened the door wide but remained outside the room, using another towel to try to catch her own drips.

Ryland sent her an inquiring look while he sat in the chair to pull on his scratched and scarred boots.

"There was a bit of a scuffle in St. James's Square, but there's no way of knowing for certain if it was her or not. There was a woman on foot and a man in a curricle, and they left together."

"Gregory."

Jess froze. "Beg pardon?"

He stomped his foot the rest of the way into his boot and snatched his jacket from the back of the chair. There was no time to bother with the cravat or anything else. He was sure to be wet again soon anyway if he had to run after his errant cousin.

"Gregory. He took his curricle to the club earlier."

"In this weather?"

Ryland shrugged as he slid past Jess into the passageway. "He didn't have to go far. And it does have a top."

"And you think Greg . . . er, Mr. Montgomery took Miranda? Why?"

Why was a very good question. What could Gregory hope to gain by stealing Miranda away? Ryland slid his fingers slowly across the polished newel post at the top of the stairs. He couldn't run off into the night, hoping to track Gregory's curricle across London. He needed information.

And he knew just the person who had it.

"Are you sure you want to do this, Your Grace?"

Ryland glanced at Price's worried face and nodded. "Positive."

"But . . . the brocade, Your Grace. It will be ruined." The big man's head shook back and forth, a look of grim resignation tightening the corners of his mouth.

Ryland swallowed a chuckle as he turned

back to the couch upholstered in green brocade and currently holding the limp form of his aunt. Rope stretched from each of the four legs, ensuring she would remain sitting upon the furniture after she awoke.

"Perhaps smelling salts?" Price tried once more to dissuade his employer.

Ryland lifted one eyebrow as he looked his butler up and down. "Do you have any?"

"Er, no."

"Then water it is."

With that he threw the flowers from the nearby vase onto the floor and upended the remaining contents on his aunt's head. She flew up, sputtering, trying to fling her arms over her head, only to find their movement limited by her constraints.

There was something satisfying about being comfortably dry while water dripped from her rapidly blinking lashes.

"Where is he?"

She stared up at Ryland, her eyes darting to the empty vase in his hand. Outrage replaced surprise on her angular features. She spit at him.

He tsked at her, handing the vase to Price before leaning down, just out of reach of his last-remaining female relative. "Such manners. What would the ladies at Almack's say if they could see you now?"

"Get away from me!"

Ryland straightened and forced himself to maintain a casual appearance. His heart pounded in his chest, the blood roaring through his ears, urging him to hurry. But calm would be his greatest weapon in fighting his aunt. It always had been. When things didn't go her way, she grew agitated and flustered. He was counting on that now.

"I'll ask you again." Ryland leaned his hips against the arm of the chair that sat at an angle to his aunt's cushioned prison. "Where is he?"

"Who?"

"Your son. Gregory."

"I believe he went to his club. With the rain he probably decided to stay there."

His eyes narrowed as he watched Lady Marguerite — he refused to call her his aunt anymore — try to straighten her skirts and sit with all the poise and restraint of a lady calling upon her social enemy.

"He's not at his club, but that's not the real matter. He has no real friends so that only leaves a few places he could go. Checking them won't take long at all." He looked deep into her eyes, praying for the key, the one thing that would cause her to break. "Price, go ready the weapons. I want as many outriders as we can muster. Make sure we are all amply armed."

"At once, Your Grace."

Price's footsteps echoed from the hall as the color began to fade from Lady Marguerite's cheeks.

"I'm going to find your son, and when I do, things will not go well for him."

"Maybe they won't go well for you."

Ryland tried to looked surprised. He was certain he failed, achieving a sort of mocking self-confidence instead. Either would serve to anger her. "Are you threatening me?"

She spat at him again. "Of course I'm threatening you. I tried to have them declare you dead, but without a recognizable body, they refused to do so."

The fact that he frequently communicated with King George and then the Prince Regent might have had something to do with that as well, but she didn't need to know that. "Seeing as I am very much alive, I'm glad to hear it."

"You shouldn't be."

"Glad?"

"Alive."

This was getting good now. Ryland resisted the urge to rub his hands together. "God has blessed me by extracting me from more than one tight situation, so He apparently has a different view of the subject."

"It should be Gregory. He's the eldest."

Ryland couldn't keep the surprise from his face. She did remember that she had married the younger brother, didn't she?

"Gregory was supposed to be the duke. Gregory should be the duke! He's older than you. He has stayed in London, has seen the many things this country needs."

Now he knew that she was out of her mind. The only reason Gregory was staying in London was because Napoleon made traveling to France a life-threatening venture. And the only thing the man ever saw in London was his club, Tattersall's, and the interior of a scattering of well-to-do drawing rooms.

"With you gone, Gregory would have been able to take his rightful place as heir! He was the eldest, but Richard kept insisting the next duke would be you, you insolent pup."

Somewhere along the way Lady Marguerite had lost touch with reality. She sat shaking her fist at the ceiling, yelling at a dead man. "Look what you've forced me to become, Richard! I begged you to see to this before you died, but you refused! I suppose that makes me the fool for believing you loved me! You never loved me or Gregory. It was always about *him.* Making sure *he* got to Eton and played on the best teams for the best houses. Making sure *he* had a mother figure. You left me with a son and no future. Curse you, Richard! I hope you and your faithless lies are in hell!"

Ryland backed away, eyes growing wide as the woman he'd always pictured as cold and controlling thrashed on the sofa, years of constrained bitterness spilling forth in a torrent she was unprepared to handle.

She lunged for the side table, the ropes causing the couch to drag behind her and impede her balance. The empty vase crashed to the floor, sending shards of fine porcelain in every direction. She clawed at pieces, dragging them against her skin in an effort to cut through the rope.

The first sight of blood drew Ryland from his stunned stupor. "Jess! Price! Jeffreys!"

He heard footsteps scramble down the corridor as he tried to restrain his aunt. The couch kept him from approaching her from behind, and her convulsions made it dangerous to come from the front. She hauled the couch another foot, madness making her stronger than he could have imagined. It was going to cost him a scrape or two, but he had to stop her.

Ducking his head to escape any blows to

the face, he dove in and wrapped his arms around her thin torso.

"No!" she screamed. The piercing sound drove to the middle of his brain.

With her arms pinned to her sides, chest heaving with sobs and exertion, she inspired nothing so much as pity. Ryland looked up at his faithful servants, his trusted inner circle. For the first time in a very long while, he was at a loss. "What do I do?"

"Let me go, Richard! I hate you! You practically made me your wife. Why couldn't you make Gregory your son?"

Ryland struggled to maintain his hold on the madwoman. One rope had worked its way around his leg, threatening to send them both toppling in a dangerous tangle.

Price and Jeffreys looked as clueless as he felt. In all of their years, they'd never been faced with a predicament such as this.

Jess strode forward and swung a fist straight into Lady Marguerite's jaw. Her head snapped back, cracking against Ryland's cheek. The sudden limp weight of her still body sent Ryland stumbling back to sit on the couch. He looked at Jess and saw that Price and Jeffreys were also staring in her direction.

She shrugged. "It's not as if all of you haven't wanted to do that very thing before."

They all had to acknowledge the truth of that.

Ryland extricated himself from the tangle of ropes and his aunt's skirts and laid her out on the couch. "We'll need someone to watch her."

Price nodded and left the room. "I'll get Archibald."

"Any word on Gregory?" Ryland asked the remaining occupants.

"He's not at his club or his, er, lady friend's," Jeffrey said.

Ryland coughed. He really didn't want to know about his cousin's indiscretions.

"None of his acquaintances have granted him shelter either," Jess added.

Ryland nodded. That didn't leave a whole lot of options. A roadside inn would tax Gregory's pockets after a few days. He was due to receive his allowance next week, so he had to be running low. Inns offered too many chances for witnesses; someone who would notice and recognize Miranda and come to her aid.

Which meant there was really only one place Gregory could go with any kind of confidence.

CHAPTER 35

Marshington Abbey was beautiful. Miranda wished she were seeing it for the first time under better circumstances. Arriving bound, gagged, and bruised in a curricle designed for town travel was not her ideal introduction to the place.

Early morning sunlight glinted off the many windows, turning the abbey into an exquisite jewel. The gardens radiated from the house, providing what was sure to be a stunning approach from any direction.

Miranda couldn't appreciate the beauty right now, though. She was too busy trying to extricate herself from Ryland's imbecile of a cousin. What was he thinking by bringing her here? This was Ryland's country home. Wouldn't the man think to look here?

She would remind him of that, but he'd grown tired of her talking within an hour of London and gagged her with his cravat. It was enough to make her sympathize with every horse she'd ever ridden. The fabric cutting between her lips and pulling at the back of her head was far worse than Jess's mittens stuffed in her mouth.

As they pulled up to the side of the house, Mr. Montgomery jerked the sodden hood of her cloak forward to where it flopped into her face and stuck to her cheeks and chin. She tried to shake the dirty wool off.

The sharp barrel of his gun poking into her ribs stalled her movements.

She sat in blindness, listening as a door opened and the slow shuffle of footsteps approached the curricle.

"We weren't expecting you, Mr. Montgomery. I'm afraid there's no one here but me. The rest of them are staying the week in the village to prepare for the fair."

Miranda ducked her head to try to see around the edge of the cloak, but all she could see were her own feet. The man sounded older but not feeble. If she could convey her plight to him, he might be of some help. She shifted in her seat, hoping he would ask about her.

Mr. Montgomery wrapped a hand around her arm and began dragging her from the curricle. She was sure to have bruises there in minutes, but it was better than a gun to the ribs.

She tripped after him, searching for some way to let the servant know all was not as it should be.

"Do not fret, Mr. Blakemoor. We've no need for much. A simple stopover on our way elsewhere. If you could see to the horses and prepare a bit of food, that will be more than enough."

Miranda dug her teeth into his cravat. How could the man be so calm about abducting her? She wanted to stomp on his foot or kick him in the shins, but she didn't know where that gun had gone.

"We had a very successful crop of tomatoes last year. Have you seen those, sir? The missus says she heard they're poisonous, but I think they're too tasty for that. Will you be staying the night, sir?"

"No. There will be no need for that."

Until that moment Miranda had been more irritated than truly afraid. But the coldness of those words stabbed through her, and fear made her tremble.

What did Mr. Montgomery plan to do to her?

Ryland was running on nerves and fear. He'd ridden all night, changing horses as often as he could. He felt the shakiness that came from too little sleep and too much energy. A deep breath, a prayer, and a long drink of water from the wineskin he carried and he felt himself begin to calm.

Where was everyone? Even though it had been years since any family had occupied the abbey, it required a certain number of staff to keep it from falling into disrepair. Ryland had often said he cared so little for the place that he wouldn't mind seeing it as a heap of rubble, but that wasn't true.

Even though his memories weren't worth recalling, the last several dukes had used this as their home. He owed it to them to keep the place in good condition. It wasn't their fault that Aunt Marguerite had made the years here awkward with her attempts to treat Ryland and Gregory like brothers. It wouldn't have been so bad if she'd shown them equal affection, but she'd never had anything but reprimands for Ryland.

It didn't — couldn't — matter what had happened within those walls. All that concerned him now was whether or not Miranda was within them. Was she inside somewhere, screaming for him to rescue her? She had to know he was coming.

In the distance he saw the old caretaker, Mr. Blakemoor, leaving the barn.

It was the first stroke of luck he'd had in a very long time.

■ ■ ■ ■

Ryland was coming. Miranda didn't know when, how, or from where, but she knew he was coming for her. It was up to her to do what she could to make things easier for him when he got here.

The best thing she could do was be nowhere near Mr. Montgomery.

So she put every one of her lady lessons to use and became the exemplary hostage. She perched on the edge of a sofa covered in a white dustcloth, watching her captor pace in front of the window in an upstairs parlor. Nary a peep had crossed her gagged lips in more than half an hour.

She knew because she'd been counting the seconds. It was the only thing she could think of to occupy her mind.

After ten minutes he'd slid the gun into the waist of his pants.

After twenty minutes he'd stopped glancing her way at all.

She gave it another fifteen minutes to be sure he'd all but forgotten her.

Then she moved. Slow, steady steps. The soundless graceful kind her mother had made her practice for hours before her debut. She had her excuse ready if he caught her. He couldn't question her looking for the chamber pot. That excuse was only going to work once, though, so this was her only chance to get away and remove Mr. Montgomery's advantage.

Because Miranda knew if it came down to it, Ryland would sacrifice anything to keep her safe.

Possibly even his own life.

The door was ajar but not enough for her to fit through. Praying the hinges wouldn't creak, she eased a foot into the crack, followed by her leg and then her body, holding her breath and pulling everything in as tightly as she could. As her shoulder met the doorframe, Mr. Montgomery slammed a hand against the windowsill.

She jumped, pushing the door open enough to slip the rest of the way through. The hinges had indeed creaked, but Mr. Montgomery's yelling about Ryland taking too long to arrive had covered the noise.

Free of the room Miranda moved faster. Her hands were bound behind her, so they were all but useless. She could gather up her skirt in them though. But in order to raise the skirt in the front she had to pull up the back indecently high. Her cloak still covered her, though, and there was no one around but Mr. Montgomery and the caretaker. Decency was going to have to take a holiday.

Knowing he'd expect her to take the main stairs when he discovered her missing, Miranda headed for the servant stairs. She was partway down the first flight when she heard Mr. Montgomery yell again. This time it was her name mingled in with a selection of blush-inducing curse words. Forsaking quietness for speed, Miranda flew down the rest of the back stairs.

A large wooden door with iron hinges stood at the base of the stairs. Miranda grinned around the cloth in her mouth. She'd found a way out if she could just get the door open. Dropping her skirt, she turned around to work the latch with her quickly numbing fingers. Whatever he'd used to bind her hands seemed to be tightening as it dried.

Finally the latch gave, and Miranda shoved the door open, expecting to fall into the precious freedom of sunlight and fresh air.

Instead she found herself in utter darkness, the heavy wooden door slowly swinging shut behind her.

She'd managed to trap herself in the cellar.

Several minutes passed while Miranda focused on breathing.

Closing her eyes — useless, really, but it made her feel better — she prayed. And prayed. And prayed some more. She lost track of everything she prayed for, not really paying attention to the words, just focusing on the fact that God could hear them and she wasn't alone.

Peace finally settled around her, bringing a calm assurance with it. Yes, her situation was dire, but at the moment, with a large door between her and her captor, she felt safe. Her eyes remained squeezed shut though. It was much better to think the darkness was of her own making.

With the sense of calm came a determination to do something, anything, to better her plight. One foot inched forward. The floor below was roughhewn stone. Her toes crept forward some more. One agonizingly slow step at a time, she crossed the floor until her foot bumped into something. Pressing her body forward she realized it was a wall, also made of rough stone.

She eased her face forward, desperate to remove the gag but vain enough to not want her face scratched up in the process. It took some work and her cheek stung a bit from a slight scrape, but the gag finally fell to hang around her neck.

Her body sagged into the wall, joy at the

simple pleasure of moving her jaw filling her heart. Somewhat renewed by her small success, she began the considerably more difficult task of unbinding her hands. Before she could get to the bindings she had to take care of the cloak, which involved some very ridiculous-feeling twists and painful rubs against the wall to get the garment pushed over one shoulder.

She was exhausted, thirsty, scared, and about twenty other feelings she'd only thought she had experienced before. As much as she wanted to curl up and cry, she knew there was a man in the house who intended to kill Ryland and very likely her as well. Quitting was not an option.

Her fingers were sure to endure more cuts and scrapes than her face. She had lost too much feeling to be delicate about the operation. Hours seemed to pass, though it might have been mere minutes. She'd stopped counting. Her arms ached from the constant up-and-down motion. She began to rise and fall on her toes so that her arms could rest and the binding would still scrape against the craggy rocks.

A loud crack broke the thick silence with an almost physical punch. Light suddenly filled the room, causing Miranda to squeeze her eyes shut and curl her face toward her chest. "There you are."

A hand wrapped around her sore elbow and jerked her away from the wall. She stumbled after her captor, presuming it was once again Mr. Montgomery. He had been running through the house, if his harsh breathing was any indication.

He started dragging her toward the door but stopped after only two steps.

"Ah, Ryland. As you see, I have the winning card. A pretty queen, I grant you, though the sister shines a bit brighter. Time to fold, Marshington." He spat his cousin's title out as if it were uncooked poultry.

Miranda eased her eyes open a crack, blinking furiously at the light. How was the room so bright?

"I look for more than a pretty face, Gregory."

Her heart leaped at the sound of Ryland's voice. She couldn't bring herself to rejoice in his presence, though, knowing that Mr. Montgomery wanted to kill him.

"Ah, yes, you're going to tell me you admire her brain as well."

"If you wish to hear it."

Miranda fluttered her lashes furiously, trying to adjust her eyes so she could see what was going on. She could almost stand to keep them open a crack.

After a heartbeat of silence, Mr. Montgomery spoke again.

"Unless you'd like to see those lovely brains in a more splattered manner, I suggest you stop right where you are."

Finally! Miranda eased one eye open just as Mr. Montgomery's words registered in her brain. She found herself looking straight into the barrel of a pistol.

CHAPTER 36

Ryland had faced down men with guns before. He'd had guns pointed at himself, guns aimed at partners, and even one memorable time where the gunman was threatening to shoot himself. He would have considered letting him continue, except that they needed the secrets locked away in the crazy man's head.

No past experience prepared him for seeing a gun held to Miranda's head.

Her eyes fluttered open and then continued to widen as she took in the barrel of the gun. Two lanterns rested on the floor, blazing light into the storeroom. It was long and narrow, with shelves lining the wall behind Gregory and Miranda. The caretaker must be using the room for storing a portion of the farm's production. The shelves were loaded with various vegetables and foodstuffs, waiting to be preserved for the winter or eaten in due time. Bins of flour, sugar, and other household needs lined the wall behind Ryland.

"What do you want?" he asked. Anything to save Miranda.

Gregory let out a harsh laugh. "I want to be you."

Ryland jerked his eyes from Miranda's face to Gregory's.

"It should have been me! I'm older. My schooling was completed. I've always been more refined, more dependable, certainly more visible than you. I'll be doing England a favor replacing the lost duke with one who actually cares what's going on in London."

Ryland wasn't sure how to respond. He couldn't risk having Gregory crack the way Aunt Marguerite had. Who knew what nonsense the woman had been feeding Gregory over the years? He had to get Miranda out of there. Maybe Ryland could placate his cousin, make him think he'd won. "You want to be Marshington? You can have it. Just let Miranda go."

Gregory's laugh grated down Ryland's spine. "You think me a fool? Mother wanted to kill you years ago, but then you disappeared. We tried to have you declared dead, but they kept asking for the body."

"And now you intend to give them one?" Ryland shifted his weight, debating his best move to draw Gregory away from Miranda.

"Yes. With an abundance of grieving over the hunting accident, of course."

Was Miranda crying? No, it appeared to be sweat. How amazing was she, holding her composure together with a gun to her head?

Gregory. He had to focus on Gregory. What had he said? He meant to make it look like a hunting accident? "No one will believe we went hunting together."

"Of course they will. You've returned to London, eager to reconnect with your family. What better way for gentlemen to bond than over a hunt?"

"In the middle of the Season?"

Gregory shrugged. "You've already been labeled eccentric. I might as well use it to my advantage."

Ryland's fingers curled into fists. He felt the ache in his knuckles and the bite of fingernails. Once he got Miranda out of this, he was going to pummel Gregory to bits.

"Let her go, Gregory. This is between you and me."

Gregory's smile was evil. There was no other way to describe it. "I have the girl, and I have the gun. What do you have?"

That was a very good question.

"A bigger gun."

Ryland turned to see Jeffreys coming through the doorway, a blunderbuss poised to fire. The scene had turned almost farcical. If Jeffreys fired that gun in this small room, they would all be feeling the bitter sting of smoke for weeks.

He turned back to Miranda. Better the bitter sting of smoke than the painful stab of death.

Miranda cut her eyes to see who had joined Ryland. Until then she hadn't been able to look at anything but the cold metal barrel pointed in her direction. Seeing a bigger gun also aimed in her direction was not comforting. Even if she wasn't the intended target, her proximity was very disconcerting.

"Get back! I'll shoot her." Mr. Montgomery's grip on her elbow was sliding. She could feel the sticky sweat coating his palm. "I'll shoot you!" The gun was now swinging erratically between herself and Ryland, waving through the air, shaking with the trembling of Mr. Montgomery's arm.

She looked at Ryland and at a glance he looked calm, controlled, but little things gave away his nervousness. His hands clenched and released, as if he were directing all of his fidgeting to his fingers. The skin around his eyes tightened, his mouth turning down as his eyes followed his cousin's hand.

A shaky finger could pull the trigger, even if he didn't mean to.

"I'll shoot her!" Mr. Montgomery repeated, obviously believing that to be the more impressive threat.

"Then I will shoot you. Either way you won't be leavin' here the duke." Jeffreys' voice was much calmer than Miranda would have suspected for a valet. Then again, Ryland wasn't likely to have hired the average valet. He must be like Price and Jess, one of Ryland's former cohorts.

The gun swung around once more and steadied in Ryland's direction.

"I may not leave, but I will be Marshington."

Miranda told herself to look away, to push him over, to scream, to do *something.* But time held her captive, wrapping her in icy ropes of fear as minutes slowed to a crawl, allowing her to watch each detail as Mr. Montgomery curled his finger more securely around the trigger.

Fear has a smell. A combination of sweat and bad breath mingled with an unexplainable bitter undertone. Slightly metallic. A bit like the smell that clings to the soot-blackened men leaving the steel factory after a long day of work. Ryland was familiar with the smell — had even noticed it on himself when he'd been on the wrong end of a pistol before.

Never had the odor filled his nostrils to this extreme. There was more at stake than ever before for every person in that room. A part of his brain, the logical part that made it possible for him to face life as an agent of the Crown, realized that fear wasn't really tangible and the combination of spices and food in the storeroom was mixing with the stench created by rivulets of sweat he could see rolling down Gregory and Miranda's faces.

A puddle formed in his ear. Sweat was pouring off of him as well.

Gregory's hand shook visibly. He was going to pull the trigger, whether he meant to or not. At this distance it wouldn't matter that Gregory had never been much of a marksman. The bullet would find Ryland's chest anyway.

So he dove.

The crack of the pistol was joined by the roar of Jeffrey's blunderbuss. In the close proximity, the noise reverberated through the storeroom, slamming into his ears as his shoulder rammed into a heavy storage barrel.

He rolled, scooting behind the barrel for shelter, shaking his head in a futile effort to clear his hearing.

Smoke from the dual gun blasts filled his face as he stood. It hit the back of his throat, stung his eyes, and made his nose itch. Lantern light bounced through the dust-filled air, making everything a giant blur. He couldn't see a thing.

"Miranda!"

"Ryland." Her voice trembled and the end of his name dissolved into a shaky sob. Crying was bad but sound was good. Sound meant she was alive.

He rushed around the barrel and into the cloud of acrid smoke.

Jeffreys' shape loomed in the smoke, rushing across the room. "Ryla — oomph!"

Years of training, experience, and practicality urged him to go help Jeffreys. Ryland could make out the shadowy forms as his valet wrestled with his cousin. Fists were flying erratically as they struggled. Miranda's whimpers were quiet but consistent, proving that not only was she alive, but at least well enough to remain so for the foreseeable future.

He had time to knock Gregory out cold.

He tripped over Jeffreys, but it didn't slow him down. Three swift moves had him grabbing Gregory by the collar, kneeing him in the stomach, and sending him headfirst into the same heavy barrel Ryland had hid behind moments before. Gregory went limp in his grip. Ryland didn't wait for him to hit the floor before he rushed to Miranda's side.

Dirty and bedraggled, she appeared unhurt as she stood at the edge of the light from one of the lanterns. Her eyes were squeezed tight, and her body was shaking with the effort to control her sobs. Tears rolled in a steady stream down her cheeks as her breath shuddered in and out between trembling lips. Her hair was a tangled mess, her face was scraped, and her dress was nearly as muddy as the day they'd hiked across the countryside.

She was beautiful.

"Miranda," he whispered as he wrapped his arms around her, holding her tight to his chest, tucking her head beneath his chin.

"Ryland?" she whispered in return, her voice still shaking with hiccups and tears.

"It's me. Don't worry. Jeffreys has Gregory." Ryland slowly ran his hands over her body, trying not to think of anything but whether or not she was injured. His hands encountered a thick glop of gooey substance that had him pulling back and dragging Miranda closer to the lantern.

She was gaining control of her breathing, and the tears were only occasional. More of the wet, pink substance resided in her hair. Her clothing was wrinkled and crusty from all the rain and travel, and more strings of goo covered her skirts.

"What on earth?" Ryland looked back to find a similar mess on the floor and wall near where Miranda and Gregory had been standing.

He slid his hands down her arms, looking around as he pulled a knife from his boot and sliced through her bindings. She'd been tied with a strip of leather, so it took some effort to cut through. As the strap came loose, his gaze zeroed in on the now-busted shelf high on the wall behind where Gregory and Miranda had been standing. Jeffreys must have aimed high in order to avoid hitting Miranda with his shot.

Miranda rubbed her hands up and down her arms. "You can tell Mr. Blakemoor that I have had quite enough of his tomatoes."

Ryland blinked. After everything she'd been through, she'd have been well within her rights to cling, scream, cry, or even faint. He wouldn't have blamed her.

Instead, now that both of them stood hale

and hearty with the danger behind them, she was talking about tomatoes. Ryland threw his arms around her and laughed.

Chapter 37

Mr. Blakemoor was as steady and competent as Ryland's steward had claimed. By the time the group emerged from the cellar, they found him returning from town with the magistrate, the rest of the staff, and a small army of people who set about cleaning the most necessary rooms and preparing food.

There was a bit of a power struggle between Mr. Blakemoor and Price, who had arrived with Jeffreys. In the end, they settled on Price directing things from the yard while Mr. Blakemoor handled things inside the house.

Ryland leaned against the window in the freshly aired drawing room. Furniture he hadn't seen in years surrounded him, but the hated memories of childhood only licked at the edge of his mind. He was too busy grappling with a new outlook on life to worry about the past.

Three hours after the magistrate had hauled off a bound and whimpering Gregory, Miranda walked shyly into the drawing room. Like Ryland and Jeffreys, she'd bathed and dressed in clothes borrowed from some of the summoned villagers. Without the aid of a proper maid or hair pins, she'd left her hair loose. The damp waves hung halfway down her back in a glorious flow of gold.

"You are beautiful," Ryland whispered. Now that nothing stood in the way of him proposing to this woman, he felt unsure. Had the ordeal been too much? Was his life too tainted with destruction to appeal to her?

She fingered the rough woolen skirt. "I never thought I'd be grateful for such a garment, but I confess it felt wonderful just to be clean."

Ryland shook his head. She'd probably never worn such coarse clothing in her life. "It isn't too itchy?"

Her quiet smile shifted to an arrogant smirk, complete with disdainfully arched eyebrows. "A lady never reveals the discomfort caused by her clothing."

With a laugh that chased the last black memory from the rafters, he scooped her up and carried her to the settee, where he settled with her ensconced in his lap.

A tray of food had been delivered, complete with a sliced tomato. Ryland adjusted the table and tray so they could reach it all without leaving the settee. He wasn't letting her up anytime soon.

"This is your fault, you know." Miranda smiled, but she avoided his eyes as she set aside an empty teacup.

His heart plummeted. She was going to tell him that too much danger marred his life and she couldn't live with that. He couldn't let that happen. She had to see that he had not caused this disaster.

Ryland cupped her chin and turned her face toward his. "You can't mean that. I've done everything I could for Gregory, all these years. I saved his life in France!"

Her soft hand cupped his cheek, giving him hope. "I'm talking about your refusal to include me. If we had talked about it at your house in London, I would never have gone into the rain looking for you to tell you Mr. Montgomery had been to our house."

Ryland dropped his head back to stare at the ceiling. Didn't she see he'd been protecting her? He'd been trying to keep her safe and pure, innocent and untouched by the merest hint of danger.

And failing miserably. Perhaps she had a point.

Miranda gripped his hair and pulled, forcing him to look at her. "This danger and action — it's part of who you are, Ryland. Part of what drew me to you even when I thought you a servant. Don't take it away from me."

She wasn't going to leave him. She still wanted him. Relief made him light-headed, and he anchored himself by pulling her into a deep kiss. Miranda melted against him, making it difficult to remember they were not yet married, this was not officially her home, and half the village was still traipsing through the rooms, making the place hospitable.

She wrapped her arms around his neck, running her fingers through his short hair. He pressed his hands to her back, pulling her more fully into the embrace. Who cared about the village?

After several moments, maybe seconds, possibly minutes, could even have been an hour, Ryland tucked her head against his shoulder and smoothed a hand up and down her back.

"All of me then? Even the converted smuggler for a butler?"

Miranda giggled. "Especially the smuggler

516

butler." She paused. "Though the former spy as a parlor maid might be up for discussion."

He hugged her tight, and tilted his head for another kiss.

A loud commotion rose from the outer yard, but Ryland ignored it. Price and Jeffreys were out there, assisting in the airing and beating of rugs and other household items. Ryland had tried to get them to rest, but both had claimed to have too much energy running through their muscles to sit still.

They could handle whatever situation had arisen.

The front door burst open. Instinct had Ryland rising and shoving Miranda over the back of the settee.

Her outraged screech as she landed in a heap on the floor made him wince, but the stream of disheveled people filing through the drawing room entrance made his eyes widen.

Griffith led the way, his face grim as his eyes searched the room. Tension visibly departed as he spied Miranda rising from behind the settee. The look he sent Ryland was curious and accusatory.

Trent was immediately behind him, though he was pushed aside before he could say anything. The petite brunette he'd met at Riverton rushed into the room. "Are you all right?"

Lady Raebourne was chased by a man Ryland had never met before, but assumed was Lord Raebourne. He didn't look happy. "Amelia, I told you to stay in the carriage until we had a chance to look around."

The little woman waved a hand in the air as she scooted around the settee to hug Miranda. "Nonsense. I asked Mr. Price, and he said everything was safe."

Ryland couldn't stop the surprise from showing on his face. This little bit of a woman had approached Price? Voluntarily? He'd seen grown men cross the street to avoid the burly butler.

Lord Raebourne looked disgruntled but said nothing.

Lady Georgina swept in, showing more emotion than he'd ever seen from her. She went straight to Miranda to wrap her in a hug. "We sent word to Mother and Lord Blackstone, but I don't know when they'll get it. She'll be beside herself until she sees you again."

"They'll be a bit slower, I'm afraid," Griffith said. "After all of you and then our two carriages came through, the posting houses will be out of fresh horses."

Ryland looked back to the door to see Colin saunter in and lean against the wall. He grinned at Ryland and then looked over the room with a raised eyebrow.

Ryland followed his gaze, taking in the chaos that filled what had been a deserted room only one day prior.

Lady Raebourne was busy smoothing Miranda's hair into a simple braid, pulling pins from her own coiffure to secure Miranda's. Georgina was patting her sister's hand and prattling on about the latest London gossip as if Miranda had been gone for weeks instead of hours.

Lord Raebourne had wandered over to the window and seemed to be inspecting the house and grounds. Griffith exuded his normal calm control, though he looked a bit unsure about what he was supposed to be doing. Trent helped himself to the food tray and Colin still stood in the corner, grinning.

"What are you all doing here?" Ryland sputtered.

Griffith's eyebrows shot up. "You woke my butler to see if Miranda had made it home. Did you expect me to simply go to sleep after that? I sent word to Trent, but I couldn't wait and I left without him."

"I woke Anthony to borrow his carriage."

Trent shrugged.

Lady Raebourne looked up. "I wasn't about to leave her to the tender ministrations of you men. I knew she would need a woman present."

"Hear, hear." Lady Georgina nodded her agreement.

Lord Raebourne shrugged. "I wasn't letting her go without me."

Colin grinned. "I offered Trent a ride home from the club."

Then Price peeked around the doorframe, trying to hide his bulky body behind the wall while he surveyed the room. Jeffreys' head appeared around the other side of the doorframe. Then Jess appeared, looking the model of a quiet servant girl, with another full tea tray in her hands. When had *she* gotten here? Had they simply left Lady Marguerite tied to the couch?

Ryland started laughing.

He couldn't stop it, didn't want to stop it. Minutes ago he'd been planning a life with Miranda, looking to her to help him build the family he'd never had. But here, in the house he'd dreaded as a child, he saw all the ways God had already provided.

Griffith, who'd taught him all the lessons his own father had imparted, providing guidance and accountability so Ryland didn't end up a dissolute reprobate.

Colin had never questioned Ryland but stood with him when he needed it — and knocked him down when he needed it.

Price, Jess, and Jeffreys, outstanding examples of life after grace.

Even Lord Raebourne and Trent with their unconditional acceptance were examples of Christian brotherhood.

God had provided.

Ryland had never actually been alone. Feeling freer than he could ever remember, Ryland grabbed Miranda in his arms and swung her around in the middle of the room. Her stunned face matched everyone else's.

Griffith recovered first. "That's two overnight adventures you've taken her on."

Ryland grinned down into Miranda's face. The rough fabric under his hands reminded him how easily this adventure could have ended differently. But it hadn't. He smoothed a stray hair away from her face. "I suppose I'll have to come to your rescue, won't I? It is a good thing I have already procured a license. We can be married as soon as we return to Town."

Several men coughed to cover their laughter.

Miranda's eyebrows rose. "You procured

a license without asking me?"

"I believe we should see to the bags, gentlemen." Lady Georgina herded everyone out the door. Griffith and Colin grumbled, though Colin objected more to the cessation of what he considered an entertaining show than he did to Ryland being alone with Miranda. Lady Georgina looked from him to her sister. Whatever she was planning on saying dissolved into a sad smile. "Congratulations," she whispered before closing the door behind her.

"I love you." Ryland's voice was barely above a whisper, but it felt loud. He couldn't remember the last time he'd said those words to anyone, and he'd certainly never meant them in this way.

"I've felt alone all my life," he began.

Miranda's eyes became wet. "Oh no, Ryland, you're not."

He briefly kissed her lips. "I know. I know that now. Though I've always tried to do everything alone, I see now how many times God provided aid in one way or another. I'm not broken, like I thought I was. I have everything I need. Marry me, Miranda, and I'll have everything I could ever want."

She nodded, even as tears dripped from her long lashes. "All of me for all of you."

Her lips curved into a mischievous grin.

"It has occurred to me that I have encountered more life-threatening situations since I've met you than ever before."

Ryland laughed and leaned down for another quick kiss. It wasn't enough, and he returned for a longer one. "I promise to make the rest of our lives as adventure-free as possible."

Miranda smiled. "That's one promise you'll never be able to keep."

EPILOGUE

One Month Later

Miranda stood at the window, looking out across the rolling fields surrounding Marshington Abbey. Ryland was coming across them, returning home from a survey of the farm. After they'd married, they'd elected to spend some time at the abbey building new memories there for Ryland and setting the foundation for their future.

Love swelled in her heart as she spied the bouquet of bright wildflowers poking out of his saddlebag.

She left the window and crossed to her desk. There were a few household matters to attend to before her family arrived for a visit. A corner of familiar blue paper caught her eye. She pulled the folded note from beneath the stack of books.

With trembling fingers, she opened the note. The first letter had been on her dressing table the night they'd returned to

London. Since then they'd shown up in various places, once even in the folds of her towel after a bath.

They were stories. Ryland's stories. Sometimes they were tales of his childhood, occasionally he shared a story from school, but most of the time he told her about his spying days. He never divulged details, but she learned how he met Jess, Price, Jeffreys, and most of their other servants. She saw the world through his eyes, what he'd learned about people and what really mattered.

She always cried for the hurt behind the words, but she treasured the love and trust that led him to share with her.

The door closed in the main hall below, and Miranda wiped her tears and slid the letter into the decorative chest with all the others.

With a wide smile on her face, she skipped down the stairs to meet him. He was wind-blown from his ride, and the clutch of flowers was half broken from the trip in the saddlebag, but Miranda loved the messiness of it all. It was real. And it was hers.

With his free hand, Ryland snagged her waist and pulled her in for a kiss. As the kiss continued, Miranda realized he had no intention of stopping anytime soon and was likely to suggest she take the flowers up to their room.

"Ryland." She smiled indulgently even as she chided him. "My family will be here soon."

"Hours yet. It's not even noon."

She bit her lip. Ryland groaned. "You have that serious look on your face."

"I found a letter."

He swung her around the hall. "I hid a letter."

"It was about your cousin."

His eyebrows rose. "I know what it was about. I wrote it." He scooped her up against his chest and dropped the flowers on her belly.

She swirled a finger through his short hair. "Do you think we'll ever bring your family here again? I mean, after Gregory has served his time in jail."

Ryland started up the stairs. "My *blood relations* are taken care of. When he gets out, Gregory will join my aunt at the house in Northumberland. There is a doctor for my aunt and a staff of servants doubling as guards to make sure they live the rest of their miserable lives far away from me. A priest visits them every Tuesday."

He pushed open the door to their room and walked in, shutting the door again with a swift kick.

"I owe them nothing else other than my forgiveness. Certainly not my company, a glimpse of my happiness, or my attention."

He paused beside the bed. "My *family,* however, is expected to arrive within a few hours, so I do hope you'll welcome them."

She didn't try to stop the tears or temper the wide smile of joy that graced her face. There was no fear of overexpressing her emotions anymore, not when she was in private. No matter how loud she got or how often she cried, Ryland never hushed or reprimanded her.

After all, he frequently told her, a lady should always be herself.

ACKNOWLEDGMENTS

If you've ever been to a play, you'll notice that during the curtain call someone, usually the lead cast member, will make some gestures toward different areas of the auditorium during the clapping. They aren't thanking you for being a great audience. They're indicating the out-of-sight people like lighting and prop technicians that made the play possible. As a backstage worker for several high-school productions, I appreciate the awkward wave.

These acknowledgments are my curtain call, and here are my seemingly random but entirely purposeful hand gestures.

To God, in whom I find my worth and my purpose, thank you.

Much appreciation to Jacob, who supports me enough to push aside the furniture and reenact a fight scene so that I can get it right. Thank you for letting me tie you up with a jump rope.

Thank you to my wonderfully supportive kids — particularly Blessing 1, who has saved her pennies so she can buy Mommy's first book. I hope you like it, sweetie.

My eternal gratitude goes to every author, agent, editor, librarian, reader, or bookseller that has taken their time to judge a contest. You have provided insight, encouragement, and the occasional hard-to-swallow truth. Those victories kept me going. Without you, this book wouldn't be here.

A little bit less gratitude goes to my brother, who stole my phone so I couldn't find out if I'd won.

A shout out to Google Images, for providing hours of procrastination in the name of research, and to Pinterest for giving me a place to store it all so I could claim to be productive. Also props to the guy who put a video on YouTube of him shooting a tomato. Even though the scene turned out completely different than originally written, I still love the exploding tomatoes.

To Alana, my beta-reader extraordinaire,

thank you for keeping my characters straight and not being afraid to tell me what works and what doesn't.

Hugs to the editorial staff at Bethany House who took a book I was proud to have written and helped me turn it into something I can't believe I get to put my name on. You guys are the best. Even if I said some not nice-things about you under my breath when I first got my revision letter.

To Delaney Diamond and the Georgia Romance Writers, thank you for the Gin Ellis critique. Even though the prologue you had me add has bitten the dust, it was enough to grab the right people's attention. Also Victoria Vane, who spent an hour showing me how to improve my writing. It was a different manuscript, but the lessons still applied. Thank you to Debby Giusti for being the biggest cheerleader a girl could hope for, even if when I couldn't figure out what to do with a character you told me to kill her.

To Patty, Ane, Lindi, Brandy, Meg, and the rest of the ACFW North Georgia peeps, thank you for celebrating as if this contract were your own. For my Regency Reflections sisters, your support has meant everything.

Finally, thank you to my readers. Without you my labor of love would have a lot less meaning.

ABOUT THE AUTHOR

Kristi Ann Hunter graduated from Georgia Tech with a degree in computer science but always knew she wanted to write. Kristi is an RWA Golden Heart contest winner, an ACFW Genesis contest winner, and a Georgia Romance Writers Maggie Award for Excellence winner. She is a founding member and the coordinator of the Regency Reflections blog and lives with her husband and three children in Georgia. Find her online at www.kristiannhunter.com.